AMONG THE CLOUDS ABOVE

A NOVEL OF THE BATTLE OF BRITAIN

JOHN RHODES

AMONG THE CLOUDS ABOVE
A NOVEL OF THE BATTLE OF BRITAIN

iUniverse books may be ordered through booksellers or by contacting:

iUniverse
1663 Liberty Drive
Bloomington, IN 47403
www.iuniverse.com
1-800-Authors (1-800-288-4677)

ISBN: 978-1-5320-5316-0 (sc)
ISBN: 978-1-5320-5318-4 (hc)
ISBN: 978-1-5320-5317-7 (e)

Library of Congress Control Number: 2018909662

Print information available on the last page.

iUniverse rev. date: 08/24/2018

I know that I shall meet my fate
Somewhere among the clouds above

—William Butler Yeats

While this is a work of fiction, I have described certain historical characters and given them imaginary dialogue. I hope I have done so respectfully. I have also used real locations when applicable. All other people, places, and names are fictitious, and any similarities to real people, places, and names are coincidental and unintended.

JR
Wilmington, North Carolina, 2018

PART ONE

AUGUST 18–20, 1940

What General Weygand called the Battle of France is over. I expect that the Battle of Britain is about to begin …

The whole fury and might of the enemy must very soon be turned on us. Hitler knows that he will have to break us in this Island or lose the war. If we can stand up to him, all Europe may be free and the life of the world may move forward into broad, sunlit uplands …

Let us therefore brace ourselves to our duties, and so bear ourselves that, if the British Empire and its Commonwealth last for a thousand years, men will still say, "This was their finest hour."

—Winston Spencer Churchill, June 22, 1940,
speech to the House of Commons

AUGUST 18, 1940

0430 hours, Sunday, August 18, 1940
RAF Christhampton, Surrey, England

Johnnie Shaux awoke an hour before dawn. His tiny cubicle felt dank. He groped for his uniform and pulled it on in the darkness, fumbled into his heavy sheepskin flying boots, and clomped down the darkened corridor, still half-asleep, unshaven and unwashed. Snores emanated from unseen cubicles on either side.

Outside the hut the night was still as black as pitch. There were no stars. The air smelled clean, in sharp contrast to the pervasive odor of unwashed clothes inside his sleeping quarters. No stars meant clouds, and clouds meant, perhaps, no flying.

He waited, yawning and rubbing his eyes until he could detect vague gradations in the blackness around him, and then set off to walk along a muddy track, stumbling occasionally into unseen ruts. The breeze was warm and soft, and somewhere to his right he heard the first tentative chirpings of the predawn chorus.

He reached another hut. It was barely visible in the gloom, and its windows were tightly sealed with blackout material. The glare of naked light bulbs dazzled him when he opened the door. This hut was also crudely constructed, like the sleeping quarters, and contained a haphazard array of battered furniture. A young airman, scarcely more awake than Shaux, wordlessly handed him a mug of hot, sweet tea. Shaux retreated back into the darkness. He felt his way to a decaying armchair on the veranda and sat down. The tea scalded his tongue, and the seat was damp with dew. He lit a cigarette and inhaled deeply. The smoke tasted harsh and acrid in his throat.

He sat with his eyes closed, gathering his senses, slowly stretching his limbs one by one, taking an inventory of his brief life, wondering dispassionately if he would still be alive to do so tomorrow.

The Royal Air Force station gradually awoke around him. A truck growled to a halt nearby and disgorged members of the ground crew. Shaux could follow their movements by their flickering flashlights and the muttering of their sleepy curses as they inspected the invisible aircraft parked around him.

The eastern sky grew perceptibly lighter, and the graceful outlines of Supermarine Spitfire fighters emerged from the darkness like wraiths, their long noses lifted skyward as if scenting the early-morning breeze for prey. The silence was shattered by a whine and a whirr and a bang and a clatter and another bang and then a staccato roar as the ground crew started a Rolls-Royce Merlin engine, the supercharged heart of a Spitfire.

More engines started. The ground crews would run them for five minutes to warm them up—"to splash the oil about a bit," as they said. Additional trucks appeared: an elderly civilian tanker to top off the fuel tanks, a truck with oil cans and bottles of hydraulic fluid and oxygen tanks and batteries and all the other innumerable supplies that Spitfires consumed, and finally a five-ton lorry loaded with long, snaking ammunition belts for the eight Browning .303-caliber machine guns mounted in each Spitfire's wings.

Other pilots materialized from the gloom, as drowsy as Shaux, and took their places silently beside him. The telephone inside the hut began to shrill at regular intervals.

"Readiness at dawn, chaps. B Flight first, A Flight later. Let's get a move on," Flight Lieutenant Debenham, the B Flight commander, announced through the doorway. "Chop, chop, fingers out," he added unnecessarily.

Shaux and the other pilots stood up like automatons and walked behind the hut to urinate.

"The wind's from the northeast, gentlemen," someone said, and they formed a row to piss downwind. In the past two weeks—a lifetime—it had become something of a 339 Squadron tradition. A new kid—Dalton, or Haughton, or some name like that—fresh from Central Flying School and Spitfire conversion training up in Lincolnshire, threw up on his uniform. The others ignored him—all fighter pilots had an intimate familiarity with fear in all its manifold expressions and did not demean those who exhibited it.

Shaux pulled on his orange Mae West life jacket and his parachute. He adjusted the parachute straps so that it hung awkwardly behind his backside; it was designed for the user to sit on instead of a seat cushion. He put on his leather flying helmet with the corrugated rubber tube for his oxygen and the trailing wires for his earphones and microphone. He arranged his goggles on his helmet and pulled on his gloves—first silk ladies' gloves and then fur-lined leather gloves on top. It would be very cold at twenty thousand feet.

He searched the lightening sky. Overhead a stately convoy of clouds was headed toward the south coast at five thousand feet, but otherwise the sky was clear. There would be no reprieve.

"Okay, chaps, time to go," Debenham called. "B Flight will patrol over Hastings, or so I'm told. Four aircraft. You, er, Dalton, stick to Shaux's tail. Remember—he's Red Leader and you're Red Two. Keep your eyes wide open, and no heroics."

The pilots walked out to their waiting Spitfires in an untidy gaggle. The fighters were slippery with dew. Shaux clambered onto the port wing of his aircraft and stepped into the tiny cockpit, easing himself down so that he sat on his parachute. The cockpit stank of 40-grade oil. One of the ground crew helped him strap in and wished him luck perfunctorily. Shaux went through his preflight routine methodically, testing the control surfaces one by one, and then started the engine, muttering his private catechism as he did so.

"Generator switch on—generator switch on. Magneto switches on—magneto switches on. Radiator flaps open—radiator flaps open. Fuel switches on—fuel switches on. Primer—one, two, three. Throttle one-third—throttle one-third. Starter."

He pressed the starter, and the twelve-cylinder Merlin engine spluttered reluctantly to life. The propeller blades rotated jerkily as the exhaust manifolds emitted burps of gray smoke and the fuselage lurched and shook in protest. Then the engine caught, missed, and caught again, and the propeller disappeared into a gray circle. Shaux ran the Merlin up to fifteen hundred revs, and it settled into a smooth roar. He tapped his instrument gauges one by one to make sure the needles weren't stuck.

The eastern sky was brightening as the four Spitfires formed a messy line and straggled across the wet grass to the southern end of the field in order to take off into the wind. Shaux's Merlin grumbled and burbled as it bounced and swayed across the field, emitting clouds of high-octane exhaust fumes. Dalton was far too close behind him, and Shaux hoped the kid's prop wouldn't chew up his tail. At the far end of the field he stamped on his left brake, and the aircraft swerved abruptly into the breeze. Somehow the kid also managed to turn without hitting him. It must be beginner's luck.

A green flare from a Very pistol shot up from the makeshift control tower at the other end of the field. Without permitting himself the least moment for doubt or fear, Shaux opened the throttle, and his Merlin howled as the revs spun up to 2,600 rpm. The airscrew dragged his Spitfire along the bumpy turf as if it were a toy kite in a gale, a thousand screaming horsepower pulling a six-thousand-pound, thirty-foot-long aircraft. The tail came off the ground within seconds. The bumps grew harsher as the Spitfire accelerated, and the springs in the undercarriage legs creaked in protest. Engine torque tried to drag him off path to the right.

Behind him, Dalton was having difficulty keeping his Spitfire straight. Shaux had heard a Spitfire described as a large Rolls-Royce engine with a small Supermarine aircraft stuck on the back. The engine housing ahead of the cockpit was over twelve feet long, and therefore much of Dalton's forward view was blocked; he literally couldn't see where he was going.

Shaux held the control stick forward until it became light in his hand, waited a heartbeat, and then eased it back. Instantly his Spitfire rose into its natural element, as sure and elegant in the air as it had been ungainly and awkward on the ground, a transformation that never failed to move Shaux regardless of how many times he witnessed it. He cranked the wheels up into their slots beneath the wings, and the rumble of air turbulence subsided. The sun rose rapidly above his horizon, bathing the Spitfires in pink light even while the ground beneath them remained in gray predawn shadow.

He glanced over his shoulder. Dalton was miraculously in the right place, a hundred feet behind his port wing. With only four aircraft in the formation, they were flying in the loose finger-four formation used by the German Luftwaffe instead of the rigid arrowhead vic formation that RAF Fighter Command insisted on.

There was little to do for the next eight minutes but to follow the flight commander as their droning engines pulled B Flight higher and higher. A Spitfire had a climbing rate of twenty-five hundred feet per minute, and they were headed for twenty thousand feet. Shaux closed the canopy and buttoned on his mask. There was nothing but static in the earphones.

He fiddled with the oxygen supply and inhaled a sweet whiff of oxygen combined with the smell of damp rubber. Oxygen, rubber, and oil merged into the sickly taste of imminent danger.

Southern England stretched out below him. Trees etched long shadows across a patchwork quilt of green meadows and golden wheat fields as the sun rose above the ground horizon. It could have been a moment to marvel at the immutable beauty of the English countryside. It could have been a moment to admire the grace of the Spitfire's lines and the thundering precision of the Rolls-Royce Merlin effortlessly lifting him higher and higher. But Shaux had locked away such inessential emotions as marvel and admiration long ago; he knew all too well that a fighter pilot who paused to savor life would very soon be dead.

They climbed into the band of cloud at five thousand feet, and the world disappeared into blinding white. Shaux kept his eyes on his instruments to ensure he was flying straight and at the right rate of climb, hoping the pilots around him—Dalton in particular—were doing the same.

They emerged into brilliant sunlight at nine thousand feet. Most of B Flight was still in formation, although Dalton had wandered off and was at least half a mile away. Shaux began to search the sky methodically, sweeping the horizon and then the four quadrants of the sky above him. This was the most dangerous moment of the patrol so far; if there were German Luftwaffe Messerschmitt 109 fighters above them, the Spitfires would be clearly visible against the clouds, sitting ducks for 109s howling down upon them out of the rising sun. Dalton, alone and inexperienced, would be a particularly easy prey.

Shaux's earphones crackled. The sector controller directed—"vectored"—them toward Chichester in Sussex. A force of twenty or more Luftwaffe bombers—"bandits" or "EA" (for "enemy aircraft") in RAF parlance—was crossing the south coast of England over Selsey Bill at fifteen thousand feet. Fighter Command preferred to send its slower Hurricane fighters to attack bombers while Spitfires flew higher to engage any fast 109s that might be flying cover above the bombers. In this instance Shaux assumed there were no Hurricanes close enough to reach the bombers before they flew far into England and reached their targets.

Whatever the case, it sounded like a cock-up—four Spitfires would engage twenty enemy bombers. God help the Spitfires if there were 109s waiting above the bombers.

The enemy appeared on cue as a line of tiny black dots, scarcely visible in the morning glare, crawling across his windshield from right to left. As the distance closed, the dots grew larger and sprouted wings, engines, and fuselages.

"EAs are Dornier 17s," crackled Green Two's voice in his earphones. Green Two was a newish pilot named Digby, blessed with phenomenal eyesight.

"Red Leader and Red Two, take the left," said Debenham. "We'll take the right."

The RAF, like the navy, used *port* and *starboard* instead of *left* and *right*, but experienced pilots knew that novices like Dalton had trouble finding their own balls on a clear summer's day, let alone translating *port* into *left* in the excitement and fear of battle.

The enemy dots further resolved themselves into twenty-four distinct gray-black aircraft flying in tight formation, heading northeast at fifteen thousand feet. Shaux could now recognize the Dornier bombers by their glass cockpits, like long, narrow greenhouses stuck on top of the aircraft, and their slim fuselages, which gave them the nickname of *Bleistifts*— flying "pencils."

Each bomber was carrying two thousand pounds of bombs—twenty-four bombers, twenty-four tons of high explosives to rain down on southern England, probably on some RAF station, perhaps Shaux's own.

Shaux calculated. His closing speed on the enemy would be fifty yards every second. If he opened fire at 250 yards, he would have five seconds to engage his target before passing slightly above him. As soon as he disengaged, he would make a rapid circle to come around behind the Dornier formation for a second attack. His tightest turning circle in level flight had a radius of about three hundred yards. Therefore, he computed, the circumference of his circle would be two times pi times three hundred, equaling eighteen hundred yards—roughly a mile—or about thirty-six seconds of flight time. The EAs would have flown away from him for thirty-six seconds at 250 miles per hour; therefore he would be two miles behind them. It would take a minute and a half to catch up. Therefore he and Dalton could engage them for five seconds every two minutes. That assumed something else didn't happen in the meantime, although something else almost always did.

Shaux chose his target—the Dornier third from the left in the rear row. He would approach the enemy from the rear and slightly above and fire into the center of the aircraft, where the wings joined the fuselage, and then "walk" his guns forward to the canopy and the engines. The Dorniers had a dorsal machine gun at the rear of the greenhouse. If he could knock that out, the Dornier would be just about defenseless; the rest of its armament was little more than dead weight.

"Red Two, Dalton, stay with Red Leader and do what he does," Debenham instructed.

Shaux could see Dalton a hundred yards behind him, flying erratically as he gripped the controls too tightly. Shaux guessed the new pilot's heart rate was at least two hundred beats a minute.

"Watch for 109s above us, chaps," the flight commander said. "Tallyho!"

The enemy aircraft swam toward them. The distance was closing fast. Shaux spared a long look above them for a fighter escort but could see nothing; perhaps there had been a Luftwaffe cock-up to match their own. Debenham and Green Two were away to his right. He could see the white phosphorus sparkle of tracer—incandescent white-hot shells so that the pilots could see where they were aiming—as the flight commander opened fire.

Shaux picked the optimal angle of deflection to intersect his chosen target and flew straight and level, partly to give himself the steadiest possible aiming platform and partly to let Dalton sort himself out.

The rear gunners of the nearest Dorniers opened fire. Shaux imagined their cries of "Achtung! Achtung! Spitfire! Spitfire!" as they saw his slippery gray shape growing rapidly behind them, playing hide-and-seek behind their tailplanes.

Shaux watched bright lines of enemy tracer arcing toward him. Most of them disappeared to his rear and below him, but the gunners' aim would improve as the distance closed. A rapid mental calculation in the trigonometry of congruent triangles told him how wide the wingspan of a Dornier should appear to be in his gunsight at 250 yards. He waited fifteen long seconds as the Dornier grew larger and larger. The sky seemed full of enemy tracer, like a fireworks display on Guy Fawkes Night, and the tracer seemed to accelerate as it approached him. He heard a sudden *whack-whack-whack* behind him as enemy fire hit his rear fuselage or tailplane. Shaux hoped they hadn't hit anything vital. The unarmored Spitfire had not so much as quivered; so far, so good.

Shaux depressed the big brass firing button on his control stick and heard the harsh coughing of his machine guns, four in each wing, firing six rounds every second. His tracer flashed on the Dornier's wing roots, one round of tracer followed by four invisible live rounds, gradually converging on the canopy as he flew closer. Five seconds to fire, six rounds per second, eight guns; that meant 240 rounds were pouring in among the four members of the enemy crew crowded into the narrow, twelve-foot-long greenhouse.

Clang-clang-clang sounded from his engine housing as the Dornier gunners found him again, followed by *whack-whack-whack* somewhere in his port wing.

Shaux continued firing until the last possible moment and then made a radical left turn, feeling the centripetal forces pushing him back into his seat as the Spitfire stood on its port wing. He could see Dalton attempting to copy his maneuver with a sloppy, skidding turn that would take him far out of the battle. Shaux continued to turn until he had completed a circle. The Dorniers crept back into his field of vision, and he began to chase them. The enemy formation seemed to be splitting into two. A Dornier in the center was trailing smoke and losing altitude, turning right, forcing the bombers to its right to take evasive action. Debenham or Green Two would claim a victory.

Ninety seconds to catch up. There was a fighter far behind him—either Dalton or even possibly an enemy 109—but at that distance it was impossible to tell. Whoever it was wouldn't catch him. He searched the sky methodically, quadrant by quadrant. Now there were aircraft wheeling and turning above him at twenty thousand feet, trailing glistening contrails like random white scribbles across the sky. These must be Luftwaffe 109s being engaged by another squadron of Spitfires. So the Dorniers still had no immediate cover, and it was still safe to attack. Far to Shaux's right the flight commander and Green Two were completing their second attack.

The Dorniers had again grown large in his gunsight. This time there was no defensive fire from the rear gunner of his chosen target; perhaps he had been wounded or his weapon was jammed or damaged.

Shaux took one more glance around and opened fire. Again he could see tracer striking the cockpit canopy. The bomber abruptly banked to the left—Shaux must have struck the pilot or severed a vital control line—and the Dornier beside it reacted too slowly. The port airscrew of Shaux's target struck the starboard wingtip of the other bomber, shredding the wing like a giant buzz saw before becoming locked in the wreckage. Shaux flashed over the two aircraft, opened the throttle wide, and began another radical turn.

The sky was empty above him. Shaux was not surprised; as often happened in a dogfight, formations of aircraft could dissipate in seconds or be miles away on some other course. Halfway through his turn, he saw a fighter spiraling earthward, trailing smoke; he couldn't tell if it was friend or foe. Perhaps it was Dalton.

He completed his turn. The two Dorniers were still tangled together in a deadly embrace, losing height and trailing oily smoke. It was a miracle they were still capable of flight. He glanced downward. There was a small town to the north, perhaps five miles distant. It was too small to be Petersfield, he thought; it must be Midhurst.

The remaining Dorniers, now a ragged cluster rather than a tight formation, were continuing doggedly northward. He had enough fuel and ammunition for at least two more attacks. The lone fighter was still behind him, either Dalton or a 109. Behind that fighter were several more black dots—perhaps the remnants of the dogfight far above him. They represented no danger to Shaux, and he was closing rapidly on the Dorniers. But if that lone fighter was Dalton and the dots behind him were 109s, Shaux could not abandon him; Dalton would have zero chance—zero—against 109s.

Shaux gave up the chase and turned again. The lone fighter again turned to follow, showing him its outline as it banked, and Shaux saw immediately that it was indeed Dalton. As Shaux completed a semicircle, they were now on a reciprocal course with the black dots that had been chasing Dalton, with a combined closing speed of seven hundred miles per hour—a mile every five seconds. The dots took form and substance and rapidly resolved themselves into the frontal silhouettes of Messerschmitt 109s.

Shaux knew the chances of shooting down a small fighter aircraft in a head-on attack were ludicrously low, but he had no time to maneuver into a better tactical position, and he doubted Dalton could keep up if he tried something too unusual. This entire encounter would be over almost before it began—Shaux might well be dead in the next twenty seconds.

The 109s were slightly above him and would dive into the attack. Shaux would climb toward them to minimize his size as a target and then try to fly beneath them at the last moment and fire upward into their exposed bellies. It would be a highly risky maneuver. Unlike the ponderous Dorniers, the 109s were agile, fast, and heavily armed, and they held the tactical advantage. The entire engagement would last only a fraction of a second.

It would be cannons versus machine guns, and Shaux didn't like the odds. The 109s were each armed with three cannons firing explosive rounds, one in each wing and one firing through the propeller hub. Shaux counted five 109s growing in his sights—fifteen cannons in all. The destructive force of a cannon shell was far greater than machine-gun ammunition. Most of Shaux's machine-gun rounds would pass harmlessly through the enemy—assuming he managed to hit them at all—doing no more damage than sewing neat little holes in their skin. Cannon rounds, on the other hand, exploded on impact and tore up everything nearby. Thus these 109 pilots simply had to hit his Spitfire to do damage, whereas Shaux had to hit something important.

Regardless of the odds, the enemy was immediately upon him. Shaux opened fire at extreme range, hoping to unnerve an inexperienced pilot in one of the 109s or to score a lucky hit. Tracer poured from the 109s. *Whack-whack-whack-clang-clang-*CRACK-BANG*!* The leading 109 raked him with fire, the final cannon shell ripping through his canopy and tearing through his seat back beside his right shoulder. The Spitfire staggered. The sky was full of 109s, and the howling gale through his cracked canopy was deafening. The 109 leader pulled up as they closed, flinching away from a head-on collision, and Shaux flashed beneath him.

Suddenly he was clear. He began another stomach-wrenching turn, just in time to see the hapless Dalton ram a 109 and both aircraft explode in a fireball.

Another 109, presumably the one Shaux had fired at, was spinning earthward out of control, spewing smoke. He saw the pilot jump clear of his tiny cockpit, but his parachute cords must have opened too quickly and become entangled on the tail, for Shaux saw him following the 109 down, his spread-eagled arms and legs rotating as the aircraft spun, pulled to his death by his stricken aircraft.

The remaining 109s were turning to pursue Shaux.

The controls felt spongy in his hand, and, looking back, he could see loose metal flapping on his tail. A shred flew off, and then another. The entire aircraft was vibrating. What the hell was wrong? Then he saw it—the radio aerial, normally a taut wire stretching from behind the cockpit to the top of the tail, had torn loose from its mounting and was whipping the rudder like a flail. The cannon shell that had ripped through his seat back must have smashed the aerial's anchor.

The Spitfire decided to turn right. Shaux tried to coax it back and eased off the throttle to reduce the strain on the tail. He had absolutely no chance against the remaining 109s. The reduced speed seemed to allow him to control the aircraft, more or less, but he was losing height, and his airspeed had dropped to 250. The 109s were forming up behind him to take turns at blowing him out of the sky.

He watched death approaching. He applied more throttle, but the Spitfire started vibrating violently and turning right again. He throttled back. He couldn't climb at these revs, and he couldn't turn. The only way out was down, but the 109s were vastly superior to Spitfires when diving, since the Merlin engine had a nasty tendency to stall in that attitude.

The canopy handles were smashed and immovable, trapping him in the cockpit. He couldn't bail out.

The 109s grew behind him as they chased him down. Shaux wondered if he should say a prayer, but he didn't believe in God and it seemed implausible to start to do so now.

There was a verse about a fighter pilot dying somewhere among the clouds above, by the Irish poet William Butler Yeats: "I know that I shall meet my fate / Somewhere among the clouds above ..." *Well, this is my fate*, Shaux thought. These were Yeats's clouds. There was just about time for one last, deep breath before the shock of cannon fire.

Abruptly the 109s banked away, and beyond them Shaux saw fresh Spitfires—another squadron—arcing in pursuit. Perhaps it was time to start believing in God after all, but it seemed more practical to find a speed and attitude of flight at which he could persuade the Spitfire to fly under his control.

He looked down and found he was still over Midhurst. There was a huge fire just to the south of the town—perhaps that was where his Dorniers had crashed. He turned northeast toward home, wondering if the Spitfire would shake itself to pieces before he could land.

He touched down twenty-seven minutes after he had taken off.

0900 hours, Sunday, August 18, 1940
Air Ministry, London, England

Flight Officer Eleanor Rand of the Women's Auxiliary Air Force (WAAF) waited while the two men bemoaned the suspension of international cricket matches for the duration of the war. It was, she learned, intolerable.

They sat in the air minister's elegant, book-lined office in Whitehall before a magnificent Adams fireplace, sipping tea. The minister and his guest, Gavin Maxwell, who was the personal representative of the Australian prime minister, sat in large leather armchairs, while she perched on an uncomfortable wooden chair facing them.

It was further testimony to the horrors of modern warfare that the meeting was being conducted on a Sunday.

"Please continue, Mrs. Rand," said the minister at length, as if they had been waiting for her.

He was a decent enough boss, she supposed, although his constant amazement that a young woman could comprehend military matters—far less master them—was becoming progressively more irritating as the weeks passed. Nominally she was a member of the liaison team between the minister and RAF Fighter Command—naturally the chief liaison officer and the deputy chief liaison officer were men—but her competence and dedication had propelled her into a role as the minister's general factotum and maid of all work.

Having her available at times like this relieved the minister of the need to prepare for meetings or reveal his lack of command over the details.

"Certainly, sir," she said with due humility. "This phase of the German aerial offensive began six days ago, on August 12, when the Luftwaffe attacked the Chain Home station at Ventnor on the Isle of Wight."

"Chain Home, Mrs. Rand?" asked Maxwell. "What is Chain Home?"

He was a large man with a face bronzed by the sun, set beneath an unruly crop of white hair. He would make a wonderful Santa Claus at children's parties, she thought, complete with twinkling blue eyes. Only his twanging Australian accent didn't quite fit the part to her English ears—"Chine Home, Mrs. Rind?"

She glanced at the air minister.

"It's all right," he said. "Mr. Churchill was quite specific; he wants our Australian partners fully briefed—no secrets between allies."

She nodded and turned back to the Australian. "Chain Home is a string of special radio stations along the south coast, sir. They use a new invention called radio direction finding, or RDF for short. I believe the Americans are calling it 'radar.' The stations broadcast radio waves, which, just like light waves, bounce back off any solid object they strike, such as an enemy bomber. The RDF stations have receivers, and by pointing their antennae, they can determine where the returning signal is coming from. If two stations pick up the signal, they can triangulate and locate the enemy. The strength of the returning signal indicates the size of the enemy force."

"That's amazing," said Maxwell. "The wonders of modern science!"

"Indeed, sir. RDF allows us to locate Luftwaffe raids as they're forming up, over France and Holland and the English Channel, even in darkness, so we can get our squadrons of Hurricanes and Spitfires up before they reach us. We also have observers all along the coasts, of course, to spot them visually. It doesn't work perfectly, but it's infinitely better than nothing. Even ten minutes' warning can make all the difference."

"This is a new kind of warfare," Maxwell commented. "Aircraft were little more than toys in my day. Never saw them in Gallipoli."

She saw him glance at his empty left sleeve, tucked neatly into the side pocket of his jacket, and guessed this was his own personal memento of the 1914–18 war—the war that had been supposed to end all wars.

"Well, Gavin, air power is now the key," the minister said. "Whoever controls the air controls the English Channel. If the Luftwaffe can defeat the RAF, they can bomb the Royal Navy out of the English Channel. That will permit the Germans to launch an invasion across the Strait of Dover, the Pas de Calais, which is only twenty miles wide. Our army is in terrible shape after the evacuation from Dunkirk in June and wouldn't be able to resist an invasion for more than a week or two at best. Most of our soldiers were evacuated from Dunkirk successfully, but we had to abandon all our equipment. We have virtually no tanks and no artillery."

He shook his head. "If the Luftwaffe defeats the RAF, you'll be able to look out that window and see panzer tanks and goose-stepping SS formations, and Hitler will celebrate Christmas in Buckingham Palace. There's nothing except the RAF to stop him."

"Will the Luftwaffe defeat the RAF?" Maxwell asked.

Clearly the minister did not wish to answer so blunt a question directly; he glanced at Eleanor.

"It's impossible to say, Mr. Maxwell," she said. "Over the past week the Germans have been carrying out an intensive bombing campaign against RAF airfields and the Chain Home RDF stations. First they send formations of fighters as decoys to try to draw our own fighters up. Then formations of bombers follow them in and try to reach their targets, supported by additional fighters. Cumulatively they're sending hundreds of aircraft every day, often bombing the same targets repeatedly. They're trying to drive the RAF out of southern England."

"But, Mrs. Rand—"

"It's a question of mathematics, sir," she continued, overriding him. "We have approximately seven hundred fighters to defend the entire British Isles. They have, we estimate, a thousand fighters and fifteen hundred bombers. If we shoot down three of their aircraft for every one of ours, we'll lose. In fact, we're shooting down less than two of theirs for every one of ours. At the rate we're currently losing aircraft, the last remaining Spitfire will go down three weeks from now, and the enemy will have close to a thousand aircraft left."

"Good God, Mrs. Rand, you make it sound hopeless!"

"Not hopeless, sir, but victory is mathematically improbable."

"Are you a mathematician, Mrs. Rand?"

The tone of his question implied a joke, for how could a woman possibly grasp the pure reason and the cold logic that formed the foundations upon which mathematics was built?

"I am, sir," she answered, and his eyes widened a trifle.

The minister intervened.

"I fear Napoleon said that God is on the side of the big battalions, if I recall correctly," he said.

"It was Voltaire, sir," Eleanor said. Having taken a mild poke at the Australian's male chauvinism, she was unable to resist a similar poke at the minister's ample complacency. "However, as you will recall, Voltaire also said, 'God is on the side of those who shoot straight.' That's the quotation I prefer to remember in this situation."

"Ah, yes, indeed he did." The minister nodded, as if he were familiar with the works of the eighteenth-century French philosopher, and seemed to search for safer territory. "Please continue with the briefing, Mrs. Rand. What happens after enemy aircraft have been detected by RDF?"

"All the available RDF and Observer Corps information is relayed to RAF Fighter Command Headquarters at Bentley Priory in Stanmore—just north of London—where it's combined into a single assessment of the situation. It's called filtering, to eliminate contradictions and erroneous information. Once they're satisfied with the information, it's put into a map of where all RAF and Luftwaffe forces are and passed down the chain of command for action. Fighter Command is divided into five groups, each of which is responsible for defending a geographic area of the British Isles. Each group is divided into sectors, and each sector has a number of squadrons. I hope I'm being clear, sir?"

"Quite clear, thank you, Mrs. Rand."

"Air defenses in southeast England are the responsibility of 11 Group, commanded by Air Vice-Marshal Park. The information from Fighter Command is relayed to 11 Group Headquarters in Uxbridge, west of London, which in turn relays it to the sector airfields, who then dispatch the fighter squadrons in their sector—preferably Hurricanes to attack bombers, and Spitfires to attack fighters. The sector controllers tell the pilots where to fly using RT—that's radiotelephone. The controllers know where our fighters are because our aircraft transmit special identifying high-frequency radio signals called 'pip-squeak.' These signals are picked up by special defending fighter radio detectors. I hope that's also clear, sir?"

"Very clear, thank you, but why do Hurricanes attack German bombers, rather than Spitfires?" Maxwell asked.

"The best German fighter is the Messerschmitt 109, sir. It's very comparable to the Spitfire in terms of performance. The Hurricane is ten percent slower than the 109, so we prefer to use it against slower targets. Ten percent may not sound like much, but in aerial battle it's a huge margin. Also, as a practical matter, we have far more Hurricanes than Spitfires, and there are more German bombers than fighters, and so …"

"And so we're back to arithmetic, Mrs. Rand?"

"Precisely, sir."

1030 Hours, Sunday, August 18, 1940
RAF Christhampton, Surrey, England

Shaux completed his report to the squadron intelligence officer. Debenham had seen his two interlocked Dorniers and could confirm that victory. The IO looked very dubious about the 109, but Shaux knew exactly where it had gone down, and perhaps the Home Guard would find the crash site. The IO, a middle-aged RAF Volunteer Reserve (RAFVR) officer with heavy spectacles and a pedantic manner, pursed his lips in manifest doubt and said he'd look into it.

Shaux, unlike more ambitious pilots, didn't care about victories, and he didn't care whether he was accredited or not. All he cared about was, well … he couldn't really come up with anything on the spur of the moment.

There was not much to say about Haughton—it turned out it was Haughton, not Dalton, after all—because newly trained pilots had less than a 50 percent chance of surviving five sorties, or less than two days at the rate 339 was flying. Haughton's entire fighting career had consisted of spending fifteen or twenty minutes trying to follow Shaux through the skies before being rammed and incinerated. Tomorrow some other kid would arrive to take Haughton's place and might still be alive by midweek.

Shaux wandered out to inspect his reserve aircraft, which had a reputation for being a bastard, and then on to his own Spitfire. It was peppered with shell holes, and the canopy had been wrenched off with a crowbar to let him out. He could see how the radio aerial had flailed the skin of the rudder down to the raw spars—no wonder he couldn't fly straight.

"It's nothing much, just a scratch or two," a ground crew flight sergeant said dismissively. "We'll have her ready by teatime."

"Piece of cake, Flight." Shaux grinned, offering him a cigarette.

The sergeant ran his oily hands through his stubbly hair and then cupped them around the guttering match Shaux held out to him. A large notice on the fuel truck beside them read, "High-octane fuel. No smoking under any circumstances. *This means you!*"

"Cheers," the sergeant said, inhaling deeply. He turned to supervise his men. "No, no, Dobson—don't use a wrenches, adjustable; use a wrenches, torque, half inch."

RAF quartermasters maintained their inventory lists using descriptive phrases such as "Bolts, machine, 5/8th." Descriptions were often clarified by describing the purpose of the object, as in, "Sheets, bedding, for the use of." This phraseology had passed into general 339 vernacular, so that someone might complain that the squadron had run out of "papers, toilets, for the use of."

Shaux had an urge to grab a wrenches, torque, and help. He was a trained fitter—as the RAF referred to mechanics—but he knew the ground crew would be deeply insulted. They were fiercely proud of their aircraft and worked sixteen hours a day or more to keep them in the air; all were skilled craftsmen who considered themselves to be in a deadly battle with their unseen Luftwaffe ground crew opponents. In their opinion, this battle would be won or lost on the ground; a Spitfire could only beat a 109 if it was in perfect mechanical and aeronautical condition—flying was the relatively easier part. Shaux couldn't really disagree.

He turned away; he knew they hated to be watched as they worked, particularly by pilots. Indeed, the mechanics and repairmen who worked on the aircraft were careful not to develop any affinity for the pilots, because otherwise the stress of high pilot mortality rates might become too great to bear. Of the eighteen pilots who had made up this squadron when it was formed three weeks ago, only seven were still left, and fifteen others, like that kid Dalton—no, Haughton—had come and gone in the meantime. In 339's brief twenty-one-day history, twenty-six young men had fallen to their deaths, or been sprayed with high-octane petrol and set ablaze in their cockpits, or drowned in the chill waters of the Channel, or been shot dead at their controls.

The air-raid sirens began to howl. Shaux immediately ran to his reserve aircraft and clambered into it. The sergeant, on his heels, helped to strap him in and jumped down to pull away the wooden chocks holding the wheels. No time for a leisurely preflight checkout. Shaux flicked the magneto switches, raced through the rest of the starting sequence, and banged the starter. The Merlin started without hesitation, and Shaux gunned it to get the Spitfire moving.

Everywhere there were men running, swerving to avoid aircraft, getting fuel trucks and ammunition lorries started, tripping over discarded equipment—a disturbed ant heap of activity. Shaux narrowly avoided Debenham's prized Alvis motorcar and bounced across the grass, holding the stick between his knees as he pulled his helmet on.

He skidded into the wind and opened the throttle wide, struggling to get his gloves on. The tail came up, and as it did so, an enormous explosion erupted somewhere to his right, and then another, and he felt the Spitfire flinching away from the blasts. He saw the silhouettes of Luftwaffe Heinkel 111 bombers passing low over the field, their open bellies disgorging bombs.

The ground ahead of him lifted itself into a towering pillar of dirt and dust. Evasive action was impossible—he just had to sit there and hope his aircraft would become airborne without damage.

The controls became light, and he held the nose down until the last possible moment before pulling the stick back. The Spitfire vaulted off the ground like an athlete and flew through the pillar of smoke and debris at twenty feet, rocking violently. The engine coughed and hesitated as the air intake sucked in clods of flying turf. The Spitfire lost flying speed and fell. It bounced violently, almost flipping tail over nose, the propeller scything through the grass like some manic, giant mowing machine before the Spitfire regained an upright attitude.

The trees at the far end of the field were rushing toward him. He could not possibly stop in time. The Merlin was vibrating fiercely; either one of the propeller blades had been bent, or the main engine crankshaft had been distorted out of true. The aircraft was at flying speed but lacked the bite to lift. The ground at the end of the airfield ran sharply downhill toward a stream that meandered among the trees, out of Shaux's field of vision below the long engine housing. As Shaux careened down the hill, the ground literally fell away beneath his wheels. The Spitfire finally became unstuck and lifted reluctantly into the air. Treetops snatched at the wheels as he roared over them.

He steadied the aircraft and began a climbing turn, cranking up the wheels as he did so. The protesting Merlin pulled him up reluctantly. The Heinkels were at two thousand feet, he guessed; at this rate it would take him five minutes to reach that altitude, and he'd be highly vulnerable to attack all the way up. All he could do was aim for the nearest alternative airfield at Biggin Hill, try to stay out of trouble, and limp in when the coast was clear. He altered course toward Biggin at a mere one thousand feet.

He jumped in shock as a savage *whack-whack-whack* sounded somewhere in the fuselage behind him. Instinctively he turned hard right, into the Merlin's torque, to maximize the turn. He jumped again at a *whack-whack-whack-whack-whack* somewhere in his port wing.

Over his shoulder he saw a big, black twin-engine Messerschmitt

110 fighter hard on his tail, tied to him by lines of orange tracer. He turned even more sharply, and the tracer couldn't keep up with him. A 110 was too clumsy to present a challenge to an agile Spitfire under normal circumstances—but the circumstances were not normal, and Shaux's Spitfire was far from agile.

His laboring Merlin could not drag him through the sky fast enough to keep him in level flight during a turn this tight; the altimeter was unwinding. Behind his head the 110 was also wheeling as the pilot tried to pull its nose round far enough to bring the machine guns and cannons bristling in its nose to bear. Shaux dragged the stick back still farther into his stomach and turned tighter. At some point in an underpowered turn like this, without enough lift to counteract gravity, the Spitfire would stall out—drop below flying speed—and cartwheel earthward.

Shaux wrenched the stick over into an opposite turn. The Spitfire trembled and hesitated at the point of stalling before obeying him. Behind him the 110 followed his turn. Shaux continued to turn and continued to lose height. The ground rose beneath his left wing, and so did the elegant spire of St. Mary's Church, towering above the local village of Christhampton. The spire flashed past just beneath him, and he was now forced to straighten out or fly sideways into the ground. The gun-encrusted nose of the 110 followed him, spitting tracer as its guns bore anew, and flew into the spire.

There was a puff of gray dust and flying stonework as the top ten feet of the spire—built four hundred years ago in the reign of King Henry VIII, Shaux recalled irrelevantly—disintegrated, but the 110 flew on without a nose or canopy. Shaux could see its pilot, still at the controls, still flying by ingrained instinct, sitting in the open air in a howling two-hundred-miles-per-hour headwind surrounded by flapping shards of jagged metal. The body of his decapitated flight engineer sat neatly beside him.

Shaux crawled up to a thousand feet, and the 110 passed beneath him, headed for home. Its white-faced pilot stared up at him as they passed. Shaux should have turned for Biggin Hill before the Merlin shook itself to pieces, but something made him follow the 110. He tried never to think of the enemy in personal terms—he knew he couldn't fire at another aircraft if he ascribed any fellow humanity to its occupants—but this particular man seemed so alone, so vulnerable, that Shaux felt compelled to follow him, so that he wouldn't have to die unwitnessed and unremarked.

The 110 flew steadily southeastward, slowly losing height, while Shaux kept vigil above it, until at long last it flew just as steadily into a wooded hill near Liphook, where a pine tree impaled the unprotected pilot and plucked him from his aircraft. The 110 scythed through the treetops for another quarter mile before it crashed and exploded. Shaux turned laboriously, passing over the remains of the white-faced pilot spread-eagled in the branches, and coaxed his Spitfire northward.

He wondered whether Yeats had been translated into German.

1200 hours, Sunday, August 18, 1940
Air Ministry, London, England

Flight Officer Rand replaced the telephone in its cradle and stared at her notes. She turned to her typewriter and began her report.

Interim Battle Report for the Rt. Hon. Air Minister; 1200 hrs., August 18, 1940:

1. 3 airfields attacked—2 inoperable, 1 damaged with limited operations
2. 16 of our aircraft shot down, plus 14 damaged/destroyed on the ground
3. 22 victories claimed—16 bombers, 6 fighters

The Luftwaffe has launched 5 bombing raids and 2 fighter sweeps so far today:

1. 0600: 30+ Me 110, with 50+ Me 109 cover, conduct fighter sweep over Sussex and Surrey.
2. 0615: 40+ Do 110, with 30+ Me 109 cover, attack RAF Biggin Hill (Sector C) (32 Squadron, Hurricane; 610 Squadron, Spitfire) damaging runways and buildings.
3. 0630: a second wave of 50+ He 111, with 30+ Me 110 cover, attacks Biggin Hill. Airfield inoperative for 24+ hours with many unexploded bombs reported on the field.
4. 0800: 30+ Do 110, with 30+ Me 109 cover, attack RAF Croydon (Sector B Satellite) (111 Squadron, Hurricane) damaging buildings and aircraft.
5. 0845: a second wave of 50+ Do 110, with 50+ Me 109 cover, attacks Croydon. Armoury exploded with severe damage. Airfield inoperative indefinitely.
6. 1015: 40+ Me 110, with 50+ Me 109 cover, conduct fighter sweep over Sussex and Surrey.
7. 1030: 30+ He 111, with 30+ Me 110 cover, attack RAF Christhampton (Sector C Satellite) (339 Squadron, Spitfire)

damaging buildings and grass field. Airfield degraded but possibly operational.

She totaled the numbers. Assuming that the RAF victories were overstated, as they always were, due to two pilots claiming to shoot down the same enemy aircraft, damaged aircraft escaping, and ambitious pilots trying to advance their prestige and reputation, then Fighter Command had suffered a significant defeat.

This was the sixth consecutive day of attacks on RAF stations. If the Luftwaffe continued to pound the airfields, it was only a question of time—measured in days, rather than weeks—before 11 Group would be forced to withdraw north of London, beyond the range of 109s, ceding air superiority over southern England and the Channel to the Germans.

In those circumstances the Luftwaffe would blast the battered British army—still reeling from its catastrophic defeats in Belgium and France and its miraculous escape back across the English Channel from Dunkirk—out of Kent, Surrey, and Sussex, and the German army could invade with secure ports and little opposition. The rolling hills and broad fields of southern England offered no natural defenses against panzer tanks—no mountains, impenetrable forests, impassable marshes, or wide rivers—and the German army might advance to the suburbs of London within a week.

She shook her head and completed a report on pilot availability, a painful exercise involving crossing out the names of pilots who had not survived the day's battles and adding up the dead, squadron by squadron. Even though she knew almost none of them, the act of drawing a line through a name seemed like an act of execution. Who was—who had been—Pilot Officer Willoughby, K., of 501 Squadron, for example? Had he played the clarinet or sung tenor in a choir? What color had his hair been? Did his parents even know he was dead? Had he been married or engaged? Had he labored over poetry he composed for his truelove? Her pen hovered above his name. If she didn't cross it out, would he still be dead?

Well, goodbye, Willoughby, K., I hereby excise you from the list. I'm sorry, I really am, but I have absolutely no choice. Requiescat in pace. Rest in peace.

She almost held her breath when she came across the handful of names she did know. A few weeks ago she had drawn a neat line through her own husband's name. She came to 339 Squadron. There were several casualties, including a Haughton, C., but at least Johnnie Shaux, her friend from Oxford, did not need to be expunged.

At last the report was finished. She glanced back at her summary of the morning's battles. The equation was clear. It required the RAF to be able to put up twenty squadrons of aircraft, 250 Hurricanes and Spitfires, at any time. At this very moment, she calculated, 11 Group had twelve fully operational squadrons at best. A thought occurred to her, and she totted up neat columns of numbers. She started a fresh paragraph.

As the following chart indicates, the Luftwaffe flew approximately 960 aircraft over the 6-hour period. There were not less than 100 enemy aircraft over southern England throughout the morning, with a peak of 230. The Luftwaffe lost 2 percent of the aircraft it deployed, or 1 percent of its total force, while 11 Group lost 6 percent of its entire force.

Time	0600	0700	0800	0900	1000	1100	Average
Fighters	110	140	80	50	120	120	104
Bombers	90	90	80	50	30	30	62
Total	200	230	160	100	150	150	166

Since 11 Group lost almost as many aircraft on the ground as it did in the air, the Rt. Hon. Air Minister may wish to consider the feasibility of strengthening airfield defenses.

She lit a cigarette and stared at her report. It was, as usual, a recitation of attrition, but she had the nagging feeling it showed something else as well, something about the balance of forces above southern England ... True, she was no expert in aerial warfare, God knew, but these were numbers, and she *did* know mathematics. There ought to be more ... She was certain there was more ...

She pulled the report from her typewriter and took it to the minister's office before she made herself late.

1300 hours, Sunday, August 18, 1940
RAF Christhampton, Surrey, England

Shaux surveyed the damage caused by the Heinkel 111s. There were several deep bomb craters scattered across the field, and hesitant parties of ground crew and civilian volunteers were cautiously walking the grass expanse looking for unexploded bombs. The far side of the field was clear, or so they said, in case they had to take off in a hurry.

All the buildings had been damaged, and the officers' sleeping quarters were a pile of firewood. Shaux clambered over the debris but could find none of his personal belongings. He now owned nothing but the clothes he wore. He found the thought oddly liberating. His most treasured possession, a grainy sepia photograph of his parents on their wedding day, was safely in his wallet.

The villagers and local farmers had emerged from their cottages to help. Shaux watched a team of magnificent Clydesdale plow horses pulling a heavy cart laden with earth to fill in the worst of the bomb craters. The ramshackle control tower was listing at a drunken angle; the local blacksmith and assorted villagers were trying to reinforce it with wooden beams. The vicar of St. Mary's stood watch over a line of rudimentary coffins.

Several aircraft had been destroyed on the ground and riggers and fitters picked at them, scavenging for spare parts. Debenham's prized Alvis Speed 20 motorcar, spotless and shining, stood miraculously unharmed amid the wreckage.

Shaux had decided he couldn't reach Biggin Hill in his damaged Spitfire and had risked landing back here, picking a line between bomb craters like a snooker player picking a line between balls scattered across a table. The ground crew had already removed the propeller from the reserve Spitfire he had flown off when the Heinkels attacked. The tips of two of the blades had been distorted when he struck the ground during takeoff; it was a wonder it had flown at all. The crew was now wrestling with a replacement, which was dangling from a derrick and refusing to seat itself on the hub.

"Half an hour, sir," the sergeant said briefly, glancing nervously at the sky, fearful of a second attack. "They say they got Biggin and Croydon, too."

"So I hear," Shaux said.

"Murdering bastards," the sergeant said, turning back to the propeller. "Not *that* way, Brown, for Christ's sake—you'll bloody well ruin this one and all."

Shaux turned and found Debenham bearing down on him.

"Dave Johnson's dead," he told Shaux without preamble, referring to the 339 Squadron commander. "Bought it during takeoff."

He paused, but neither of them felt it necessary to comment.

"Anyway, they've put me in charge—acting squadron leader. We're being transferred to Oldchurch, in Kent; obviously this place is a complete mess."

He glanced around the field at the toiling ground crews and civilians and seemed to dismiss their efforts as futile. Shaux noticed that he had managed to find time amid the chaos to put squadron leader's rings on his uniform sleeves to denote his new rank. Or perhaps he'd had this uniform already, kept secretly in hope of professional advancement.

"We have seven serviceable aircraft and seven pilots. I've put Henderson in charge of A Flight; he'll have four chaps including himself. You'll be temporarily in command of B Flight until someone arrives to take it over. At the moment that's only you and Digby. Group has promised us replacements in Oldchurch tomorrow; perhaps they'll show up, perhaps not."

He flicked his cigarette into a pile of rubble. "Let's get cracking, Shaux; I've told group that 339 is fully operational, and by God I'll see to it that we are."

He strode away, pausing to yell unnecessary orders at a hapless farmer with a horse and cart, exulting in the mantle of command. It apparently did not occur to him that the farmer had voluntarily abandoned his harvesting in order to help.

At 1330, 339 took off for the short run to Oldchurch. Shaux half expected his hurriedly replaced propeller to fly off during the stress of takeoff, but it behaved perfectly, and the Spitfire felt like a Spitfire instead of a wounded bird. They were supposed to fly over to Oldchurch at five thousand feet, but they had been in the air less than five minutes when the voice of the sector controller rasped in their ears.

"This is Sapper calling Shadow leader. Vector to Canterbury at angels twenty. Over." Under RT protocol, "angels" meant thousands of feet, "Sapper" was the code name for the Biggin Hill sector, and "Shadow" was 339's call sign.

"This is Shadow leader, Sapper," Debenham's voice crackled back. "Vector to Canterbury at angels twenty, understood."

Shaux saw the nose of Debenham's Spitfire lifting. He applied more throttle and followed suit. They rose through a band of wispy clouds into the clear air above, and Shaux began his endlessly repeated search of the sky, horizon by horizon, quadrant of blue by quadrant of blue.

Above Canterbury, Debenham ordered him up to twenty-five thousand feet, and he and Digby, his wingman, continued to climb. At this altitude—about as high as a Spitfire could operate, almost as high as Mount Everest—he'd be able to spot incoming 109s before Debenham and dive down again to support the rest of 339 if necessary.

He could see Debenham far below him, leading the remainder of the squadron in a lazy circle with the gray mass of Canterbury Cathedral at its center. Shaux positioned himself a couple of miles farther south, squinting through the brilliant sunshine toward the coast, searching the thin air for the little back dots that could turn into 109s in seconds.

Twenty minutes of monotony ensued as Shaux tried to maintain his concentration. Canterbury Cathedral was the seat of the archbishop of Canterbury, the head of the Anglican Church. King Henry II had had Saint Thomas à Becket murdered there in 1170 and subsequently done penance before Thomas's tomb. Henry had been a great warrior, the most powerful man in Europe. What would he have thought of Spitfires defending his realm?

A second squadron of Spitfires appeared a little to the west at twenty thousand feet, and below them a squadron of Hurricanes. Obviously 11 Group was preparing for a major encounter. He wondered what would go wrong this time—he'd lost half his tail and half his prop so far today. Anyway, Henry II—

The controller's voice jerked Shaux back to reality. "This is Sapper calling Shadow leader. Bandits to your southeast crossing the coast at angels fifteen and twenty."

"Message received and understood," Debenham replied.

"This is Green Two," said Digby in Shaux's earphones. "EA visible ten miles southeast."

Shaux stared toward the sea once more, and now he could discern two thin, dark lines, as if a black pencil had been scribbled across the sky.

"Follow me," Debenham's voice sounded, and Shaux saw 339 turning north as Debenham maneuvered into a favorable position from which to launch an attack.

The higher line in the sky was resolving itself into individual small dots, while the lower line had become a cluster of larger blobs.

"This is Green Two," Digby added. "Forty-plus 109s at angels twenty; thirty-plus twin-engines at fifteen."

Digby really must have outstanding eyesight, Shaux thought.

From his vantage point at twenty-five thousand feet, Shaux watched the battle play out beneath him. The other Spitfire squadron to the west began a flank attack on the 109s. A dozen Messerschmitts broke off from the main formation and turned to face them. Within seconds the neat formations had unraveled into a whirling kaleidoscope of fighters, wheeling, turning, climbing, diving, rolling, intersected by streams of tracer, locked in a brief, furious dogfight. It was impossible to tell what damage was being done or which side was winning.

Another dozen 109s peeled off from the main group and descended on the squadron of Hurricanes, which was just closing with the bombers. A second dogfight erupted far below Shaux. The 109s held the advantage in height and speed over the Hurricanes; the outcome would not be good, and in the meantime the bombers could cruise on toward their targets unopposed.

The remaining 109s ignored these engagements and swept on over Canterbury, shepherding the bombers. Shaux saw that Debenham had completed his maneuvering and had formed 339 into line abreast for a frontal attack on the 109s. Johnson, their previous CO, had despised such formations—"long on drama, short on effectiveness," he had said—but clearly Debenham had different opinions.

The five 339 Spitfires flew straight at the twenty 109s. Shaux watched as the two formations swept through each other. One Spitfire collided with a 109, and the two aircraft spiraled earthward, but the 109s seemed otherwise unharmed.

"This is Green Two," Digby's voice crackled in his ears. "Another thirty-plus 109s at angels twenty; another thirty-plus Dorniers at fifteen."

Shaux looked toward the coast. Two more formations were emerging from the harsh brilliance of the sky, two more neat rows of dots. He thought he could see sunlight reflecting on the characteristic glass domes of Dornier 17s.

The Luftwaffe had sent 130 aircraft in the two waves; 11 Group had been able to muster less than 30 fighters to oppose them.

He looked down. The squadron of Spitfires, the Hurricanes, the remnants of 339, and the formations of 109s that had attacked them had all disappeared, leaving only a scattering of vapor trails to suggest they had ever existed; sixty aircraft had gone *poof!* in the sky, as if some celestial magician had cried "Abracadabra!" and waved them away.

Now only he and Digby stood between the new arrivals and their targets. This time it appeared that the Luftwaffe had successfully punched a breach in the line of 11 Group's defenses. The first thirty Dorniers were already through the gap, and another thirty were approaching. If the latest arrivals got through, over a hundred tons of high explosives would soon be raining down on the airfields of southern England.

He had no chance of seriously disrupting these new formations, but he also had no choice but to try. There was no regulation in the Fighter Command pilot training manual specifying that one shouldn't attack when the odds were thirty-to-one against. At least he had the advantages of height and surprise; the sun was behind him, and the 109s probably didn't realize he and Digby were all the way up here.

"Once more unto the breach," he muttered to himself, recalling his schoolboy Shakespeare.

"Message not understood; say again," Sapper responded, and Shaux smiled briefly.

He led Digby down in a shallow dive to meet the 109s, keeping in the glare of the sun. The 109s were dawdling, tied down to the speed of the Dorniers below them. He and Digby would have an airspeed advantage of well over a hundred miles per hour. The 109s were flying in six or seven formations of four fighters—*Schwarms*, as the Luftwaffe called them—with plenty of space between them; he could only attack one group, and all the other *Schwarms* would jump on him and Digby as soon as he did so. He picked the leading group hoping he could make them scatter and therefore disrupt, or at least disturb, the entire formation.

He swept down, still apparently unobserved, and fired a long burst at the leader and then the 109 behind him and then the 109 behind that. The probability of doing any serious damage was minimal, but at least he'd given them a shock.

As soon as he roared over them, he jammed the throttle wide open and executed a vertical loop, hoping Digby would have the wit to follow him.

A loop was a flamboyance best reserved for air shows—"not a gentleman's maneuver," his flight instructor had once told him primly—and usually self-destructive in combat, since the aircraft lost most of its speed in the climb; however, on occasions such as this, when the enemy had been taken by surprise and his initial airspeed was so much higher than theirs, it was worth a try.

He could see the 109s all the way through his loop. The leading *Schwarm* was breaking up, as he had hoped, and the remaining groups were wheeling round, assuming that there was at least a squadron of Spitfires on their tails. As Shaux came roaring back down out of his loop, another *Schwarm* flew conveniently into his gunsight. He fired at them at random.

The pilot of the last 109 must have been a novice, for he put his aircraft into a steep dive. This was the standard way of escaping attack since 109s could outdive Spitfires; 109s had fuel-injected engines, whereas Spitfires had carburetors that had an unfortunate tendency to run dry in a steep dive. On this occasion, however, the novice had succeeded only in keeping himself in Shaux's sights.

Shaux half rolled his Spitfire onto its back so that gravity would force fuel into the carburetors and followed the 109 down. He fired another long burst as they plunged earthward, more to frighten the 109 pilot than anything else. The 109 skittered one way and then the other as the pilot sought to escape. The pilot would not be getting more than occasional glimpses of Shaux behind the 109's tail, and he daren't pull out if Shaux was still there.

The rolling hills of southern Kent were racing up to meet them. Shaux broke off the attack and pulled his aircraft out of its inverted dive in a gut-wrenching maneuver. The 109 pilot, alas, was so focused on Shaux in his rear mirror that he failed to look elsewhere until too late. Perhaps he was disoriented by Shaux's inverted silhouette. His aircraft plowed a deep gash into a meadow before exploding.

Shaux was now far out of the battle and far too low to make any useful contribution. Digby appeared beside him and sketched a wave; he'd followed him faithfully through the frantic twists and turns.

Shaux waved back and then flew low until he could find a landmark— the ancient port town of Hastings, on the sea—and turned toward Oldchurch, wondering if it had been on the target list of the bombers that had pierced 11 Group's defenses.

1500 hours, Sunday, August 18, 1940
Air Ministry, London, England

Gavin Maxwell, the Australian prime minister's representative, returned to the Air Ministry in a somber mood. He had also visited the War Office for an assessment of the state of the British army following the evacuation of Dunkirk, and the Admiralty for an update on the status of the fleet.

He had lunched with Mr. Joseph Kennedy, the American ambassador, who had told him flatly that Britain would be defeated and that the American public was in no mood to come to the rescue, regardless of President Roosevelt's sympathy toward the British cause.

"Churchill should stop all this foolish fight-to-the-death nonsense and stop deluding the public into thinking there's a chance," Mr. Kennedy had told him. "The sun is setting on the British Empire, and the sooner Churchill finds out what terms Hitler will accept, the better. You Australians should conserve your strength and worry about Japan."

Maxwell pondered. Australians were indeed watching Japanese belligerence throughout Southeast Asia with increasing alarm. It would be foolish to send Australian men and supplies halfway round the globe to support a doomed Britain, only to subsequently fall prey to a Japanese onslaught on their own vast and ill-defended continent.

Unless Britain showed it could withstand and survive against the strength of Germany, it might have to be written off as a lost cause. All Australians felt loyalty to the mother country and the king, despite their fierce independence of spirit and despite their horrible losses in the Great War. But if England didn't stand a Buckley's chance, then Australia would have to look to its own best interests. The Australian prime minster, Robert Menzies, was still supporting Churchill, but Menzies was clinging to power by his fingernails and lacked Churchill's ability to rally his countrymen with towering rhetoric.

Maxwell privately regarded Churchill as not much better than a highfalutin, vainglorious, flimflam man who saw victory around every corner. The disastrous Gallipoli Campaign in the Great War had been one of Churchill's overreaching ideas. It had cost Australia and New Zealand over a hundred thousand casualties and Maxwell his left arm. Now, instead of bowing to the inevitable, Churchill was fighting a quixotic battle against unstoppable German forces instead of doing the obvious thing and suing for peace. Churchill seemed to have subordinated England's best interests to his own obsessive and pugnacious personality.

After all, no European country had been able to withstand the Nazi onslaught—dramatic armored advances spearheaded by Panzer tanks combined with devastating airpower, which the Germans called *blitzkrieg*—for more than a few weeks. The whole of western continental Europe had collapsed in May. Most of the British army had escaped by sea from Dunkirk, saved by civilian ships in Operation Dynamo, but the Germans had taken over two million—two *million*, Maxwell wondered in awe—prisoners of war from their defeated enemies.

In addition, RAF fighters had been unable to protect the skies over Belgium, Holland, and France against the Luftwaffe, and there was no reason to imagine that the formula had changed.

If the key to Britain's survival was the aerial battle now raging in the skies of southern England, then the chances looked very dodgy. Maxwell had pretty much decided to advise Mr. Menzies to take Joe Kennedy's advice, and he felt it was only fair to warn the air minister.

When he arrived at the ministry, however, he discovered the minister had been called away on urgent business and found himself being entertained by Mrs. Rand.

"The minister sends his apologies, sir," Eleanor told him as a tea lady old enough to be her great-grandmother perilously served them with shaking hands. "The Luftwaffe has been very active today, I'm afraid."

"Not to worry, Mrs. Rand," he replied, taking his teacup firmly before the tea lady spilled the contents over his impeccable trousers. In truth, he'd much rather talk to this young woman than the minister. She clearly had a better brain, and she surely had better legs.

"I'm interested in your mathematical approach to things, Mrs. Rand. You seem to cut through all the hoopla and get to the point. Tell me more about your analysis of the situation."

"Certainly, sir. Where would you like me to start?"

"Explain again why control of the air over the Channel is necessary for an invasion."

"Very well, sir. To conduct a successful invasion, the Germans need to be able to shuttle a very large number of slow, poorly armed or completely unarmed ships back and forth across the Channel for days and days on end—troop ships, supply ships, tankers, everything you can think of. It would be an armada of undefended barges. We could attack them with our navy or strafe and bomb them with aircraft."

Maxwell's mind again went back to the chaotic shores and blood-soaked beaches of Gallipoli, and he shuddered.

"The Germans have a smaller navy than ours, so they can't risk a sea battle against the Royal Navy, but they have far more aircraft. They could bomb any British ship that comes within fifty miles of their invasion fleet, and modern dive-bombers—particularly Luftwaffe Stuka dive-bombers—are highly effective against naval targets. Stukas have been successful at driving our civilian convoys out of the English Channel."

"I see."

"However, the Luftwaffe can only dive-bomb our navy if there are no RAF fighters to attack their bombers. Stukas are just about defenseless. Therefore, they have to exclude the RAF from the Channel and the North Sea, which means forcing 11 Group north of London, where they'd be too far away to defend the Channel and the Channel ports."

The tea lady almost spilled a bowl of sugar into the Australian's lap—but not quite.

"Once the Germans have done that—if they can do that—their invasion fleet will be safe from attack from the Royal Navy and from the RAF as well. Therefore, they're trying to shoot down our fighters and destroy our southern airfields. That's the whole point of the current battle in the air; it's to establish the conditions for an invasion, or, from our perspective, to deny them."

"You make it sound so logical, Mrs. Rand. Let me see: the Royal Navy can attack and defeat the invasion fleet; the Luftwaffe Stukas can attack and defeat the Royal Navy; the RAF fighters can attack and defeat the Stukas. Therefore, if the Luftwaffe drives the RAF fighters away, then the Stukas can drive the Royal Navy away, and the invasion force will safe. Amazing, Mrs. Rand; it's so logical—so mathematical!"

"I'm afraid it is, sir. Hitler can never be secure in Europe until he's defeated England."

She had lost some of her prim reserve, he noticed, as if she found logic exciting. He smirked inwardly—he had seduced women in many ways but never by logic. It really was a pity she was married.

"Why not? Even if he leaves England alone, your army has already been defeated, and there's not much you can do to damage him. He controls the entire continent."

"That's true, sir. But we control the seas. Napoleon was in a similar position of overwhelming power on the continent, but the British navy blockaded his ports and prevented him from importing everything he needed. Eventually his armies were sucked dry of supplies and lost. We can do the same and deny Hitler vital raw materials and supplies."

"And what are the odds for the air campaign?" he asked. "How do you calculate the odds in the middle of a battle?"

"You accumulate past statistics and project them forward to forecast an outcome. You project who will win and who will lose."

She paused and seemed suddenly lost in thought.

"And who will win, Mrs. Rand?"

"Actually you shouldn't project who will win, you should project who won't lose," she said, as if speaking to herself.

"Who won't lose? What do you mean? Can you do that?"

She appeared to be experiencing some private epiphany. To his secret delight she nibbled her bottom lip.

"What have you concluded?" he asked, reluctantly breaking into her thoughts.

"Concluded?" Abruptly she seemed to emerge from her reverie and refocus on their conversation. "Well, sir, 11 Group is theoretically capable of putting a maximum of twenty-four squadrons of twelve fighters into the air at any given time; that's a total of three hundred and sixty aircraft. For a variety of reasons—mechanical difficulties, pilot shortages, supply difficulties, mistakes, adverse local weather, and so on—it's hard to get more than ninety percent of the squadrons into the air, with ninety percent of their aircraft, so in real life the maximum is two hundred and ninety fighters. That's not all, however; we need to keep several squadrons in reserve, to provide coverage while other squadrons are refueling and rearming, so it's very unusual for us to have more than one hundred and fifty aircraft in the air."

"How many airplanes do the Germans send over?"

"It varies from day to day, of course, and the weather plays a major role. But, to answer your question, never less than one hundred at one time and sometimes five or six hundred."

"Then the odds are heavily against you!"

"Yes and no; we shoot down approximately five percent of the aircraft they send, while they shoot down three percent of ours."

"Then the odds are with you," he said in confusion.

"On a given day, they are; over a period of weeks, they're not. You see, this battle is being fought as much in the aircraft manufacturing plants as it is in the air. If they shoot down ten aircraft per day, we must replace them at the same rate to break even—seventy aircraft per week. In fact, we're producing about twenty Spitfires and twenty-five Hurricanes per week, so our reserves are steadily dwindling, at a rate of thirty-five aircraft per week. That's two whole squadrons."

He wrinkled his brow, as if attempting to calculate.

"That means 11 Group will run out of aircraft six weeks from now, assuming present trends continue," she told him. "The Germans, on the other hand, started with eleven hundred fighters. Even though we're shooting down more of theirs than they're destroying ours, statistically they're positioned to withstand heavier losses and still win. A similar set of statistics applies to pilots, sir—we're losing more than we're training, and the average novice is only surviving five hours of fighting."

"Only five hours? They must be suicidal!"

"On the contrary, sir," she said, very firmly. "For example, my late husband loved life, and he had everything to live for, but he still climbed into his Hurricane whenever the order came."

"I'm sorry, Mrs. Rand. I didn't realize ..." he mumbled.

She brushed his embarrassment aside impatiently. "A friend of ours at Oxford, now a Spitfire pilot, says you play the hand you're dealt. That's exactly what we're all doing, as best we can."

"But your own statistics ... You're a mathematician. Surely—"

"Benjamin Disraeli said there are lies, damn lies, and statistics. If that was true in the nineteenth century, it's even truer today."

She lit a cigarette, as if deciding that polite diplomacy would not persuade him. "Look, sir, if I may be frank, Australia—like America—has the luxury of deciding if it wants to sit this one out. We do not."

He felt offended without knowing why.

"Let me tell you a fairy tale, sir. There was a condemned man brought before a king. He told the king that if the king spared his life, in one month he'd teach the king's favorite horse to talk, or he'd go to the gallows without complaint. The king loved his horse and promptly agreed."

The Australian snorted.

"The condemned man's friends thought he was crazy—he should have accepted his fate rather than dragging out his misery. But the man said he'd made a good deal and had three ways of escaping execution. One, the king might die in the next month, and his successor might forgive him. Or, two, the condemned man himself might die of natural causes, in which case he'd have lost nothing."

"That's only two ways, Mrs. Rand. What was the third?"

"The man told his friends the horse might talk."

The Australian snorted again. "That's just a fairy tale, Mrs. Rand—the war is real. The Luftwaffe will defeat the RAF—your calculations prove it—and the German army will invade and conquer Britain."

"Wait a month and find out, sir. It's August 18. By September 18 we'll know if you're right or wrong."

"I'm right!"

She shrugged. "Current trends project that result, certainly, but all statistical projections contain a margin of error."

"Fairy tales, margins of error—baloney! England will fall!"

"Perhaps, sir; and perhaps the horse will talk."

1600 hours, Sunday, August 18, 1940
RAF Oldchurch, Kent, England

Shaux parked his Spitfire near Debenham's and clambered out unassisted. The ground crews and all their paraphernalia must still be on the road, somewhere between Christhampton and Oldchurch. He counted the Spitfires and found they had lost only one over Canterbury.

And then there were six, he thought.

He ambled out across the grass to inspect the airfield. Three months ago RAF Oldchurch had been a collection of sheep meadows surrounding a meandering stream. One of the meadows had doubled as the village cricket field; a local rule gave an extra run to any batsman who struck a sheep, and four runs if the sheep fell over. Then RAF engineers had surveyed the land and found it flat enough to serve as an auxiliary landing field. Bulldozers had arrived and carved off the gentle hillocks and used the scraped-off earth to fill in the streambed.

There had been no time or money or energy to dam the stream or channel out an alternative course. A soggy marsh had therefore appeared on the upstream side of the airfield where the irresistible forces of water and gravity were slowly cutting through the muddy fill, reclaiming the streambed, so that more than one unwary pilot had found himself flipped over on takeoff or landing as his wheels encountered a line of sticky ooze.

Still, the field was wide and reasonably flat, allowing aircraft to take off and land in any wind condition. Fighters could fly off five or six abreast, saving precious minutes when they scrambled.

RAF Oldchurch had no permanent buildings, he saw. A series of large tents served as an ammunition store, a hangar for major repair work, and a mess hall for the ground crews. A long line of smaller tents made of rotting, ancient canvas provided sleeping billets, latrines, a makeshift command post, and a rudimentary field kitchen. Shaux found a vacant cot in one of the drier tents and tossed his flying jacket on it to mark his ownership. He had no other possessions.

He wandered back outside. A line of Boulton Paul Defiants was parked at the edge of the woods. This type of aircraft looked like an oversize Hurricane with a rotating turret with four machine guns located behind the cockpit. It could not fire directly forward, backward, or downward. Early in the war it had achieved considerable success, surprising enemy fighters that attacked it from the rear quarters in traditional fashion, but the Luftwaffe had quickly learned its blind spots, and the weight of the gunner, the turret, and all the extra equipment made it too slow and clumsy to evade 109s or 110s.

Shaux had flown Defiants in the Battle of France and looked on them with affection despite their dangerous limitations. He noticed that one of them carried the identification code S for Sugar, the same code as the aircraft he had flown in France. Perhaps it was the same one. He'd had successes in his S for Sugar against the frightening but even more vulnerable Junkers 87 Stuka dive-bombers.

Defiants were now flown only in emergencies, and their crews were sitting out the battles raging above them, some in envy and some in relief. The most practical effect of the Defiants on RAF Oldchurch seemed to be that their pilots and ground crews had established proprietary claims over the least unpleasant facilities and accommodations.

"This is an *outrage!*" Debenham's strident tones came through the thin walls of a dilapidated tent. He emerged and stood toe to toe with another squadron commander, presumably the leader of the Defiants.

"I'm not going to strip my chaps of fuel and ammo just to satisfy you," the Defiant leader said to Debenham. "We've only got enough for two sorties."

"When were you scrambled last? Easter Sunday? In the last bloody war? I'm telephoning Biggin Hill."

"Be my guest; they've been out of contact for three hours."

Shaux walked away from the argument and entered the hangar tent. The Defiant ground crews were reading, sleeping, or playing cards, according to their characters. He recognized one of the card players—a burly flight sergeant whom he had last seen in the panicked evacuation of France.

"How's it hanging, Flight?"

The sergeant looked up and recognized him. "Fair to middling, Mr. Shaux. A bloody sight better than Arras."

They shook hands, both lost for a moment in the last days of the Battle of France two months before. In the chaotic collapse of the French army and the British Expeditionary Force, the few RAF squadrons in France had been savaged by overwhelming numbers of Luftwaffe aircraft, bombed and strafed out of airfield after airfield and driven back toward the sea. Shaux had been flying S for Sugar, searching for Stukas and trying to evade 109s.

The sergeant had been frantically scrounging for spare parts, fuel, and ammunition—everything it took to keep S for Sugar operational.

Their last airfield had been outside Arras in northern France. German tanks had been less than five miles away when the squadron received orders to retire to England. The pilots and air gunners would escape by air, but the ground crews were sure to be captured and locked away in POW camps, probably for years. Shaux had squeezed the sergeant into the narrow space behind the pilot's seat in his Defiant. His fitter, a diminutive Welshman named Jones, had sat on Shaux's lap. His armorer had crawled into the rear fuselage, where he'd lain flat on his face in the thundering darkness. The Defiant had barely made it off the ground with six hundred pounds of extra weight, and they had crawled across the Channel fifty feet above the waves.

"Any chance of some fuel and ammo, Flight?"

"Of course, Mr. Shaux," the sergeant replied, rising to his feet. He raised his voice. "Lively, now, you lads; let's get these Spits fed and watered."

Shaux thanked him and walked back to the squadron commanders, who seemed on the verge of blows, trying to think of some way of keeping the Defiant officer's attention diverted while his ground crews worked.

An airman emerged from one of the better tents, which was festooned with telephone wires. "Biggin's back on the phone, sir," he called.

The two squadron commanders jostled as they entered the tent, each determined to get the first chance to complain about the other. Debenham reemerged, his face like thunder.

"Bloody Biggin took their side," he whined.

Shaux led him out of earshot and nodded his head toward the Spitfires, now surrounded by the Defiant ground crews.

"Can you keep him occupied another ten minutes?" Shaux murmured.

Debenham smiled and turned back to the tent. "This is bloody *unacceptable!*" he roared as he entered.

Ten minutes later the ground crews were back in their hangar. Shaux sauntered into the operations tent. The airman was listening on the phone.

"Sector asks if you can go to readiness, sir?" the airman asked Debenham.

Debenham glanced at Shaux, who nodded fractionally.

"Tell them we can," Debenham said. "We have only six aircraft, but we're ready."

He struck a pose and turned to the Defiant commander. "We'll fly with half-empty tanks and half-empty ammunition belts," Debenham told him grandly. "I wouldn't take your bloody help for all the tea in bloody China."

Five minutes later 339 took off for the fifth time that day. Or perhaps it was the sixth time—Shaux couldn't be certain. He found it hard to concentrate and was surprised when they crossed the coastline within five minutes, forgetting how far south Oldchurch was. The sector controller vectored them to Folkstone at twenty thousand feet, and Shaux began to search the sky once more; northern horizon, western horizon, southern horizon, eastern horizon, forward down past the port wing, back down past the port wing, forward down past the starboard wing, back down past the starboard wing, northern sky, western sky, southern sky, eastern sky, northern horizon, western horizon, southern horizon, eastern horizon …

"Aircraft approaching Folkstone from the sea, at our altitude," Digby's voice sounded, and Shaux couldn't tell if there was static or his voice was cracking. "Sorry—I mean this is Green Two; EA south, angels twenty."

Shaux had looked there not five seconds before and failed to see them; now he could see them clearly. He blinked several times to clear his eyes. Thank God for Digby …

"Follow me," Debenham said, turning his Spitfire sharply. The depleted squadron wheeled round, and the incoming aircraft assumed the shapes of twenty Messerschmitt 110s. The 110s turned away from 339— either as a preplanned navigational course change or to avoid 339, Shaux could not tell—in the direction of Hastings. Shaux estimated they were ten miles away and it would take six minutes to chase them down.

He resumed searching the sky. The 110s might well be bait, with 109s above them waiting to pounce on any Spitfires doing as Debenham had done. Northern horizon, western horizon, southern horizon, eastern horizon, forward down past the port wing, back down past the port wing, looking back along the coastline … He blinked twice and refocused. Another formation was approaching the coast far below them.

"Green Leader calling, twenty-plus bandits to the southeast at angels ten," he said, speaking slowly and clearly. It seemed the 110s were trying to draw them away from a low-level bomber formation. If there were Hurricanes in the area, they'd continue chasing the 110s; if not, they'd be redirected back to the bombers.

"Sapper calling Green Leader, acknowledged. Shadow, continue on present course."

Five minutes later the 110s turned toward France, and Debenham reported their new course. Shaux guessed there were 109s waiting for them out over the Channel, and sector must have reached the same conclusion; the controller ordered the depleted 339 to break off and return to Oldchurch. As they turned for home, Shaux saw another squadron of Spitfires in pursuit of the 110s.

A wave of exhaustion swept over him, and he could not stop yawning, as was often the case at the end of a sortie. The squadron doctor said it was something to do with adrenaline levels, whatever they might be, just a normal human reaction, but for Shaux it was a sign of danger; more pilots died on the journey home when they were relaxed and less vigilant than on the journey out. Enemy fighters liked to stooge around airfields looking for tired, unwary pilots returning home with their minds on the first pint of beer at the local inn. He'd done the same thing in France around Luftwaffe bases.

He tried to maintain his disciplined sweeping of the sky, but his eyelids felt like sandpaper. The subdued thunder of the Merlin was a lullaby. How many more times could he sustain severe aircraft damage and live to tell the tale? The flailing radio aerial, the bent prop blades … He'd only survived by luck. His number would come up on the next patrol or the one after that. There were simply too many enemy aircraft, too many chance encounters, too many things that could go wrong. He was fated to die somewhere among the clouds above, as Yeats had written. If not today, then tomorrow. Tomorrow and tomorrow and tomorrow …

Enough of that nonsense. He shook his head and blinked his eyes, adjusted himself on the uncomfortable parachute, and resumed his surveillance.

1700 hours, Sunday, August 18, 1940
11 Group Headquarters, Uxbridge, Middlesex, England

Eleanor stood on the balcony overlooking the operations room at 11 Group Headquarters in Uxbridge, a few miles west of London. 11 Group occupied Hillingdon House, and the operations center was located in a bombproof bunker deep underground.

The large room below the balcony was dominated by a vast map of southeastern England painted on a table some thirty feet square, so that the controllers, who sat in windowed balconies, could look down on the entire battleground. WAAFs stood around the table wearing telephone headsets, listening to reports of aircraft movements relayed to them from the RDF stations and the Observer Corps. They pushed small plaques across the map as the battle developed and fresh information came in; each plaque showed the identity, size, and height of Luftwaffe and RAF units.

On the opposite wall were tall displays showing the status of each squadron in each sector, with lights indicating if they were stood down, at readiness, or in the air. The displays were known as the "tote board," and the lower the lights on a squadron's readiness "ladder," the higher its state of readiness. The highest state was "Enemy sighted." She saw that more than half of 11 Group's squadrons were flying.

She was in distinguished company. In addition to the air minister, the commander in chief of Fighter Command, Air Chief Marshal Sir Hugh Dowding, was discussing the situation with Air Vice-Marshal Keith Park, the commander of 11 Group, and Air Vice-Marshal Trafford Leigh-Mallory, the 12 Group commander. The four men controlled Fighter Command and perhaps the fate of England.

Dowding was universally acknowledged to be a brilliant organizer and visionary thinker. This control room, indeed the entire Fighter Command organization, was his brainchild—the "Dowding system." It was he who had championed the Chain Home RDF stations and all the other communications innovations, devised the command system of group and sector controllers, and fought for the development of the Spitfire and the Hurricane.

All this he had done in the four years before the war, despite the prewar Chamberlain government's reluctance to spend money on military investments and despite the naive belief that Hitler could be accommodated and there would be "peace in our time."

Well, Eleanor thought, Chamberlain had made that prediction only two years ago at Croydon airfield, waving a letter signed by Hitler for the press photographers, and Hitler had bombed Croydon airfield this morning.

More controversially, Dowding had resisted demands that Spitfires be sent to France to support the British Expeditionary Force and the French army in the face of the German onslaught in the spring, insisting—prophetically—that they must be kept in reserve to defend English skies. He had been pilloried for abandoning the BEF to its fate at Dunkirk; in fact, he had committed more than two hundred fighters, although not the magical Spitfires. The RAF had shot down 150 Luftwaffe aircraft, but Dowding had not been forgiven in the popular imagination. Eleanor's husband had given his brief life in that endeavor.

Dowding was known as a morose and formal man, a private soul who seldom left his office in Fighter Command Headquarters at Bentley Priory, a few miles away, trusting Air Vice-Marshal Keith Park, the commander of 11 Group, to manage the tactics of the battle.

Park was a New Zealander, the man who stood here all day, every day, watching the map spread out beneath them and deploying 11 Group forces. He, too, was accused of being overly cautious, of not throwing the full weight of his command into every battle. He was a counterpuncher, a conserver of strength, a boxer intent on denying the enemy ultimate victory, preferring to harry and weaken the Luftwaffe rather than be drawn into a pitched battle against vastly superior German forces.

Eleanor saw the mutual respect that flowed between Dowding and Park; she could see it in their clipped sentences and the way they could communicate by gestures and inferences. She saw a stubborn determination, a fatalistic acceptance that the survival of England rested in large part on their shoulders and that a single misjudgment could lead to disaster.

"Kesselring's trying one last time before it gets dark," Park said, his casual tone belying the strain etched into his features. "He has 110s trying to draw us west, so he can slip his bombers into the gap. They may take crack at Hawkinge or Manston or Lympne or even Oldchurch or the Chain Home stations at Dover and Foreness. We'd better take precautions."

Generalfeldmarschall Albert Kesselring was the commander of

Luftflotte 2, based in the Pas de Calais. She had heard it said that the mutual respect between Reichsmarschall Herman Göring—head of the Luftwaffe—and Kesselring was similar to that between Dowding and Park.

Kesselring was throwing everything he could at 11 Group that day, but 11 Group still had as many fighters in the air as it had at dawn.

Park picked up the phone and ordered a squadron of Hurricanes to the extreme southeast corner of England.

The last member of the distinguished group was very different from Dowding and Park. Air Vice-Marshal Trafford Leigh-Mallory, the commander of 12 Group, which defended central England, did not attempt to hide his scorn for Park's tactics.

"Dammit, Keith, why do you insist on scattering your squadrons across the map?" he demanded. "Why send one squadron to defend four targets? You should be concentrating three or four squadrons into a single wing and smashing their formations. Instead, you're swatting at flies with a lace handkerchief!"

"If you can tell me where the enemy will be in half an hour, I'll send my squadrons there," Park said icily, keeping his eyes on the map below. "Further, I'll request you to send yours also. Where exactly is that, Trafford? Will it be southeast Kent, or will they come north to West Malling or Biggin Hill again?"

"That's not the point! You're—"

"That's precisely the point," Park said, cutting him off. "It takes time to assemble a Big Wing, and it leaves the rest of the map vulnerable. Unlike you, I don't have a crystal ball."

"If you were better organized—"

"I'd be better organized if your so-called Big Wings did a better job of defending my airfields. Can you have four squadrons over Biggin thirty minutes from now?"

"Gentlemen, please!" Dowding interjected mildly. "We've had this discussion several times before."

"Yes, we have," Leigh-Mallory replied hotly. "Furthermore, we'll continue to have it until you concede I'm right and do it my way."

Eleanor had heard that there was bad blood between Park and Leigh-Mallory, but this was the first time she'd seen it in person. Dowding and Park had been distinguished fighter pilots in the 1914–18 war, while Leigh-Mallory had commanded a bomber and reconnaissance squadron. Perhaps that was why his views on fighter tactics were so different from Park's, she thought.

Park broke off the interchange to answer a phone call.

"Park speaking … Good afternoon, Freddie … Yes, 339 should stand down for the rest of the day. They can't have more than half a dozen aircraft ... I'll make them the top priority for replacements tomorrow."

"We're here to discuss reinforcements," said the air minister hurriedly as soon as Park hung up and before the argument could start again. "How many operational aircraft do you have, Park?"

"Oh, somewhere between two hundred twenty-five and two hundred fifty, Minister, I should say."

"You had two hundred thirty-seven operational Hurricanes and Spitfires at 1500 hours, sir, including one squadron from 10 Group at Tangmere," Eleanor said, forgetting she was a humble note taker.

Park's eyes left the map below and focused on her. He looked exhausted, she thought, rather than irascible.

"Did I?"

"I called all the sectors at that time, to give the minister an update, and that's what they reported, sir."

She waited for an explosion, but none came.

"Thank you," he said. "In that case, Minister, in the immediate future I'm more concerned with pilots than aircraft. If I could get my squadrons up to full muster, the pilots wouldn't have to fly four or five times a day."

"Exactly," Dowding said. "We're supposed to have eighteen pilots for every squadron, but with such heavy losses over the last few days …"

"Do you know how many pilots there are?" Park asked Eleanor, with no sarcasm she could detect.

"Not exactly, sir. There were two hundred sixty-three available at 1500, but there's bound to be twenty or so strays one way or the other."

"She's a walking adding machine," the minister said with a proprietary smile. "I've never known her wrong."

"I see," Park said.

"I'm often wrong, sir," she said to Park. "Accurate data are hard to obtain, and people have more important things to do than count."

"I see," Park said again.

1800 hours, Sunday, August 18, 1940
RAF Oldchurch, Surrey, England

A t 1800 the Defiant squadron emerged from their quarters and clambered into three dilapidated lorries.

"Where the hell's the mess? Where do we eat?" Debenham demanded as they prepared to depart.

"It's in the village hall. You'll have to walk, but it's only half a mile," one of the Defiant officers called back, and the convoy departed with grinding gears and belching exhaust fumes.

Debenham jumped into his splendid Alvis and roared off in pursuit of the lorries. He did not offer anyone a lift. The rest of 339, the pilots still in their flying equipment and the newly arrived ground crews in their overalls, set off to follow in a bedraggled column. Shaux was torn between hunger and exhaustion.

They emerged from the woods that surrounded the airfield and came to the village. The hall stood beside a tiny Norman church. Inside the hall the Defiant squadron was finishing its dinner. Aromas of roast chicken and mashed potatoes filled the air. The ladies of the Women's Volunteer Service, who managed the makeshift canteen, were apologetic but helpless when 339 trooped in; they had not been informed of 339's arrival and had no more food to offer them.

Debenham, who was just completing his meal, exploded with rage, and the WVS ladies cringed before his wrath, reduced to tears.

"We've been up since dawn," he ranted. "We've flown five missions today. We've lost good men. We've been defending you with our lives, for Christ's sake, and now we're bloody well hungry!" He did not let the fact that he had already eaten hold him back.

"It's not our fault," one of the women wailed.

"It's not our fault," Debenham whined in cruel parody. "It is your bloody fault, you stupid cow! It's your duty to feed us. We've done our duty; now you bloody well do yours!"

"But—"

"You're nothing but a bunch of useless bitches!" he roared. "You make me bloody sick!"

He turned on his heel and strode from the room.

A long silence followed. The men of the Defiant squadron scraped back their chairs and left, some chuckling at the practical joke they had played on 339 and some shamefaced.

The pilots and ground crew of 339 stood in a forlorn huddle.

"Look, of course it's not your fault," Shaux said finally. "Forget what he said—he's had a difficult day, that's all."

"Nobody told us you'd be coming," one of the women said. "How were we supposed to know?"

"Do you have anything you can spare?" Shaux asked. "A few loaves and some cheese for sandwiches? Anything like that?"

"Well, we could ask in the village to see if anyone's got anything spare," the woman said doubtfully. "But what with the rationing and all …" Her voice trailed away.

"I've got half a loaf and a bit of cheese," said another.

"Mrs. Watkins may be able to help," said the first woman. "She's the vicar's wife. We've still got plenty of tea; you sit down and have a cuppa, and we'll see what we can do."

"That's very kind of you," Shaux said.

"You're welcome, I'm sure," she replied, and her face lit up with a smile. "Come on, ladies, let's organize a picnic."

They returned in half an hour with diced potatoes in beef broth— "almost stew, if you shut your eyes," their leader said—as well as bread, cheese, and tomatoes for grilled sandwiches; pickled onions; and an assortment of half-eaten homemade fruitcakes. It was a far better dinner than Shaux had grown used to in the mess at Christhampton, and he told them so; the ladies blushed and smiled and promised to do better tomorrow.

The men of 339 crossed the street to the village inn, a long, low, rambling building with unexpected gables set at odd angles. A plaque on the wall informed visitors it had been rebuilt following a fire in AD 1342. *Six hundred years ago*, Shaux thought. The public bar was long and narrow, with massive hand-hewn beams supporting the upper floor, and the air was redolent with beer fumes and thick with tobacco smoke. The room was crowded with the Defiant squadron, who were already in a raucous mood, and a selection of locals, who talked in softer tones and watched the antics of the airmen with tolerant amusement.

Shaux navigated his way through the crush and ordered a pint of bitter.

"You're with the new Spitfire squadron?" the publican asked.

"Yes, we were bombed out of Christhampton this afternoon. My name's Shaux."

"Well, the RAF is always very welcome here," the publican told him. "Jack and Mabel Winslow at your service. Mind you, I have to say your CO's a bit of a handful. Marched in here demanding room and board like we're the Royal Hotel in Brighton. Told me to garage his car in case it rains. Upset the wife and all."

"Well, he had a difficult day," Shaux responded vaguely, wondering whether Debenham had ever entered a room without grating on at least one of its occupants' nerves; an image of an infant Debenham disrupting a nursery leaped into his head.

Digby, his new wingman, joined him at the bar.

"I owe you a pint, Diggers," Shaux said. "Thank God for your eyesight—nobody else saw those buggers coming in over Folkstone."

"Thanks—actually I'm a bit of an ornithologist, so I've spent half my life trying to see things in the sky."

"A bird-watcher? That's very appropriate in this business."

One of the Defiant pilots joined them. "Catch anything up there, chaps?"

"No. There was some trade up there, but sector gave it to other people. I can't say I'm sorry."

"Busy day?"

"Four outings, I think."

"Five," said Digby. "Four out of Christhampton and one from here. What about you?"

"Oh, we only take off if they think we're going to be bombed. Never have been, so we've never taken off."

"I see," Digby said politely. Shaux could tell he was contrasting the nonstop action of a Spitfire pilot, flying all day, every day, until the rivets shook themselves loose, with the leisurely life of the Defiant crews.

"The Defiants did their bit in France, while the Spits stayed safely at home," Shaux told him. "The Defiant was a good idea but not quite good enough."

"Bloody death trap, if you ask me," the Defiant pilot said. "I can't wait to get transferred to Hurribirds or Spits."

"Another pints, bitter, drinking, for the use of?" Digby asked, using 339's private argot.

He and the Defiant pilot began a technical discussion of the relative merits of different types of fighters. Shaux found he was losing track of the conversation. He excused himself and walked wearily back to the station, barely able to drag one foot after the other. The events of the day blurred into one long, amorphous dogfight, a cavalcade of near disasters.

He fumbled his way to his cot—he hoped it was the right one—and collapsed upon it. A variety of insects greeted him.

2100 hours, Sunday, August 18, 1940
Air Ministry, London, England

Eleanor Rand removed her glasses to rub her weary eyes, sipped her tea, lit a cigarette, and turned to the next report. She glanced through it and noticed that 339 Squadron had been posted to RAF Oldchurch until RAF Christhampton could be repaired. Seeing mention of 339 made her think of Johnnie Shaux and Oxford.

In her last year at Oxford she had been drawn into the glittering social set—*the* social set—that revolved around Rawley Fletcher and George Rand, and her friend Johnnie Shaux had followed in her wake.

Rawley Fletcher was her first love. He was handsome, debonair, and elegant; he was the heir to an ancient peerage and carried himself as she imagined the cavaliers of old England had done, floating through life far above the hoi polloi; a man with, perhaps, an exotic past and doubtless a glorious future. Everyone knew who he was. She and half the girls in Somerville College were half in love with him before they even met him.

George Rand was his companion and opposite. While Fletcher was an indifferent and uncaring scholar who seemed to view ignorance as a virtue, Rand was brilliant. While Fletcher resembled a Greek god, Rand was rotund and slothful. Rand had a sharp and cruel wit, rapacious appetites, and was given to extravagances—he was said to be absurdly rich. He was known for his habit of consuming champagne and caviar for breakfast, for the composition of erotic poetry, and for hosting parties with a bacchanalian reputation.

Eleanor's mother saw Oxford solely as an opportunity for finding a suitable husband. She dismissed Eleanor's academic interests as a tiresome and unladylike eccentricity. Women did not need to know anything for themselves, because men would tell them whatever they needed to know. She ridiculed Eleanor's tentatively expressed ambitions to apply her mathematical talents to a professional career, perhaps in the novel and exciting field of quantum mechanics or the new American zero-sum mathematical theory.

Young ladies in the upper reaches of society did not *work*, and they certainly did not *think*, for goodness' sake, her mother insisted—they found a suitable husband so that they could breed. Eleanor's sisters were already suitably married and breeding appropriately, and she half believed her mother's dire warnings of arid and aimless spinsterhood.

Rawley Fletcher singled her out at a ball, as if hailing a taxi, and she responded to his advances partly out of curiosity and partly out of duty to her mother. A candlelit dinner followed. In the next days, there were punting expeditions on the river and outings in his outrageously fast Bentley motorcar. There were even exhilarating trips in airplanes, for Rawley and George were members of the exclusive Oxford University Air Squadron. Sometimes she paused to wonder whether she was actually dazzled or simply trying to be dazzled, but this was all new and extraordinary, and she let herself be swept onward.

Two weeks after their first meeting, Rawley seduced her in a sunlit meadow, an energetic performance that left her puzzled by its brevity, his apparent disregard for her comfort, and her own lack of emotion or satisfaction.

The moment he had finished, he sprang up. "The first time's always the worst for a girl," he told her cheerfully. He reached down to pull her up. "You'll get used to it—practice makes perfect, as they say. I'll tell you what: we'll do it again later. Now let's get back to Oxford; we're supposed to meet George for tea. Get a move on!" He patted her rump, as he might have patted a horse he had ridden, and pulled on his clothes.

Back in Oxford, he casually mentioned the encounter to George, and she burned with humiliation. George smirked, and Johnnie Shaux—their silent fourth, as always—looked outraged.

"Game, set, and match, old chap! Well done, Rawlers!" George said to Rawley, who grinned modestly as if he had just won a tennis tournament.

Thereafter Rawley would come to see her every few days, sometimes staying no more than fifteen minutes. She felt she was an observer rather than a participant, as if she were watching him play polo. He moved with athletic grace and steady, purposeful rhythm, his eyes closed in concentration. As the end of his exercises approached, he would cry "Tallyho!" and his movements would become swifter, like a runner making a final sprint to the finishing line.

"Splendid, old girl," he would say, with a peck on her cheek and a pat on her rump, before hurrying off. He called it "humping," a term she had not heard before.

Lacking any experience of men, she assumed his physical attention to her would turn into love, and then he would seek to give pleasure as well as to take it, and "humping" would evolve into "making love." At times she wondered whether she really loved him or simply the idea of him. She was twenty-one, and her mother's voice rang loudly in her mind. She considered that perhaps she should resist his advances until he proposed, but she feared to take the risk—humping seemed to be his primary interest in her, and he might seek an alternative humpee.

Shortly before the end of their last term at Oxford, the four of them—Rawley, George, herself, and Johnnie Shaux—went punting on the river. Their final examinations were over, for better or worse, and George had provided a lobster and champagne picnic. They reclined on cushions in the flat-bottomed boat amid a variety of hampers and ice buckets while Johnnie, as usual, was relegated to the task of punting, standing on the stern and thrusting the punt along with a twenty-foot pole.

"Farewell to youth, farewell to innocence," George drawled as Johnnie propelled them smoothly up the River Cherwell. "The real world, whatever that may be, beckons us. What shall become of us, when we become real? I, for one, will go to Paris, where I will attend the Sorbonne, exploring nineteenth-century French literature as a subterfuge for exploring Gallic decadence in all its many-faceted glory. Á recherché de la grande epôche and so forth; shades of Henri de Toulouse-Lautrec etcetera. Indeed, I propose a toast to decadence, long may it seduce us. Vive la décadence!"

They drank to decadence, and George refilled their glasses.

"I shall delay my departure until after your wedding, of course, Rawley, old chap."

"Wedding?" Eleanor gasped, her heart in her throat. How typical of Rawley to confide in George that he intended to marry her and fail to mention it to her! Sometimes, in the dark of night, she had wondered whether he were just a cad, using her as a humpee of convenience; but no, here was evidence his motives were noble after all. She glimpsed a hopefully golden future, in which Rawley's love for her would be as complete as she supposed hers would be for him and in which she would earn her mother's delight and even admiration at her accomplishment.

"Oh, yes, I've been meaning to mention it, old girl," Rawley said to her. "You know Jessica O'Leary, the American girl? Her father's filthy rich, railways or oil wells or something, and with her money I'll be able to put Fletcher Castle back in shape."

He saw her expression.

"Well, it's the right thing to do," he said, as if annoyed that he had to justify himself. "It's a matter of family honor. Father lost most of our money in the crash of '29, and the old coot had to mortgage the estate up to the hilt. We're practically paupers—I might have to give up the polo ponies, and I can't even afford an airplane of my own! Now, with Jessica's money, oodles of American dollars, I'll be able to restore the family fortunes."

She could not speak.

"Don't worry, old girl," he told her, patting her hand. "I won't drop you—you can still be my mistress."

The boat shook violently as Johnnie missed his stroke and fell into the water with a mighty splash. Rawley and George collapsed in gales of laughter. She helped Johnnie to pull himself from the water, his muddy splashes hiding her tears. He grasped the side of the boat and stared into her eyes, seeing her anguish, and his face mirrored her pain.

Johnnie Shaux had been their humble follower; Jeeves to their Bertie Wooster, Boswell to their Johnson, Sancho Panza to their Quixote.

She had met him a year before when they had attended the same mathematics seminars, and they had begun to work together in the library. He was a placid companion, happy to listen to her chatter, and over the months he had become her confidant. He made no attempt to seduce or impress her, and he respected her brain. Unlike all the other men she knew, he never used the phrase "for a woman"—as in, "You're very good at calculus, for a woman"; "You're very practical, for a woman"; "You're surprising strong, for a woman."

He shared her dawning realization that mathematics was not just a science of number manipulation but a tool for understanding the world and even the universe. He'd introduced her to the work of von Neumann, the Princeton mathematician, whose analyses of probabilities fascinated her, particularly his application of mathematics to calculating competitive advantages in his zero-sum minimax theory of games.

She'd gathered that Johnnie was an RAF officer on special leave to attend Oxford, or something of the sort, but she never bothered to ask him the details, and he did not volunteer them. He was sufficient unto himself, cut from whole cloth, and needed no background or history or explanation. He was simply Johnnie.

When Fletcher and Rand had taken her into their circle, Shaux had tagged along. He was a carrier of picnic baskets, a changer of flat tires, a fetcher of another round of drinks, a punter on hot afternoons, and now an empathetic feeler of pain.

On one recent drunken evening, George had offered a long, slurring monologue on philosophy.

"Hedonism is the only honest philosophy," he had concluded. "We all want to be happy, and a hedonist is frank enough to admit it. I propose a toast to the moral integrity of the hedonist, king among philosophers."

They had drunk.

"What about you, young Johnnie Shaux?" George had drawled. "What guiding light does your soul follow?"

Shaux had looked uncomfortable in the spotlight. "Oh, I don't know; I suppose you just play the cards you're dealt," he'd responded.

"A phlegmatic pragmatist? A dour determinist? A stolid stoic? Does nothing stir your passionless persona or melt your celebrated sangfroid?"

Now, as she helped to haul him back on board the punt, filthy with river slime, Eleanor saw in his eyes a veritable kaleidoscope of passions, although perhaps she simply saw a mirror of her own.

Rawley married his American as soon as term was ended and departed on the ocean liner *Queen Elizabeth* for America. George set off in search of decadence, and Shaux returned to the RAF, wherever that might be.

Eleanor found herself adrift and friendless, struggling to come to terms with Rawley's betrayal, and temporarily goalless now she had received her coveted degree—first-class honors, no less, a distinction she shared with Shaux. She thought listlessly of returning to Oxford to take her doctorate, but quantum mechanics had lost its attraction. Perhaps she'd take a risk and go to Princeton in America to study under von Neumann and Albert Einstein, but she lacked the energy to reach a decision.

Her mother was most displeased that she had left Oxford unengaged and subjected her to long critiques in which the phrase "After all I've done for you" featured prominently.

Her expectations for the future had been pinned on Rawley and her love of mathematics; now both had deserted her.

A sympathetic letter from George drew her to Paris—"There's more to life than mathematics and viscounts, or so I am assured"—and she set out, in methodical fashion, to explore the city. She discovered George had shed his acerbic exterior like a snakeskin, revealing an amusing and amiable companion beneath. His satire had become a wry humor, his arrogance had mellowed into self-confidence, and his intellect had lost its iconoclastic edge.

His penchant for the erotic had survived, however, and he would linger before the paintings and statues of unclad feminine forms with which every museum abounded, and he dragged her to a drawing class featuring nude female models.

The rhythms of Parisian life fitted her mood perfectly—lazy meals beneath the bright awnings of outside cafés, where she and George would make up fantastic life stories for passersby; slow strolls along the banks of the Seine, watching the fishermen and innumerable artists painting innumerable impressionist renderings of Notre Dame; candlelit dinners in tiny bistros tucked away in obscure alleyways. She bought a beret and wore it at a rakish tilt, wishing she could acquire the casual chic that seemed to belong to French girls by birthright.

George developed the amusing notion of aping the extravagant hand gestures that seemed to accompany every French conversation, and they would gesticulate and giggle as they ate.

"*Sacré bleu!* I have swallowed a cherrystone," he said, spreading his arms wide.

She placed her hands on her cheeks. "*Quel dommage!*" she exclaimed in mock horror. "I am devastated for you."

He shrugged theatrically. "*C'est la vie!*"

"*Mon dieu!*"

"*À la recherche du temps perdu.*"

"*Arrivederci, Roma!*"

On other occasions he was thoughtful and serious. She was surprised by his extensive knowledge of international affairs and politics, subjects she routinely ignored.

"There'll be war before winter," he told her over dinner in Montmartre. "Hitler has set his heart on conquering Europe, and soon even Neville Chamberlain will have to admit it. We might argue that Austria and Czechoslovakia don't matter, but if Hitler takes Poland, we'll have to fight."

"What will you do?" she asked, not questioning his analysis.

"Oh, join the Auxiliary Air Force, I suppose."

The Oxford University Air Squadron was not just an exclusive flying club, she realized; the university air squadrons were also used to train future pilots in case hostilities broke out, providing airmen for the AAF as a reserve. She recalled one of the rare occasions when Shaux had expressed a personal opinion, when the Oxford University Air Squadron had rejected his application for membership, even though he was an RAF officer.

"Don't be silly, old chap," Rawley had told him. "It's just that they maintain certain social standards, and you, frankly—well, anyway, no offense, but surely you see what I mean? It's the way things are, old chap, and rightly so; best to accept them."

"And what will you do?" George asked her, bringing her back to the present.

"Oh, volunteer for something useful, I suppose," she said vaguely. "What will Rawley do, do you think?"

"Oh, Rawley, Rawley, Rawley, always Rawley! It's time you moved on, my dear Eleanor. There's plenty more fish in the sea, I assure you, and they'll treat you a damned sight better."

"Will they?"

"Not all men are fools, I promise you."

George's international predictions were proven accurate within a month. Hitler invaded Poland, and England and France declared war on Germany. Rawley returned across the Atlantic and, through his father's connections, secured a commission in the exclusive Dragoon Guards, attached to the War Office. George was accepted into the prestigious 601 Squadron AAF and departed to the north of England to be trained on Hurricane fighters.

In contrast to these glittering appointments, Eleanor volunteered for the Women's Auxiliary Air Force (WAAF) and found herself in the dusty bowels of the Air Ministry, compiling lists of squadrons and aircraft. She was not filled with patriotic fervor, but volunteering allowed her to avoid both having to make a decision on what to do next about her career and having to live with her mother.

Rawley came to see her. He looked dashing in his uniform, and she noted he had already risen to the rank of captain and wore the red epaulettes of a staff officer. She let him take her out to dinner, against her better judgment.

"How is your wife, Rawley?" she asked. "How is married life?"

"Oh, splendid," he answered vaguely. He glanced at her and plowed on. "Look, old girl, she's over there, and I'm over here. A chap needs what a chap needs—you know what I mean. That's why I wanted to see you."

She knew all too well. "But, Rawley, you're married—you took a vow to be faithful."

"It's only humping—it doesn't mean anything," he said dismissively. "We did it before, and there's no reason not to now. It's not as if I've met someone else and fallen for her; after all, it's only you. So it doesn't count. We'll go back to my flat after dinner."

She found she was still helpless to resist him, humper and humpee reunited; or perhaps, in the vacuum of her aimless existence, she had no reason to resist, for she was only her.

Rawley was soon sent to France, as part of the staff planning the new British Expeditionary Force.

"Where will you be?" she asked him after his pre-departure hump.

"I can't tell you, old girl—official secrets and all that." He made it sound as if she were not to be trusted.

George reappeared from flight training, somber beneath his habitual banter. He had lost weight and seemed older. Perhaps service life, with its rigid disciplines and unappetizing food, was good for him. He, too, took her to dinner, in an opulent restaurant in which his wallet banished the very concept of wartime food shortages. Unusually, he came straight to the point.

"Eleanor, I know you've taken up with Rawley again, but I'd ask you to consider your alternatives, particularly now we're at war."

"What does the war have to do with it?"

"Everything. Not to be maudlin, but there's a distinct chance I'll die."

"Oh, come, George, aren't you being a little melodramatic?" She smiled. "Besides, you're not the dying type."

He shrugged. "Perhaps not, but I've come to realize that aerial combat is not without risk. Up there it's you or him, and if there are enough hims …"

"*Quel dommage,*" she said in a weak attempt to lighten his mood.

"Eleanor, for once I'm being entirely serious," he said, and she saw that it was so. "I'm twenty-four, and I wouldn't want to die without expressing my profound admiration for you."

She found it difficult to comprehend his meaning.

"I know Rawley is—or was, might be more accurate—my friend," he plunged on. "But I also know he's treated you like a cad. In a nutshell, I intend to bend my suppliant knee and beg your hand in marriage."

"George …"

"I'm well aware of my manifold faults and weaknesses. Money has the trick of bringing out the worst in one. You, on the other hand, are the only person I know who can bring out the best in me—a best of which I was unaware. If I am to die, I'd rather die better than worse. I'd rather die devoted to someone else, rather than drowning in a sea of self-indulgence."

She married him within the week.

In part she married him to shut her mother up. George's background raised her mother's eyebrows in disdain—his father was an undistinguished Russian émigré who had anglicized his name from Randovitch to Rand—but, on the other hand, George's father had also been immensely successful in business, and George's inherited wealth reduced Eleanor's mother to awed silence, asking humbly if seven zeros really meant ten million.

In part she married him to spite Rawley, who would henceforth have to hump elsewhere.

In part, she married George to bring out the best in him and, as a consequence, perhaps the best in herself.

He gave her an engagement ring with a square-cut diamond wider than her finger, leased an Olympian flat in Mayfair, and gave her a Rolls-Royce as a wedding gift. He treated her with great consideration, sought constantly to fulfill her slightest wish, and encouraged her to apply her intellect to her job in the Air Ministry—"You've got the sort of brain that can really help the war effort; I don't know how, but I'm sure of it."

In contrast to Rawley's robust exercises, George approached her with an unexpected and welcome tenderness but was, alas, as unable to arouse her passions in his way as Rawley had been in his. Perhaps passions—feminine passions—had no real role within the institutional framework of marriage, or at least the institutional framework of marriage as practiced by the English upper classes.

Within a month George's squadron was ordered to France, and shortly thereafter she received a telegram that informed her she was a widow. He had died over Dunkirk on his very first operational mission, and her life was once more emptied of meaning or purpose.

"Do you want some dinner sent up, ma'am, or not?"

"What?" she said, startled.

"Do you want some dinner sent up, ma'am?" an elderly civilian clerk repeated. "It's after nine o'clock."

She was sitting in the converted closet that served as her office in the Air Ministry. She suspected she had been staring at the same report with unseeing eyes for an hour or more.

"Oh God, I had no idea!" She stood and stretched. "No, thanks, Mr. Smith. I'll walk home. The night air will do me good."

She packed her things, put on her uniform raincoat, and set off for George's ornate and echoing flat—now her flat, she reminded herself.

AUGUST 19, 1940

0730 hours, Monday, August 19, 1940
Air Ministry, London, England

Eleanor finished her phone calls and tabulated the results. The war cabinet was meeting later that morning to hear an assessment of the situation from Dowding, and she wanted her minister to have the latest statistics at his fingertips. Park and Leigh-Mallory would also be there; she wondered whether the animosity between them would surface in Churchill's presence.

She yawned and drained her teacup. She had slept poorly, risen early, walked through the deserted streets of London in the earliest glimmerings of dawn, and been at her desk since 0600. She would stay there until late in the evening, in part because she felt she should be making a better contribution to the war effort and in part because, since George's death, there was nothing else to occupy her time.

In some senses the work she was doing was trivial—telephoning people and adding up numbers—but she had a gnawing feeling that the data she was amassing could be put to a more valuable use than simply making her boss, the minister, appear well informed. Was her data merely a record of what had happened, or could it be used for some deeper analysis? Was there something she could add to Dowding's strategy or Park's tactics that they weren't already doing by instinct and experience?

Take von Neumann's zero-sum minimax theory, for example. She'd fooled around with the notion of applying it to the aerial battle before, but never seriously. Could she apply to it the dispute between Leigh-Mallory and Park? Could she construct a mathematical model of the effectiveness of Leigh-Mallory's Big Wings in comparison to Park's independent squadrons? Or dare she risk addressing the actual battle itself, the clash of fighter against fighter, and fighter against bomber … Now there was a thought—were there asymmetries beyond the Luftwaffe's obvious numerical superiority?

She frowned and went in search of another cup of tea. Mathematics had always delighted her; it had an irresistible logic and a sense of balance, of completeness, that the real world lacked. It was a place to escape into, a place where people and events didn't matter, because mathematics was timeless and without emotion.

She had never attempted to apply her knowledge to a real-world problem. The idea of trying to analyze some aspect of the war in the air was forbidding, and the idea of doing it on her own, without a mentor, was disconcerting. She was, she supposed, an intellectual follower, rather than a leader or innovator. She had followed other men's logic and admired it, as one might listen to Beethoven and marvel at his vision. The notion of composing her own symphony seemed ludicrously implausible.

Yet she had the raw skills and tools, and she had a real problem to apply them to. Even though her reports were trivial in themselves, men like the minister and Park found them interesting. If she could move beyond mere data, to what the data *meant* …

She returned to her office with a fresh cup of tea. She could not tell whether Park had been pleased or annoyed by her precision on the previous afternoon. Some people—her mother, for example—found exactitude very annoying; "little miss know-it-all" was one of her mother's names for her least favorite daughter. Others, like the minister, found accuracy extraordinary and unexpected, as if a lifetime in government had taught him that factual information was unimportant in determining national policies and, in any case, unobtainable through government channels. Park, on the other hand, she guessed, was a believer in facts.

"How many aircraft do I have this morning?" Park asked from her doorway, as if conjured up like a genie by her imagination. She almost jumped out of her skin.

"Good Lord! Sorry, sir, you startled me."

He grinned, and his mask of tension lifted for a moment.

"You have three hundred twenty-five fighters, sir," she told him, adjusting her glasses. "Eighty Spitfires and two hundred forty-five Hurricanes."

He squeezed his way into her tiny office, removed a stack of papers from her visitor's chair, and sat down.

"I'm here for the report to Churchill," he said. "However, I also wanted to see you."

"Me, sir?" she asked. Perhaps her numbers really had annoyed him.

"Indeed, yes. I admire exactitude, and I need as much correct information as I can lay my hands on. Regardless of all the information available to me—Stuffy Dowding's foresight in building the control system was nothing short of brilliant—I still operate on guesswork. Poor intelligence leads to poor decisions, and I can't afford a single bad one."

He glanced around. "Is it safe to smoke in this cubbyhole, or will I asphyxiate us both?"

"I smoke in here all the time, sir; I've never quite lost consciousness." She grinned, and he offered her a cigarette.

"To come straight to the point, Mrs. Rand, I'd like to transfer you to my staff."

She stared at him.

"Your job will be to collate all available operational information, just as you do for the minister. But I want more than that. I want you to analyze the data and tell me what it means. I'm told you're a mathematician—I want you to apply your knowledge to the battle."

This was precisely what she had been thinking when he walked in.

"I'll certainly try, sir, of course, but whether I can come up with anything useful ..."

"I'm sure of it, Mrs. Rand. I'll give you a free hand. I'd like you out in the field too, visiting the airfields, talking to the pilots and so on, seeing things your own way. We're balanced on a knife edge; anything that can tip the scales in our favor, however minor, will be invaluable."

She felt he had just transformed her from irrelevance to relevance.

"I'd be delighted to help in any way I can, sir, but I'm not sure how the minister will react."

"Oh, I'm sure he won't like it; but, on the other hand, you're in Fighter Command, not the Air Ministry, so technically we can transfer you whether he likes it or not. I'll speak to him this morning. I'll grovel a little to ease his pain."

Park was not prickly, as everyone said. He was just very determined to do his job, and he was not going to let anyone stand in his way.

She wondered what his opponent, Generalfeldmarschall Albert Kesselring, the commander of Luftflotte 2, was like. His nickname was Smiling Albert, she knew. Who would win the first great air battle in human history: Smiling Albert weighing in with over 1,000 aircraft, or Prickly Park with 325?

Park stubbed out his cigarette and rose. "I think I'd better promote you, so the chaps in the field won't brush you off. Most of the RAF is still foolish enough to think that WAAFs have nothing to offer but typewriting and stenography skills. I'll see you at Hillingdon House this afternoon, Squadron Officer."

He grinned at her surprise.

"And now, if you'll excuse me, I go a-groveling."

1030 hours, Monday, August 19, 1940
RAF Oldchurch, Kent, England

Chaux was awoken by the sound of Merlins droning in the distance. He sat slumped in a battered deck chair just inside his tent, the canvas awning of which was losing its battle with the persistent drizzle. He had tossed and turned all night in his unfamiliar and uncomfortable cot and had spent the morning dozing, half-aware of the squadron around him and half-adrift in formless dreams.

He saw he had fallen asleep still clutching a mug of tea, and an endless succession of rain drips was falling into it with a rhythmic splat. He wondered how long it would take for the drips to fill the mug. There was probably one and a quarter cubic inches worth of empty mug at the top, assuming the mug was a bit less than three inches in diameter and the tea was a quarter of an inch from the top, but what was the volume of a drip? His heavy eyelids closed as he calculated. If a drip was a sphere of water, distorted by gravity but held together by surface tension, and the sphere had, say, a diameter of a sixteenth of an inch, for the sake of argument, then $4/3\pi r^3$ would be ... 0.001 cubic inches. At a drip rate of ten drips per minute, it would take less than two hours for his mug to overflow.

Well, he had nothing else to do for the next two hours ... Of course, he'd have to allow for losses when the splat of a drip falling on the surface of the tea caused some tea to splash out of the cup. Now that was more like it. How much tea would be lost? That might be an application of Archimedes. Drip volume net of splash loss ... Drip volume would be constant, but splash loss would rise as the cup filled, until splash equaled drip when the cup was full. Suppose, for the sake of argument, V was the volume of fresh rain gradually filling the cup, D was the volume of a drip, S was the median volume of all preceding splashes, and R was drip rate. Then at any time T, $V^{(T)}$ would be equal to $R(D - S)$. Now he was finally getting somewhere ...

He closed his eyes. In contrast to yesterday's continuous action, 339 had not yet been called to readiness, and it was already close to 1100. The skies were overcast, and heavy rain was forecast for this afternoon. It must also be raining in France and over the Channel, preventing the Luftwaffe from flying. Doubtless the Luftwaffe crews—who were, it was universally believed, coddled by Hermann Göring—were catching up on their sleep in luxurious leather armchairs in elegant, dry surroundings, before being summoned for a pre-luncheon glass of schnapps.

The sound of the Merlins became louder. He opened his eyes again to observe a ragged line of Spitfires making their final approach to the airfield. Judging by their sloppy landings, these must be raw pilots straight from flying school and Spitfire conversion training at an operational training unit. It was like putting apprentice jockeys on derby winners, he thought. One chap landed so hard Shaux was certain his wheels would get buried in the mud and he'd finish up ass over teakettle, but he righted himself by some miracle after a long and improbable moment during which the aircraft seem to teeter in the point of equilibrium.

The aircraft taxied haphazardly toward the line of tents, like a waddling line of geese, and Shaux stood up, ready to run for his life if these chaps were really as inexperienced as they seemed to be.

Debenham and the other pilots emerged into the drizzle to watch. The Spitfire that had almost flipped over seemed to be aiming straight for Debenham's Alvis motorcar, its propeller slicing through the air. Debenham ran to his car in panic and jumped in. The Spitfire came on. Debenham started the engine and drove off, his wheels spinning in the muddy grass. The Spitfire unwittingly turned to follow. Everyone—339, the Defiant squadron, the assembled ground crews—howled with laughter as Debenham zigzagged across the field to avoid the scything propeller blades and finally set off down the lane toward the village.

The pursuit ended when the Spitfire's wings encountered the trees lining the lane, bringing the plane to an abrupt halt. The pilot opened the canopy and removed his helmet. *He's just a schoolboy*, Shaux thought.

"Gosh! I'm most frightfully sorry," the pilot piped in a youthful falsetto. "I'm sure I'll get the hang of it soon."

When at long last Debenham finished berating his pursuer, it transpired that these were indeed their replacements, bringing 339 up to full strength, at least on paper. In addition, these were the new Spitfire Mark IIs, with the more powerful Merlin XII engine, which added almost twenty miles per hour to the top speed and four hundred feet per minute to the rate of climb. The Mark IIs even had armor plating behind the pilot and on each side of the cockpit, and a hydraulic system to raise the wheels instead of cranking them up by hand.

Debenham immediately allocated the new aircraft to the experienced pilots and reorganized the flights, assigning most of the new recruits to

Shaux and Digby in B Flight, including the youth who had chased him, whose name was Potter.

"That gives me one good flight in A Flight," Debenham told Shaux. "You'll have to make do as best you can with B Flight, until I can get an experienced flight commander to take over from you."

"Can I take them up north for some training?" Shaux asked. "If this weather holds for a day or two, we'll be stood down, and I could try to teach them some basics."

"No mollycoddling, Shaux, and no shirking off to safety," Debenham said, shaking his head emphatically. "They'll have to bloody well sink or swim, just as we all did. I'm not prepared to compromise 339's state of readiness—under my command 339 will be ready, willing, and able, at all times."

"Basic tactics …"

"Shaux, dammit, this squadron will be at full strength, and that's final. It will fly whenever called upon. I'm not going to jeopardize my reputation just because of a few recruits."

It struck Shaux that Debenham was only acting squadron commander. He must be desperate to get his promotion confirmed and willing to risk the lives of the new pilots if that was what it took.

"Surely, Skipper, we'd be more successful if they were better trained …"

Debenham paused. More training might produce more enemy aircraft shot down, which would enhance his standing at group, but, in the meantime, 339 might miss a dramatic day like yesterday, when the reputations of fighter commanders were made or broken. Even worse, 339 might be replaced in the order of battle by some other squadron and sent to rot in Scotland or some other godforsaken hellhole far from the action.

"No, Shaux," he said. "If you want advancement, you're going to have to learn to take calculated risks. You're going to have to lead boldly. That's the difference between a leader and a follower; perhaps you'll understand that, someday."

He stalked off to inspect his Alvis. He had ordered Potter to polish it until it shone—regardless of the drizzle.

Shaux returned to his tent. He had carefully positioned his mug beneath the drip, and the tea was perceptibly closer to the rim. *Let's see, it must be about 11.35, give or take a couple of minutes.*

1200 hours, Monday, August 19, 1940
11 Group Headquarters, Uxbridge, Middlesex, England

Eleanor arrived at Hillingdon House at noon. Park had placated the minister by promising him that all Eleanor's figures would be telephoned to him immediately so he would be as up to date as ever.

She felt she was finally joining the battle. Here, with Park, she would be able to see the situation developing as the WAAFs moved their indicators across the board. She would see Park and the controllers analyzing the unfolding battle and ordering squadrons into position. She would experience the ebb and flow of fortunes, the thrill of victory, and the pain of defeat.

She was now on a war footing. At night she would no longer return to her luxurious flat and its obsequious, geriatric servants. She would endure the hardships of barracks life, crammed into a dilapidated hut with twenty other women, eating unappetizing institutionalized food and sleeping on a lumpy mattress. If she wanted to go out, she'd have to walk or bicycle—nothing could have compelled her to bring her grandiose Rolls-Royce to this fortress of utilitarianism.

Her new office was even smaller than her old closet at the ministry, but it did have a small window, and through the grimy panes she could see aircraft taking off and landing at RAF Uxbridge.

She picked up the phone.

"Yes, sir?" asked the operator.

"Can you connect me to Biggin Hill operations, please?"

"Yes, ma'am."

Eleanor settled down to wait while Biggin Hill decided whether it really had to speak to her. She heard a couple of clicks and a male voice with a strong cockney accent.

"Biggin Hill," said the cockney voice.

"Group for Sector Ops," the 11 Group telephone operator said.

"Immediately, Group, hold the line," the Biggin Hill operator replied. Two more clicks.

"C Sector Ops, Rogers here," said an urbane voice.

"Group on the line, sir," the Biggin Hill operator said.

"Squadron Leader Rogers speaking."

Eleanor took a deep breath. "Good afternoon. This is Squadron Officer Rand, 11 Group Air Officer Commanding staff." She almost added "sir," but that was no longer necessary.

"Good afternoon, SO. What can I do to brighten an otherwise rainy noontide for the AOC?"

Eleanor felt a moment of exultation—she was an insider, connected to the sector controller in less than a minute. She was group AOC staff, an extension of Park himself.

She spent the next hour calling all the sectors, asking them to call Uxbridge every three hours, every day, with the information she requested. Not one of them demurred. She had been no more than an annoying bureaucrat in the Air Ministry, wheedling information for the minister, an irritant from outside the system who had to be placated, just as one must placate the emissaries of dangerous and unpredictable gods. Now she was asking on behalf of Park, and the sectors were eager to oblige—if Park had asked for it, it must be useful. He was obviously held in high regard, indeed with affection, by those directly in the front lines.

"How did he get on with Winston this morning?" asked one sector commander.

"I don't know, sir—I haven't seen him since."

"I hope the old ruffian appreciates the job he's doing."

"I hope so too."

"Was Leigh-Mallory there, do you happen to know?"

"Yes, so I understand, and the AOC in C, of course."

"Well, Stuffy will back the AOC up."

"I'm sure of it," she said, hoping she was not implying she was the intimate confidante of the powers that be.

She completed her tabulations and waited for Park to summon her. After an hour she went in search of him. The warrant officer outside Park's office door directed her to the underground operations room.

"He ordered me to issue you with a pass, ma'am, so you can come and go as you please."

She left the building and crossed the lawn to a grim concrete doorway, through which she could see steps leading down to the bombproof operations bunker. Two RAF policemen stood guard, and she could see the tip of a machine gun protruding from a pillbox in the woods. Unlike the soldiers on guard at the ministry in London, these men gave her the distinct impression they'd shoot unauthorized visitors without a qualm.

She descended the long flights of concrete steps and entered the control room, which was more than sixty feet beneath the surface of the lawn above. Park was on his balcony staring down at the map.

"Please don't wait for me to call for you," he told her. "Come and find me when you need me, wherever I am, at any time."

"Very well, sir."

"It's pretty quiet today," he said, pointing to the map. "Bad weather from here to Brussels. Gives both sides a chance to regroup from yesterday. The forecast is for several days of rain. I'm trying to decide whether I can risk sending some of the chaps off for a twenty-four- or forty-eight-hour pass. In the meantime, I'll send the weakest squadrons off for a couple of hours of training. That way I can get them back in a few hours if the weather breaks. What do you have for me?"

"Not good news, sir. According to my figures, since August 8 we've lost one hundred forty pilots in 11 Group, and we've only had fifty replacements."

"I know," he said, shaking his head. "I've been trying to get the chief of air staff to light a fire under the training schools, so far without success. We should be training twice as many as we are. We'll have to use the Polish squadrons and the Czechs. I've been holding them back as a last-ditch reserve, and we may be in the last ditch. That's over a hundred pilots all together, and they hate the Nazis with a passion."

More than a hundred Polish pilots had escaped the Nazi onslaught the previous September and made their way to England. Although the Polish Air Force, equipped with obsolete aircraft, had been crushed by the Luftwaffe, their pilots were well trained. Two special Polish squadrons had been formed, and other Poles, along with a number of Czechs, had been distributed out to the operational squadrons. There were even some Norwegians who had escaped the invasion of their country; it seemed there were refugee pilots from every crushed country in Europe, all thirsting for revenge.

"The aircraft situation is almost as bad as the pilots, sir. In the same period we've lost almost two hundred and received only a hundred fifty replacements, predominantly Hurricanes."

Park pounded the balcony handrail in frustration. "Kesselring isn't beating us in the air, but our own supply lines are starving us to death. The PM places great faith in this chap Aitken, who runs the *Daily Express*, to beef up fighter production. We'll have to see. The Spitfire factory at Castle Bromwich is now under Lord Nuffield's control—he's the chap that founded Morris cars. Let's hope he can mass-produce fighters as efficiently as he can churn out motorcars."

Eleanor had visited the Morris factory in Cowley, close to Oxford, and seen the endless lines of cars being assembled piece by piece. Could something as complicated as a Spitfire be built the same way?

"Let's hope so, sir."

"Have you had a chance to think about your new job?" Park asked her. "Any ideas? After all, you've already been on my staff for four hours!"

She smiled. "I've been arranging for you to get the statistical information automatically. I'd like to have an assistant for that purpose, if I may?"

"Certainly. See the adjutant and tell him I approved it."

"Thank you, sir. As far as applying mathematics to the job, I'd like to see what I can do over the next few days."

"How will you tackle it?"

"I'm afraid it's all a bit abstract and academic, sir, and very far from the reality shown down there on the map."

"Try me."

This morning she had been thinking about von Neumann's minimax theory in the context of asymmetries. The thought was somehow tantalizing, however ill formed. She summoned up as much conviction as she could muster.

"Well, sir, it strikes me that the fundamental issue is asymmetry. There are many of them and few of us. Each side has asymmetrical advantages and disadvantages. We have the advantage of fighting over friendly territory, for example, and they do not. Each side has opposing objectives—one to attack, the other to defend—and different tactics. If we can model those differences and apply statistical values to them, something useful might emerge …"

She shook her head apologetically. She thought she sounded like a stuttering first-year student who hadn't studied her textbooks. "As I said, it's hopelessly vague …"

"Don't worry," Park told her. "When I was a young man, an engineering chap tried to explain to me why an aircraft can fly. I couldn't follow his formulas, but he was able to say exactly why one design would be better than another. He was invariably right. I've respected science ever since. So keep going."

"Very well, sir, but I may come up with nothing."

"But you've already come up with something."

"I have?"

"Dozens of people give me advice every day; give me their views of the battle and tell me what I'm doing right or wrong—mostly wrong. Members of Parliament make speeches telling me what to do. Newspaper editorials, letters from veterans of the Great War, schoolboys, academics, pensioners—they all know how to win. Ninety-nine percent is rubbish. But you've already given me something to think about—no one's ever described the situation as asymmetric, but that's exactly what it is."

He turned to the map, leaning his elbows on the balcony rail, lost in thought.

Eleanor slipped away and sought out the group adjutant, a bookish but clearly competent officer of indeterminate age, who assigned her a WAAF sergeant with a bookkeeping background to manage the reports from the sectors.

"WAAF Sergeant Millicent Smith looks as if she doesn't have a brain in her head, but she's very competent," he assured her, gazing at her across mounds of paperwork piled on his desk. "What else can I do for you?"

She laughed. "Well, since you ask, I need a mathematician who has studied at Princeton in America in the last five years," she blurted out.

"Do you, by Jove! Does it have to be Princeton, specifically? Isn't that where that chap Albert Einstein is?"

"Yes, but I need someone who studied mathematics under a colleague of his, another refugee named von Neumann, who has a theory of games."

"Did you say games, Mrs. Rand?" he asked.

"Yes."

He adjusted his glasses and scribbled a note. "The name is von Neumann? That may take a bit of doing, but I'll look into it."

"Thank you, sir."

1230 hours, Monday, August 19, 1940
RAF Oldchurch, Kent, England

A battered Morris Cowley motorcar rumbled to a halt in front of the pilots' tents, and a rotund, elderly wing commander extracted himself from the driver's seat. Shaux glanced at his overflowing mug—it must be about 1230, he calculated—and stepped outside. The new arrival wore a Royal Flying Corps pilot's badge and a row of medal ribbons from the 1914–18 war. He walked with a limp and supported himself with an ivory-handled cane.

"My name's Pound, Harry Pound," he announced in a deep, resonating voice. "I'm the new station CO, for my sins."

He looked around doubtfully. "I assume this is an RAF station? It looks more like a Boy Scout camp led by an inept scoutmaster. Are you chaps 339?"

Debenham advanced toward him.

"Are you Squadron Leader Richard Debenham, by any chance?" Pound asked.

Debenham stared down at him. "This place is a complete shambles, to be frank," he said, unwilling to let the courtesies of greeting a senior officer outweigh his pent-up complaints. "How are we supposed in fly in this dump? No permanent facilities, no officers' mess, no running water, and my tent leaks like a sieve." He made it sound as if he slept at the airfield, rather than in the comfort of the inn. "Sector promised us a mobile canteen for lunch, and it hasn't turned up. Bloody typical. Modern warfare requires modern facilities and services. With due respect, sir, Spitfires aren't Sopwith Camels."

Pound looked up at him mildly. "Indeed they're not, Dickie, if I may call you that—I believe you're known as Dickie?" Pound responded mildly. "Far too advanced for an old codger like me. Well, I suggest you take care of the flying, and I'll take care of the shambles. Is that reasonable?"

Without waiting for a reply, he turned to the pilots. Shaux could see he was distinguishing between the new arrivals in smartly pressed uniforms and festoons of equipment, engaged—despite the rain—in a game of cricket using a broken tennis racquet instead of a bat, and the lounging veterans in deck chairs beneath the awnings of their tents.

"I hear you chaps have had a busy time."

Debenham took breath to voice new complaints, but Pound beat him to it. His face lit up with pleasure.

"I say, is that your Alvis motorcar, Dickie? Is she a Speed 20 or a 25? A magnificent machine, if I may say so. Can she really do a hundred?"

Debenham refused to be mollified. "She's a damned sight faster than a Morris," he said, eying Pound's undistinguished, mud-splattered car.

"I expect you're right," Pound said, shaking his head. "No, I'll tell you what—I'll race you to the end of the field and back, just to prove it."

"Don't be ridiculous," Debenham snorted. "You don't stand a chance."

"Come on, I'll bet you a shilling. I've tinkered with my old Cowley over the years to give her more go—don't be deceived by her looks. Let's prove it; I'm a great believer in proofs."

He laughed infectiously, a deep, booming sound, full of the joy of living, and Shaux warmed to him instantly.

"A shilling or a fiver—it's still ridiculous," Debenham said, in a voice approaching a sneer.

"A five-pound note?" Pound pondered aloud. "Goodness gracious! That's a great deal of money! Still, my dear wife insisted I take a fiver with me—'You never know if you'll need it,' she said—so I can accommodate you."

He turned to his car and clambered in.

"This is *absurd*," Debenham said. "You can't be serious."

"Come on, sir, are you afraid of an old Bullnose Cowley?" one of the pilots jeered. He had orders to be transferred to another squadron and had no reason to fear Debenham's wrath.

Shaux stared at the Cowley and then at Pound, who winked back, and Shaux had a premonition.

"I'll bet a fiver on the Morris too," he said.

He *never* bet under any circumstances, having been poor all his life. He also made a point of not antagonizing Debenham. Five pounds was a vast amount. And yet, Pound's car hadn't sounded like an elderly Morris when he'd arrived …

"Jesus *wept*," Debenham snapped. "You're both stark, staring mad. *Oh, very well, if you insist!*"

He stomped to his car, clashed the gears, and drew up beside Pound, revving his engine dramatically.

"I expect to be paid in full, Shaux," he said. "A gentleman does not welch on his bets."

Pound started his engine also, and Shaux was too focused on its rumbling sound to respond to Debenham's insult. The pilots improvised a starting flag from an oily handkerchief.

"On your marks ... get set ... *go!*"

Debenham gunned his engine and let out the clutch abruptly. The Alvis jerked and stalled. Pound started forward at a stately pace, slowly gathering speed. Shaux noticed that the tires were wider than the standard tread and grinned in delight. Pound's Cowley was a Trojan horse!

Debenham cursed and struggled to restart the Alvis as the Cowley, now emitting a powerful roar, receded into the middle distance across the airfield. The Alvis spun its wheels in the soft ground, sending a spray of mud back into the group of mocking pilots, and lurched off in pursuit, followed by catcalls.

The Cowley approached the far end of the field, and the Alvis, zigzagging wildly as its rear wheels gained and lost their grip, was closing the gap. Pound executed a stately half circle and headed for home. Debenham, close on his tail, swung sharply to overtake Pound in the turn. Both Debenham's rear wheels lost traction, sending the back of the Alvis skidding wildly in a complete, mud-spewing circle, and Debenham and his motorcar disappeared sideways into the trees beyond the end of the field.

It took the ground crew thirty minutes to extract the Alvis, with the help of a mobile crane normally used to change aircraft engines, and to tow Debenham ignominiously back.

"Ah, there you are at last, Dickie," Pound said. "Thanks for the race."

Debenham appeared to be incapable of speech.

"Group's been on the phone while you've been, er, completing your lap," Pound continued. "The weather's going to be lousy all day, and half of 11 Group has been stood down. 339 should undertake training flights to get the new pilots acquainted with combat situations—simulated attacks and that sort of thing. I thought the Defiants should come along and play the enemy."

He looked at his watch. "Take off will be at 1400 hours. There's clear blue sky over the Bristol Channel and South Wales, if we can believe them."

A staccato banging noise sounded from the village lane, and a motorcycle and sidecar erupted into view. The driver was enveloped in a flapping canvas raincoat, a leather helmet, and a large pair of goggles. The bike advanced toward them, its unmuffled exhaust sounding like machine-gun fire, and drew up.

The driver turned off the engine, which emitted a couple of explosive backfires before shuddering into silence. The driver removed helmet and goggles, revealing not, as Shaux had expected, a dispatch rider from sector or something of that sort but the leader of the WVS ladies.

"I've improvised some lunch," she said. "We were told a mobile canteen was coming, but you never know, do you?"

She opened the top of the sidecar to reveal a mound of sandwiches in brown paper bags and a tea urn.

"About bloody time," Debenham snapped and grabbed a sandwich.

When the men had helped themselves and wandered off to eat, Shaux approached the WVS lady.

"We're very grateful," Shaux told her. "It seems the RAF canteen let us down."

"It's my pleasure." She smiled. "Oldchurch is always at the bottom of the RAF's list. I suppose it's because it's only an emergency field, but that's silly, because there are always fighters here, one way or another. It's not fair on you, and it makes the village look bad. We're just as much a part of the war as the station at Tangmere, you know, with all their stuck-up airs and graces."

It had not occurred to Shaux that civic pride might be involved.

"When we hear the fighters taking off, we count you out, and then we wait and count you in. That's the hard part, if everyone doesn't come back."

A new world of vicarious hopes and indirect mourning opened up.

"There should be a big sign in the lane—RAF Oldchurch—with one of those painted crests," she added. "All we've got is an old noticeboard for Oldchurch Cricket Club; it's just not right."

Shaux had considered this to be a temporary and unpleasant lodging, a jerry-rigged pasture to be used in emergencies, but through the WVS lady's eyes he glimpsed the war in civilian eyes, with the vapor trails of fighters in the skies, sightings of droning formations of Luftwaffe bombers passing overhead, occasional errant bombs falling at random, shortages of supplies, food rationing, depressing news of successive defeats in the newspapers, and a sense of general foreboding. If Czechoslovakia, Austria, Poland, Norway, Luxembourg, Denmark, Holland, Belgium, and even France had been consumed, if the British Expeditionary Force had been defeated—crushed—and forced to flee at Dunkirk, what was there to stop England from meeting a similar fate, with young German soldiers drinking at the pub and fearsome Gestapo officers speeding through the village in black

Mercedes-Benz motorcars on unknowable missions of cruelty? What was to stop the onslaught, except for the fighting words of the prime minister on the radio, growling through the static, and a handful of Spitfires and Defiants up the lane at the dilapidated, ramshackle emergency airfield?

"My name's Dorothy Brown, by the way," the WVS lady said, breaking into his thoughts. "Everyone calls me Dottie; you should too."

She smiled again, and Shaux was not certain what to say.

"Well, thanks again," he managed to mumble.

"Yes, indeed," Pound boomed, joining them. "You're a positive angel of mercy, Mrs. Brown, riding to our rescue astride a fine BSA Gold Star, no less. A 1938 model, if my eyes do not deceive me."

"It's my husband's pride and joy, sir. He taught me to drive, and when he was captured, I decided to put it to use in the war effort."

"Captured, Mrs. Brown?" Pound asked, his booming voice suddenly soft.

"He was in the rearguard at Dunkirk. He's Royal Artillery, and they had to stay behind to spike the guns."

"Ah, I see." He said no more, for there was nothing else to say.

Shaux thought of the limbo of uncertainty she must be living under. The Red Cross said that the Germans were following the Geneva Convention for prisoners of war, but even so it must be a hard and dreary life, and she must feel she was a captive just as much as he. No wonder she had volunteered for the WVS and took a fierce pride in the airfield, however pathetic it might be.

"Another cuppa, sir?" Mrs. Brown asked Pound.

"Thank you, I don't mind if I do. Look, Mrs. Brown—Dottie, if I might be so bold—I need your help. I must try to get this place fixed up a little—better tents, or even huts, for example. I'm sure you know everyone locally and could point me in the right direction."

"I'll certainly try, sir, but you should speak to Jack Winslow down at the pub. He knows everyone."

"I will, Mrs. Brown, I will. I'll go in this evening; perhaps you'll join me?" He produced an ancient tobacco pipe and lit it expertly despite the rain. "Thank you again, Dottie; it was very thoughtful of you," he boomed, puffing luxuriantly. "One day I'd love to try your Gold Star, if you'll let me. In the meantime, if you'll excuse Shaux and me, we have a sortie to fly."

"You're flying with us, sir?" Shaux asked.

"I wouldn't miss it for the world."

"Are you serious?" Debenham's voice broke in. "With due respect, we can't be weighed down with excess baggage."

"I'll fly in the gunner's seat in one of the Defiants," Pound said. "From there I'll be able to observe the advances made in aerial combat since my day. I'm sure I'll learn a great deal from watching you handle 339."

"Well," Debenham began, searching for a reason to object. He could find none and stomped off in high dudgeon.

"I hope that man's a better pilot than he's a human being," Mrs. Brown said succinctly.

"I'll let you know, Dottie." Pound smiled. "I'll give you a full accounting when we meet this evening to plot the renaissance of RAF Oldchurch."

1500 hours, Monday, August 19, 1940
11 Group Headquarters, Uxbridge, Middlesex, England

Eleanor stared unseeing out of her office window, trying to find an application of von Neumann's zero-sum minimax theory to the battle between 11 Group and Luftflotte 2. Perhaps the approach was purely statistical—aircraft available, loss rates and replacement rates, and the same for pilots and supplies. That would suggest that the battle was a "zero-sum game," to use John von Neumann's phrase, in which one side's gain was exactly proportional to the other side's loss.

On the other hand, looking at the battle only in numerical terms ignored the objectives and strategies of each side. A zero-sum game was symmetrical, like a teeter-totter, one side up and the other down, but, as she had said to Park, the battle in the air was not. Perhaps it was symmetrical but weighted, like a heavier parent sitting close to the point of balance on one side of a teeter-totter and a lighter child sitting at the far opposite end. There were exact formulas to calculate such effects, dating back to Newton and even Archimedes.

If, for example, the battle was defined as a function f such that $(f)x = \ldots$

Her phone rang, and she lost her thought.

"Rand speaking," she said distractedly.

"It's me," answered Rawley's unwelcome voice. "I've had the devil of a time tracking you down. What the devil are you doing in Uxbridge, Eleanor, of all places?"

"I've been transferred," she said. "Look, I'm sorry, but I can't talk at the moment."

"Not to worry, old girl; I'll tootle down and pick you up for dinner at seven."

"That's not convenient—" she began, but the line went dead as he disconnected.

Rawley Fletcher was the last person she wanted to deal with. She most emphatically did not want to be humped, as he would inevitably demand, and she needed to focus all her attention on Park's project. She paused, realizing that this was the first time in a very long time that deference to Rawley's wishes was not her automatic if reluctant response. Her marriage to George, however brief and ephemeral, must have weakened her habit of reflexive submission, and the war and her desire to make a contribution now claimed her time and allegiance. Park wanted her data and her ideas. However unlikely it seemed, 11 Group actually needed her. She would submit to Rawley no more.

Perhaps on balance it was a good thing he'd telephoned; she'd see him tonight and end the relationship for good, concluding their zero-sum game in which he had always won and she had always conceded defeat.

She returned to her analysis. What had she been thinking about? She had rejected simple statistical comparisons as too incomplete … Instead, she had thought of couching the battle in terms of—

"Squadron Officer Rand, ma'am?" asked a voice behind her.

She swung around ready to bite someone's head off and saw a buxom young WAAF sergeant in her doorway.

"I'm Millie Smith, ma'am. The adjutant told me to report to you, about something to do with numbers."

"Oh, yes," Eleanor said, swallowing her irritation. "Come in and sit down, and I'll explain it."

Miss Smith perched on the visitor's chair. She had blonde hair and blue eyes and a perfect complexion—just the features Eleanor wished she possessed herself.

"Can you do arithmetic?" Eleanor asked her.

"Well, I'm pretty good at adding and subtracting, ma'am," she said, smiling brilliantly and displaying faultless teeth. "I can do multiplication and long division if I have enough time."

Eleanor's heart sank. Instead of someone to relieve her of the job of gathering Park's statistics, she had gained the task of teaching someone how to tabulate information. Her thought—whatever it had been—had vanished.

"Well, let's get started," she said.

Millie was quick-witted but poorly educated, Eleanor discovered. She grasped the concept of a table displaying the vital statistics of the readiness and strength of each squadron, and she transcribed the numbers Eleanor had recorded during her phone calls accurately. She was, as she had said, pretty good at adding and subtracting—"I'm a bookkeeper in a factory, and that's all adding up, and I keep the scores for the darts club down the local, ma'am, and that's all taking away, and you've got to be quick and get it right, or there's hell to pay."

She even understood the concept of a rate of change, as soon as Eleanor explained it to her, so that the table could include percentage increases and decreases from one report to the next. Unfortunately, rate-of-change calculations required division, a slow and painful process during which Millie furrowed her smooth forehead and bit her full lips in concentration.

"I'll practice at night, ma'am; I promise I will. Just give me a chance."

Eleanor controlled her impatience and decided to give her a day or two—at least she was trying.

"They didn't teach the girls arithmetic in secondary school," Millie explained. "They said we didn't need it, so we stopped when we was—when we were—eleven. We did cooking and needlework and housework instead."

And thus the servitude of working-class girls is preserved, Eleanor thought, *set upon a course toward a lifetime of ill-paid or unpaid domestic drudgery.* At least Rawley had never asked her to darn his socks.

1600 hours, Monday, August 19, 1940
RAF Oldchurch, Kent, England

Shaux coaxed his flight into a loose formation over Wales—the novice pilots were far too erratic to risk anything tighter—and turned for home. The training exercises had been a disaster. The new kids could scarcely fly, let alone fight, and Debenham's jeering criticisms and barking orders had destroyed what little self-confidence they had started with.

Pound had crammed his ample frame into the gunner's seat of one of the Defiants and observed the carnage. In the first part of the exercise the Defiants had pretended to be Dorniers, and 339 had simulated various forms of attack, including, at Debenham's insistence and to Shaux's horror, head-on attacks, which had resulted in several near misses as the novices attempted to maneuver in a situation involving closing speeds of six hundred miles per hour.

In the second part of the exercise the Defiants had simulated attacking Messerschmitt 110s. Had Shaux's flight really been attacked by genuine Messerschmitt 110s, he would have no flight to lead.

Now they were homeward bound. Even the kids could fly more or less straight and more or less level, and Shaux wondered how on earth he was going to turn them into something other than cannon fodder. They flew eastward toward England, toward the clouds that had given them a day of respite from the Luftwaffe. It was a rare moment of peace in the air, a moment to enjoy his new Spitfire. Debenham had given him one of the new Mark IIs this morning, and the ground crews had already painted the code letters KN, the 339 Squadron code, and J, his own unique letter, on the side. K-King N-Nuts J-Johnnie was officially his aircraft.

He felt he was sitting above the Spitfire, rather than in it. The graceful elliptical wings stretched out from the bottom of the fuselage eighteen feet on either side, the nose stretched before him twelve feet, and the tail was twenty feet behind. The Spit had a clear canopy like a bubble, affording an excellent view in every direction but down. All the other aircraft he had flown had heavily framed canopies, and the pilot sat lower, so that one seemed to be inside the aircraft poking one's nose out of a barred window at the top.

The Messerschmitt 109 was significantly smaller but heavier than the Spitfire and must have been even worse than the Hurricane or the Defiant in terms of visibility. Messerschmitt 109s, so it was said, were all engine, all brute force, and, in contrast to the smooth elegance and fingertip control of the Spitfire, 109s were said to be twitchy and to require significant force to maneuver.

Even so, the 109s were shooting down a lot of Spitfires and a lot more Hurricanes. Shaux knew the figures of Fighter Command victories published in the newspapers were gross exaggerations. The sole margin of victory in favor of 11 Group, he guessed, was the success of the stable and reliable Hurricanes against the Luftwaffe's lumbering bombers.

It also seemed to him that the German pilots were more experienced than the average kid now occupying an RAF fighter cockpit, and their tactics were definitely superior. The only reason that the Spits were keeping up with the 109s was that the experienced pilots were quietly abandoning official Fighter Command tactics and formations in favor of those they saw the Germans using. He had heard that the Luftwaffe called the officially prescribed Fighter Command formations *Idiotenreihes*—"rows of idiots." Well, that certainly jibed with Shaux's private view of Debenham's tactics.

But for the moment there were no 109s, and he could sit all alone, high on his Spitfire, reveling in the way it freed him from the earthbound chains of mere mortals, soaring as on wings like eagles, as the Bible said. The awesome power of the twelve-cylinder Merlin before him, twenty-seven liters of engineering perfection, propelling him through the sky … The elegant wings, each square foot lifting twenty pounds of aircraft in defiance of gravity … One of the fastest, and arguably the best, aircraft in the world … Who could ask for more?

The cockpit was spartan. The control stick rose between his legs; the diminutive oval wheel on top of it was off-center, designed to be held in the right hand. The throttle lever was situated to his left, perfectly positioned for him to rest his left hand on it. Most of the other levers—the elevator and rudder trim, the fuel-mixture control, and so on—were also on his left, so that he could fly with his right hand and adjust the other controls with his left.

The instrument panel was immediately ahead of him, almost touching his knees. The flight instruments—the altimeter, the bank-and-turn indicator, the rate-of-climb indicator, and the rest—were in the center. The dials for the engine were all neatly arranged to the right, but all the others—like the flap control, for example, and the oxygen-flow indicator— were jumbled together on the left. The instrument panel was half-obscured by the bulky and complicated gyroscopic gunsight in front of his face, and the cockpit was so crammed with instruments and controls that the compass was stuck underneath the control panel between his legs, half out of sight. The whole cabin had a rough-and-ready, utilitarian look, as if designed by an engineer with a cost accountant looking over his shoulder. The reason that the cockpit was painted a sort of pale, creamy green, so Shaux had heard, was that the RAF had found a lot of cheap pale, creamy green paint in a bankruptcy auction.

Shaux felt at home, like a mechanic in a machine shop. He felt as if he were part of the aircraft, part of the mechanism, slotted in amid its intricate apparatus like another component—or, inversely, as if the aircraft were an extension of himself, so that he could almost feel the air flowing over the wings, the forward thrust of the engine, the subtle deflections of the airflow as it streamed over the control surfaces, the perfect balance of forces in all three dimensions that permitted him to swim through the liquid air ... He could feel the balance of forces between the lift of the wings and the thrust of propeller and the attitude of the airframe in space ... a balance melded into a perfect harmony. This was as close to heaven as he would ever get.

Tomorrow morning he would wake up and stretch each of his limbs and wonder whether it would be the last day of his life. He had been flying against the Luftwaffe almost every day since May—the Blitzkrieg in Holland and Belgium, Dunkirk, the Battle of France, and now what Churchill was calling the Battle of Britain.

He had flown well over a hundred sorties in all, well over two hundred hours in the face of the enemy, and increasingly against 109s. He was so far beyond the range of statistical probability, so far into the realm of pure luck that he couldn't last much longer. Even the best pilots—and he wasn't one of the best—ran out of luck eventually. He had been shot down over Dunkirk and survived unscathed. The next time he couldn't possibly be so fortunate.

An engine failure at the wrong moment, an unlucky stray bullet from a terrified Dornier rear gunner, a chance encounter with too many 109s or with a Luftwaffe ace like that chap Adolf Galland, and that would be that. Hell, yesterday alone he'd had half his tail torn off, a cannon shell within a couple of inches of his head, and a takeoff with a bent propeller.

The margin between life and death was measured in millimeters and milliseconds. If the radius of that 110 pilot's turning circle had been 1 percent greater or less, he'd have missed the church spire. If that 109 pilot's parachute cords had been an inch farther from his aircraft, the tail wouldn't have hooked him and pulled him to his death. Tomorrow or the next day the margin would be against Shaux.

He knew he shouldn't think like this. He'd seen pilots laughing in the pub in the evening and incapable of getting out of bed the following morning, paralyzed by fear. A somber procession of visitors would come—the flight commander, the squadron commander, the chaplain, the doctors—and the verdict would be passed. "Shell shock" they'd called it in the last war. He'd heard that the Americans called it "battle fatigue." In the RAF it was called, with a singular brutality, "LMF"—"lack of moral fortitude." If it happened to him, Shaux would be stripped of his rank and consigned to cleaning toilets for the rest of his career, an object of universal contempt. Debenham would sneer as he signed the verdict.

And yet he wasn't frightened. When things went wrong, he calmly sorted them out. Logic and experience triumphed over panic even with a 109 up his ass. His heart would pump, and his palms would sweat, but his brain continued to function. No, he wasn't frightened; he was resigned and very, very tired—and in that frame of mind the truth was that he didn't really care whether he lived or died.

"Yellow Three," he said, "if you'd relax and stop gripping the stick so tightly, you'll fly straight and level."

"Understood," Yellow Three piped in his earphones.

"Cut the chatter," Debenham snapped. "No unnecessary messages."

Yellow Three was the unfortunate Potter. What chance did the poor kid have? Shaux would make him his own wingman, the safest position in the flight. Digby could take the next worst as his wingman, and that would leave the two recruits who seemed to have some inkling of what they were supposed to be doing. They'd make up the third pair and try to take care of each other.

As they flew farther east, Debenham led them down to one thousand feet, under the cloud cover and into the rain. The Oldchurch field was turning into a muddy bog. Miraculously they all landed safely, their wheels sending up long plumes of spray, and managed to taxi without mishap.

Debenham called a squadron meeting, the principal purpose of which was to berate Potter. Shaux saw the kid's shoulders were shaking and realized he was fighting back tears. This was completely unfair …

"Quite right, Skipper," Shaux broke in when Debenham paused for breath. "I agree entirely. Perhaps this is a good point to break up into flight meetings so you can call sector? You've more important things to do than waste your time on fools like Potter. My tent, B Flight, right away."

"Well, I suppose so," Debenham said, annoyed at Shaux's presumption but mollified by his deference.

B Flight crammed into his tent, and Shaux briefly announced his plans for their pairings. Then he sent the others away so he could talk to Potter in private.

"Look, Potter, forget everything Debenham said, and remember only what I tell you."

"But …"

"But nothing! Listen to me. I'll teach you only one thing each day, so it will be easy to remember. Do you understand?"

"Yes, sir, but …"

"Don't call me 'sir.' You're a Fighter Command pilot, and all pilots are equal. You should call me Shaux. You call Debenham 'Skipper.' You can address Pound as 'sir' out of respect for his age and experience. What's your Christian name?"

"It's Clarence, sir, er, Shaux."

"I see. Do you like that name?"

"I hate it! At home the family calls me Froggie, and that's what my friends called me at school."

"Very well, Froggie it shall be," Shaux said. "Now, for your first lesson: your Spitfire knows how to fly."

"You mean …"

"You don't have to fly it—it knows how to fly all by itself. It was designed to fly, and it does it beautifully. You don't have to fly it. All you have to do is tell it where to go. It's like riding a bicycle. You don't consciously steer the handlebars; you just sort of lean. It's the same with a Spit; just hold the stick lightly and lean—left, right, up, down, whatever you want. The Spit will do the rest."

"If you say so," Potter said doubtfully.

"I do say so, Froggie. Now, what's the first lesson?"

"My Spitfire knows how to fly."

"Exactly, Froggie! Now, go and get cleaned up for dinner, and repeat 'My Spit knows how to fly' one hundred times."

Shaux lit a cigarette and watched Potter's retreating back. If only the kid could live long enough to discover it was true …

1900 hours, Monday, August 19, 1940
11 Group Headquarters, Uxbridge, Middlesex, England

Rawley Fletcher arrived at the main gates of RAF Uxbridge with a dramatic squeal of tires and an imperious honk on his horn. Eleanor detached herself from a line of women huddled beneath the overhang of the guardhouse roof and hurried to Rawley's Bentley through the worsening rain. One of the other WAAFs—they were all waiting for their escorts for the evening—emitted a piercing wolf whistle, and the girls giggled. Rawley grinned and waved to them with noblesse oblige.

Eleanor entered the car feeling cheap and humiliated.

He took her to a famous pub on the Thames in Marlow and made an unnecessary fuss over the poor selection of dishes and wines available. They had dined there with George and Johnnie Shaux in the long-ago days of peace, taking a motor launch down the river from Oxford. Rawley had humped her in the tiny cabin on the way back, she recalled.

Having upset the staff and downed three glasses of whiskey, he led her to the dining room, and they sat down at a table overlooking the water in the gathering dusk. She had not seen him since George's death, but he did not offer his condolences or speak well of his friend; indeed, he did not speak of him at all.

He seemed full of nervous energy, in contrast to his usual debonair self, and he had developed the unattractive habit of glancing away as he spoke. He was wearing a major's crown on his epaulettes, she noticed, and the white-and-mauve ribbon of the Military Cross was sewn onto his left breast.

"Oh, Dunkirk," he said casually when she congratulated him. "A lot of chaps got the MC. Besides, by luck the old man knows the chaps who deal with these kinds of things and mentioned me. It'll help if I stay in the army and make it my career."

"We have to win the war first," she said, thinking of the tens of thousands of men who must have acted with stoic and unrecorded bravery on those awful beaches, fighting rearguard actions to protect their comrades, fearful of death or capture and the ignominy of surrender, waiting in patient lines for a day or more, and then wading into the breakers for the little ships to pick them up and carry them to safety—and the privileged handful, like Rawley, whose father happened to know the right chaps to whom to mention him.

"Oh, we'll win," he said, as if it was self-evident. "The British always win—Agincourt, Waterloo ..."

"How did you come to be at Dunkirk, Rawley? I had no idea you were there."

"Oh, they sent some of us War Office chaps over to Belgium to make an assessment of the situation when the Germans were breaking through. The damned transport aircraft broke down and left us stranded—typical bloody RAF incompetence. Then we commandeered a lorry from some of our infantry, but it ran out of petrol. We actually had to walk the last ten miles. Walk! Outrageous! It was pitch-black, and none of the locals spoke even a single word of English! A complete bloody shambles!"

"It must have been awful! Waiting endlessly on the beaches, not knowing if you'd be rescued or captured."

He glanced away as he replied, "Well, we were general staff, so we were able to get on the first available ship, of course."

"Oh, I see. How long were you on the beach?"

"About ten minutes, I should think ... bit of luck, that."

"Indeed," she said, pondering a military system that required fighting men to make way for staff officers. Had some private soldier lost his freedom because Rawley had taken his place? If so, how did that strengthen Britain's defenses?

"I ruined a perfectly good pair of boots," he said, perhaps sensing her thoughts.

"Oh, dear," she murmured.

"I noticed your friend Johnnie Shaux there, waiting, as a matter of fact," he hurried on. "Do you remember him from Oxford?"

"Johnnie was there as well? Goodness, I had no idea about him either!"

"Must have got himself shot down, stupid bugger! No wonder the RAF's in such a mess, with pilots like that. How can you expect to fly an airplane if you can't manage a punt without falling in?"

George had also been shot down over Dunkirk; unlike Johnnie, he hadn't survived. Something told her not to mention it; she may not have loved George, but she didn't want to give Rawley the chance to make a disparaging remark. She made an effort to push the conversation on.

"What have you been doing since, Rawley?"

"Oh, this and that. Scouting the south coast for good defensive positions when the Germans invade."

"You think it will come to that?"

"Bound to; the RAF was useless over there, and they're losing here," he said with a shrug. "It's only a question of time."

"We haven't lost yet," she objected, taking personal offense at his dismissal of Fighter Command.

"No? A bomb fell near the castle and killed a couple of cows. Upset the old man. That wouldn't have happened if the RAF was winning, would it?"

"We're giving as good as we get—better, in fact."

"I doubt it; you wait and see. Fighter Command is on its last legs—everyone says so. Then it will be up to the army. But don't you worry—we'll drive the Germans back off the beaches, and that will be that."

She marshaled her arguments and then dropped them. There was no point in trying to convince him, and she found she didn't really care what he thought.

"Look, don't bother yourself with all that—strategy and so on is men's work," he said. Even as she absorbed this insult, he continued, "Speaking of which, I booked a room, old girl. After dinner we'll go upstairs."

She had hoped to escape without this, although she'd known it was a futile hope. She had to reject him and end it once for all. She shouldn't have come.

"I can't stay, Rawley. I have to get back to Uxbridge; I've a lot of work to do."

"Nonsense!"

"I'm sorry, Rawley, but I really do have work to do."

"It can't possibly be important, old girl," he said with utter conviction.

"I'm afraid it is."

"Look, really, it'll only take ten minutes. Just a quickie, then, if you really have to get back and do some filing, or whatever it is you do. A quickie's the least you can offer after all this time, dammit, after all I've been through."

His voice had risen in indignation, and she feared they could be overheard by their fellow diners. He almost sounded like her mother.

She should be deeply offended. She was newly widowed, and he knew it. She should give way to outrage. She should deliver a stinging rebuke. Instead, she was overwhelmed by the sheer magnitude of his self-absorption and his utter lack of respect for her as a fellow human being.

On the other hand, she wavered, if it meant so much to him and nothing to her, why not? One last farewell hump, for old time's sake; it was not as if she had any self-respect to lose.

Bizarrely she thought of Chamberlain giving way to Hitler's demands in Munich: appease and pretend the future will be better, give way and delude oneself that he won't be back with fresh demands.

She stared at him as he ordered another drink and fumbled for the glass. It was an amazing coincidence that Rawley, George, and Johnnie had all been at Dunkirk … the three men in the boat with her at Oxford. George had fought and died; Johnnie had fought and survived, which she knew because he was now on the squadron list for 339; and Rawley, who hadn't fought, had pulled rank and been there only ten minutes and used his connections to receive a medal that was supposed to represent "gallantry during active operations against the enemy."

There were three men in a boat …

"Come on, old girl, be reasonable," he said with a slight slur but thankfully in a lower tone. "I haven't had it in ages."

"How is your wife?" she asked, wondering whether he was capable of shame. "Does she write often?"

"Oh, well, I'm afraid there's been a bit of a muddle in that regard. Jessica's filed for divorce."

"A divorce?"

"Adultery."

"But I never told anyone!"

"No, not you, silly girl! She knew all about you in Oxford. You don't count."

"I see." Should she be irked or relieved that her role as an extramarital humpee fell beneath legal scrutiny? "Then who …?"

"Well, the fact is, to be blunt about it, I humped her best friend, Fanny, on the ship over there." He grinned sheepishly at the memory. "It wasn't my fault—she offered. It's not the man's fault if the girl offers. Anyway, Jessica found out—in fact that silly cow Fanny actually told her. Jessica's father took a very dim view of it, and I've started getting letters from his lawyers. Apparently America is full of lawyers, and divorce is very fashionable."

"You committed adultery in the first few days you were married?"

Again he glanced away. "Well, Jessica didn't like humping, as it turned out, and, as I said, Fanny offered to take up the slack, as it were. After the wedding we all went to America together on the *Queen Elizabeth*, and one thing led to another. Naturally a chap expects to hump on his honeymoon—that's the whole point of getting married, after all—and if Jessica didn't want to and Fanny did, it seemed perfectly fair. Besides, there's not much else to do in the middle of the Atlantic, and Fanny was very keen on it."

"But—" she began, almost speechless.

"I had to be quite firm with Jessica on the first night, and then after that she kept crying every time—it made my teeth stand on edge. She kept pretending to be seasick instead of doing her duty. Fanny, on the other hand, was as easy as you are—no questions asked, knew what was expected of her. So what's a chap supposed to do?"

"But—"

"Yanks just aren't as civilized as us, I suppose."

"But—"

"Anyway, that's what I wanted to see you about, in a way."

"It is?"

The conversation—the entire evening—was turning out to be very different from the one she'd planned. She had disliked him before this sudden, crude revelation; now she abhorred him. He had *forced* his bride against her will. He was despicable. She must cut to the chase and get it over with. No appeasement.

"Look, Rawley, I insist you listen. There's something I have to tell—"

"By the way, did George leave you his money in his will?" he interrupted.

"What? Yes," she said, confused. It was his first reference to George.

"I'd heard that, but I wanted to be sure. All of it?"

"Yes, of course. What has that—"

"Good." He seemed to relax for the first time that evening "Well, then, I'm a free man, or I will be soon, and so are you—a free woman, I mean."

Her heart, already low, began to sink yet lower. Surely he couldn't mean …

"I've decided we'll get married," he said, immediately confirming her worst suspicions. "I can use George's money to set the estate to rights, instead of Jessica's, and George was filthy rich. You can set that brain of yours to work on the estate—facts and figures, investments, all that sort of thing. It'll give you something useful to do while I make a go of it in the army. I should tell you the old man's sick; I'll inherit pretty soon, I'd say."

She said the first thing that came into her head. "I can't possibly give up what I'm doing."

"Nonsense! Women can't help the war effort, except as nurses, and you're not the nursing type. You should be doing something more useful, like helping to sort out the estate. Look, to be frank, chaps like me represent the England we're fighting for—the peerage *is* England! So, preserving the estate and bearing my son and heir and so forth is your patriotic duty."

"But …"

"Look, old girl, I know what you're thinking: I can have my pick of the litter, so why pick you?"

It was not what she'd been thinking—far from it—but he pressed on to answer his own question.

"Well, you're clever for a girl, and you're not bad looking in a certain way. You don't yak endlessly like most women do, and I don't mind humping you. So now you've got George's money, I could do a lot worse, frankly, and I know you always wanted to sink your hooks into me. Well, now you've got me!"

She could find nothing to say to him.

"I've worked it all out," he continued. "We can't get married until the divorce is final, but in the meantime you can leave the WAAF and go up to Fletcher Castle. You'll be able to help out with the old man—he's going a bit gaga, to be frank—and you can give me some of George's money until we're married and I get the legal right to all of it. You can start getting the castle fixed up, and you can come up to London for a hump a couple of times a week. The sooner I can get you pregnant, the better, as a matter of fact; the line of inheritance will be assured, and you'll have plenty to keep you busy, what with the old man and a baby and the castle and all."

He grinned at his own brilliance. "Pretty good, eh? The future Lord and Lady Fletcher!"

She stared at him.

"You're speechless!" he crowed. "I knew I'd sweep you away! Make your dreams come true and so forth."

He leaned across the table and squeezed her hand. She could tell he meant it as a sign of affection, even of generosity.

"Eleanor, Viscountess Fletcher!" he chuckled. "Who'd have thought it?"

Something snapped.

She stood up, wondering how she could get back to Uxbridge at this time of night; if she couldn't get a taxi, she could try to get to the A4 main road, she supposed, and hitchhike eastward from there. She doubted there'd be any buses.

"I have to get back to the station now, Rawley," she heard herself say. "We'll never marry, never hump, and never see each other again."

There were one or two curious faces turned in her direction, but she would not—dare not—stop.

"What do you mean?" he stuttered. "It's what you always wanted!"

"Perhaps, a long time ago. But now I have people who depend on me, and I don't want to let them down."

"Being my wife is a very important position," he said, also rising. "You should be grateful I'd consider you."

He looked at her closely, bleary-eyed. "I say, are you playing hard to get, now I've declared my intentions? Is that it? Make me beg before you yield and all that girlish nonsense?"

She held her voice low, praying they were not being overheard. "I have to leave now, Rawley. I have work to do."

"Leave? This is very unfair of you. Perhaps you're in shock. Perhaps you don't think I'm serious. Look, I told my father our financial problems were over—you can't let me down! He'll be upset, and it'll be your fault."

"Goodbye, Rawley."

She crammed her uniform cap on her hair and fled to the bar to ask the landlord how to get back to Uxbridge. Her stomach was in knots, and she was almost panting for breath. Rawley appeared, weaving as he pursued her, perplexed and argumentative.

The landlord seemed to assess the situation at a glance.

"Bertie," he called down the bar. "Have you got half an hour before your shift starts, to drive this young lady to Uxbridge?"

The designated driver was a young and very large police officer, preparing to go on duty as an air-raid warden by consuming a couple of pints of beer, which, he claimed, improved his night vision if drunk at a steady pace. The landlord whispered in his ear, and the policeman nodded.

Rawley reached out for Eleanor's wrist. "Look, come upstairs and be reasonable," Rawley began, but the policeman intervened.

"Now then, sir, the young lady has to leave," he said to Rawley, standing very close in front of him, and Rawley had the good sense not to argue.

She slumped into the back seat of the police car and attempted to obliterate the evening's events by recalling her thoughts on minimax theory. Mathematics didn't ask for her money; it didn't ask to hump her; it just wanted her time and attention.

2030 hours, Monday, August 19, 1940
RAF Oldchurch, Kent, England

The bar of the Oldchurch Inn was packed. Pound had taken Shaux with him to meet Mrs. Brown—"My dear wife doesn't like me meeting women in pubs unescorted," he'd said with a twinkle in his eye—and they sat at a table with Jack Winslow, the publican, hatching schemes for finding all the facilities the airfield lacked.

"Well, there's those big tents—'marquees' they call 'em—they use for the annual agricultural show," Winslow offered. "I could speak to Sir Ronald, the lord lieutenant—I know him slightly—to see if he'd offer them, since it's an emergency."

"That would be splendid," Pound said. "If they're big enough, forty feet square or so, they could be hangars for repairing aircraft. A Spitfire would fit in forty feet square, if we could make the doorways high enough for the tail."

"My husband works—worked—for a road-building firm," Dottie Brown said. "They've got all sorts of bulldozers and mechanical shovels. Maybe they could do something about damming the stream better, so the field doesn't flood."

"Excellent," said Pound, his pipe emitting smoke like a locomotive at full speed. "We'd have to repair it in stages, so a part of the field is usable at all times."

"They've got portable lavatories for the fair as well," Winslow said. "It's really a portable village, with all kinds of amenities that could be put to good use up at the airfield. And kitchens, I think, for refreshments."

"They've got well diggers, like giant corkscrews, on the back of lorries, at the construction firm," said Dottie. "I wonder …"

"I don't see why not!" Winslow replied enthusiastically, grasping her point. "Well done, Dottie! We'll give you hot and cold running water before the week is out, Mr. Pound, or my name isn't Jack Winslow—well, cold running water, anyway."

Debenham joined them and listened to the conversation listlessly.

"Waste of time, if you ask me," he said. "It's a dump and always will be. The sooner we get transferred to a real station, the better."

Dottie bridled, but before she could reply, Winslow offered drinks all around, on the house, and the moment passed.

Pound and Dottie had their heads together like conspirators, and she took out a paper and pencil to make notes.

"Let's see," she said. "Suppose there are two squadrons and each squadron has forty men, counting the ground crews, and each man needs space for a bed ..."

"Good," Pound said enthusiastically. "Actually, there are ninety-seven men at present, I believe. Let's suppose we can fit four men in a hut ..."

"You'd need, let's see ..."

"Twenty-five four-man huts, leaving three spare beds," Pound said.

"Goodness, you're a quick one with numbers," Mrs. Brown exclaimed. "Are you a mathematics teacher?"

"Oh, something of the sort," Pound replied vaguely.

England's leading mathematician was also named Pound, Shaux thought, H. W. A. Pound of Cambridge, and the new CO had mentioned proofs earlier in the day ... He wondered whether this Pound was a relative.

Winslow was called away by his wife to change a keg. Debenham quickly became bored and retreated to his room upstairs, muttering about useless exercises, while Shaux looked round the bar and found Digby in the center of his newly formed flight.

"Ah, there you are," Shaux said. "Pints, bitter, all round to celebrate B Flight's inevitable success?"

He wondered whether these schoolboys should really be drinking beer and whether they'd have hangovers in the morning. At twenty-one he felt old enough to be their father.

"Diggers saved my bacon yesterday," he told them. "He's got absolutely the best eyesight in 11 Group. He can tell a Dornier from a Heinkel at five miles and see a fly on a horse turd—turds, horses, as we refer to them in 339—at fifty yards."

Shaux was not a conversationalist, nor a maker-up of tall stories, but he wanted these young men to feel part of a team, part of something special, members rather than aspirants.

"Can you really?" one of them—Shaux thought his name was Ash—asked Digby.

"Well, sometimes," Digby responded, looking amazed at Shaux's bonhomie but apparently understanding its purpose. "It depends on the weather, of course, and the size and color of the fly. Obviously a brown-colored fly is harder to spot on a brown turd. If it's misty or raining, like today, my limit's no more than twenty yards—twenty-five tops—for your average flies, brown, on your average turds, horses."

"You're joking, aren't you?" Potter asked him.

"I wouldn't bet against him if I were you, Froggie," Shaux said. "They don't call him Hawkeye for nothing."

He kept it up for ten minutes, spinning an improvised history of 339 made up of prodigious feats and amusing pratfalls, a history in which fighter pilots never seemed to die, hoping the kids would be alive in two weeks to invent such stories for the next set of replacements. Digby played along, and Shaux reflected that Digby himself had joined the squadron as a raw trainee only a week ago but was now, if not a seasoned fighter pilot, at least a survivor.

Pound completed his plotting with Dottie and joined them, and they asked him what he had done to his motorcar.

"Oh, very little, really," he said. "I merely bored out the engine; added twin carburetors; replaced the gearbox, the brakes, and the differential; modified the suspension; and put on broader tires—just tinkering, really. I wanted to give her a little more oomph—the wife is very partial to a touch of oomph."

"It sounds like you replaced the entire car, sir," Potter said.

"Oh, no, Froggie, the ashtray and the door handles are original."

Ash asked him about flying in the Great War.

"Well, the Sopwith Camel took a bit of getting used to. Tail-heavy in level flight. Turned right if you put the nose down and left if you put it up—a bit unnerving until you got the hang of it. Needed left rudder regardless of which way you turned. Spun like the devil. Tended to stall on takeoff. That sort of thing. It had a rotary engine like an enormous gyroscope."

"It sounds extremely dangerous," Ash said.

"It was a beauty! The Germans had nothing like it. It could outmaneuver anything in the sky."

Shaux wondered what it must have been like to fly in a plane weighing a thousand pounds, made of creaking wood and canvas and held together by wires, with a cranky engine delivering less than one-tenth of the power of a Merlin. At a maximum speed of 120 miles per hour, dogfighting must have been an intimate arabesque of tight turns, swooping dives, and desperate climbs, fighting the limitations of the aircraft as well as the enemy—all without, in a bizarre display of official bravura run amok, a parachute.

It must have been intensely personal, like a bare-knuckled boxing match—the enemy pilot would have been clearly visible, close enough to see him flinch when your guns bore or to see his grim satisfaction as he raked you with his own.

"I couldn't have done it," he said to Pound. "I'm not that good a pilot."

"Oh, come on, sir, someone said you shot down five Germans yesterday, all in one day," Ash said to Shaux.

"Really?" Shaux said. "That sounds highly unlikely; I thought it was at least fifteen."

Ash seemed about to press the point, but Shaux wanted to give them confidence, to win their trust rather than their admiration.

"Look, chaps, wake-up's at 0430. I suggest we call it a night. The weather's supposed to be lousy, but you never know."

"I assume you gentlemen are sufficiently flexible of limb that you can fit into my Cowley?" Pound asked. "If so, I'll give you all a lift."

"You're not staying here, sir?" Shaux asked, looking up at the ceiling, above which Debenham would be tucked into a warm and comfortable bed.

"Absolutely not," Pound said, knocking the ashes out his pipe. "When you chaps have a decent place to sleep, I will too. In the meantime, sleeping in a tent will remind me of my long-lost youth."

They downed the last of their beer and stepped out into the total darkness of the village street, stumbling until they gained their night vision.

"Damn!" Digby exclaimed.

"What's the matter, Diggers?"

Digby pointed toward the invisible church in the impenetrable gloom. "See those four baby house martins nesting up in the church tower, just to the left of the clock?" Digby asked. "It would make a wonderful photograph, but I'm afraid the light's too poor."

2130 hours, Monday, August 19, 1940
11 Group Headquarters, Uxbridge, Middlesex, England

The police car drew up at the main gate of RAF Uxbridge. The deep shadows on either side of the guardhouse seemed to be a general trysting ground, Eleanor noticed. People were still people, even in the direst of national emergencies.

The young policeman insisted on escorting her to the gate, and Eleanor wondered what her reputation would be—she had been picked up in style by a Bentley and brought back in a police car.

She decided not to go straight to bed for fear of tossing and turning and second-guessing herself over Rawley. She had refused a man who had offered to make her a viscountess and give her a place in the upper reaches of society—her mother would think her mad—but she had also refused a man utterly dedicated to his own self-interest. The probability of future happiness with Rawley was zero. She was no more to him than an easy hump with £10 million in the bank.

It was true she had married George without loving him, but he was amusing and pleasant company and anxious to please her. She had hoped that, over time, love would evolve from companionship; even if not, she thought, companionship was not a bad premise for marriage.

She walked through the quiet halls of Hillingdon House—even 11 Group slowed down at night, it seemed—to her office. She could make a start on minimax without interruptions and write everything down as she went, so that she wouldn't forget her thoughts, as she had this afternoon.

The light was on in her office, and Millie sat hunched over her desk, a pencil behind one ear, another pencil between her perfect teeth, her eyes half-closed in concentration.

"Oh, ma'am, it's you," she said, looking up with a start. "I'm practicing division."

She had found a school textbook on mathematics, God alone knew where, and had the page open to calculating divisions.

"I'm very slow, I'm afraid, ma'am, but I'm sure I'll get better with practice."

"That's very good, Millie," said Eleanor, impressed by the girl's determination. The neatly written columns of numbers marched on for several pages; Millie must have been at it for three hours or more. She had been prepared to give Millie a day or two and then replace her; now she decided to stick with her, come what may.

"I'll show you another way of doing it tomorrow; it's called synthetic division of polynomials, and it was invented by a man called Paolo Ruffini."

Millie looked at her apprehensively.

"Don't worry, Millie," she laughed. "It's actually much simpler and faster. It uses addition and multiplication instead of division."

"If you say so, ma'am," Millie said doubtfully. "Can I get you a cup of tea? The canteen stays open all night."

"Tea would be excellent, thank you."

Alone with her thoughts, Eleanor returned to statistical theory and discrete mathematics. On her way home with her police protector—he hadn't uttered a word in the entire journey, God bless him—she'd decided that her existing statistics would form a baseline for any given calculation, a way to assign values to variables like the relative strengths and weaknesses of the Luftwaffe and the RAF.

And, as she'd realized in the car, she'd need to extend her data collection to fighter production, spare parts availability, pilot training schools, and so on, so she could predict trends into the future. In fact, she needed to incorporate many things—everything—that built up to the moment when Park ordered his squadrons into battle.

Now, she thought, *that's all very well and good, but how does that help Park?* She'd noticed he'd study the huge map in the operations room, intently staring down from his balcony, guessing the enemy's intentions, and then assign his squadrons accordingly. But what were the enemy's intentions? How could he know what was in Generalfeldmarschall Kesselring's orders for Luftflotte 2?

She sat back and lit a cigarette. The enemy's intentions were … were … to bomb targets. *Yes,* and 11 Group's mission was to *prevent* attacks, and the German fighters' mission was to *prevent* 11 Group from preventing the attacks. An attack by Luftflotte 2 bombers, a counterattack by 11 Group, a counter-counterattack by Luftflotte 2 fighters.

That was the asymmetry—not the numbers, not that the two sides were fighting to control the same airspace, but the fact that the two sides were fighting to control the same airspace for *completely different reasons.*

She crushed out her cigarette and scribbled down her thought before it could escape her and then compulsively reached for another cigarette.

The mathematician John von Neumann of Princeton had theorized that the way to win a zero-sum game—a game in which a positive for one player was a negative for the other, like the game of checkers—was to prevent the opponent from winning it, to minimize the opponent's maximum benefit, which he called "minimax." Park was parrying Kesselring's thrusts. If Park could cover all possible targets with enough fighters to disrupt Kesselring's bomber formations, Park would win, because Kesselring couldn't. No, Park wouldn't *win*; strictly speaking, he would *not lose* …

Victory lay not in defeating the Luftwaffe but in denying it victory. It wasn't necessary to shoot down all the Luftwaffe bombers but simply to stop them bombing accurately.

That left the Messerschmitt 109 fighters, which swarmed above the bombers like clouds of angry mosquitoes, waiting to swoop down on Park's fighters. But Eleanor decided she already had enough to specify before tackling that. Sufficient unto the day …

She took a fresh piece of paper and drained her cold teacup. God knew how many cigarettes she was smoking …

She wrote:

Stage	Action	German Objective	British Objective	British Strategy
1	German fighter sweep prior to bombing attacks	Deplete 11 Group resources by drawing 11 Group up to fight fighters, instead of bombers	None	Best ignored[i]
2	German bombing raid with fighter cover	Reach and destroy targets	Disrupt bomber formations and prevent successful bombing	Reach bombers as quickly as possible, before they reach their targets[ii]
3	German fighters break up British attacks	Permit German bomber formations to continue to targets	Tie up covering fighters so they can't defend bombers	Reach fighters and distract them, leaving bombers to continue uncovered[iii]

Notes   i   RDF cannot distinguish a fighter sweep. Requires direct observation by Observer Corps or reconnaissance patrol.

           ii   Best done by Hurricanes. Targets unpredictable. How to cover all possibilities without wasting resources hanging about?

           iii   Best done by Spitfires, so the Hurricanes can get the bombers, but there aren't enough Spitfires.

Note to self: Consider the element of time.

She frowned. How could Park identify targets so that he could position his scanty forces where they were needed? If Park had an area one hundred miles wide and sixty miles deep to defend, and a fighter could fly for two hours before refueling and rearming, which took an hour, then—she scribbled a calculation—Park had one fighter for every three square miles of territory. If the Luftwaffe put five hundred aircraft into an area ten miles wide and fifty miles deep, say, the possible courses from the southern coast of Kent to the outskirts of London, then Kesselring would have one aircraft per square mile, or a tactical advantage of three to one.

Obviously it all depended on knowing where the enemy was going, so that Park could concentrate his resources. That had been Park's own point against Leigh-Mallory's Big Wings when they argued yesterday.

She could review all the places the Luftwaffe had attacked in the last ten days, but that would leave open thousands of other possibilities. Perhaps she shouldn't attempt to list all possible targets, or even all probable targets; perhaps she should work backward from the targets most valuable to Britain. Clearly London was a target of immense value, because there were millions of lives to defend, but what would von Neumann, the father of minimax theory, say?

"What would you say, Jancsi?" she asked aloud.

"In a zero-sum game, minimax theory assigns the greatest value to the targets most capable of denying the opponent an advantage," she answered herself in what she imagined was a comic-opera Hungarian accent. "Remember, my little pomegranate, the objective is not to win but to prevent the enemy from winning. That is why you take the middle space in tic-tac-toe."

She wrote that thought down, almost giddy with excitement and fatigue.

"Therefore, Eleanor, my little cherry blossom, my tiny minimax disciple, the answer to your question is the RAF airfieldzz, and the Chain Home RDF stationzz. London has no practical value in the context of winning or losing."

She giggled and reached for another cigarette. The pack was empty. She looked at her watch; almost three hours had flown by.

Exhaustion struck her like a blow. She itched to start turning these thoughts into discrete equations; she yearned for rest. Should she continue while her ideas were flowing, or should she make sure she'd written everything down and make a fresh start in the morning, less than four hours from now? The answer was clear; Park would want his availability statistics in the morning, and she'd have to be bright-eyed and ready with them. Yawning prodigiously, she tidied up her notes and set off for the WAAF quarters.

Her unfamiliar cubicle was one foot wider than the bed, and the door could not open fully without hitting the tiny wardrobe. The bedclothes felt rough and damp, and the mattress was as hard as iron. Through the thin walls came the sound of her neighbor snoring like the engine of a London bus. The bathroom down the hall was a testimony to the slovenliness of women en masse. Nothing could be a greater contrast to the palatial flat she had left that morning.

She had never felt happier.

AUGUST 20, 1940

0430 hours, Monday, August 20, 1940
RAF Oldchurch, Kent, England

Shaux awoke in the confines of his damp cot, stared into the darkness, and stretched his stiff limbs one by one. He'd read that people who'd lost a limb could still feel their toes or fingers, and he wondered whether what he felt was real or imaginary. He sat up and placed his feet on the ground; the dampness was real.

It had rained during the night and more was forecast, so with a bit of luck there'd be no operational flying today. Perhaps they'd be able to get more training in; if it rained for a week, the kids might have a chance of surviving when the skies cleared and the Luftwaffe reappeared.

He sneezed and hoped he wasn't getting a cold. Quite apart from slowing down a pilot's reactions, a runny nose was pure misery when you had an oxygen mask covering your face. He dressed quickly—it was the third day he'd worn the same clothes—but he didn't feel any warmer. It occurred to him that he had no other clothes, and he doubted that Oldchurch had any supplies. Perhaps the ground crew sergeant could lend him a spare set. He couldn't remember when he'd had a bath, but it had to have been back at Christhampton.

He stamped out into the night and down the line of tents, his boots squelching on the invisible muddy turf, aiming toward a faint glimmer of light seeping through the walls of the tent where the ground crew worked.

Dottie Brown was there, stirring a large saucepan of porridge. The aroma sent him back to breakfast in the orphanage.

"Good morning, Mr. Shaux," she said brightly, and he forced himself to be polite, even though he loathed talking at that hour.

"A bowl of porridge to keep the damp out?"

"Please."

"Milk with your porridge, Mr. Shaux?"

"Yes please, Mrs. Brown."

"Sugar?"

"Thank you."

"Some nice fresh tea?"

"That would be wonderful."

"One sugar or two?"

"Two, please."

"Ah, a man with a sweet tooth has a soft heart, so they say."

"So I've heard, Mrs. Brown. I must say, it's very kind of you to look after us like this."

"Not at all; it's the least I can do. You can thank me by calling me Dottie, if you please!"

Shaux noticed she had a strange look in her eye as he mumbled her name self-consciously, and the look extended itself to a strange smile in one corner of her mouth.

He escaped before she could say more, carrying his bowl and mug and his soft heart to a rickety card table, where he discovered he was starving. He would have gone back for another bowl of porridge, but the effort of making more conversation seemed too onerous. The woman must have arisen at three o'clock to have breakfast ready by now, he thought; it was really very decent of her. He just wished she didn't smile in a way that made him feel vaguely uncomfortable.

He lit a cigarette and closed his eyes, pondering the day ahead and his chances of surviving it. If it kept raining, pretty good; if not, who knew?

The tent gradually filled: pilots alone with their thoughts; ground crews silently recalling their maintenance schedules and wondering how soon the remaining Mark I Spitfires would be replaced with Mark IIs so they wouldn't have confusion over spare parts; members of the Defiant squadron wishing group would finally declare them nonoperational and send them north to be retrained on Hurricanes or Spitfires, so that they didn't have to sit uselessly on their asses all day while the battle raged above them.

The loudest sounds were Mrs. Brown's cheerful voice and the clatter of her pots and pans, a kernel of activity surrounded by sleepy men contemplating the new day with various causes and levels of uncertainty.

Shaux kept his eyes closed and hid within the solitude of his mind. It was all so *pointless*, he thought. Why was he fighting? He felt no hatred toward the Luftwaffe pilots or any particular love of England. He had no family to defend. His death or survival would make no difference to the outcome of the war, or to anything else, for that matter. It was all so *pointless*. Then why? Well, the brutal truth was, he had to admit, that he had nothing better to do.

At 0530 Debenham's Alvis arrived from the village with a roar. He entered the tent and surveyed the scene. Shaux opened his eyes reluctantly and saw Debenham's brow furrow with displeasure. He wondered what Debenham could possibly find to complain about on this occasion.

"Since when do officers and other ranks mess together?" Debenham barked. "I want all officers out of here, on the double, if you please. Warrant officers, NCOs, and other ranks in here only. Just because we're stuck in this dump it doesn't mean we ignore basic RAF rules and regulations."

The offending pilots, too sleepy to resist his pettiness, rose to their feet.

"You chaps should know better," Debenham said. "339 keeps up the proper standards, regardless of conditions."

Pound appeared behind him. "Ah, Dickie, good morning. You wouldn't know, of course, since you weren't on station. Last night I decided that we'd all share facilities until we can arrange additional accommodations. It's a more efficient arrangement, don't you think? Sorry you weren't informed."

Shaux knew Pound had issued no such order. He watched Debenham trying to think of a rebuttal, to no avail. Shaux sat down again, only to have Potter ask him a question.

"There's no talking before dawn," Shaux cut him off.

"Is that RAF rules and regulations?"

"No, mine." He closed his eyes.

"More tea, Mr. Shaux?"

Shaux groaned inwardly and accepted the offer as graciously as he could.

Pound returned. "Group says we're stood down until 1200. That means 339 can do more training. We'll send one flight at a time, just in case the weather clears. It's 0600; I suggest you take A Flight at 0700 and 1100, Dickie, and Shaux can take B Flight at 0900 and 1300, assuming the stand-down continues."

Debenham again tried to form an objection without success. In frustration he turned on Mrs. Brown; it seemed his porridge had been cold and lumpy. Pound intervened, and Shaux returned to his tent, where, he was reasonably confident, the bedbugs were mute.

He sat in the open door flap to watch the sky brighten. He stretched his limbs again, searching for an inner point of balance at which he could face the potential dangers of the day with equanimity, a fulcrum of fatalism in which he could conquer fear by abandoning hope.

He had no past to speak of. If his years to come would be a waste of breath, as he suspected they might be, then his death, if it came—when it came—would be insignificant. In such circumstances he could face death with equanimity and climb into his Spitfire with complete indifference.

At 0700 he stirred himself to watch Debenham and A Flight take off on their training mission. He guessed the cloud cover was at a thousand feet— safe enough, even for the trainees. He wandered down to the operations tent to find Pound, who was apologizing profusely into the telephone.

"Once again, Hankerhome, I do apologize for telephoning at such an early hour. I very much appreciate your offer to help us out."

He listened for a minute.

"Well, that's most generous, if I may say so. We'll go over today to take a look. Thank you so much, and good day to you."

He replaced the receiver, beaming.

"Ah, Shaux! I recalled, during a long and extraordinarily uncomfortable night, that I was acquainted with Lord Hankerhome. I telephoned him in connection with our scavenger hunt. It turns out he's the chairman of the local racecourse, which is closed for the duration of the war. Anyway, he gave us a free hand to go over and borrow anything we can use—very decent of him, I must say."

"That's very promising, sir," Shaux said, admiring Pound's enthusiasm but doubting there was anything on a racecourse that could be useful on an RAF station.

"I've been meaning to have a word with you, Shaux," Pound continued. "I knew a Shaux in my old squadron who spelled his name the same way. It's an unusual name—Scottish, I believe—so I wondered if he might be a relative."

A cold shaft of apprehension struck Shaux. He had just concluded, as he did each morning, that he had no past—he had slipped through his twenty-one years unnoticed and unremarked, like a wraith. He didn't *want* a past.

And yet he found himself saying, "You did, sir? What did he look like?"

"Oh, it was a long time ago, I'm afraid."

Shaux took out his wallet. He noticed his fingers were trembling. He unfolded the old sepia-colored photograph of his parents on their wedding day, his sole connection to the rest of the human race, and silently handed it to Pound.

Pound took an eon to put on his spectacles.

"Good Lord—that's him! That's Jack Shaux, beyond a shadow of a doubt! Is he your father? And this must be your mother, I assume? Good Lord, how is he?"

Shaux took the photograph and began to fold it up again. "He died in 1918 in France, sir, before I was born. My mother died shortly after I was born, so I literally know nothing about either of them."

"Good Lord," Pound said. "I didn't know."

Shaux was far from certain he wanted to know more. A two-dimensional sepia image of a smiling man his own age, a complete stranger, was something he could handle, something that allowed him to stay securely within his protective shell of fatalism. But if the image took on character—if he had a good sense of humor, or if he was athletic, or if he was a good pilot or a mathematician, if he was whatever he might have been—then he ceased to be an image and became a man who was no longer a complete stranger, someone to be mourned although never met, someone to be missed although never known.

Shaux did not need—could not afford—real people in his life. An actual father might create the obligation to go on living, to explore a manhood his father had never known, in which case his life would cease to be a waste of breath … If he asked Pound for details, he'd be drawn into a universe where life and death had meaning and the future held purpose and perhaps even hope.

Even if he merely asked Pound if he was indeed Professor H. W. A. Pound, as he now suspected, or a relative of his, then he'd be drawn into a discussion of mathematics, and Pound might suggest something interesting for him to study, something he'd look forward to …

Shaux saw Pound looking at him, as if expecting questions.

"If you'll excuse me, sir, I have to round up the chaps for training. I thought I'd get them to do a little taxiing while, er, while things are quiet."

"Good idea," Pound said. Shaux had a feeling that Pound knew he had really intended to say, "While Debenham's not here to criticize," but the CO said nothing.

B Flight taxied, playing follow-my-leader, while Shaux taught them the tricks of leaning far out of the cockpit to see past the engine cowling and lining up on tall trees in the far distance and all the other techniques he'd learned through trial and humiliating error.

Then, when Debenham and A Flight returned, they flew down the coast to Devon, where Shaux broke them into pairs to practice formation flying.

"You lead, Green Three," Shaux said to Potter. "See where I position myself. Fifty yards back, twenty yards out ... Now let your aircraft turn right ... Straighten out, Green Three. Remember your Spitfire knows how to fly; now, let it turn right while you watch."

They flew for thirty minutes, and Potter's flying gradually smoothed itself out. They changed places, with Shaux taking the lead.

"Your Spitfire knows how to follow mine. Sit back and watch it follow."

Potter followed him erratically, like a kite lurching back and forth in a high wind.

"Hold the stick lightly with just your thumb and first finger, Green Three, as if you were a grand lady holding her teacup at a garden party. Rest your left forefinger on the throttle, nothing else. Now, let your aircraft follow mine."

He kept it up for twenty minutes. Then Shaux called up the rest of B Flight, and they turned for home.

"Green Three, you have the lead. Vector is two-niner-zero. Straight and level."

B Flight arranged itself like a flight of migrating geese and headed east.

"B Flight, look down at your instruments. Fly straight and level. Trust each other."

B Flight took on the appearance of a gaggle of drunken geese, lurching hither and yon.

"Look up. Rearrange yourselves ... Straight and level ... Now look down. Trust each other."

By the time they reached Oldchurch, the geese were still inebriated but no longer dead drunk. As he took the lead for their final approach—God alone knew whether they understood the correct glide path—Shaux suddenly wondered whether his father had been a Potter, willing, enthusiastic, but totally inexperienced, so busy wrestling with the controls of his Camel that he had failed to notice a brace of German Albatross fighters behind him, until it was too late ...

0630 hours, Tuesday, August 20, 1940
11 Group Headquarters, Uxbridge, Middlesex, England

Eleanor had been at her desk since 0530, determined that her first full day working for Park would begin with a prompt and accurate report. Last night's minimax notes sat to one side beckoning her seductively, but she resisted the call of higher mathematics in favor of the grind of data gathering and tabulation.

It was also her first day post-Rawley, although she refused even to consider personal feelings until her work was done. Well, that was not entirely possible; she felt as she'd felt when she had appendicitis and an unnecessary and harmful piece of herself had been removed, a source of poison expunged. I'll *chose the next man*, she promised herself, and if there wasn't a next man, her life was fully absorbed by the challenge of making a contribution—a genuine contribution—to Park's efforts. Besides, after Rawley and George she very much doubted men were worth the effort.

Millie also arrived before dawn, listened attentively to Eleanor's phone calls to the sector control offices, and helped her tabulate the results. In spite of the early hour, she was vivacious and seemed as fresh as a daisy. She had managed to cajole a pimply young airman to bring them tea from the canteen instead of fetching it themselves, an unheard of concession; the youth appeared frequently and gaped at Millie, who smiled politely but seemed unaware of the adoration that he radiated.

It occurred to Eleanor that Millie might have an allure that men found irresistible; if that was the case, she might be the better person to telephone the controllers, all of whom were men, of course. Eleanor decided to take a chance and let Millie call Biggin Hill; Millie would be an eighteen-year-old working-class girl talking to a wing commander, but perhaps charm knew no class barriers.

Millie requested a connection to Biggin. Eleanor noticed immediately that Millie had a trick of projecting her voice so that the person she was talking to imagined she was there in person. Eleanor could tell the sex of the person at the other end of the line based on how Millie spoke; Millie's voice was crisp and formal when she was talking to a woman and lower and throatier when she was talking to a man.

"You're dreaming," Eleanor heard her say to an operator—obviously a man. "Let's see if the connection is as quick as your line of chat."

The telephone conversation with the Biggin sector controller was efficient although punctuated by unprofessional giggles. The information was delivered promptly and fully, and the report was completed ahead of schedule. Eleanor wondered whether she was being unethical in taking advantage of Millie's attributes. *But all's fair in love and war*, she thought, smiling to herself, *and the cause is noble.*

At 0630 Eleanor went to the control room in search of Park.

"Winston Churchill's going to make a speech about Fighter Command today," he told her as he scanned her newest statistics. "After yesterday's meeting and these figures, it will probably be another dose of 'hard and heavy tidings,' as he said a few weeks ago. He never evades bad news, I must say; that's one reason people believe in him."

"He's always supported the RAF, sir," she said. "Even after Dunkirk, he spoke at length about our contribution, even when most people thought we'd let the army down."

She noticed she'd said "we" and "our"; the shift from the marble corridors of the ministry to the drab concrete of the underground control room had made her feel part of Fighter Command for the first time.

"That's true," he said, folding her report and placing it in his tunic pocket.

"It looks as if it's going to be another quiet day, thank God," he continued, glancing down at the map, which was almost bare of indicators. "The weather's forecast to be rainy and overcast all day. If this keeps up for a week, we'll be able to make a lot of progress on the ground; after the pounding we've taken, it's a golden opportunity to regroup."

He pondered for a moment.

"I'd like you to visit a couple of stations, to get the real feel of things. Talk to the controllers and the pilots, see if there's anything else we should be doing."

"I will, of course, sir, but I'm not really qualified to offer—"

He waved away her doubts. "Doctors, psychiatric specialists, university professors, business efficiency experts, engineers, land surveyors, financial wizards—almost anyone you can think of—have visited the airfields, very few of them at my request, I might add, but no mathematicians. You've approached the battle in an innovative way, and you've already offered me one valuable insight—asymmetry. Just take a look and see what you can see."

"Then, certainly, sir, if you think it will help. Where shall I go?"

"Go to a big station, a sector station like Biggin Hill. We've tried to make the sectors as good as they can be. Then go to a small satellite, like Oldchurch, for example. I sometimes worry they're the ones bearing the brunt and getting the least attention."

"Very well, sir. I'm afraid I won't be able to give you the statistics if I'm not here."

"That's quite all right, Mrs. Rand. Hopefully it'll be a quiet day. I'll probably visit a couple of stations myself."

Eleanor knew that Park had his own Hurricane, which he used to visit RAF airfields. He had even flown over to Dunkirk at considerable personal risk to make a personal assessment of the best way to defend the beaches—another reason why the criticisms that he had abandoned the British Expeditionary Force were so unfair. He'd ordered 11 Group to try to establish a perimeter twenty miles around Dunkirk, to hinder the German army from bringing up supplies and reinforcements. Everyone assumed the Germans had stopped short of Dunkirk due to stupidity, and perhaps that was true, but Eleanor believed it also had a lot to do with Park's aerial defense.

"None of this is real, you see," Park said, looking down at the map. "All this is just little markers on a map and colored lights. Reality is what happens in the air, how the aircraft perform and how the pilots fly, how the squadron and flight commanders plan their attacks and handle their chaps, how the ground crews work to repair and turn around the aircraft between sorties, how we overcome attrition rates and losses and maintain morale. Those are the critical issues. That's the real battle. A place like Biggin is as close as I can get you without actually flying; that's why I want you to go."

If the map isn't real, she thought, *then my calculations will be even less real. Unless …*

"I'll do my best, sir."

1200 hours, Monday, August 20, 1940
RAF Oldchurch, Kent, England

"Well, Froggie, how did it feel up there?" Shaux asked Potter. "You appeared to be a lot more relaxed than yesterday. Did you let your aircraft do the flying?"

"I tried to; it seemed easier, somehow, as if there's less to worry about."

"Good!" Shaux said. "Now for today's lesson: search the skies. Your Spitfire knows how to fly, but it doesn't have eyes—that's where you come in. The Spitfire flies; you look. Search the skies—always and always again. Most trouble arises because the pilot literally didn't see it coming and it was too late to react. You should be spending eighty or ninety percent of your time searching, even when there's an enemy aircraft in your sights or on your tail."

"Always search the skies," Potter repeated slowly. "The Spit flies; I look."

"Exactly. If we can get in another training flight this afternoon, that's what I want you to concentrate on. It will help to relax your flying too, because you'll be busy searching."

"The Spit flies; I look," Potter repeated like a mantra.

"A glance at our formation, a glance at the enemy, if any, and then you sweep the horizon, sweep the sky above you, glance downward on each side, forward, and back. Then you start over again."

"Okay," Potter said. "But what about—"

"B Flight at readiness in ten minutes," Oldchurch's only loudspeaker blared.

Potter and the rest of B Flight began to run to their Spitfires.

"*Whoa!*" Shaux called. "Calm down! First, check your gear—life jacket, parachute, helmet, goggles, gloves. Now, line up in a row facing downwind. Everybody pees."

B Flight lined up solemnly and urinated downwind.

Pound emerged from the operations tent. "Interesting," he said mildly, observing B Flight in midstream. "Sector says it's a reconnaissance patrol—your mission, I should clarify, not your current activity."

Debenham was still away in the west with A Flight. Shaux was sure that he would find some way to be affronted when he returned.

Shaux led them to their Spitfires at a deliberately lazy pace. "Readiness" meant they had to be in their aircraft and ready to take off within five minutes; half the time the call to scramble never came, and they'd be stood down again. A possible reconnaissance patrol for a single flight meant that Chain Home might or might not have picked up a weak RDF blip somewhere out over the Channel that might or might not be a flight of enemy aircraft or a flock of seagulls or merely the result of a loose wire somewhere in the apparatus. Shaux checked his aircraft and sat back for a long and fruitless wait.

On this occasion, however, the warrant officer in charge of the operations tent emerged and fired a Very pistol into the air, meaning "prepare for takeoff." Shaux started his engine, checked the gauges, and turned into the wind. He rolled slowly forward, thanking God for this morning's taxiing sessions, so that B Flight could sort itself out. A second Very flare arced into the gray sky—"clear to takeoff"—and Shaux opened the throttle. His Merlin XII howled, and the Spitfire picked up speed at an astonishing rate—the extra one hundred horsepower made an enormous difference.

The stick grew light in his fingers, and his Spitfire jumped into its natural element. The controller's voice directed him to vector to Dover at angels twenty-five. Shaux watched his compass swing round to the correct bearing, verified that B Flight had not flown into itself, and climbed toward the clouds. They had conducted this maneuver over the Bristol Channel yesterday, and he hoped B Flight could control its excitement.

They broke through the clouds at ten thousand feet. Shaux was glad he had chosen "search the skies" as his lesson for the day, and he also took comfort in knowing the hawkeyed Digby was with them.

Still, this was emphatically *not* a good situation. The kids were novices. If they actually encountered the enemy, they'd probably either freeze in fear or scatter in panic. It was grossly unfair to send helpless schoolboys against the enemy—it was dramatic evidence of England's desperate straits. It struck Shaux for the first time that 11 Group was losing the battle. He never thought about the battle as a whole; the "battle" had always been no more than a series of discrete but repetitious events in which 109s suddenly appeared out of nowhere and tried to kill him, and vice versa. Other than that he drank tea in his damp tent or beer in the village pub.

When they were overhead Dover—Shaux assumed that was their location, for below them there was nothing to see but cloud—sector instructed them to patrol the coast as far as Hastings. Without landmarks this meant they would patrol west for twenty miles and then back again. Presumably another flight from some other squadron was patrolling west from Hastings, and another east from Dover. It was a tight patrol pattern—only five minutes each way—so Shaux guessed that group had decided the blip was real, and was headed in B Flight's general direction.

After four or five laps monotony set in. Pretty soon, the kids' attention would wander, for there was nothing more boring than endless reconfirmation of negative results. The sky over the Channel was clearer, and the kids would tend to favor searching in that direction. The enemy was seldom courteous enough to present himself in clear visibility, however, and Shaux wished he had added that to his lesson—"look where you least want the enemy to be," or some such instruction.

"This is Yellow Leader; aircraft, angels ten, bearing one-niner-zero," Digby snapped in his earphones, and Shaux, like the rest of B Flight probably, jumped. He searched in the direction Digby had given them but could see nothing.

Shaux wondered whether he should turn away. He'd be court-martialed and branded as a coward, but at least the kids would still be alive.

"Follow me," he said, feeling like an executioner leading the kids to their deaths. He turned to Digby's bearing, maintaining their altitude; if there were enemy aircraft down there, and Digby was seldom wrong, he wanted to keep B Flight high in the sky, where the enemy would fail to spot them against the glare.

"Search the sky," he added. This would be a classic situation were all his pilots would be staring down at the clouds below them, searching for the enemy, oblivious of any 109s that might be using the lower aircraft as bait.

"This is Yellow Leader; EA are ten 88s at bearing one-niner-five," Digby said. He'd already identified the aircraft and counted them, and Shaux hadn't even seen them … Perhaps his own eyesight was deteriorating and his value to the war effort, whatever that might have been, would come grinding to a halt.

Where the hell were the Junkers 88s? The bombers must be just above the cloud tops; they'd descend through the murk as they approached their designated target and hope to catch British defenses napping.

The tactical situation was dog shit. If he attacked them now—assuming he could see them—they'd slip into the clouds and disappear. If he waited for them to descend into the clouds, he'd never find them. If he descended to their height, tailed them at their speed, and then followed them down—they wouldn't risk a turn in the clouds—B Flight would be prey to any 109s waiting for them to do precisely that. If he delayed a decision, the bombers would do whatever they planned to do unmolested.

He had planned "always act decisively" for tomorrow's lesson, but here he was, pissing away the initiative. He'd been dithering for ten seconds.

Then he saw something. At first he thought Digby had been mistaken, thinking that the 109s five thousand feet below them were much-larger Junkers 88s fifteen thousand feet below them. But these were definitely 109s … The picture resolved itself—the 109s at angels twenty were shadowing Digby's 88s flying at one-oh.

"This is Green Leader," he said. "Twelve bandits at angels twenty, bearing one-niner-five. Follow me."

He put the nose down and rolled left, putting his Spitfire into a shallow dive. Then he rolled right, to put B Flight in line for an attack on the 109s' rear quarter. His altimeter wound down, and his airspeed indicator wound up. His kindergarten class followed in his wake.

He calculated. The Spitfires would close on the 109s at twenty-five yards per second, giving him a long ten-second firing opportunity. When the 109s saw them, they'd dive—the one attitude in which they could easily outperform the Spitfires—and they'd probably turn right, to make it harder for the Spitfire guns to bear. So … a deflection shot, anticipating the turn.

The Spitfires would be flying a hundred miles per hour faster than the 109s and would race past them; there'd be no chance for a second attack. On the other hand, they'd be perfectly positioned to attack the 88s, which Shaux finally spotted, looking down past the 109s.

"Yellow Section, follow Yellow Leader and stay on the 109s. Green Section follow me."

Hopefully the 109s would be shocked and disoriented by their attack. Digby would stay with them and keep them busy while Shaux went after the 88s. Digby would be outnumbered, but if the 109s scattered, he'd have a good chance of holding his own, and he could always escape down into the cloud cover if things got too hot to handle.

Perhaps the kids would have beginner's luck and survive.

B Flight was keeping remarkably good formation—even two days of training had paid off. They were bearing down on the 109s, which still hadn't spotted them. The enemy grew larger and larger in his sights. Digby opened fire at three hundred yards, and Shaux followed suit a second later.

He saw Digby's tracer playing around the leading 109 and an immediate eruption of oily smoke.

Shaux was aiming to the right, betting that he had correctly anticipated the 109s' reaction. The rightmost 109s dove and turned into his tracer, while the left part of the formation turned left. By splitting their formation, the 109s had immediately given up their numerical advantage. Shaux guessed Digby had disabled their leader or knocked out his radio, so that he couldn't keep his formation together. Or, perhaps, this particular squadron of 109s was as inexperienced and undertrained as B Flight.

Shaux knew he was hitting his target 109, but it absorbed his fire apparently unscathed. It was diving hard, and he flashed over it. Potter and Ash were staying with him; Digby and the other kids and the 109s had vanished. Shaux bore down on the 88s, searching behind him in case some of the 109s were following, but could see nothing but Potter and Ash.

He maneuvered to attack the 88s from dead astern, flattening out as he did so, and then climbed a little to shed airspeed. The 88s opened fire at half a mile—an absurd distance—and Shaux was pleased that Potter and Ash did not respond. He hoped they'd have the wit to avoid hitting him when they did open fire.

Eight seconds later, at three hundred yards, he fired a ranging shot, lifted his nose a trifle, and then fired a burst into the midsection of the 88 he'd selected. It was one of those days when his guns seemed to be loaded with rubber bullets; the 88 appeared to be as impervious to his fire as the 109 had been.

He saw Potter firing into the left end of the formation, and Ash to the right—excellent! Then they were past the 88s. Shaux led Potter and Ash into a tight left turn, just as they had done in training three hours before. The kids stayed with him—clumsily, but with him. The 88s were diving for the clouds on divergent courses as the Spitfires completed their turn. Potter's 88 was flying crabwise, smoke streaming from its left engine, its left wing sagging, slowly but inevitably slipping into a spin from which there was no escape.

It was highly unlikely that the scattering 88s would be able to descend through eight thousand feet of cloud, reorient themselves, reestablish their formation, and continue to their target. One or two might try, but the raid would not be effective; more likely they'd jettison their bombs at random and head back across the Channel.

Shaux left them to their fate and led Green Section back up in search of Yellow Section.

"Yellow Leader, this is Green Leader," he called.

"Yellow Leader," Digby's voice crackled. "EA have scattered."

"Return to base, Yellow Leader."

He turned for Oldchurch, gulping oxygen in relief. The kids had survived their first encounter with the enemy—and Froggie Potter had undoubtedly achieved his first victory.

1230 hours, Monday, August 20, 1940
RAF Oldchurch, Kent, England

Eleanor had spent the morning at RAF Biggin Hill, just to the south of London. Like Uxbridge, Biggin was a large, permanent RAF station with concrete runways and extensive brick buildings. It had suffered widespread bomb damage but still gave the impression of bustling efficiency.

Smartly uniformed guards studied passes at the main gate, a squad of airmen marched down the main camp road as if they were Grenadier Guards in front of Buckingham Palace, WAAFs scurried to and fro carrying files, machine guns barked in the firing range as the guns of a Hurricane were calibrated for 250 yards, a Merlin grumbled and burbled in an engineering hangar, and two squadrons of fighters were lined up to perfection on the wet expanse of tarmac. She would not have been surprised to see a gang of airmen painting over the bomb damage.

Biggin was home to 32 Squadron flying Hurricanes and 610 Squadron flying Spitfires, an Auxiliary Air Force squadron with an impressive record. Biggin was also the sector station for Sector C, in control of satellite stations at West Malling, Lympne, Christhampton, and Oldchurch—a fifth of Park's command. The sector control room was almost as impressive as 11 Group's in Uxbridge, with its own large map table tended by hovering WAAFs. But there was something about the map that wasn't quite right … What was it? The station commander arrived and introduced himself, and Eleanor lost her thought.

Eleanor had brought Millie with her on the spur of the moment, and it was very clear from the sector controllers that there would be absolutely no difficulty in providing the statistics she sought; indeed, Biggin would be glad to assist the process by telephoning the other sector stations on her behalf. When an elderly wing commander asked Millie how she was enjoying life in the WAAF and questioned whether there was anything he could do to ease her path, Eleanor left them to it.

She sought out the squadron commanders, who gazed into the overcast sky with studied resolution and assured her that everything was top-notch and that their squadrons were hitting the Luftwaffe for six. Career officers, it seemed, never complained to higher authority.

"What can be done to improve the odds?" she asked.

"More Spits, less 109s," said one of them, and the other chuckled at his wit.

"And if that isn't the case?"

"More Hurris, less 110s," said the other, and the first roared with laughter.

"And if neither is the case?" she asked patiently.

"We'll carry on," said the second officer. They both gazed down at her through a haze of male superiority. Park had been wrong to promote her, she thought; if he'd wanted her to be taken seriously, he should have given her a pair of balls.

Eleanor returned to the sector control room in frustration. She'd learned nothing. Worse, she had nothing to offer; her mathematician's eye would provide Park with no insights.

The wing commander had offered to drive Millie over to Kenley, the home of Sector B. Eleanor again wondered whether it was ethical to use Millie's charms to ease the flow of statistical information and again decided that the ends justified the means.

She arranged to go on to Oldchurch by herself and pick up Millie on her way back.

An hour later Eleanor wondered whether her driver had become lost; they had passed through the sleepy village of Oldchurch and were following a narrow lane that wound through dense woods. Eventually they came to open grass ahead, and she saw a decrepit sign announcing the Oldchurch Cricket Club.

They entered a large and muddy field. A weedy gravel track led off to the right along the side of the woods. After a quarter of a mile they came to a long line of elderly tents, a ragamuffin collection of canvas of various shapes, colors, and sizes. A line of half a dozen Spitfires were parked at odd angles beyond the tents, with ground crews working on them. The Spitfires each had a big KN painted on their sides—the identification letters for 339.

Two decrepit marquees stood beyond the Spitfires. One was filled with engineering equipment and boxes of ammunition; the other was a makeshift canteen, with WVS ladies in attendance. In the distance she could see a row of dispirited Defiants.

A group of pilots sat on an assortment of decaying garden chairs outside the canteen, in attitudes of acute boredom, and her driver drew up in front of them.

"RAF Oldchurch, ma'am," he said, without apparent irony.

She clambered out of the car and walked over to the group, noting the appraisal and speculation in their eyes. She approached a squadron leader, who sat a little apart from the others; something in his bearing reminded her of Rawley.

"Good afternoon," she said. "My name's Rand. I'm from group."

"Ah, yes," he said, in a tone meant to be nonchalant but succeeding only in being boorish. "You must be here to perpetuate one of the three great lies of modern civilization."

He definitely reminded her of Rawley.

"I beg your pardon?"

"There are three great lies. One is 'The check is in the post.' The second cannot be repeated to a lady. The third great lie is 'I'm from headquarters; I'm here to help.' Is that clear?"

"As crystal," she said. She guessed he was rude to everybody. "In that case I'll bother you no more."

She turned her back on him and faced the pilots. "Can you tell me where to find Wing Commander Pound?"

"You've found him," said a rotund officer emerging from one of the tents. "You must be Squadron Officer Rand."

He shook her hand briskly and led her away from the lounging officers.

"Keith Park telephoned me this morning to say you'd be showing up," he said. "He has a great deal of confidence in your abilities."

"I only met him two days ago," she protested.

He chuckled. "Well, he makes his mind up very quickly. Don't worry—I've known him for over twenty years, and he's always been an excellent judge of character."

"I see," she said uncertainly.

"Look, Keith telephoned me last week and asked me to come back to the RAF. We flew together in the last war, and we've stayed in touch over the years. He told me he wanted me to be a spare tire, as it were, a twelfth man, an extra pair of arms and legs."

He gazed out over the muddy expanse. "This station is an emergency field, but it's getting a lot of traffic. There's one or two squadrons most of the time, plus a few stragglers passing through. He sent me here to see what I could do. I arrived yesterday."

He was animated and energetic, belying his frame and his cane. "The point of this long recitation is that I've no idea how to be a station commander and I haven't been in the RAF for over twenty years. However, if Keith Park thinks I can do it, then I can do it. If he thinks you can be helpful, then you will be helpful."

He had a knack of making it seem as if she'd known him a long time, like a favorite uncle.

"Thank you, sir. That's kind of you to say; it's been bothering me, and I don't want to let him down."

"Neither do I," Pound said.

They strolled past the long line of Defiants and continued to follow the edge of the woods. The ground was getting soggier, she noticed. Pound paused to light his pipe, and she took out a cigarette, which he lit for her effortlessly, despite the damp breeze.

He continued his line of thought. "However, how an old mathematics teacher like me is supposed to run an airfield, I don't know! Apply logic, I suppose … Keith has a naive belief in mathematics … He says it's a ray of purity in an impure world."

"You're a mathematician, sir?"

"Yes, I teach at Cambridge."

"Really? Excuse me for asking, sir, but you're not H. W. A. Pound, are you?"

"Yes I am," he said, raising his eyebrows in surprise. "Very few people know my work—I'm astonished you've heard of me."

"I studied Poundian harmonics at Oxford, sir."

He grinned. "Good Lord—poor old you! I must say it's very flattering that people call them 'Poundian harmonics,' but the equations aren't really mine, in the sense that they were always there, inherent in mathematics; I just happened to be lucky enough to unearth them, like a treasure hunter finding a trove of golden pieces of eight."

So much for one of the great intellectual leaps of the twentieth century, she thought, *a leap that illuminated and almost reinvented discrete mathematics.*

"I think you're being far too modest, sir. I wish I could be a leader and not just a follower."

He waved away her admiration. "What's your field of interest, if I may ask?"

"John von Neumann's game theory, sir. I've just started to try to apply it to Fighter Command."

He stopped abruptly, and his face lit up in a grin of enthusiasm. "Great Scott—what a capital idea! The Battle of Britain as a zero-sum game!"

"I literally started yesterday; God knows if there's anything there … You know von Neumann's work, sir?"

"Indeed I do; I spent a term—a semester, as they call it—at Princeton. Jancsi is an amazing man—brilliant at half a dozen different subjects and the host of the most extraordinary parties."

"Perhaps I'll be able to study there after the war," she said. "I've been thinking of it."

"Excellent idea! You'll love it—and, of course, Einstein's there as well, although I'm afraid his best days are over. He asked me to give him advice on constants, although I know very little physics … Tricky things, constants, I've always thought … Nettlesome, and to be approached with extreme caution, as Newton and Einstein knew all too well. Seductive! Be warned, young lady! Never trust a constant unless you know it really, really well! But I digress. Although Einstein may be past his prime, von Neumann is firing on all twelve cylinders, like a Merlin engine."

"There's another mathematician here, sir, did you know?" she asked. "John Shaux of 339 Squadron was at Oxford with me."

"Shaux's a mathematician? Good Lord!"

"He's a lot better than me," she said, articulating what she had often thought but never admitted. "Is he here? I'd like to see him if he's not busy."

"He's flying at the moment. They took off shortly before you arrived."

They reached the far end of the field and turned back.

"How is 339 doing, sir?" Eleanor asked, remembering that she was supposed to be discussing the war, not mathematics. "I know they've had a lot of replacements."

Pound pursed his lips. "Two days ago they were bombed out of Christhampton, and they were down to seven or eight pilots and a half a dozen Spits. Their squadron commander was killed. They've got an acting squadron commander—that charming chap you encountered—and two acting flight commanders, one of whom is your friend Shaux. Yesterday they got six replacement aircraft and six pilots straight out of training school."

He removed his uniform cap and scratched his head. "So, how are they doing?" he mused. "Pretty well in the circumstances, I'd say. Keith asked me this morning if he should pull them out of the line. I told him that if the weather stays bad and they can get some more training, they might muddle through … Keith is so short of aircraft and pilots, I thought we should take the chance … I hope that was the right decision."

"What about the facilities here? It looks a bit primitive."

"It's positively Neanderthal, my dear," he laughed; his informal address did not seem the least offensive. "However, I have formed a cabal of local worthies, and we are going to ransack the countryside. Our first foraging expedition is this afternoon. I have four priorities: working facilities, accommodation, the quality of the field, and defense."

"Group can't help?"

"Group has fifteen or twenty airfields to worry about. They have to focus on repairing key stations like Croydon and Christhampton. In the meantime, God helps those who help themselves."

They were almost back to the meager encampment. She looked around her. Only the aircraft seemed in good order. Eleanor had no doubt of Pound's energy and creativity, but what could one man do without RAF resources behind him? Perhaps she should tell Park that Oldchurch was beyond redemption.

"Give me a week," Pound said, as if he had read her thoughts. "Come back and see us then."

As she was driven back to Biggin Hill, Eleanor reflected that she should add another variable into her minimax calculations—the quality of leadership. Park, worrying over his map, distributing his razor-thin resources across the table like a gambler putting his bets on a roulette table ... Pound, plucked from academia and deposited on an overgrown cricket field, foraging for the basics that could turn Oldchurch into a real fighter station ...

She found it hard to stay awake, and her mind seemed to be jumping from minimax, to Pound, to the orderliness of Biggin, to Park, to the disorder of Oldchurch, to the strange feeling she'd had looking at the map in the Biggin control room, to the thought that she was now a free woman—free of Rawley, free of poor George—to an unexpectedly sharp sense of disappointment at missing Johnnie Shaux, and back to minimax.

How did one assign a numerical value to the intangible quality of leadership? Was Göring a better leader than Dowding, or Kesselring than Park, or Hitler than Churchill? What precisely was leadership in a zero-sum game? The act of not losing?

1500 hours, Monday, August 20, 1940
RAF Oldchurch, Kent, England

Shaux led B Flight back to Oldchurch—considering the low cloud base, he was pleased he'd found it on his first try—and walked over to Potter's aircraft as the new pilot climbed down.

"How do you feel, Froggie?"

"Do you think that 88 went down?" Potter asked immediately.

"I'm certain of it," Shaux replied. "It had developed a spin that it couldn't get out of."

Potter's eyes filled with tears. "Then I killed four chaps. I'm a murderer."

"Walk with me, Froggie," Shaux said, taking him by the arm and leading him away from the camp. "We don't know if they got out; they certainly had time to. We do know they'd come to England with the express purpose of killing English people by blowing them apart with high explosives, very possibly RAF people on this or some other station. You prevented them from doing so."

Potter took out a dirty handkerchief and dabbed his eyes. "I didn't feel scared; I didn't feel brave; I didn't feel *anything*."

"I know."

"I kept saying to myself, 'My Spitfire knows how to fly; I just have to tell it where to go,' and the next thing I know there's an 88 right in my sights."

"Look, you did your job, Froggie. It's a horrible job, but it's also an honorable job, defending people you do not know from being harmed."

As Potter blew his nose very loudly, Shaux wondered whether he should be giving himself the same lecture.

"I have to tell you that it doesn't get any easier, and it shouldn't. If you became blasé about shooting down aircraft, you'd lose your humanity. You just have to remember that you had to take lives in order to save a lot more lives."

Potter blew his nose again and wiped his eyes. "Thank you, sir; I knew you'd understand. I know it's my duty, and I'll do it again, but it's just that they were probably like me, with sweethearts and friends and parents and a career to think about ..."

"They were probably exactly like you," Shaux said. "They were probably decent young chaps that didn't believe in Nazism. Before the war their biggest fear was probably Latin exams. They're just like us. They're not our enemies; our enemies are the chaps that send them. Unfortunately we're the ones that have to stop them."

Potter shuddered and blinked very rapidly.

"Now come back, and we'll report your victory," Shaux said firmly, before Potter could be overcome again and before Shaux could be swept into a vortex of despair.

"You won't tell Debenham I cried, will you, sir?" Potter asked, taking deep, quavering breaths.

"No, of course not." Shaw smiled. "But you know what? If I told Debenham, he'd think the worse of you; on the other hand, if I told Pound—which I won't—I'm sure he'd think the better of you."

They walked back slowly to give Potter time to collect himself and then reported the details of the sortie to the IO. Debenham found it incredible that Potter had gained a victory on his very first sortie, but Shaux was very firm, and Ash had also seen the 88 plunging earthward.

"I'll record it as a probable," the IO said, with a frosty glance at Debenham. "If it crashed on land, it will be a definite; but two witnesses to a 'forced down out of control' still counts as a victory. Congratulations, young man."

Pound arrived to add his congratulations. He then informed them that 339 had now been stood down for the rest of the day. "That leaves us free for our scavenger hunt," he added enthusiastically. "Anyone coming along?"

Debenham snorted in disdain and turned on his heels. Potter excused himself and headed for the privacy of his tent.

"I'll come, sir," Shaux volunteered.

They set off in style in the rumbling Bullnose Cowley, leading a procession of lorries driven by enthusiastic local farmers. A huge brewer's dray, pulled by a magnificent team of Shire horses, brought up the rear. Pound lit his pipe, which emitted clouds of dense smoke; the combination of inadequate windshield wipers and the smoke made it almost impossible for Shaux to see the road.

"Incidentally, I met a friend of yours today, Shaux," Pound said, swerving to avoid a stray chicken. "A very interesting young lady named Eleanor Rand."

"Eleanor was here?" Shaux felt he'd been struck by lightning.

"She's been assigned to Keith Park's personal staff, and he's sent her out to visit operational stations."

"Good Lord!" Shaux said, as mildly as he could. The thought that she'd been here, actually here …

The past was taking on far too much form and substance. His father had evolved from a two-dimensional photographic image into a three-dimensional man that Pound had known, a man Pound could tell him about, if he dared to ask. Eleanor was not, as he had sternly taught himself, a figment of his imagination, a false memory, but a real woman to whom Pound had talked an hour ago.

"No man is an island entire of itself," John Donne had written long ago, but Shaux wanted to be an island; he *needed* to be an island.

"She's a very fine mathematician," he said, lest Pound think it strange he had fallen silent.

"She said you're better," Pound chuckled.

Shaux could have kicked himself—there was no longer any question in his mind that Pound was indeed Professor Pound, the creator of the elegantly simple Poundian harmonic equations—but he said nothing, for fear of being drawn into further conversations that threatened his vital insularity.

"She's applying von Neumann's zero-sum game theory to the battle," Pound said. "I must say, it's a very intriguing notion. If she can quantify the situation in minimax terms, it could be very helpful to Keith Park."

"Good Lord," Shaux said again, his brain racing. "She'd need to be able to apply Turing states to … She'd need to deal with asymmetry … She'd need … Good Lord!"

The battle, as far as he was concerned, was about young men like Potter and his German equivalents, climbing into Spitfires and 109s and flying into extraordinarily hazardous situations, and about the combination of luck, judgment, and guts necessary to determine whether they landed safely again. The notion that Eleanor could deconstruct a thousand such encounters to determine minimax strategies, to create an abstract, logical set of probabilities …

"Ah, this must be it," Pound said, breaking into his thoughts.

They had arrived at a pair of large white gates; beyond stood a set of low buildings and a grandstand. The Cowley led the armada of farm vehicles in and drew up near the grandstand.

Wickham racecourse was a large grass oval with a white grandstand opposite the finishing line, and a long row of single-story buildings between the grandstand and the road. The place had a forlorn, deserted air. Racing had been suspended for the duration of the war, like all other professional sports. Shaux tried to imagine Wickham with crowds of bettors filling the stands and buildings, horses pacing nervously in the mounting ring, bookmakers shouting their odds, the air filled with the smell of hot meat pies and roasted chestnuts; but in silent reality Mother Nature was reclaiming her own, and weeds sprouted where the crowds had stood and the horses had once strutted.

Pound was examining the foundations of the nearest building, which had a fading sign announcing Jockeys and Trainers Only.

"Aha!" he cried. "Just as I hoped—all these buildings are prefabricated. The walls and roof are simply bolted together. They were brought in by lorry and set on concrete blocks. Excellent!"

"You can't mean …" Shaux began.

"Indeed I do! 'Help yourself to anything useful,' Lord Hankerhome said; what could be clearer than that?"

"Surely he didn't mean …"

"He has a literal mind—I taught him at Cambridge." He looked around. "Now, what we need is a crane …"

Within an hour the jockeys' changing room had been disassembled and maneuvered, in seven creaking pieces, onto the dray. Two other lorries carried the components of a snack bar, and the stewards' office had been taken apart.

"Let's see," Pound said. "There are thirteen buildings in all … Four more trips should do it … And then we'll start on the stables—they'll make excellent accommodations, sleeping, for the use of."

Shaux shook his head in admiration. It took many skills to fight a war—Froggie's grim determination to do his duty, perhaps Eleanor's application of minimax, and now Pound's architectural ingenuity.

"I'm not sure the grandstand will fit on a cart, sir." He grinned. "If it did, you could put on an air show to raise money for ammunition and spare parts."

Pound laughed. "Not on *one* cart, I grant you, Shaux, but it's made of wooden beams and planking—I'm sure we'll find a use for it. The stairs will come in handy in a control tower."

1700 hours, Tuesday, August 20, 1940
11 Group Headquarters, Uxbridge, Middlesex, England

Eleanor and Millie returned to Uxbridge. Millie, it seemed, had the entire 11 Group sector system eating out of her hand. Indeed, when they reached Eleanor's office, they found a comprehensive 1500 hours status report waiting for them, delivered by a dispatch rider from Millie's Biggin Hill wing commander.

The ends were honorable, Eleanor reminded herself, even if the means were antediluvian. Millie seemed to take it for granted that men would do whatever she asked and appeared completely innocent about the reason—although that could not be possible. It must be extraordinary to have that kind of power, Eleanor thought with a pinch of jealousy, like one of those American Hollywood actresses on the cinema screen. Eleanor was sure Millie would never have submitted to Rawley's self-absorbed humping. She'd have seen through Rawley in a flash and dismissed him out of hand, leaving him groveling in her dust.

"If the reports come in automatically, ma'am, it'll free me up to calculate rates of change, if that's acceptable to you?"

"What? Oh, of course, Millie, and that reminds me—I have to show you how to do synthetic division." She'd been hoping to get back to minimax, but there never seemed to be time.

"Paolo Ruffini's polynomials?" said a voice. "You just gotta love that little guy, don't you!"

A corporal stood in the doorway. He had blond hair cropped in a crew cut, rimless spectacles that made his blue eyes seem larger than they were, a grin revealing perfect white teeth, and a baggy uniform at least two sizes too large for his slender frame.

"Kristoffer W. Olsen Jr., ma'am, corporal, RAFVR," he announced himself in a voice like warm honey. "I've been posted to you to work on minimax equations. You are Squadron Officer Rand, are you not, ma'am?"

He drew himself up and gave Eleanor an extravagant salute. She and Millie stared at him as if he were an apparition.

"Yes, I am," she managed. "This is Millie—er, Sergeant Millicent Smith, I should say."

"Sergeant Millie," the apparition said and saluted once more.

"You studied at Princeton?" Eleanor finally managed.

"That's affirmative, ma'am. I am—I was—a postdoc under Jancsi von Neumann."

"Postdoc?"

"Postdoctoral student, ma'am. I did my first PhD in physics, and then I thought, what the heck, I'll do one in math as well, just for balance."

"What on earth are you doing in the RAF?" Eleanor asked.

"Well, ma'am, a bunch of us volunteered to fight the Fascists. My parents immigrated to North Carolina from Norway, and we don't like Nazis one little bit. No, ma'am, we do not."

Eleanor knew the German SS had invaded Norway in April in spite of Norway's neutrality. Norwegian and Allied resistance had collapsed by June. King Haakon VII had escaped to London, and the Fascist Vidkun Quisling had formed a puppet government. It was reported that the Nazis were ransacking the country and treating the population with savage brutality.

"I've been flying since I was twelve," Olsen continued. "So I got myself over to Norway to shoot down some Nazis. But it was all too late by the time I got there, and we had to be evacuated to England. Anyway, I was sent to RAF flying training school, but they rejected me because I wear spectacles, which is ludicrous in several dimensions."

"I see."

"It was kind of a bummer, ma'am," he said cheerfully. "Then they weren't sure what to do with me. They listed me as RNoAF on loan to the RAFVR. There's talk of forming a Norwegian Spitfire squadron or two; there's enough of us, and I already passed the RNoAF eyesight test, so it may still work out, ma'am."

"Well, er, Corporal, welcome," Eleanor said.

She had not remotely expected the group adjutant to find her an actual von Neumann–trained mathematician. She had been wondering whether she should ask Park if Johnnie Shaux could be freed up to work with her for a week or two, although it seemed unreasonable to ask for an experienced pilot when Park was so dreadfully short of aircrew. On the other hand, Park considered her work very important, and perhaps he'd have done it.

Shaux and she would make a good team, she thought, and he always seemed to know what she was thinking; it was such a pity she'd missed him at Oldchurch.

The phone rang. Park wanted to see her at 2000 hours to discuss her findings from her visits—so much for an undisturbed evening with minimax.

"Look, I have to write a report. Perhaps Millie can show you the statistics we're collecting, and you can show her synthetic division. We need that to calculate rates of change. The stats will be inputs to a minimax model."

"It would be my pleasure, ma'am," the corporal replied, his blue eyes sweeping Millie. "What's our overall objective, if I may ask?"

Eleanor paused. "I don't know" would have been the honest answer. Instead she said, "We're going to build a model of the air battle to try to determine non-losing strategies using minimax principles, a model that can be recomputed several times a day to determine the optimal immediate moves based on the latest situation."

God! How bombastic that sounded—how outrageous!

His eyes narrowed. Perhaps he was debating whether she was sane.

"Gotcha," he said finally. "Sounds like fun."

Eleanor found herself believing him.

"Would you like a cup of tea, Kristoffer?" Millie asked him, and something in her voice made Eleanor glance at her. Oh, no, surely not? Had the smiter of men's hearts been smitten, and so quickly?

"Tea is the last, desperate resort of a coffee drinker cast away in an alien land, Sergeant Millie." He smiled.

"I'll show you where the last, desperate canteen is." Millie smiled back and led him away.

Eleanor frowned, smiled, shook her head, sat down at her typewriter, and began to compose her report to Park.

The report seemed a bit thin when she had finished it, but it was the best she could come up with. She set it aside and read over her minimax notes. They were fine, as far as they went, but they didn't really add anything, any insight that would assist Park in his battle against Kesselring.

"Consider the element of time," she had written to herself. "Vell," she muttered in her fake von Neumann accent, "let us consider it, my little peach blossom."

Time—where did she start? Well, all mathematical calculations of time began with a notional time T, the start of any process.

A raid started when RDF sensed a formation of enemy aircraft— Dornier 17 bombers, for example—over Calais, the part of France closest to England where the Channel was only twenty miles wide. That would be time T. She knew from watching the map in the control room it took a few minutes for the bombers to get organized into their formations; she'd have to find out exactly how long, but she guessed five minutes at a minimum.

The Dorniers crossed the Channel traveling at four miles per minute, taking five minutes to reach the English coast at time $T + 10$. If the Dorniers' target was within fifty miles of the coast—an airfield south of London, such as Biggin Hill, for example—it would take the bombers ten more minutes to reach their target, at $T + 20$. Therefore Park had a total of twenty minutes to stop the raid.

If Park scrambled a squadron at readiness at time T, when RDF picked up the raid, at $T + 10$ the fighters would be climbing through fifteen thousand feet—the operational ceiling of the Dorniers—as the enemy was crossing the coastline.

Spitfires and Hurricanes flew at six miles per minute in level flight. In ten minutes, from $T + 10$ until $T + 20$, they could fly sixty miles. Therefore, even if they were directly behind the Dorniers, they could catch them before they reached their target.

Thus it followed that if the fighters were located south of London at an 11 Group station, they could intercept any possible raid in Park's 11 Group territory.

She reworked her numbers assuming the fighters were flying from 12 Group's area, north of London. She found that the RAF fighters could only reach areas immediately to the south of London in time to prevent an attack.

Therefore, the winning strategy for Kesselring was to force 11 Group north of London so that he could bomb targets across southeastern England unimpeded. She'd known that already, of course, but she liked having a precise mathematical basis instead of simply common sense. If Kesselring forced 11 Group north, he would gain control of the approaches to London and would have air superiority over the coastline when an invasion came. That meant his bombers could bomb not only static targets like the docks at Southampton and the naval harbor at Portsmouth but also British army units attacking the invasion force.

In addition, the Ju 87, the notorious Stuka dive-bomber, had played an insignificant part in the battle so far because it was highly vulnerable to Spitfires and Hurricanes. If, however, Park's squadrons were forced north of London, the Stukas would have time to attack in southern England

and retreat back to France unmolested. This was particularly significant because the Stukas had proved themselves to be highly effective against small targets such as tanks. If the Stukas were free to roam southern England, the army would literally have to hide in wooded areas.

She sat back and lit yet another cigarette. She realized she'd have to cut down or she'd develop a hacking cough and chest pains like her uncle Bertie, but tobacco seemed to help her think.

What had she accomplished?

She had started with a mathematical basis for determining a winning strategy for Kesselring and therefore a defensive strategy for Park. She could use her statistics, including fighter production and pilot training, to calculate how long, if ever, it would take for Kesselring to win by shooting down all Park's fighters.

That, however, was a simple projection of the effects of attrition. Park already knew all about that, and Max Aitken and Lord Nuffield were already doing everything possible to improve fighter production.

But, far more importantly, she had translated the dynamics of the battle into a time analysis. Time measured the actual battle, the dynamics of winning or losing. Time gave a rigorous logical basis—a minimax basis— for translating strategy into tactics. Her former work had counted up how many pawns Park and Kesselring had on the chessboard, but it hadn't helped to evaluate whether to move a specific pawn at a specific time or how close or far apart the squares were.

"We're going to build a model of the air battle to try to determine nonlosing strategies using minimax principles, a model that can be recomputed several times a day to determine the optimal immediate moves based on the latest situation," she had told Dr. Kristoffer W. Olsen Jr. in a grandiose flourish. Now perhaps she had a basis for making her promise true.

Better write it down before I forget, she thought and tugged her typewriter into the center of her desk.

Zero-Sum Analysis		
	Luftwaffe	11 Group
Objective	Gain air superiority.	Avoid losing.
Method	Defeat RAF by shooting down fighters.	Avoid fighters.
	Bomb airfields, forcing RAF to retreat north of London.	Prevent bombers from bombing airfields, thus remaining in southern England.
	Bomb Chain Home RDF stations to reduce early warning of attacks.	Prevent bombers from bombing RDF stations.
Time constraints and estimates	Bomber formation assembling over Calais takes 10 minutes to reach south coast. Bomber flying from south coast at 250 mph needs 12 minutes to reach London, total 22 minutes.	Requires 15 minutes to fly from London to south coast, plus 8 minutes to reach operational height, plus 9 minutes to take off, total 32 minutes.
Time results		Therefore, if squadrons withdraw north of Thames, Park has ceded 2/3 of southern England to Luftwaffe.

She paused before continuing.

| Conclusions | Optimal minimax strategy:

Destroy RDF stations, thereby denying 11 Group 10 minutes' warning. Ignore all other targets.

Once accomplished, target the RAF stations. | |

Could that be right? Could the whole battle depend on the survival of the RDF stations? But Kesselring's attacks against Chain Home had been declining, as if he'd lost interest … Holy Moses! Had Kesselring made a mistake? Without Chain Home, Park's fighters didn't have time to stop the bombers. Without—

"Excuse me, ma'am," Millie interrupted her from the door. "I think you're supposed to meet Mr. Park in half an hour."

"Oh God, Millie, thanks. I've lost track of time." She smiled at her unintended pun.

"We've brought you a meal, just in case you'd forgotten," Millie said.

Kristoffer W. Olsen Jr. stood beside her, carrying a tray.

"This gray, lukewarm mass of semisolids may possibly be a source of animal proteins and other amino acids, ma'am, although I admit it seems unlikely," he said. "The greenish viscous fluid, I'm told, consists of organic molecules and is possibly derived from vegetative materials. You'll also notice that the random arrangement of these substances on the plate resembles the face of Donald Duck. *Bon appétit*, ma'am."

"*Merci beaucoup, m'sieur.*" She grinned, and out of nowhere sprang the answer to the riddle of the Biggin Hill operations map.

2030 hours, Tuesday, August 20, 1940
RAF Oldchurch, Kent, England

The public bar at the village inn was crowded. The kids were cheerfully buying Potter drink after drink in celebration of his unexpected victory. Shaux sincerely hoped his luck would last—indeed, he hoped Potter would evolve into the kind of pilot the newspapers wrote about, a "warrior of the skies" and all the other nonsense they printed that served to disguise the basic truths: the guts to climb into the aircraft, the skill to get the guns to bear on target, and the sheer bloody luck to come back unscathed.

Shaux abandoned Potter to his alcoholic fate and went to sit with Pound, Dottie Brown, and Jack Winslow—the plunderers in chief. Debenham, sulking over his drink, was also there, perhaps because no one else seemed willing to accept his company.

Pound was exulting over the afternoon's scavenger hunt, and Shaux felt a growing affection for him. He was completely committed and enthusiastic, utterly without guile.

"Well, I have to say his lordship said 'help yourself to anything useful,' and we simply took him at his word," he chuckled.

"You certainly did, sir." Shaux smiled.

"This is supposed to be an airfield, not a racecourse," Debenham commented sourly.

"I'd better telephone Hankerhome in the morning and confess," Pound said, still smiling.

They were interrupted by Mrs. Winslow from behind the bar, raising her voice to the level of a bullhorn. "Winston Churchill's going to speak on the radio at nine o'clock. They just announced it; they said it would be about the air battle."

"Stupid old fool," Debenham muttered. "Christ, the man must be seventy if he's a day. No wonder we're in a mess if he's the best we can do."

"Mr. Churchill's a wonderful man," Dottie Brown objected. "You shouldn't speak ill of our leaders like that; it isn't right at all."

Debenham scowled and tossed back his drink. He was drinking whiskey, Shaux noticed, unlike the other pilots.

"He's a dinosaur," Debenham muttered. "He rode in a cavalry charge, for Christ's sake." He lurched to his feet and went to buy another drink.

Shaux knew Churchill had a checkered history. He'd been a famous soldier and war correspondent in his youth and then a cabinet minister for twenty years during the Great War and the 1920s. Then, perhaps falling victim to his many excesses, or so Shaux had read, he'd lost power and influence and become a lonely figure of fun, obsessed by the rise of Nazi Germany and bitterly opposed to the Chamberlain government's policies of appeasement.

He was larger than life, a man of passionate beliefs and hatreds, extravagantly gifted, but unable to find a way of turning his prodigious talents to a useful end.

Then just three months ago, in May, when it became obvious that Chamberlain could be trusted neither to fight Hitler nor to negotiate with him, Churchill had been brought back in from the cold as prime minister.

British policy had changed abruptly. Churchill had said in his very first speech as PM that he had nothing to offer but blood, toil, tears, and sweat. Shaux had heard that speech sitting in an elegant château in the north of France, where his Defiant squadron was waiting for the expected German onslaught.

Churchill had gone on to say that Britain would fight to the end; since then, the whole of Western Europe had collapsed, and the British army had been defeated and forced to flee from France, Holland, and Belgium. Norway had collapsed. Now the end seemed very close.

In those three months, Shaux had flown dozens of sorties against the Luftwaffe over France, Belgium, and Holland, during which it had become painfully obvious that the Luftwaffe was stronger, better equipped, and better trained than the RAF; he had flown his Defiant out of France with German tanks only ten minutes from the airfield; had been shot down by three 109s over Dunkirk; had waited for thirty-six hours on the beach to be rescued by an elderly tugboat that had thereupon been bombed and sunk by a Stuka in mid-Channel; had floated in his life jacket all night until he was rescued by a sailing schooner the following morning, blue with cold and racked by thirst; had been retrained on Spits and posted to 339 for more blood, toil, tears, and sweat.

On a larger scale, England's experience had been as catastrophic as Shaux's.

But, in spite of disaster after disaster, in spite of Hitler's overwhelming strength, Churchill seemed unshakable. He had said, in another speech, that people would remember this as Britain's finest hour. Finest hour!

Shaux smiled to himself; as Eleanor used to say at Oxford, maybe the horse would talk.

"Look, all I'm saying is that the longer we fight, the more we'll piss Hitler off," Debenham was saying to Pound, clutching a fresh large whiskey in his hand. "If we're going to have to come to terms, better to do it now than when he's invaded. Maybe he'll leave us unoccupied, with our own government, like southern France and Vichy."

"We should fight to the end," Dottie Brown insisted.

"That's easy to say," Debenham sneered. "What's that expression? *You'll* fight to the last drop of *my* blood!"

"That's not fair! I'd fight if I—"

"Now, now," Winslow intervened. "Let's not fight among ourselves. Better get another round in before he comes on the radio."

The bar drew silent as Mrs. Winslow turned up the radio and an announcer intoned an introduction to the prime minister.

Shaux listened to the gravelly voice with rapt attention. The long, flowing sentences rolled out with irresistible power. It was like listening to poetry:

"Rather more than a quarter of a year has passed since the new Government came into power in this country. What a cataract of disaster has poured out upon us since then!"

"Damned right," Debenham said.

"Shut *up!*" Dottie growled back.

"The great air battle which has been in progress over this Island for the last few weeks has recently attained a high intensity. It is too soon to attempt to assign limits either to its scale or to its duration. We must certainly expect that greater efforts will be made by the enemy than any he has so far put forth …"

If that was the case, Shaux thought, he wondered how much longer he could go on … waking up every morning and trying to compose himself … flying all day every day, encountering the enemy for a few seconds of vicious, kill-or-be-killed action … counting the dead but not remembering them … pretending that the enemy aircraft were not flown by young men just like himself … waiting for the day he'd fly once too often …

Churchill's voice rolled on. "We may be sure, therefore, that he will continue as long as he has the strength to do so …"

As, I suppose, will I, Shaux thought, *until I reach a pointless end to a pointless life. After all, I don't really have anything better to do.*

"We believe that we shall be able to continue the air struggle indefinitely and as long as the enemy pleases, and the longer it continues the more rapid will be our approach, first towards that parity, and then into that superiority, in the air upon which in a large measure the decision of the war depends ..."

How could he be so sure, so confident that this battle would not end in defeat, one more disaster in the cataract? Didn't Churchill understand how hard it was to fight just one more day, let alone "indefinitely"? Didn't Churchill understand that eighteen-year-old Froggie Potter would almost certainly come to a horrible fate while Churchill continued his indefinite struggle? Parity? Superiority? On what basis—that Churchill was prepared to sacrifice more Froggie Potters than Hitler was?

"The gratitude of every home in our Island, in our Empire, and indeed throughout the world, except in the abodes of the guilty, goes out to the British airmen who, undaunted by odds, unwearied in their constant challenge and mortal danger, are turning the tide of the World War by their prowess and by their devotion ..."

Shaux shivered. It seemed that Churchill was speaking directly and solely to him, stiffening his sinews and summoning up his blood. *Undaunted by odds, unwearied in their constant challenge and mortal danger* ... But Shaux *was* daunted; he *was* weary!

Yes, he thought Churchill might have answered, *but you also have prowess and devotion, for you climb unhesitatingly into your Spitfire every time you're called upon to do so.*

Yes, that's true, Shaux might have answered, *but only because ...*

"Never in the field of human conflict was so much owed by so many to so few ..."

Surely not—he was no hero, just a man indifferent to his fate; there was nothing heroic about risking a valueless life. Besides, the pilot in Yeats's poem had not fought because of duty or because of the inspirational speeches of politicians, and nor did Shaux, who fought because he just happened to be in the RAF, and in the RAF you fly.

"All hearts go out to the fighter pilots, whose brilliant actions we see with our own eyes day after day ..."

Shaux looked down at the table, sensing Dottie Brown's burning eyes on him. He knew the locals in the bar were staring at the pilots, and he felt as if half the world were staring at him too. Shaux felt ashamed; he didn't want the burden of other people's gratitude. He didn't want them to think he was being selfless. He didn't want people to think that his actions were brilliant. Giving up a life not worth living—a waste of breath—was not a sacrifice deserving credit.

He stole a glance at the other pilots, their boisterous drinking set aside while Churchill spoke. Digby was looking sheepish; Potter was rapt; Ash was puffed up with pride, even though he'd been in the battle less than a day.

Debenham, Shaux saw, looked at things in a very different light.

"Damned right!" Debenham growled. "It's the very least we deserve."

2045 hours, Tuesday, August 20, 1940
11 Group Headquarters, Uxbridge, Middlesex, England

Eleanor presented her report to Park in the study of his quarters. As a senior officer he was entitled to a comfortably furnished, substantial house, in sharp contrast to her minute room in the WAAF officers' grim quarters, and she looked jealously at the overflowing bookcases and the innumerable photographs of family and colleagues. Even the carpet beneath her feet was to be envied in contrast to the dusty floorboards of her cubicle. He invited her to sit, and she sank into the luxury of a comfortable armchair beside the fireplace.

"What did you learn today, Eleanor?" he asked as he also sat.

She had made notes on a number of topics; the most important—from a pretty thin haul—was that the sector control room at Biggin was housed in a conventional building at ground level.

"If Biggin is bombed again and loses the control room, the whole of C sector is out of the chain of command, sir. The other sectors can't pick up the slack easily, because the sector radios can only talk to four squadrons. Other controllers can't communicate with each other's pilots."

"That's an excellent point," Park said. "We'll get the control room—all the sector control rooms—moved underground immediately. I'm surprised nobody's pointed that out before."

"You may also want to consider building additional control rooms as backups, at other stations, so that it's impossible to knock out a sector."

"That in itself is well worth your trip. Anything else?"

"Well, sir …" She hesitated.

"Out with it!" He grinned.

"I was looking at the map at Biggin Hill, sir, and it occurred to me that it shows 11 Group's area."

"Yes, of course; what's wrong with that?"

"Nothing, sir, but it made me think about the map here. It occurred to me just now that you can only see the south of England and a bit of France."

He raised his eyebrows in perplexity, and she hurried on, feeling as if she were entering a minefield.

"If, however, you could also see 12 Group's area, and vice versa, it would make it a lot easier for you and Air Vice-Marshal Leigh-Mallory to coordinate your forces. He'd be able to see raids developing and gaps in our coverage and would be able to scramble earlier."

She waited for an explosion. She had poked at the festering wound of Park and Leigh-Mallory's mutual dislike. She had implied criticism of Dowding's brilliant control system. She would be back in the bowels of the Air Ministry by midnight.

Park looked as if he'd been struck by lightning. "What exactly are you suggesting?" he demanded.

"He'd be able to offer more assistance if he could see what was happening, sir. Fighter Command has created an artificial division in our defenses."

Again she waited. Park sat deep in thought, staring into space. At length he roused himself and stood up.

"Mrs. Rand," he said slowly while Eleanor waited with bated breath, "many people have said that the rift between Trafford Leigh-Mallory and me is caused by the fact that he's an arrogant so-and-so and I'm a prickly bastard. While that may well be part of the answer, I've tended to see it as differences of opinion on fighter tactics. Nobody has suggested that we don't cooperate more fully because the system doesn't permit us to. I find that observation deeply illuminating."

"I hope I haven't—"

"I need to think about it, Eleanor," he interrupted her. "If you were going to ask if you've offended me by bringing up a sore subject, you certainly haven't—quite the contrary. Once again you've seen something that others haven't."

He sat down again. "By the way, what did you think of Oldchurch?"

"I met Professor—I mean, Wing Commander—Pound, sir," Eleanor said, glad to be back on safe ground and doubly glad Park hadn't bitten her head off. "He struck me as a very able man, if I may say so."

Park smiled. "Harry Pound is absolutely first-rate; he and I flew together in the last war. What did you think of the station?"

"It's an enlarged, marshy cricket field with a row of Spitfires and Defiants parked along one side, sir."

"I'd heard as much; I haven't been there yet. What are the facilities like?"

"Dreadful, sir. They have nothing but old tents that leak like sieves.

No engineering facilities, no proper latrines or washrooms, no canteen, no first aid post, no defenses. They have to walk down to the village to eat. They only have electricity because the local vicar redirected the power lines from the church."

"Well, we need it as an emergency field," Park said. "It's in an excellent location, right on the south coast, smack on Kesselring's best routes to London. If the facilities are really bad, we'll move the squadrons elsewhere and use it only during the daylight hours."

"Wing Commander Pound said to give him a week, sir. He believes he can fix it up."

Park chuckled. "Pound is not only a brilliant mathematician, as I'm sure you're aware, but also an amazing fixer-upper. He's got an old family car that he's worked on over the years, and it can do a hundred miles per hour. It's the most amazing sight!"

"You also need Oldchurch as an operational station in case one of the main stations is damaged, sir."

"That's very true too, particularly if Kesselring keeps attacking airfields. Very well; we'll give Harry Pound his week and see what he can do."

He stood up. "Can I offer you some refreshments, Eleanor? The prime minister's going to speak in a few minutes, and you're welcome to stay and listen. Whiskey and soda?"

"Thank you. A little whiskey and lots of soda water, please. Do you mind if I smoke, sir?"

"Of course not—how thoughtless of me! Please help yourself to the box on the table."

Park fiddled with the radio controls. "Churchill's going to be talking about us, I'm told," Park said. "After yesterday's briefing, it'll take all his rhetorical skills to make the situation sound hopeful."

They sat down by the fireplace, as Eleanor imagined millions of people were doing, all over the country, to listen to the one man in England who was convinced the war could be won—would be won.

"Rather more than a quarter of a year has passed since the new Government came into power in this country. What a cataract of disaster has poured out upon us since then!"

"He doesn't mince his words," Park commented.

It struck Eleanor that Park had taken enormous criticism over his handling of Dunkirk and the fall of France—two major disasters in the cataract—for refusing to send over the Spitfires, the one aircraft capable of beating the enemy back. In the popular mind, or at least in the army's mind, Park had condemned the army to death and destruction. And now he held the responsibility for defending Britain itself.

"The great air battle which has been in progress over this Island for the last few weeks has recently attained a high intensity. It is too soon to attempt to assign limits either to its scale or to its duration. We must certainly expect that greater efforts will be made by the enemy than any he has so far put forth ..."

Park was staring into the fireplace. Watching him, Eleanor realized that the raging battles of the past ten days, the huge toll in men and machines, were simply a prelude to what was to come. Churchill's voice rolled on.

"We may be sure, therefore, that he will continue as long as he has the strength to do so ..."

"And so will I," Park murmured. "And so will we all."

Hitler and Churchill, Göring and Dowding, Kesselring and Park, bloodied prizefighters battering at each other in a primeval battle of attrition, until one side could stand no more ...

"We believe that we shall be able to continue the air struggle indefinitely and as long as the enemy pleases, and the longer it continues the more rapid will be our approach, first towards that parity, and then into that superiority, in the air upon which in a large measure the decision of the war depends ..."

"I showed him your analyses," Park said to her. "I'm sure he's referring to those. He asked that copies be sent to the aircraft factories. However, he's a great deal more optimistic about the future than the numbers warrant."

Oh God, what had she started? She imagined sweating foremen staring at her numbers ... *"Come on, lads, let's get one more Spit finished before we knock off!"*

"The gratitude of every home in our Island, in our Empire, and indeed throughout the world, except in the abodes of the guilty, goes out to the British airmen who, undaunted by odds, unwearied in their constant challenge and mortal danger, are turning the tide of the World War by their prowess and by their devotion ..."

Park was lost in thought, Eleanor saw. It was his hand, his voice on the telephone, that sent those airmen out, again and again.

"Never in the field of human conflict was so much owed by so many to so few ..."

"Amen," Park said, and Eleanor saw there were tears in his eyes.

"All hearts go out to the fighter pilots, whose brilliant actions we see with our own eyes day after day ..."

Park was a fighter pilot himself, she thought, and knew exactly what he sent his men to face. Perhaps only a fighter pilot had earned that right. Perhaps the aircrews would accept commands only from a man who knew, from direct experience, what he was asking them to do.

She thought of poor George, scarcely a warrior, shot down and killed on his very first operational sortie. His military efforts had seemed so futile, his death so pointless—but not, she realized, in Churchill's eyes. On the contrary, in Churchill's eyes George was a hero in a noble cause, a man of prowess and devotion, a fighter in a struggle unparalleled in the field of human conflict.

The prime minister's words had redeemed George and consecrated his death; George was no longer a sweet but listless libertine, a carefree hedonist, but one of the "few." What had Shakespeare written? "We few, we happy few, we band of brothers"—or something like that. In Churchill's eyes, George stood with the Spartans at Thermopylae, with Horatius at the bridge, with Henry V's archers at Agincourt, with Travis and Bowie and Crockett at the Alamo, with the Light Brigade in the valley of Death.

Her eyes filled with tears. She had always seen George through the prism of his weaknesses, his all-to-human follies, she realized. She had thought of him with fond forgiveness. Now she saw his strengths. In the future she would remember him a strong man, in the company of other strong men, taking the place he had earned in the hall of Valhalla.

She thought of Rawley, so confident that Park and his pilots would not stem the German tide; what would he be thinking now?

And finally she thought of Johnnie Shaux. She hadn't seen him since Oxford, and yet in her mind's eye she saw him vividly—silent, dependable, always there when he was needed, a friend she had always taken for granted, a companion of whom she had almost no knowledge, because she had never bothered to ask.

Was Johnnie listening to Churchill? What was he thinking? Was he undaunted by the odds and unwearied by the constant challenge and mortal danger—a man to whom so many owed so much, but not enough to give him a decent place to sleep or even a proper toilet to use?

She'd missed him today; suddenly she feared she'd never see him again.

"Amen," she echoed.

PART TWO

SEPTEMBER 6–8, 1940

I have nothing to offer but blood, toil, tears and sweat. We have before us an ordeal of the most grievous kind. We have before us many, many long months of struggle and of suffering.

You ask, "What is our policy?" I will say; "It is to wage war, by sea, land and air, with all our might and with all the strength that God can give us: to wage war against a monstrous tyranny, never surpassed in the dark lamentable catalogue of human crime. That is our policy."

You ask, "What is our aim?" I can answer with one word: "Victory—victory at all costs, victory in spite of all terror, victory however long and hard the road may be; for without victory there is no survival."

—Winston Spencer Churchill, May 13, 1940, inaugural speech as prime minister to the House of Commons

SEPTEMBER 6, 1940

0530 hours, Friday, September 6, 1940
RAF Oldchurch, Kent, England

Johnnie Shaux awoke an hour before dawn. His tiny cubicle smelled dank, like the cellars beneath the orphanage, leavened with just a faint, almost undetectable whiff of horse manure. He pulled his uniform on by feel in the darkness and fumbled his way into his heavy sheepskin flying boots, still half-asleep, unshaven and unwashed.

Outside the hut the night was still as black as pitch; there were no stars, and the air smelled of rain. He waited until he could detect vague gradations of blackness, yawning and rubbing his eyes, and set off to walk along a crudely fashioned wooden walkway beside a long row of huts. The breeze was warm and soft, and from the invisible woods that bordered the field he heard the first tentative chirpings of the predawn chorus.

He reached a larger hut, barely visible in the gloom, its windows tightly sealed with blackout material. When he opened the door, the glare of naked light bulbs dazzled him. An airman silently handed him a mug of hot, sweet tea, and Shaux retreated back out into the darkness. He felt his way to a decaying deck chair on the veranda and sat down. The tea scalded his tongue. He lit a cigarette, and the smoke tasted harsh and acrid in his mouth.

He sat with his eyes closed, gathering his senses, stretching his limbs one by one, taking an inventory of his brief life, wondering whether he would still be alive to do so tomorrow. Every day was the same, endlessly repeated. *"Plus ça change, plus c'est la même chose,"* he muttered under his breath. The more things change, the more they stay the same.

Yesterday had been a bad day, although no worse than the day before or the one before that. Each morning the bombers gathered in the skies over northern France and Belgium like a swarm of locusts. Above them rose the 109s, like clouds of angry wasps. Then they swept across the Channel, wave after wave. The first wave of bombers would swing toward some hapless 11 Group airfield, the second toward another, and so on, each wave carrying at least forty tons of high explosives to rain down on its appointed target, Manston or Lympne or West Malling or Hawkinge or Oldchurch …

Squadron by squadron, 11 Group would scramble in response to the RDF blips that foretold the coming of the enemy, climbing hard with throttles wide open and the Merlins screaming, clawing up through the thinning air, "hanging from their propellers" as the pilots said, climbing fifty vertical feet every second while crossing three hundred feet of the ground far below them; turning to the vectors given them by the tinny voices of the controllers; staring into the haze above them, trying to penetrate the incandescent blaze of the sun, desperate to see the enemy before the enemy saw them.

After four or five minutes they'd be at the altitudes favored by the lumbering bombers, but at a ground speed of only two hundred miles per hour while they were climbing at an angle of fifteen degrees, the Spitfires couldn't catch the bombers even if they saw them.

They'd continue to climb, wondering why the Merlin, spinning at forty revolutions every second, powered by five hundred controlled explosions of compressed high-octane gasoline vapor in its twelve cylinders, didn't shake itself apart; or wondering why the tips of the propellers, slashing their way through twelve hundred feet of air each second, a mile of air every five seconds, did not disintegrate.

In another three or four minutes—if they were granted that eternity— they'd be entering the thin, cold air above twenty thousand feet, the realm of the 109s, the angry wasps, each armed with three vicious canons capable of sawing a Spitfire in two.

And then what? Would there be nothing but empty sky with the controller's calm voice vectoring them back and forth and round and round in a futile search for an enemy that wasn't there? Or would there be a sudden, heart-stopping *bang-bang-bang* as the black silhouettes of 109s erupted out of the sun, canon shells ripping at the Spitfires?

And then what? A split-second chance to pour the contents of the Spitfire's eight machine guns into some hapless or inexpert enemy, stitching holes in his wings or his fuselage or chiseling bits off his engine or the pilot's body? Or would there be an eruption of oily smoke and flame from the Merlin, the heat of exploding high-octane fuel burning through the absurdly thin fire wall ahead of the cockpit? Or the surreal feeling of dead controls if the cables were cut by canon shells, utter helplessness as the Spitfire stalled and dropped like a spinning stone, converted in a split second from an elegant flying machine into six thousand pounds of scrap metal at twenty thousand feet in the sky with nothing to hold it up? Perhaps a panicked escape from the doomed aircraft, perhaps wounded, perhaps burned, perhaps blinded, into the sudden roaring of the frigid sky, dependent on a parachute that might or might not open and that, even if it did open, might or might not have been damaged by canon fire or flames?

Shaux started; his cigarette had burned down to his fingers. He flipped it away and lit another.

The Royal Air Force station had gradually awoken around him. A truck growled to a halt nearby, disgorging members of the ground crew. Shaux could follow their movements by the flickering of their flashlights and the muttering of their sleepy curses as they checked the aircraft parked around him.

Well, yesterday had been a bad day. Perhaps today would be better; perhaps not. No man controlled his own fate; resisting fate led to despair.

He knew it, accepted it, bowed to its inevitability; he just wished that fate could bloody well get it over with … except …

He had always carried the fading sepia picture of his parents as a totem, and in the last few days he'd carried another totem, a letter written in a careful, rounded hand. It wasn't light enough to read, but he'd already committed it to memory.

> C/o 11 Group Headquarters
> RAF Uxbridge
> Middlesex
>
> Dear Johnnie,
>
> I'm sorry I haven't written before, but so much has been going on that I haven't had a chance—actually, that's not true; I should have written, but I didn't. You've always written, and I never have. Mea culpa, mea maxima culpa, etc., etc.

Thank you for the kind words you wrote about George. You were always a much better friend to him than he was to you. I was astonished by his death rather than upset; he was not the sort of man to die, if you see what I mean. I hope it was instant; he feared death and couldn't tolerate even the mildest pain.

Looking back, it's hard to realize I actually married him, and I'm ashamed to say I can't really remember why I did; it all seems so improbable.

While I'm in a confessional mood, let me say that I've finished with Rawley, completely and forever. You were always too polite to say what you thought, but I knew anyway; I could see it in your eyes, and you were right, as always.

So, I find myself without past encumbrances and with a new job. I can't write about what I'm doing, but it's fascinating and consuming, and I feel useful for the first time in my existence. Of course I trust you—I just can't risk a letter going astray.

I was sorry to miss you when I was down at Oldchurch, but I'll be going down again soon and hope to see you then. Perhaps we'll get a chance to have a drink and talk, like we used to so long ago at Oxford.

Sincerely,
Eleanor

He patted his wallet to make sure he hadn't lost it. It was a simple, everyday sort of letter, he supposed, an old friend catching up, one of ten thousand similar letters written the same day, most with the classic opening phrase "I'm sorry I haven't written before." But it had struck him like a bolt of lightning, shaken the most important tenet of his belief system—that his life had no real purpose or value, "a waste of breath" as Yeats had written.

His long conversations with Eleanor at Oxford—in truth her long monologues in which she had poured out her soul and he had listened— had emphatically not been a waste of breath. They had been a glimpse into somebody else's soul, a bridge to the rest of humanity. If she was coming to Oldchurch and hoping to talk to him, then the future, at least the immediate future, was worth living for.

The photograph of his parents was a totem pointing backward. Now she had sent him a totem pointing forward. The two totems were back-to-back in his wallet, like the Roman god Janus with two faces. Ever since he'd received the letter, he'd climbed into his Spitfire hoping to come back—and fearful that he might not. But hope and fear were antithetical to his philosophy. How could he climb into his Spitfire without a second thought if he cared about the outcome? How could he be undaunted by the odds, in Churchill's words, now that he had something at risk?

Debenham's Alvis snorted to a halt in front of him, snapping Shaux's chain of thought, and for once he was grateful for the interruption. The Alvis didn't sound too good, Shaux thought, lumpy and uneven, as if the timing was off. Come to think of it, the Alvis didn't look too good in the predawn light either. Debenham had stopped washing it—or, rather, he had stopped compelling the nearest underling to wash it for him.

Debenham had changed in the last two weeks. He used to be imperious, demanding, ambitious, and sharp-tongued; now he was merely sharp-tongued. It was as if he had been worn away, as if his utter confidence in himself and his future success had somehow been eroded, like a rocky coastline pummeled by the ocean for tens of thousands of years.

Well, Shaux thought, the endless succession of days of endless fighting was grinding everyone away, until there was nothing left but the innermost man, exposed for all to see; in many cases, perhaps including Debenham's, perhaps including his own, the innermost man was too abraded, too flayed, to endure the onslaught.

Debenham had been flying less and less, Shaux had noted—his Spitfire had been unusually prone to engine trouble, causing him to turn back before encountering the enemy; he'd had an unusual number of family emergencies requiring a leave of absence; he'd been too busy with paperwork or too sick with a summer cold or too this or too that. More often than not, Charlie Henderson, the commander of A Flight, had led 339 into battle. But poor old Charlie had died over Hastings yesterday; Shaux had seen him jump from his stricken aircraft with a burning parachute.

Of all the 339 pilots that had flown into Oldchurch on August 18, just three weeks ago, only Debenham, Shaux, and Digby were still alive.

"Jesus *Christ*," Debenham roared, startling Shaux into full wakefulness. He'd tripped on the steps leading up to the hut and now was wavering as he tried to steady his balance, his arms flung wide. He caught himself and climbed the remaining step with excessive caution, and Shaux realized he was not sober. Debenham paused for a moment, clutching at a pillar for support, and then stormed inside yelling for tea while Shaux wondered what he should do.

He *had* to report it to Pound, of course; he had absolutely no choice. Debenham was a danger to himself and the whole squadron, and Pound was exactly the right man to handle the situation in an appropriate, compassionate fashion. Nevertheless, going behind one's CO's back smacked of insubordination or even mutiny. Shaux knew he would be destroying Debenham's reputation and career, and the fact that Shaux loathed Debenham made matters worse, not better.

"Jesus *Christ*," Shaux echoed quietly.

0730 hours, Friday, September 6, 1940
11 Group Headquarters, Uxbridge, Middlesex, England

Eleanor knocked and entered Park's office. He was on the telephone; he waved her to a chair and indicated, with a series of one-arm gesticulations, that she should pour herself a cup of tea, light a cigarette, and make herself comfortable. In the meantime he continued his conversation.

"Look, Harry, I've lost six squadron leaders in eight days. There's simply no reserve … I simply don't have anyone to send to Oldchurch to take over 339."

He paused to listen to the reply. Eleanor had trained herself not to listen to Park's conversations with other officers, but he must be talking to Pound, and the mentions of Oldchurch and 339 were irresistible.

"I don't know this chap Shaux," Park said into the telephone. "However, I do know Debenham—vaguely—and I don't care for him. But I simply can't afford to transfer a squadron CO in unless I absolutely have to."

He paused again. Eleanor gave up the effort not to listen.

"That's very unfortunate," Park muttered. "Still, everyone's under tremendous strain, and some people are bound to reach their breaking point … Alcohol? Poor chap; it's happened enough times before, God knows … Now, tell me about Shaux."

Eleanor eyed the extension telephone with longing, barely restraining herself from snatching it up.

"Really? Jack Shaux? Of course, I remember him very well; a good man, used to fly in his kilt, as I recall—heaven help the ladies if he'd come down on a parachute! He died at the very end, right before the armistice; I was there when he went down … So, this chap you're proposing is Jack's son? I didn't know Jack was even married, let alone had a son."

It had never occurred to Eleanor that Johnnie Shaux had parents; he had always seemed *sui generis*, created whole and complete as an Oxford undergraduate, seated in a shaft of sunlight in the Bodleian Library in Oxford, reading a mathematical text she needed to borrow. Now, it seemed, he had a father who had also been a fighter pilot, a colleague of Park's and Pound's, who had been shot down in 1918.

It was strange somehow—Johnnie, who was simply Johnnie, had

become more complicated, as if he had suddenly expanded into another, hitherto unrevealed dimension.

"Look, Harry, I trust your judgment without reservation, as you know," Park said. "If you think he can handle it, we'll give him a shot at it … God knows, we're so shorthanded I'd put a bus driver in a Hurricane, if he were foolish enough to volunteer for it."

Park stood. Clearly his conversation with Pound was coming to a close. It appeared that Johnnie was going to replace the odious Debenham, who had been extremely rude to her during her trip to Oldchurch. She opened her report and checked her notes; Park's unvarying politeness and encouragement did not mean she could be unprepared for a briefing.

"I agree entirely," Park said into the telephone. "Very well, I'll look after that as well. You can tell him if you wish to. I'll get the wheels rolling at my end … Good morning to you, Harry … Oh, it seems about the same as the last few days; they're building up over the French coast as we speak, so stand by for another busy day … Good morning."

Park hung up the telephone.

"Sorry to keep you waiting, Eleanor," he said. "And there's one more thing I must do before it slips my mind, if you'll forgive me."

He picked up the telephone again.

"Connect me to the adjutant, please … Archie, good morning, AOC here. I've just been on the telephone with Harry Pound at Oldchurch discussing 339. Post John Shaux as squadron commander, with the rank of acting squadron leader, and move Debenham to the group reassignment list, all effective immediately … Oh, Debenham's having a breakdown, I'm afraid, LMF, but we're going to keep our mouths shut … Yes, alcohol, poor bastard … Yes, it's amazing they all aren't … And one other thing; write up Shaux for the Distinguished Flying Cross—telephone Pound for the citation. Shaux is spelled S-H-A-U-X, by the way, not S-H-A-W … Yes, that's the one … Thank you; I'll see you later when Dowding arrives."

Johnnie appeared to have grown yet another dimension. He was not simply a pilot, she gathered, but a commander of pilots, a man to be trusted to lead a squadron into battle, and beyond that, a pilot whose skills deserved the award of a decoration for distinguished service.

She wasn't sure she liked the idea of a multidimensional Johnnie. The original version was so soothing, so undemanding, so comfortable, so unexceptional, so utterly uncomplicated, like a favorite pair of old slippers.

A staff officer entered with an urgent report requiring Park's immediate attention, and Eleanor was still left with her thoughts.

There were three men in a boat, she thought, remembering the punting trip during which Rawley had announced his intention to marry someone else. There were three men in a boat—one used his connections to avoid the battle; the second died before the battle had scarcely been joined, barely tested but accounted for with honor; the third went into battle and endured.

She definitely preferred the old Johnnie, she decided—the one she had known at Oxford, the one to whom she could tell anything, the one without a past or a medal, the one she didn't have to think about.

"Now, finally, Eleanor," Park said. "I'm sorry for the long delay. What do you have for me?"

"Well, sir, I'm not quite sure," she said, refocusing her thoughts. "My formulas have begun to produce results that might be useful, but ..."

She trailed away, assailed by doubt.

"Tell me what you've got; don't worry if it's right or wrong."

"Well, as you know, we've compiled statistics about the state of 11 Group and other relevant factors, such as aircraft production, pilot training, and so on. By comparing the statistics from day to day, we've developed trends. We can take the trends and project them into the future."

"Yes, I follow that," Park said. "Go on."

"Once we reached the point of projecting into the future, we were able to begin testing how accurate our assumptions are."

"By waiting and seeing if your projections turned out to be true?"

"Yes, sir, but we could also pick a day in the past and project from that day, to see if our projections turned out correctly. By studying why we were wrong, we were able to modify our assumptions and make them better. We've probably rebuilt our assumption set fifty times in the last two weeks."

"I see," Park said. "Trial and error."

"Exactly, sir. It's a bit crude, I'm afraid."

"On the contrary," Park said. "That's how the Merlin is being developed and why it's such a fine engine. The chaps at Rolls-Royce literally run it at full power until it breaks and then strengthen whichever bit broke. Then they repeat the process, over and over."

"I didn't know that, sir. It's comforting ... Anyway, we've used a similar technique to track the flight plans and timing of enemy attacks. We've reached some rather startling conclusions. It's a sort of mathematical map of the battlefield, as it were. We've used time and height instead of distance as the scale of the map."

"Time and height? I'm not sure if I follow you."

"Sorry, sir. We can say that fifteen thousand feet over Hastings is twelve minutes from the ground at Oldchurch, sir, but only six minutes from ten thousand feet over Biggin Hill, even though Biggin is four times farther away on a conventional map."

"Interesting. It's almost like a three-dimensional version of the map in the operations room? That would be immensely valuable!"

"Well, anyway, sir, we've used the statistical trends and the time-height map to project the outcome of the battle. The conclusions are mathematically correct but unlikely."

"What are they?"

"Before I waste your time with nonsense, sir, I'd like to go over my calculations with Dr. Pound—Wing Commander Pound. He's not just a mathematician; he's the best theoretical logician in England. If he thinks what I'm doing is right, I'll present it to you."

"Fine; with the way things are going, I'd like a crystal ball."

"I can only project probabilities, sir."

"I know that, Eleanor. Don't worry; I won't be demanding to know what Kesselring is going to have for lunch three hours from now. Go down and see Harry Pound—today, preferably—and let me know."

1300 hours, Friday, September 6, 1940
RAF Oldchurch, Kent, England

Shaux sat outside the dispersal hut in the warm sunshine, feigning sleep. Too much was going on, and he needed time to digest it without interruption. He had reluctantly reported Debenham's condition to Pound, who had gone to see for himself. An hour later a white-faced Debenham had hurled his kit bag into his Alvis and driven off like a madman; an hour later again Pound had taken Shaux for a stroll around the airfield perimeter, during which he had promoted Shaux and told him he was receiving the DFC.

It was not a good outcome. Although logic told him that Debenham had brought his fate down on himself, Shaux felt he had committed an act of betrayal, and now Shaux would pay by being loaded down by responsibilities he did not want and distinctions he did not welcome.

None of that mattered, of course, with the 109s waiting; it simply meant he'd torture himself even more every time a 339 pilot went down.

"Look, we don't have much time." Potter's voice intruded on his thoughts from farther down the row of armchairs, decrepit, pilots, for the use of. He was addressing two nervous new pilots, fresh from flying school. "You'll have to learn on the job, just as we all did. I'll give you just one thing to think about. Remember—you may not know how to fly very well, but your Spitfire does. So, repeat after me: 'My Spitfire knows how to fly.' Now, repeat it."

"My Spitfire knows how to fly," two youthful voices responded in unison.

"I want you to repeat it until you believe it."

Shaux smiled to himself, remembering the nervous schoolboy who had chased Debenham's Alvis into the woods and down the lane to the village. It seemed so long ago.

"My Spitfire knows how to fly," the voices repeated dutifully.

"Exactly; your aircraft does the flying, and you just tell it where to go."

"What does that mean, sir?"

"First of all, don't call me 'sir.' Call me Froggie or Potter on the ground and Green Leader in the air. We're all pilots together. What I mean is that you don't use the controls consciously; you hold them lightly and just sort of lean, as if you were riding a bike ..."

Shaux smiled inwardly again and turned to more-immediate matters—namely, 339 barely had enough qualified pilots to be operational. Digby could serve as A Flight leader; his phenomenal eyesight and inherently cautious approach to life would keep them as safe as possible. He'd be the rock upon which Shaux would build—if he had time to build.

He'd take a chance and put Froggie Potter in charge of B Flight; even though he was very young and inexperienced, he was turning out to be a natural leader. He already had seven victories under his belt, which indicated that he might have the right combination of instincts and luck to survive the battle.

What was Shaux's own new job? What was a squadron CO supposed to do? Lead by example, he guessed, but that didn't tell him what to *do*. He thought back over his former COs, wondering why some were good and some not. The best had made him feel comfortable, he supposed, had made him feel he could get the job done, despite all his weaknesses, and they'd made him feel confident in their leadership, regardless of their particular characters and idiosyncrasies.

He'd have to do the same, he thought; somehow he had to give the same feeling of confidence—enough confidence that they'd climb into their Spitfires, even though one or two of them probably wouldn't make it through the day unscathed; enough confidence that they'd remember the basics, the vital lessons about staying in formation and searching the skies and all the rest; enough confidence in their Spitfires, and the ground crews that maintained them, that they'd believe they could compete with the 109s on an even basis; enough confidence in their leaders—in him—that they'd follow him into battle, even if they were shaking with fear and peeing in their underpants; enough confidence not to flinch when the battle was joined and the 109s opened fire.

But why would they follow someone like himself, who was convinced his fate awaited him somewhere among the clouds above? Would they not see through the thin veneer of confidence he'd don like an ill-fitting clown suit? He lacked Digby's calm reliability and Potter's natural flair and even Debenham's caustic habit of command. What could he offer them? Stoicism in the face of death? What good would that do them, for Christ's sake?

Now he'd have squadron leader's rings on his sleeves and a DFC ribbon on his breast beneath his pilot's wings. He'd have the outer trappings of leadership—but surely they'd penetrate that and see the worn-away man inside the uniform, the peeled-back soul who considered life a waste of breath.

Pound had been very flattering when they'd talked, but his opinions of Shaux were grossly inflated and sadly mistaken. He had also been very unfair, Shaux thought, because Pound had singled him out, turned the spotlight on him, making him act a part for which he was not equipped. Shaux had always sought the background; he made sure he was always in the back row in group photographs, his face half-hidden behind someone else's. He was an obscure man, and he wanted an obscure life—he *needed* an obscure life, in order to accept an obscure death. He was Shaux the Obscure, a follower, not a leader, a man living on the outskirts of life.

His name had always been just one name in some long list—in the orphanage, at school, at college, in the RAF; one day soon it would be just one name in a long list on some war memorial.

Soon he'd have to open his eyes and acknowledge the world around him. He'd have to stand up and say something squadron leader–ish, something to convey the message that 339 was equal to the task, that the odds were not appalling, and that they could be confident. Should he bark an order, as Debenham would? Should he crack a joke? Should he yawn to indicate that the battle was just a tedious routine?

"I say, Jenkins," Digby's voice intruded. "There's a popped rivet on the tail of that Defiant."

Shaux chuckled to himself. This was a game they all played with new recruits and outsiders, a 339 tradition.

"Which one, sir?" Sergeant Jenkins asked, playing along.

"The one at the far end of the row."

"How can you possibly see that?" one of the new pilots gasped. "That Defiant's got to be two hundred yards away if it's an inch! Nobody can see a rivet at two hundred yards!"

"Of course they can't; that would be absurd," Digby replied. "But with the current angle of the sun, it's casting a shadow, and the shadow's at least three inches long."

Shaux stood up. "Better get it fixed, Flight," he said, keeping his voice steady.

"Right away, sir," the sergeant said prosaically. "Defiants have always been wicked rivet poppers, bless 'em, since the day they came into service."

The two new pilots' faces alternated between incredulity and awe at Digby's telescopic eyesight.

"I suggest we get ourselves organized," Shaux said to the pilots as a group, assuming the mantle of command. "We'll be going to readiness in a few minutes."

He decided not to fake a yawn.

"However, there's still time for a cup of tea, I should think."

1400 hours, Friday, September 6, 1940
RAF Oldchurch, Kent, England

Eleanor's driver navigated the lane that climbed through the woods to the airfield. The old cricket club sign had been replaced by a smart new noticeboard announcing RAF OLDCHURCH, painted in blue letters on a white background. A guardhouse, looking rather like a refurbished garden shed painted white, stood beside the gate. A guard waved them to a halt and inspected their identification. He was wearing a white canvas belt with a large pistol holster. The military precision of the scene was somewhat mitigated by hanging flower baskets at the guardhouse windows, bright with red geraniums.

The rutted track leading onto the field had been filled with fresh gravel. She saw at once that the row of dilapidated tents had gone. In their place stretched a long line of prefabricated huts set on cinderblock foundations, with new porches facing the airfield. A working party of civilians was completing the task of connecting all the huts with a long covered wooden walkway. A water tower rose behind the huts, suggesting plumbing; the words *Southern Railways* were still discernable beneath the fresh green paint.

A series of larger huts followed, with neatly printed signs: Station Office, A Flight, B Flight, Operations Room. The large tents she had seen on her last visit, housing the engineering and equipment areas, were also gone, replaced by splendid white marquees with scalloped edges hanging from their roofs, reminiscent of the grand garden parties she had attended in her youth, except that these marquees had camouflage netting stretched over them to disguise them among the trees.

Pound emerged from the door marked Station Office and greeted her warmly.

"How nice to see you again," he said, lighting his tobacco pipe. He glanced about, beaming, obviously delighted by his handiwork, and she felt a wave of affection for him.

"You've transformed this place, sir!" she exclaimed. "You did it!"

"The big change is invisible," he said, pointing with the stem of his pipe down the length of the field. "We built a culvert for the stream and covered it over. Now the airfield doesn't turn into a bog every time it rains. The entire enterprise was planned and executed by the villagers, who have refused every offer of compensation. They were somewhat vague about where they got the concrete pipes and the digging machinery; I thought it best not to press the matter. It's a wonderful contribution."

"Now it really is an RAF airfield, as good as any," she said, glancing about. "All these new buildings … I'm amazed."

"The huts are on loan from the local racecourse," he told her, smiling broadly. "Those marquees are from the county's annual agricultural fair. Once, they housed prize bulls; now, they house Merlins and radios."

He was almost dancing in delight. "It's the little things that please me: the vicar donated his potting shed for a guardhouse, the control tower was the judges' stand at the racecourse, the WVS ladies equipped the kitchen, a plumbing contractor donated several baths for the bathhouse, etcetera, etcetera. My own contribution was to take the gun turrets out of the Defiants and mount them around the airfield. They're pretty ineffective as antiaircraft guns, but it makes us feel less helpless."

"It's magic!" she said, laughing with him. "Abracadabra—instant RAF station!"

"You are too kind," he said, aping as deep a bow as his figure would permit.

She noticed a fenced-off garden. "Goodness, are you growing vegetables?"

"We are," he chortled. "Salads, some fruits, vegetables—all donated from gardens in the village. The pilots are engaged in a rather intense competition involving tomatoes, even though it's late in the season. B Flight is betting on horse manure, while A Flight swears by chicken droppings."

"But what are those buildings over there?" she asked, pointing across the field to a line of large structures, a mishmash of canvas and plywood, some still under construction.

"Aha, my pièce de résistance!" He grinned triumphantly. "Better than a rabbit out of a hat, although also based on the principle of deception. Those are dummies, made out of the old tents. You'll notice that all the new buildings on this side are set back into the trees, whereas those stand out in the field, with the toothless Defiants neatly lined up in front of them. My theory was that the enemy might bomb the decoys, rather than the real thing. Well, we've been bombed twice, and on both occasions they aimed over there."

"That's very ingenious, sir," she said. A thought struck her. "Perhaps the AOC could order all the stations to do the same thing."

"Yes, or better yet, Keith Park could build dummy airfields all over southern England, and the Luftwaffe wouldn't know the real thing from the decoys."

"Of course," she said, grasping the implications. "Kesselring is bombing airfields—more than twenty attacks in ten days. If we gave him double the targets, we'd halve his effectiveness—no, his effectiveness would decline geometrically …"

"Well, the number of new airfields would be a negative exponent," Pound said, reminding her that he was a mathematician as well as a magician. "Indeed, it would be possible to calculate precisely how many decoys would be necessary to frustrate his efforts completely."

"I'll have to put that in the minimax model."

"Ah, yes, your model," Pound said. "Keith Park telephoned to say you'd reached some conclusions but were reluctant to present them without a mathematical review. I'm looking forward to it."

Eleanor groaned. "I hope it's not all nonsense, sir; I hope I haven't built a house of cards."

"Well, let's get a cup of tea and take a look, shall we?"

She turned to follow him. "Is Johnnie Shaux here, sir? I'd like his opinion also."

"339 is on patrol. With a bit of luck he'll be back in half an hour or so."

Only then did she realize that the field had seemed empty and waiting, like a tennis court between sets. What a fool! The entire purpose of Oldchurch was to provide a home for Spitfires, and she had stupidly failed to observe their absence.

"Oh," she said inadequately.

She had been looking forward to showing Johnnie her work, hoping he'd be impressed by her originality. She noticed Pound had said "with a bit of luck." She realized with a jolt that it wasn't actually certain Johnnie would return at all … Suddenly she felt cold, and even more of a fool; she'd been admiring decoy huts while he was up there somewhere, perhaps in contact with the enemy.

"Come on, my dear," Pound said, as if reading her thoughts. "Tea, a smoke, and your von Neumann model."

She had prepared an explanation of her approach, but her mind was split between minimax theory and the crawling second hand of the clock in Pound's cluttered office as it inched its way through "half an hour or so." She simply handed him her notebook to let her work speak for itself.

Pound put on a large pair of spectacles with curly ends that wrapped around his ears. He opened her book and pursed his lips; instantly she was back in a college tutorial at Oxford, waiting for her tutor's verdict. Pound turned a page, paused to relight his pipe, and turned another. He raised his eyebrows and jotted some notes on a pad. He read another page and then turned back to refer to a previous one.

She ground out her cigarette and noticed there were already two of her butts in the ashtray. She felt as if she were gripped in a vice between the tension of Pound's silent reading and the strain of Johnnie's uncertain return.

At one point Pound frowned, scribbled a calculation, and looked at the result in surprise. Eleanor wanted to scream, "What's wrong?"

An airman entered with their tea and set it on the desk. Pound did not look up, his eyes on her pages, but he reached out one hand and picked up the brimming cup. Eleanor was sure he'd spill it on her manuscript. The cup hovered indefinitely while Pound studied an equation. He grunted, although whether in agreement or disagreement Eleanor could not tell. Finally he took a sip, and the cup, still unseen, returned to its saucer without a mishap.

Eleanor stole yet another glance at the clock; half an hour or so had passed, and still no Johnnie and no verdict either.

At last Pound read her last page, pondering her conclusions, and slowly closed her notebook.

She bit back the temptation to demand, "Is it correct? Is it incorrect but promising? Is it rubbish? Is it anything at all?"

He relit his pipe, stared at her, and prepared to render judgment.

"Well, now, my dear—"

The airman poked his head into the office. "Excuse me, sir, 339's in sight."

"Ah, thank you, Davis," Pound said. "How many?"

"Four so far, sir."

"Let's go and see them, shall we?" Pound asked her. "I like to be there in case they need me."

"Of course, sir," she said. The was no point in pressing him for an answer when he was distracted, and, besides, it would be a relief to see Johnnie climbing out of the aircraft, safe and sound.

1400 hours, Friday, September 6, 1940
RAF Oldchurch, Kent, England

It had been a classic example of the uncertainties of aerial combat. Digby spotted Dorniers attacking the RAF station at Manston. Just as 339 was approaching, a squadron of Hurricanes had thrown themselves on the bombers, and Shaux had left them to it and led 339 up through the high clouds to find any 109s that might be covering the Dorniers.

As 339 emerged above the wispy cloud tops, they had encountered a dozen 109s, also emerging from the clouds, at close range and on intersecting courses. The first engagement consisted of hasty potshots, fired at random by the less experienced pilots, as the two sides took immediate evasive action, breaking left and right, up and down. At least half the aircraft on both sides dropped back into the cover of the clouds, leaving the remnants to circle each other like gladiators.

The remaining 109s stayed in formation and began circling upward. Shaux and the balance of 339 followed them. Better to be in the open air where he could see what was going on than flying blindly in and out of the cloud tops, where so many aircraft in such a small volume of space made collision a real possibility.

The 109s formed themselves into line astern, following their leader in a steeply climbing spiral. Instinct told Shaux that these were experienced pilots and that their leader might be one of the German aces, like Adolf Galland or Werner Mölders. Whoever he was, he'd reacted immediately and sought the advantage of height; 109s could outclimb Spitfires at this altitude, and as long as the 109s stayed higher, they'd be beyond the Spitfires' reach.

Why the spiral? Shaux guessed Galland or Mölders, or whoever he was, didn't want to lose touch with the Dorniers. By climbing in this fashion the 109s were staying close to the bombers and neutralizing the Spitfires; 339 could neither catch the 109s nor attack the Dorniers.

You may be very smart, Shaux thought, *but the new Mark II Spitfire can climb almost as fast as a 109 and out-turn it.* The 109 leader had to be looking back in surprise, wondering how the Spitfires were managing to keep up. Shaux also kept 339 in a tight spiral, his head full of geometry as he calculated the effect of a smaller turning circle against a better rate of climb—a helix within a helix. He wondered whether there were any formulas describing the surface topographies of helixes, but nothing came to mind; he'd ask Pound when—if—he got back.

He couldn't catch the 109s vertically, but his turning advantage meant he could keep them in front of 339, in his general field of fire. If the 109 commander kept climbing, eventually he'd swim into Shaux's gunsight, and then it was a question of whether 339 would be close enough for the 109s to be in range.

Besides, Shaux thought that tight turns were the finest of all a Spitfire's attributes. As a matter of fact, he had explained the maneuver to Froggie Potter just last night in the inn.

"Look, a Spit's wing roots stall before the wingtips and ailerons. It's called 'washout,' and it's very unusual. When the roots stall, you can feel the air turbulence shaking the elevator, but you're still flying and you're still in control, because the rest of the wings haven't stalled. No other aircraft can do that, because they stall from the wingtips inward. So in a Spit you can sit in an ultra-tight turn, just above stalling speed, while the other chap either stalls without warning and loses control or takes a less aggressive turn."

So, instead of neutralizing 339, the 109 leader had neutralized himself; the longer he kept climbing, the longer the Dorniers would stay unprotected from the Hurricanes and 339 would stay almost in range.

Evidently the 109 leader reached the same conclusion, for he abruptly broke out of his spiral and fell away to his right, circling down the other way. Now the two groups were turning in opposite directions, giving the 109s a chance to attack.

Not so fast, Shaux thought, turning to follow the same course, keeping the 109s ahead of them.

The abrupt change of course had cost both sides height. Now they were back down among the cloud tops, catching glimpses of each other. Shaux was wondering what maneuver Galland, or Mölders, or whoever he was, would try next when three stray 109s emerged from the cloud cover a hundred yards behind him. Blind luck had presented the new 109s with a perfect firing position. Cannon shells began flashing past him and then— *whack-whack-whack*—found his tailplane.

Shaux jerked back on the stick. His Spitfire reared up on its tail. He cut the throttle, and the aircraft staggered, beginning to stall, in an almost vertical climbing position with no power. As the Spitfire began to slide backward, he rammed the throttle back open, the Merlin roared, and he caught the aircraft just as it began to fall. The two pursuing 109s flashed harmlessly past beneath him.

It was a stunt he'd often imagined but never tried, a desperate gambit to escape certain disaster, the equivalent of driving a racing car into a brick wall in order to brake quickly. He'd had no idea whether it would work—apparently it had.

The rest of 339 was scattering left and right. Somehow Galland or Mölders had caught them up—Shaux wished he knew how. He gave 339 a vector upon which they could reorganize but received no answers.

When Shaux regained full control over his Spitfire, he found he was flying beside Protherow, a kid who had joined 339 only yesterday. Oil was streaming from Protherow's engine cowling, and then a broken fuel line erupted in a whoosh of fire. Shaux could see Protherow staring and yelling at him, although he could not hear him. Shaux realized he couldn't hear *anything*; his own radio must have been hit.

He could tell that Protherow was asking him what to do, and Shaux mouthed the word "Jump!" and pantomimed opening the canopy. Protherow nodded and reached for the latches, hammering at them with his fists. Shaux could see flames beginning to lick up from the cockpit floor. They were only thirty feet apart, wingtip to wingtip. Protherow's eyes were filled with pain and terror as he wrestled with the latches. His mouth was open and screaming, and Shaux saw him form the words "Help me! Help me!" Protherow's mouth paused its screaming for breath and sucked in flames. His huge eyes, ringed with fire, pleaded silently.

The two Spitfires flew on in perfect formation while Shaux waited for Protherow—"hobbies include watercolor painting and stamp collecting; plans to become a missionary," said his personnel file—to die.

Protherow's Spitfire turned slowly out toward the sea and assumed a graceful gliding attitude. Shaux let him go. Protherow would be laid to rest like the ancient Vikings, borne away on a ship of fire.

Shaux shook his head and struggled to concentrate. Where was he? Where was Oldchurch? Where was Galland or Molders? Where was the rest of 339? Shaux had been given responsibility for 339, and he had led them into mortal danger. He searched the skies by ingrained habit, but saw only Protherow's eyes.

1430 hours, Friday, September 6, 1940
RAF Oldchurch, Kent, England

Eleanor and Pound rose and walked outside to see 339 return. She heard a gathering drone in the eastern sky and saw five Spitfires approaching in line ahead, above the trees at the far end of the airfield. They landed one by one without drama and taxied toward her and Pound. Two more Spitfires appeared in the eastern sky, and then another.

The station warrant officer, a large and impressive figure who held himself stiffly, like a guardsman at Buckingham Palace, joined them.

"Twelve went off, sir," he said, with a lilting Scottish accent. "That's eight so far."

Pound's verdict on her theories was forgotten. She watched each pilot as he clambered out of his cockpit, trying to recognize Johnnie beneath the cumbersome flying gear and leather helmet. Two of the aircraft had holes in their skin; she found it difficult to comprehend that these were the marks of Luftwaffe gunfire. She noticed how solicitous the ground crews were, offering their arms as the pilots jumped down. More than one had lit cigarettes at the ready and handed them to the pilots as soon as their feet touched the grass.

A pilot approached them, stretching and rolling his head on his shoulders, as if he had a crick in his neck. He pulled off his helmet to disclose an absurdly young face and astonishing blue eyes. He couldn't have been more than nineteen or twenty at the most.

"About twenty Dorniers were bombing Manston, sir," he said to Pound.

That's not very far from here, Eleanor thought. *It could easily have been us.*

"We saw some Hurricanes going after them," the pilot continued. "The skipper led us up, and we met a dozen or so 109s above them, above the clouds."

"Everyone okay, as far as you know, Digby?" Pound asked.

The pilot lit a cigarette and inhaled deeply. "Protherow's Spit went down on fire; I don't know if he got out or not. Poor bastard; it was his first op."

"Let's hope he's all right," Pound said quietly.

What about Johnnie Shaux? Eleanor wanted to ask but didn't.

"Froggie Potter got another 109, a definite; went straight down without a tail," Digby continued.

"Excellent!" Pound boomed. "That young man's a natural!"

What about Johnnie Shaux? she demanded silently.

"Two more coming in, sir," the warrant officer said, with binoculars to his eyes. "That's ten; that leaves Protherow and one other unaccounted for."

"Who's missing?" Pound asked.

"I haven't seen the skipper or Froggie or Blackman yet," Digby said, looking around. The rest of the pilots were clustered around a bespectacled intelligence officer, Eleanor saw, being handed mugs of tea by a WVS lady.

"That's Blackman coming in now; I can see his letters," the warrant officer said. "The one behind must be Mr. Shaux or Potter ... Let's see ... It's Potter."

The two aircraft landed, and they all searched the sky. No Johnnie. The others showed no emotion. *They must do this three or four times a day,* she thought, but for her this was a new and wholly unwelcome uncertainty.

Another aircraft appeared. It had to be Johnnie. She found she was almost sobbing in relief.

"It's a stray Hurricane," the warrant officer reported, his eyes still glued to his binoculars. "Looks a bit banged up."

Now Eleanor could see a long trail of white vapor behind the Hurricane and could hear that its engine was cutting in and out.

"Losing fuel, running on empty," Digby commented. "It's going to be tight."

The Hurricane grew larger. It seemed to be dropping more steeply than the Spitfires had done, and it dipped every time the engine stuttered. Would it clear the trees at the end of the field? For a heart-stopping moment it looked as if the Hurricane would land short, ensnared in the elm trees that lined the field, but at the last moment the engine roared, and the aircraft cleared the uppermost branches with inches to spare.

Eleanor was breathing a sigh of relief when the engine cut out completely and the Hurricane dropped steeply to the ground. Its undercarriage snapped off, and the aircraft crashed down on its belly, sending up a spray of mud and shearing off the propeller, which cartwheeled madly toward the trees. She watched in disbelief as the Hurricane bounced up into the air, flipped over, and fell twenty feet upside down. There was a flash, followed a second later by a whooshing sound, and the aircraft was engulfed in flames.

The ground crews threw themselves into every available vehicle and raced across the field in a ragged convoy, but it was clear to Eleanor that their efforts would be too late.

"Pity," Digby commented. He ground out his cigarette and walked away.

Eleanor stood staring at the funeral pyre. Her statistical analysis would add one more 11 Group loss; the trend analysis would turn a fraction to the worse. She wasn't sure whether the event would be recorded in her model as "destroyed by enemy action on the ground" or "mechanical failure / other." She had no categories for "sons lost" or "sweethearts killed."

Another pilot approached them. He tugged off his helmet, revealing a cherubic, boyish face of startling beauty.

"Well done, Froggie," Pound said to him. "I hear you got another one."

"Has anyone seen the skipper?" the youth demanded. "Three of them jumped him and Protherow."

"I'm fine, Froggie," Shaux's voice said behind her.

She jumped out of her skin.

"Where … what—" she spluttered.

"I must have landed while you were watching that poor Hurricane."

He looked exhausted. His eyes were lined with strain and endless hours of searching for tiny black dots in the sky. He needed a haircut; the breeze was brushing his hair across his forehead. He was puffing too deeply on his cigarette, and the fingers of his left hand were stained yellow with nicotine. He was thinner; his cheekbones were more prominent than she remembered. He had turned his back to the burning Hurricane, perhaps so that he didn't have to acknowledge its existence or what it meant.

"We could see Manston getting pasted by Dorniers, sir," he said to Pound. "We saw some Hurries arrive to chase them away—perhaps that chap was one of them." He gesticulated over his shoulder at the wreckage. "Anyway, we went up top and found some 109s at twenty thousand south of Canterbury."

He paused to inhale. His fingers weren't shaking, Eleanor noticed.

"We met by accident just above the clouds," he continued. "It was all a bit of a shambles. We lost Protherow, but Potter definitely got a 109, and Digby got a probable."

He was still his old, phlegmatic self, she saw, recounting death and destruction as if summarizing a football game. A stranger would have sworn he was an observer, not a participant, in the mayhem.

The WVS lady arrived with a mug of tea for Johnnie.

"Thank you, Dottie," he said and gulped half of it in one swallow.

The WVS lady was not much older than they were, Eleanor observed, and she smiled at Shaux in a manner that was not entirely to Eleanor's liking. She could not tell whether he was indifferent to the tea lady's attention or simply pretending not to notice.

"I'm sorry I missed your work," he said to Eleanor, lighting another cigarette from the embers of his old one. "What did you think of it, sir?"

His eyes were browner and richer and deeper than she remembered, like delicious hot chocolate on a winter's evening, and his forehead had a red line across it from his flying helmet.

"Let's go back so we can sit down," Pound said. "Could you manage more tea, Dottie, my dear?"

"Of course, Wing Commander, right away."

"You are an angel of mercy, Dottie, the one woman in the world my dear wife should fear."

The WVS lady smiled coyly and glanced at Eleanor; her look suggested she had proprietary rights over all the men at Oldchurch. She hurried off to fetch more tea.

"What would we do without Dottie?" Pound asked, justifying the WVS lady's glance.

"I'd fly over to Calais and surrender, sir," Shaux said.

Eleanor noticed that Pound and Shaux did not look at the burning remnants of the Hurricane as they walked toward the row of huts set back in the trees. It was not indifference, she decided; it was fatalistic acceptance of the inevitable.

They entered Pound's office. She and Shaux sat down before his desk while Pound arranged himself behind it and patted her notebook. The image of an Oxford tutorial was even stronger.

"Let me summarize this document for you, Shaux," Pound began, but Dottie arrived with cups of tea for him and Eleanor, another large mug for Shaux, and a plate of scones, which she placed on the desktop at Shaux's elbow.

Eleanor squirmed. She was coping not only with the anxiety of Pound's evaluation but also with the remnants of the ghastly uncertainty of waiting for Johnnie and the shockingly abrupt translation of her cold statistics into burned and missing pilots and aircraft. Now she added the quandary of not knowing whether fighter station protocol accorded returning pilots preferential service from tea ladies or whether Dottie was singling Johnnie out for other, older reasons.

Pound adjusted his spectacles and began to speak with studied precision.

"This document uses cumulative statistics to posit the current states of 11 Group and Luftflotte 2, termed 'Current Combatant Status,' denoted by the symbols theta and epsilon respectively. The current values of theta and epsilon therefore vary each time new statistics are inputted. The document then postulates asymmetric goals for each side—that is to say, each side's goals are not simply the inverse of the other side's goals—and in so doing the paper departs from classical von Neumann game theory."

He glanced up as if to give Eleanor the chance to disagree, but his analysis was exact. Johnnie's eyes were on the ceiling, she noticed—a sure sign he was concentrating.

"Goals are broken down into constituent subgoals," Pound continued. "Interestingly, however, despite the overall asymmetry, each individual subgoal is treated as a zero-sum game. As an analogy, one either occupies a square on a chessboard or does not, regardless of whether one is winning or losing the overall game or one's purpose in holding that square. By evaluating the current value of theta and—"

The warrant officer with binoculars poked his head into the office. "Excuse me, sir, that was sector on the phone; 339 at readiness immediately."

Shaux stood up and gathered his belongings. His face betrayed no feeling. "If you'll excuse me, sir, I'd better get going," he said to Pound. He looked at Eleanor and said, "I'm sorry for the interruption."

He walked out toward his aircraft, unhurried but purposeful.

"Good hunting, Johnnie," Pound called after him, and Shaux lifted his arm in acknowledgment without looking back.

Eleanor wanted to call out too but wasn't certain what to say. "Good hunting" was too masculine; "good luck," too trite; and "be careful" seemed absurd.

She stood by Pound outside the office and watched the pilots clambering into their Spitfires, with the ground crews hovering about them. She watched a sergeant standing on the wing of Johnnie's aircraft, helping him strap in. A Merlin engine stuttered to life, and then another and another, filling the air with a shattering roar that beat upon her with a physical force.

Johnnie's sergeant was leaning over and shouting in his ear. Johnnie gave him a thumbs-up. The warrant officer emerged from the operations hut and fired a Very pistol into the air. The roar of the Merlins rose to a primeval scream, as if they were flexing their muscles and exulting in their power. Now she and Pound were buffeted by the tornado of their prop wash, which tore at their uniforms and sent Eleanor staggering backward. Her hairpins surrendered to the onslaught, and her hair flew out behind her.

The Spitfires began to lumber forward, looking like an ungainly gaggle of geese as they rocked and bounced on the uneven surface of the field. Their tails came up, and they steadied, receding rapidly across the field. Johnnie's aircraft lifted its nose, as if sniffing the breeze, and then rose smoothly into the air, launching itself like a pole-vaulter. The other Spitfires lifted in his wake, ugly goslings no more, transformed into masters of their natural element.

The gale of 339's prop wash died away, and the sound of the Merlins weakened to distant thunder. The aircraft grew smaller as they climbed higher and higher.

As if all were one, the squadron wheeled toward the south, presenting their silhouettes to her, their cockpit canopies catching the sun like diamonds, and passed from her sight behind the trees. She noticed that every single person on the station had come out to watch 339 off, and now they stood about in awkward, angular postures as if uncertain what to do next, straining to hear the last ebbing throbs of 339's departure.

The airfield seemed shockingly empty without the Spitfires, no longer an RAF station but a large, silent field with a long row of huts beside it.

She knew that back in group headquarters in Uxbridge a calm voice would announce, "339 is airborne," and Park would nod briefly in acknowledgment, his eyes on the map table as a WAAF pushed a plaque labeled "339" toward the south coast.

Eleanor had stood beside Park and seen it a hundred times, but now, for the first time, she had seen what it meant: the young men strapping in; the attendant ground crews; the scream of the Merlins; the Very pistol commanding them into the air; the tempest of prop wash, rich with the tang of high-octane exhaust fumes; the lurching acceleration across the ground; the sudden sureness of the aircraft as they rose into the air; the elegant precision of their turn toward the enemy; the graceful silhouettes of the aircraft with red-and-blue roundels on their elliptical wings, the unconquered symbols of resistance to the all-conquering Third Reich; the emptiness and irrelevance and silence of those left behind.

Eleven aircraft had taken off; statistically only nine or ten would come back, perhaps as few as six or seven. It dawned on her that Johnnie might not come back. Perhaps "I'm sorry for the interruption" would be the last words she'd ever hear him say. He hadn't said goodbye, and she hadn't wished him luck.

Perhaps he wouldn't have good luck, because she hadn't wished it for him. Perhaps he'd encounter a Luftwaffe pilot who had been wished good luck by a girl as he took off, and that would be the decisive factor—the pilot with luck wished upon him and the pilot without.

Why hadn't she done so? Because she'd felt awkward, not knowing how to say it. How pathetic! Had he listened for it and not received it? Was that what the sergeant had said to him as he was strapping in—"Well, I'll wish you luck, sir, even if that mean bitch won't!"—and Johnnie had acknowledged him with a thumbs-up? And now he was somewhere over the coast, thousands of feet in the air, climbing toward an implacable enemy, defenseless without the protective, cloaking armor of her luck.

She tasted salt and realized it was a tear.

She saw Pound's kindly face staring at her and felt his hand on her arm.

"Time for a good cup of tea," he said. "It's the best remedy."

"What do we do now?" she asked helplessly.

"We wait."

1500 hours, Friday, September 6, 1940
RAF Oldchurch, Kent, England

Shaux berated himself silently as he passed through ten thousand feet. This kind of warfare could only be fought with absolute concentration, with every other thought or emotion utterly suppressed. He needed a complete awareness of the airspace around him, to the total exclusion of the rest of the universe.

An average patrol lasted ninety minutes. Contact with the enemy lasted two minutes at most and actual combat no more than ten seconds. Since one didn't know when those ten seconds would occur, one had to be ready—keyed up, poised for instant action, adrenaline pumping—for the other 99.9 percent of flying time.

Aerial combat was brutally abrupt and almost always without warning. One second the sky was clear; the next it was filled with 109s. There was a phrase in the Bible—"the quick and the dead," which might have been coined to describe the battle between 11 Group and Luftflotte 2.

Shaux knew he had survived so far only because he was able to focus. But now he couldn't concentrate; as the roaring Merlin pulled him higher, his thoughts kept drifting to Pound's interrupted exposition of Eleanor's paper and to Eleanor herself. If each side in the conflict had asymmetric goals and yet competed for each subgoal in a symmetric zero-sum game, how had she resolved the dichotomy? What insight had caused her to create the dichotomy in the first place? Was the scoring weighted or absolute? Was—

A burst of static in his earphones made him jump out of his skin. The controller's voice ordered 339 to vector for Romney.

If he couldn't concentrate, he told himself, he was dead; he might as well bail out now and not open his parachute. It was that simple; no dichotomies to resolve—just two alternatives: life and death.

He glanced back at 339, stretched out behind him, turning in unison for Romney on the coast, the home of a famous miniature railway built by a millionaire racing driver and now, Shaux had heard, requisitioned and used by the army to transport ammunition.

His pilots were being led by a brainless imbecile, he thought, a cretin, a moron. He was completely unfit to lead them … It was only six hours since Pound had sent Debenham packing and promoted Shaux in his stead. He should tell Pound, as soon as he got back—if he got back—to find another squadron commander; it simply wasn't fair on his men. They needed a leader, not a daydreaming nincompoop.

He shifted in his seat. Why couldn't he concentrate? They passed through twenty thousand feet. The sky was clear, perfect weather for 109s to cruise high above them. "Search the skies," he said to himself, as he had said to dozens of raw trainees. "Stay alert. Search the skies."

Eleanor had changed, he thought. She was much more confident; she had metamorphosed from a bright, fun-loving Oxford student into a competent, self-assured woman. He could tell it by the way she held herself, by her obvious conviction that her game theory mathematics were valuable. She'd taken von Neumann and moved him forward, changing a black-and-white simulation of competition into something more flexible and subtle, an intellectual leap forward. She had lost weight, he thought, and it suited her very well. The delicate lines of her cheekbones and jaw were more clearly drawn, and her figure, even in a lumpy uniform, was more definitive.

The controller's voice broke in on Eleanor's outline and told them to patrol along the coast as far as Dungeness; again Shaux's thoughts had drifted. Jesus *Christ!*

Suppose we see 109s over there—what do I do? Or over there? If they're above us? At the same height? Think! Plan ahead! Search the skies—don't rely on Digby to see them in time to react. You're swimming in shark-infested waters, and you're daydreaming!

No, she was less confident, he thought, as if life had proven to be more difficult and complicated than it had been in the carefree, secluded cloisters of Oxford. She'd been jumpy, nervous, edgy, not looking at him in her old straightforward manner but glancing at him and glancing away. It was more than being nervous about Pound's verdict, he was sure; it was as if she was struggling with some inner conflict. Perhaps Rawley was back in her life and giving her a hard time again, now that George was dead. She'd written that she'd finished with him, but could two lovers ever truly finish with each other? Perhaps Rawley wouldn't sleep with her, now that he was married. Perhaps—

"Bandits, one eighty, angels fifteen, five miles," snapped Digby's voice.

Where the hell was one eighty? What course were they on now? *Sweet Jesus, help me! Do something! The seconds are passing! Get a grip—the squadron needs direction!*

"EAs are heading northwest. Twin-engine aircraft, probably 110s."

110s? Were they flying a nuisance raid, a *freie Jagd*—"free hunt"—as they called them? Should he ignore them? Were they sneaking in for an attack on a coastal airfield? Were they decoys for 109s? What if they weren't 110s? Why couldn't he spot them? *Decide! Decide!*

"Follow me," he said and turned away from the vector Digby had given them. It would be easy to dive down on the 110s; there was a good chance they'd get three or four of them without loss to 339. On the other hand, 110s could do limited damage—all they could do was shoot up an airfield and scare the hell out of the local population. They might have been sent over to fly about aimlessly in order to draw up 11 Group, creating gaps in British defenses through which bomber raids could sneak. If that was the case, there'd be Dornier 17s or Junkers 88s or Heinkel 111s a few miles behind them, with covering 109s high above them.

By leading 339 on the reciprocal course, Shaux would be heading out to sea, toward any aircraft tailing the 110s. It was not a conventional strategy, and he wouldn't try it for more than five minutes, but it was worth a shot. At least he was thinking clearly even if incorrectly.

Within two minutes the hawkeyed Digby reported incoming bombers, far below them. Shaux's instincts had been right—at least, on this occasion. He smiled to himself: 339 would think he was a genius.

Now, where were the inevitable 109s? They should be up here, above twenty thousand feet, watching the bombers and waiting to jump any Hurricanes or Spitfires that attacked the bombers. He swept his aching eyes across the sky. Where were the 109s?

"Bandits have fighters behind them," Digby reported.

There'd been talk of a change in strategy by the Luftwaffe, under which the 109s flew close escort with the bombers, but Shaux had tended to disregard it, because it robbed the Luftwaffe of its most powerful weapon—the ability of the free-ranging 109s to sweep down on anyone attacking the bombers. Still, Digby was right, as always. Shaux spotted the dark profiles of 109s silhouetted against the shining waters of the Channel, down at fifteen thousand feet, bumbling along at a mere 250 miles per hour. What a waste …

It was so foolish it had to be a trick; there must be more 109s up here … Still, a 109 was a 109, even at fifteen thousand feet, and could not be ignored.

"Follow me," he said again. A long, arcing curve would bring 339 above and behind the 109s, shielded by the sun's glare. If he hit the 109s dead astern, they'd split left and right, allowing 339 a clear shot at the bombers ahead of them before the 109s could regroup.

He didn't need to say anything, beyond the ritual "Tallyho!" He'd always thought Debenham talked too much; additional orders might be misunderstood or confusing for the new pilots. He'd trained the kids to follow their leader, no matter what, and shoot only if something got in the way, looking behind and above at all times. He'd trained Potter to follow him, and now the newest kids were following Potter. It was a simple regimen, a default strategy; he only needed to speak if the usual pattern had to be broken.

They descended on the 109s at a ground speed of well over four hundred miles per hour. Shaux would use the extra speed 339 was accumulating in their dive to descend a little below the enemy and then use it to climb into the attack. The 109s would have most difficulty seeing them at that angle, and 339 would still have a margin of speed of fifty or sixty miles per hour.

The Spitfires were in ragged line abreast as they closed. The 109s stayed put, apparently unaware of 339's arrival, and grew larger in his gunsight. Someone—one of the new kids, Shaux assumed—opened fire prematurely, but there was almost no time for the 109s to scatter before 339 was upon them. Shaux flew straight at his selected target, pouring tracer into its after fuselage and tail. He was on a collision course but took no evasive action, gambling the 109's pilot would seek escape by diving. As it was, the 109's pilot was slow to react, and Shaux missed his tail by no more than five feet. Now the 109s were diving and breaking left and right; he led 339 straight through the center of their formation, with the undefended bombers ahead of them.

"Stay with me," he said.

He stared behind him; the sky was full of scattered 109s. One of the new kids had forgotten everything he'd be taught and was peeling away in pursuit. He'd never catch them, even if he chased them all the way to France, and alone over the Channel he'd be dead meat. Potter's voice filled Shaux's earphones before Shaux could speak, instructing the kid to turn back. Froggie was a natural; if he survived, one day people would talk about him as they talked about Douglas Bader or Sailor Malan or Stanford Tuck, great pilots and great leaders.

The Junkers 88s were growing rapidly. It spoke volumes of the Luftwaffe's iron discipline that they did not scatter as the Spitfires broke

JOHN RHODES

up their covering 109s and chased them down. They stayed in formation, like the rigid lines of goose-stepping German soldiers Shaux had seen on newsreels at the cinema, strutting in parade before Adolf Hitler. That discipline would cost several of the 88 pilots their lives, and they were still over the chill waters of the Channel.

Shaux chose his target and waited. It occurred to him they were on a course that would bring them to Oldchurch ... Eleanor was at Oldchurch ... He was filled with a cold, primeval rage. Twenty-five 88s, twenty-five tons of high explosives scattered across the airfield and the surrounding country ... The distance closed rapidly.

A quick check above and behind in case the 109s have reformed. Ease back on the throttle to maximize firing time. Check that the gun safety is off. Ignore the tracer that is beginning to arc toward us as the Junkers open fire. One more glance back. No 109s. Kids following, in decent order. Pick the deflection angle. Wait ... Wait ... Squeeze the trigger. Feel the Spitfire tremble as the eight machine guns fire in unison. Walk the tracer into the glass dome of the rear gunner's position. Hold it there. Cease firing and break left, hard, tight. Throttle wide open to maintain altitude. Hear the power of the screaming Merlin. Feel the grip of the beautiful airframe slicing decisively through the air. Feel the weight of the centripetal forces jamming you back into your seat. Keep it tight. Hope the kids are following.

The Junkers swam back into view, in a tattered formation but still together, still pressing on to rain down death and destruction on Eleanor's head. He'd been unfortunate enough to see the corpse of a young woman after a sneak bombing raid on Hastings. She'd been lying in the gutter, blown from her shattered house—in two pieces.

One of those 88s would do the same thing to Eleanor, if he gave it the chance. *Keep the throttle wide open, balls to the wall. Check for 109s. Check a second time. Close the gap. Check for the rest of 339. Pick a target. Throttle back. Match altitudes. Take a second to check the sky above and behind you—no 109s. Open fire. Walk the tracer along the fuselage to the cockpit. See the 88 stagger as its wounded pilot releases the controls. See it start to yaw. Watch the stream of white vapor streaming back from a ruptured fuel tank.* Hear ye the eleventh commandment: thou shalt not bomb Eleanor.

1530 hours, Friday, September 6, 1940
RAF Oldchurch, Kent, England

Eleanor and Pound returned to his office, where her notebook still lay on Pound's desk awaiting his verdict. It seemed trivial now and utterly remote from the real battle that was raging in the skies above them; just a handful of formulas manipulating a few columns of numbers, an arid intellectual exercise of no relevance to the world of men and machines, to the sharp tang of engine fumes and the scream of Merlins, that her formulas purported to represent.

She half expected Pound to say as much as they resumed their places and he adjusted his spectacles.

"Von Neumann's minimax theory is based on competition for common goals," Pound began, as if delivering a lecture. "In a game of tic-tac-toe, for example, each player can win by completing a line or diagonal and can force a draw by denying that pattern to his opponent."

He tapped her notebook with the stem of his pipe. "You, on the other hand, have postulated a game in which each player has a different way of winning, or, to be precise, different ways of not losing. It's as if one player could win if he completed a line, and the other if he completed a diagonal, but not vice versa, thus creating asymmetric goals. Yet although the goals are different, the players compete for the same spaces."

She lit yet another cigarette and waited. There was something surreal about listening to him explaining her own work to her.

"Once a zero-sum game becomes asymmetric, other asymmetries emerge," he continued. "For example, in a game of tic-tac-toe there are six ways of completing a line but only two ways of completing a diagonal. However, within each individual space symmetry is maintained, because only one player can occupy any given space."

She waited, and Pound squared his shoulders.

"Your document is technically correct," he said, finally delivering his judgment. "I can find no mathematical or logical flaws. Since it is consistent with von Neumann, while building on him, we can say it is a potentially valuable contribution."

She breathed a sigh of relief. "It's useful?"

"I've always wanted to say that something was a seminal work," he said somberly, removing his glasses. "Now I have the opportunity. This is a seminal work!"

"It's—" she started, but he overrode her, his austere manner set aside and enthusiasm bubbling up in its place.

"It's incomplete, but that's half the beauty. It raises more questions than it answers. It's as if you've built a foundation and the building is still in the early stages of construction. It opens the door to new vistas without exploring them."

"You like it?"

"It's the best thing I've seen in years, my dear Eleanor! Congratulations!"

She sat back. In her heart she'd known the work was good, and she'd had Kristoffer check it over and over, and refine it and refine it, and polish it and polish it, but Pound's endorsement made it officially good, like a diploma with a gold seal.

It was as if her work had acquired a separate existence of its own, quite distinct from the formulas she had scribbled late at night in a fever of excitement. Now the work was coldly logical, endowed with an inevitability she had never anticipated—"Rand's theory of asymmetric zero sums," or some such grandiosity. It would be examined by other mathematicians like a specimen in laboratory, weighed and tested, poked and prodded, praised or lampooned, accepted or rejected, all without reference to Eleanor.

He was continuing to discuss it, throwing out all kinds of ideas, talking more and more rapidly, and she knew she should be paying attention. He'd risen from his desk and was pacing up and down behind it. He'd torn off his spectacles as if they were slowing the torrent of his thoughts. He seized a piece of chalk and began to scribble on a blackboard previously reserved for a list of pilot availability.

"Like all good theories, it's testable … That's what makes it so credible … Its weakness is that people are not rational; if a coin comes up heads a few times in a row, people will bet more and more heavily on tails, even though the odds on the next toss are still fifty-fifty … It implies that Kesselring has made mistakes, and one learns never to underestimate one's enemies …"

His words faded in and out of her attention. It was as if nothing mattered until Johnnie got back—if he got back. How long had he been gone? What was Pound saying? Variable asymmetries? Was Johnnie all right? Explicit versus implicit asymmetries? Was Johnnie even still alive? Why hadn't she wished him good luck?

"Look, sir, I'm not sure I can wait until 339 returns," she heard herself saying, interrupting Pound's flow. "I apologize; I'm not paying attention. I think ... I think I'd better go to my hotel. It's been a long day ... Perhaps we can discuss it tomorrow, when I'll be able to concentrate?" She paused and then went on, "When Johnnie Shaux gets back, will you ask him to join me for dinner?"

Pound put on his glasses and stared at her closely and then removed them.

"Of course, my dear," he said without hesitation. "Let's find your driver."

He bustled her out and opened the car door for her with old-fashioned courtesy.

"I'm sorry, sir ... It's been a difficult ..."

"I understand completely," he said, and she saw that he did.

1600 hours, Friday, September 6, 1940
RAF Oldchurch, Kent, England

When Shaux landed at Oldchurch—it had not been bombed, he noted immediately—Pound told him that Eleanor had left the airfield but invited him to dinner at her hotel in Hastings. Shaux's immediate reaction was to think of a variety of excuses. He needed some time alone to digest the events of the day. He needed an early night. He needed to decide whether he should speak to Pound about commanding 339. He needed ...

Why did she want to see him? She'd written, "Perhaps we'll get a chance to have a drink and talk." At first he'd thought ... Well, he'd been wrong; naturally the motive behind her invitation was to discuss her paper. Obviously she'd be seeking out everyone in England who had even heard of von Neumann or minimax. She'd even said she couldn't discuss her work in the letter. Of course!

But a couple of hours in her company would be a further assault on his weakening cocoon of isolation and his stranglehold over his emotions. It would be another bridge to a world of pasts and futures from which he needed to be cut off.

He tried a couple of excuses out on Pound.

"Well, unfortunately I have no way of getting to Hastings, sir."

"Nonsense—I'll lend you my car." Pound beamed.

"Thanks, but it'll be too late, and I need the sleep."

"Nonsense—an early dinner, and you'll be home just as soon as if you'd stopped at the village pub for a couple of pints, bitter."

"I need to go over 339's paperwork." God—how pathetic could he get?

"Nonsense—a break from routine is as good as a tonic," Pound boomed.

Shaux gloomily concluded he'd have to go and started fretting about the state of his only decent uniform.

"Her minimax paper is remarkable!" Pound told him, dismissing Shaux's feeble social reservations and moving on to more important matters. "It's not just a mathematical breakthrough, from a technical perspective; I think it has immense potential value to the war effort."

Shaux had been so diverted by Eleanor's invitation he'd forgotten to ask Pound about her model. Pound began to expound with growing enthusiasm while Shaux, who normally didn't care about his appearance, wondered whether he'd have time to polish his shoes.

"I've been wondering if I should leave Oldchurch to work with her," Pound was saying. "She's opened up a lot of important issues that need a great deal of thought ... Besides, any fool can run a simple airfield."

Shaux remembered he'd asked one of the ground crew to sew squadron leader's stripes and a DFC ribbon on his only other uniform. He'd done it with reluctance, rather than pride, as a tribute to Pound; now he'd have to wear the damned thing in public and make a spectacle of himself. God—he needed a bath and a shave as well! Damn! He said something incoherent about Eleanor's work, excused himself, and bolted toward the bathhouse, wondering why Pound was chuckling at him.

1900 hours, Friday, September 6, 1940
Prince Frederick Hotel, Hastings, Sussex, England

Eleanor waited for Shaux in the dining room of her hotel in Hastings. Like so many other places these days, the room seemed to mourn its glorious past in the long-ago days of peacetime, in the gluttonous time before food rationing. There was an empty stage for a string quartet in the corner, from which elegant diners had once been serenaded as they sipped their sherries and chose from the extensive menu. Now half the diners were in uniform, and there was little to see but the cracks in the ornate plaster ceiling from the most recent bombing raid.

This afternoon Johnnie had been in his usual self-effacing mood, yielding the floor to Pound, passively absorbing her theories without visible reactions. She hadn't been able to tell whether he was still the same comfortable Johnnie she'd known at Oxford or whether a year of war had left unseen scars.

Well, he couldn't possibly be the same. This afternoon's events had been a rude awakening to the realities of his war: the constant, nerve-racking patrols—he'd flown three times today; the remorselessly lengthening lists of casualties; the cannon holes in the Spitfires and the stricken Hurricane immolated at the far end of the airfield; the endless flood tide of Luftwaffe aircraft, pounding southern England from across the Channel, just as the sea pounded the beaches and cliffs.

In time the waters of the Channel would grind down the tall cliffs of Dover until they sank beneath the unrelenting waves, and the sea would rush in to inundate the land. Would the Luftwaffe erode away the Spitfires and Hurricanes until they too were obliterated, so that a German invasion could overwhelm England and submerge everything that was English?

Her half-forgotten schoolgirl Shakespeare arose in her memory: *This something something, this scepter'd isle ... / This fortress built by Nature for herself / Against something something and the hand of war ... this little world / This precious stone set in the silver sea / Which serves it as a moat / Against the envy of less happier lands.*

Unfortunately, times had changed since Shakespeare's day. Hundreds of Luftwaffe aircraft could fly across the moat in less than ten minutes, and this fortress, this little world, was defended against the hand of war and Hitler's envy by 11 Group alone.

Keith Park has only eighty Spitfires and two hundred Hurricanes, she thought. *One hundred ninety-nine Hurricanes, actually, accounting for the burnt-out wreckage at the far end of the field at Oldchurch.* Less than one hundred of Park's pilots could be described even remotely as experienced. How long could they resist? How long could Johnnie resist?

Churchill had said the English would "fight on and on and on and on," but how much strain could mere mortals take?

Shaux arrived punctually. She could tell he'd gone to some trouble to press his uniform and shine his shoes, and she saw their fellow diners glancing at his pilot's badge and new purple-and-white DFC ribbon. "He's one of the few," they'd be whispering to each other as Johnnie, she was sure, tried to slip by unnoticed and unremarked.

She was conscious of how her own uniform resembled a sack of coal; she'd have to ask Millie the secret of looking glamorous in shapeless blue serge—not that she needed to look glamorous for Johnnie, of course, but it would still be nice to know. She took off her spectacles and immediately felt absurdly vulnerable. She began to put them back on, but Johnnie was already here.

"I've been thinking about your work," he said as soon as he sat down. "I haven't had time to absorb it, but it's clearly absolutely amazing. I talked to Pound afterward, and he thinks it's marvelous."

She had remembered him as passive, but now she also recalled his rare bursts of animation, in which his enthusiasm was invariably directed toward praise or admiration for others.

"You really think it's useful?" she asked, fearing Johnnie was just being nice to her.

"It's a genuine breakthrough, according to Pound, and he isn't given to idle flattery," he said. "He says that as more people get to understand it, it'll change the way strategy is developed. I wonder if they'd let you go to America to discuss it with von Neumann, or if it's too secret."

"Von Neumann? Now you're getting carried away," she laughed.

"Pound said it's highly innovative." Johnnie grinned. They'd had a tutor at Oxford who had described mathematical errors as innovations. "Only Pound meant it as a compliment."

"He really did?" If Pound truly did think her work was useful, then …

"He said he was thinking about talking to Park about leaving Oldchurch and working with you! He said it would be a more valuable use of his talents than cobbling together borrowed racecourse buildings."

She gasped at the notion of developing the minimax model under Pound's direction—it would be like hooking a supercharger onto the project. But since this afternoon she saw the world through a different prism.

"Oldchurch needs him—you and the other pilots need him, surely?"

"He's wonderful—but he said the model is a major contribution to the war effort."

Her head was still spinning at Pound's reception, but the truth was more prosaic.

"I just wanted to avoid looking stupid because I'd built an illogical mountain out of a flawed molehill."

"It *is* a mountain, it's logical, the premise is not flawed, and you're never stupid," he stated flatly. He was grinning with pleasure at her triumph.

"Even when I fell for Rawley?"

She immediately regretted the question. Rawley was the last person she wanted to think about, let alone discuss, and Shaux, who had been so enthusiastic as he talked about her work, looked as if she had just reached across the table and slapped him. Thank God the waiter arrived at that moment and took their orders from the grim wartime menu.

"What's your next step with the minimax model?" Shaux asked, as if she hadn't mentioned Rawley. "Have you thought about making it self-correcting, by comparing the predictions to actual results? What was it like to think it up?"

"It was like … I don't know … coming across something totally unexpected …"

She couldn't find the right words.

"Like a patch of wild strawberries in an old hedgerow?" he offered.

How could he know? It fitted perfectly. How unlike him to be poetic! It must be some carefully remembered childhood recollection or something from a favorite poem.

"Exactly! Something beautiful and delicious among the briars."

"It must have been amazing!"

"I sat in my office late at night and had imaginary conversations with von Neumann in a fake foreign accent—so childish!" She felt as if she was confessing an intimate secret, but she wanted him to know. "I felt I was exploring a beautiful undiscovered country."

"God, I envy you!"

The waiter brought their drinks, and Shaux toasted her success. Then he leaned back, clearly basking in her achievement, content to admire.

She wanted him to share the experience.

"I have a wonderful colleague, an amazing young American mathematician called Kristoffer W. Olsen. He came over to fly for Norway, but Norway was lost as soon as he got there, and his eyesight is too poor for the RAF but good enough for the RNoAF."

She realized she was gabbling but could not stop.

"I pour out my ideas, and he writes it all down and checks it. He's full of wonderful expressions, such as 'collateral damage' for a bad idea and 'hominy grits' for something that is perfect. I've no idea what hominy grits are, to tell you the truth."

She laughed and took another sip of her drink, half-inebriated by Pound's flattery and Shaux's admiration.

"Kris is an important contributor—that's why I put his name on the paper after mine. He has a very precise mind, and he's wonderful at getting rid of everything that's not essential—the paper's less than half the size it would've been if I'd have written it. 'Cut the crap' and 'bury the bullshit,' he keeps saying. He tells me I must think simplicity is a deadly sin, because I try so hard to avoid it."

Shaux's expression was rapt, as if he was seeing it all in his mind's eye, an observer looking in through the window.

"Then there's Millie. She was a factory worker, but her mind's as sharp as a tack. She collects and inputs all the data. We all laugh, all the time. She and Kris are developing a thing, I'm sure of it; it's so sweet to watch them together. Their children will be beautiful blonds with perfect teeth. Then there's Air Vice-Marshal Park; he bears the full weight of the battle, but he always finds time to say something encouraging. Then there are those late-night sessions, when the building's quiet, and I'm all alone … and I find … I find wild strawberries."

"God, I envy them!" Johnnie said. "Just to be there!"

She looked at him afresh. Even though they were fighting the same battle, in their own ways, his war was so different from hers, so indescribably more horrible. She remembered the awful process of watching 339 landing without Johnnie; the burning Hurricane with, God help him, a burning pilot trapped helplessly inside it; the tang of high-octane fuel; the silhouettes of the Spitfires turning in perfect formation toward the enemy.

Suddenly she was tired of minimax and game theory. Suddenly her triumph—if triumph it was—seemed trivial in comparison to the realities of battle.

"Look, Johnnie, we always talk about me. What about you?" she asked.

He looked as if she'd awakened him from a pleasant dream. "Me? Oh, nothing new—I just fly, that's all." He smiled.

"No, that's not all," she said firmly, refusing to be dismissed so easily. "It can't be all."

Rawley, George, her brothers—every man she'd ever known—talked about themselves constantly. Even Kristoffer loved to tell self-deprecating stories of his youth in North Carolina. Only Johnnie remained silent. She'd always thought of that as desirable, because he required no effort, but now she wanted a glimpse beneath his placid surface.

"Tell me something about yourself," she insisted.

"As I said, I just fly. You, on the other hand—"

"No! That can't be all!"

"I fly all the time." He grinned.

"I insist! Tell me about something before Oxford."

He lowered his head like an obstinate child. "Well ... what do you want to know?" he asked reluctantly.

"Everything—I know almost nothing about you," she said.

"That's because there's almost nothing to know."

"I won't let you get away with that," she said. Why was he so reluctant to tell her anything? "For instance, this morning I found out that your father was a pilot in the last war. What did your mother do when he died?"

He was clearly startled that she knew.

"Do? I don't know; she died three months after I was born."

"What? How?"

"I think it was a Zeppelin raid; at least, that's what I was told. She died in London on August 5 in 1918, and I know there was a raid that day—the last raid of the war, in fact."

She took a moment to absorb the fact that Johnnie was orphaned as a baby. It explained a lot, she thought—he really was *sui generis*.

"So what happened to you? You were a tiny baby—did your relatives bring you up?"

"Nobody really knew anything about my parents, I believe. My mother was in lodgings, waiting for my father to come home from France. So I was put in an orphanage."

He made it sound so mundane, as if he were talking about someone else.

"How awful!"

"Not really." He shrugged. "Besides, it's all I ever knew. We were clothed and fed and sent to school, just like all kids."

No wonder he was such a clamshell, she thought; so self-contained, so devoid of visible emotions. He must have been taught to fend for himself ever since he was a toddler.

"But you had no one who loved you," she protested. "You had no parents or brothers or sisters."

"Well …" he began weakly and his voice trailed away.

"Then what happened?" she hurried on, shying away from a discussion of Shaux's need for love. She wondered why she'd brought it up in the first place.

"Then I went into the RAF," he said. "The boys went into each of the services—army, navy, air force, police—in rotation when we reached fifteen, and the RAF was my turn."

"You left school when you were fifteen?"

"Yes, of course."

"But how did you get into Oxford?"

The waiter returned with their unappetizing meal and saved him from replying.

"I'm not trying to pry, Johnnie; I'm just interested," she said as the waiter departed. He was two different people—animated when the subject was her or her work and a clamshell when it came to himself. She wondered whether she should go on.

"I suppose I've always taken you for granted, but I've realized you are the only real friend I have. Can't I be interested in my friend?"

Shaux had lowered his head like a rebellious schoolboy, staring at her from beneath his eyebrows. He reminded her of a hooked fish, zigzagging in a desperate attempt to escape. She stared at him and knew he would answer, but against his will. With a flash of insight she knew he assumed that she had only turned to him in the absence of Rawley and George; he must think that she considered him the last and least interesting of the three men in the boat, a temporary dinner companion until someone more interesting came along.

She had hoped for a pleasant evening, and now she had ruined everything, trying to pry open a clam with a crowbar.

"Okay, Johnnie, no more questions; I'm sorry." She tried to lighten the mood and smiled. "I'll let you off for now, but not forever."

"It's just that … I just can't …" he began, and his voice trailed away.

He seemed to start again but stopped. "It literally is a waste of breath" was all he could manage.

He looked so miserable that she reached across the table to squeeze the back of his hand.

"It's all right," she said. She considered adding, "I understand," but she didn't. She didn't understand at all.

She picked up her knife and fork and took a mouthful of watery mashed potatoes.

"Park is the most amazing man," she began, returning to territory in which Shaux could happily retreat from the limelight.

As Eleanor began to describe the 11 Group operations room and the cut and thrust of Park's daily duel with Kesselring, her world, Shaux grasped for the tatters of his own. He desperately wanted to listen to her, but a cataract of memories and emotions overwhelmed him. She had unleashed a torrent.

He would not, *could* not, abandon his stoic solitude. He could not, would not, give way to hope. He had been raised to expect nothing, and he did not, would not. It was axiomatic that the past was a waste of breath, a meaningless jumble of remembrances and recollections, signifying nothing.

St. Christopher's Orphanage in southeast London had not been "awful," to use her word. It had been strict, highly regimented, and without comfort or entertainment, true—but not awful. When he had done his homework and completed his jobs—there had been more and more chores as he grew older—he had been left to his own devices. He'd occupied much of his spare time with long, solitary walks across the broad, grassy expanses of Blackheath or down the hill to Greenwich Park and the river. He had often stood on the Greenwich Meridian, the line by the Royal Observatory that separated the Eastern and Western Hemispheres, imagining himself to be bestriding the world like a mighty conqueror of yore.

The orphanage had been a place to house unwanted children until they were fifteen, when they were deemed old enough to look after themselves; at that age the boys went into the armed services, and the girls were found places in shops or domestic service.

The charity that supervised St. Christopher's saw its charter as providing children with physical support and lacked the resources to waste precious donations on the children's creature comforts and emotional well-being; the kids were lucky to have a roof over their heads and food in their bellies, and, in any case, orphans were expected to be miserable.

It had been spartan, Shaux allowed, and joyless, but it hadn't been awful.

"You left school when you were fifteen?" she had asked.

"Yes, of course," he had answered, but it hadn't been "of course" at all; it had been the occasion of the most extraordinary and unexpected uproar.

On the last day of school, Shaux had gone to Mr. Finlay, the mathematics teacher, to say goodbye. He'd loved math, and Mr. Finlay had encouraged him, lending him some of his own books and pushing him to study above and beyond the syllabus. Mr. Finlay was the only teacher Shaux had liked, and he'd overcome his natural reserve to thank him.

"What do you mean, Shaux?" Mr. Finlay had demanded. "Why aren't you coming back next term?"

"I'm going into the RAF, sir. I have to leave St. Christopher's when I'm fifteen."

That evening Mr. Finlay appeared at the orphanage to protest. To Shaux's surprise and embarrassment Mr. Finlay told Mrs. McKinley, the matron, that Shaux was exceptionally talented and it would be a "crying shame"—Shaux remembered the exact words—if Shaux were to be taken out of school.

Mrs. McKinley was a woman of strict routine; the policy of the orphanage was clear, she said, and Shaux would have to go. Mr. Finlay offered to pay for Shaux's bed and board, to no avail. He even offered to take Shaux into his own home, but Mrs. McKinley was firm; Shaux was fifteen, and it was time for him to begin repaying his debt to society for supporting him through his formative years. She chided Mr. Finlay for questioning the orphanage's policies and for requesting such a dangerous precedent.

"We do not treat our children as individuals, Mr. Finlay," she told him. "We do not encourage them to fill their heads with fanciful ideas and dreams. We do not set them up for a fall. The best preparation we can give them is to accept life as it is and get on with it—to play the cards they're dealt."

Mr. Finlay retreated, saying he'd pursue the matter with the trustees, but he was equally unsuccessful with the strict and austere board, and

Shaux went off for basic training as a boy entrant in the air force, wondering why Mr. Finlay had been so upset.

"But how did you get into Oxford?" Eleanor had asked.

Shortly after his service career began, Shaux received a letter from Mr. Finlay, in which he proposed to send Shaux the school's textbooks so he could continue his studies. Over the next three years Shaux became a qualified fitter—a ground crew air engine mechanic—and worked on the textbooks Mr. Finlay sent him.

When Shaux turned eighteen, Mr. Finlay arranged for him to take the scholarship examinations at Oxford. Having studied under Mr. Finlay's remote but intensive supervision for three years, Shaux found the exams surprisingly easy.

The RAF was perplexed, for it had no regulations governing corporal fitters attending university, and Shaux was told he could not go; higher education was suitable only for officers and gentlemen. Shaux accepted this judgment, but the redoubtable Mr. Finlay did not. If Shaux could not attend Oxford because he was not an officer, why not promote him? Mr. Finlay told Shaux's commanding officer he would write a letter to his member of parliament, and the CO, fearing career-risking controversy, promised he'd look into it. Evidently, as Shaux had found out much later, a fattening file of memoranda had circulated ponderously among administrative officers in Whitehall until a Fighter Command personnel officer, hurrying to clear his inbox before a long weekend in the country with his fiancée, had misunderstood the subject matter involved and issued Shaux an officer's commission. Shaux therefore had gone to Oxford and, in due course, met Eleanor.

He half heard her description of the dispute between Leigh-Mallory and Park. Again he wanted to listen, and again he could not. He was fascinated by the idea of assembling flights and squadrons into Big Wings, but the cataract she had undammed poured on undiminished.

How could he explain, without incurring either her contempt or her anger at his presumption? And even if he did explain and somehow escape her condemnation, how would he be able to get into his Spitfire tomorrow morning and climb—undaunted by the odds and unwearied in his constant challenge and mortal danger, as Churchill had so succinctly put it—to meet the 109s?

The utter banality of his existence, particularly in contrast to hers, had never been more apparent. She had revolutionized minimax; he wished he had done something dramatic or exciting—adventures, achievements, disasters, anything remotely interesting. The present battle didn't qualify; it was simply a monotonous prelude to death, like a fatal illness, filled with solemn but futile ceremonies, overly drawn out and endlessly tedious.

"What are you thinking, Johnnie?" her voice broke in, returning him abruptly to the present and his half-eaten dinner. God, she looked beautiful!

"Oh, nothing really," he replied. "Please go on."

SEPTEMBER 7, 1940

1030 hours, Saturday, September 7, 1940
11 Group Headquarters, Uxbridge, Middlesex, England

Eleanor was nervous as she tapped on Park's office door. She had told him she had reached a startling conclusion; she offered a fervent prayer that he would indeed find it startling—and for its insight, not its stupidity. She was even more nervous when she entered the office and found Air Chief Marshal Sir Hugh Dowding sitting in one of the visitor's chairs.

"You remember Squadron Officer Eleanor Rand, sir?" Park asked Dowding. "She's the mathematician I spirited away from the air minister."

"Yes, of course," Dowding replied with the faintest possible smile.

Clearly Dowding did not remember her or was unimpressed with what he could recall. Her heart sank. Park must have invited Dowding to the briefing expecting Eleanor's "startling conclusion" would be important enough for Dowding to hear it for himself. Perhaps Pound had telephoned Park with his support, but Pound had endorsed her methodology, not her conclusions, and had characterized her work—correctly—as a good start but certainly far from a complete, robust model.

Eleanor swore to herself she'd never use the term "startling" to describe her work again. She had been worried about making herself look like an idiot and her work look trite; now she also had to avoid making Park look like an idiot in placing his confidence in her, in spite of Pound's enthusiasm.

"Eleanor's late husband went down in his Hurricane over Dunkirk," Park added, as if prodding Dowding to be more enthusiastic because she was a member of the Fighter Command family.

"I'm very sorry to hear that," Dowding said.

She knew he meant it, of course, but it didn't seem to have broken the ice.

"Well, what do you have for us, Eleanor?" Park asked. She knew him well enough by now to see the minute lifting of his eyebrows, as if to say, "Well, I tried; your briefing will have to stand on its own merits."

She cleared her throat. "I'd like to review the current situation, if I may, gentlemen, to establish the context of my conclusions."

"Go ahead," Dowding said briefly.

"As far as statistics are concerned, I'm afraid there's nothing you don't know, and none of it is good." She glanced down at her notes, even though she knew the numbers by heart. "In the eighteen days since I first reported to Air Vice-Marshal Park, we've lost three hundred seventy-five fighters—one hundred sixty-five in the last six days alone."

Dowding closed his eyes briefly. It occurred to Eleanor that although he received her statistics every day, he was not used to having them stated so bluntly. He probably went over them alone in his office, staring at the casualty lists in grief and horror. Still, there was nothing she could do about it now; she plowed on.

"It's true that we're manufacturing replacement aircraft at an extraordinary rate, particularly Hurricanes, and it's also true that the Luftwaffe has lost far more aircraft than we have. But, from a statistical point of view, one has to ask, How much longer can we keep going, if 11 Group loses ten percent of our force every single day?"

She was not describing a battle, she thought; she was documenting carnage. Almost sixty aircraft, British and German, were falling out of the English sky every single day. If the weather was bad, it might be as few as twenty, but when the skies were blue and the sun shone brightly through the glorious late-summer days, ripening the rippling fields of golden wheat and fattening the plump red apples in the orchards and the juicy blackberries in the hedgerows, as many as a hundred crippled aircraft crashed down in a single day, like flying debris from some monstrous aerial catastrophe.

"That's not the worst of it. We're losing pilots at a slower rate, but the replacements are now down to eight hours' total flying time, so we're not keeping up with our losses, particularly if one calculates the losses in terms of hours of experience. We have nine-tenths as many pilots now as we had on August 18; however, our experience level, in terms of operational hours flown, has halved. At some point we'll simply run out of trained pilots."

"I don't doubt you've calculated that point exactly?" Park asked, with a weak attempt at humor.

"I have, sir."

Dowding cleared his throat. "If I remember my history correctly, there were one hundred thirty chaps at the Alamo in Texas, a hundred years ago, against an army of several thousand. They held the enemy off for thirteen days, I believe—extraordinary heroism—but in the end they all died. Are you suggesting this is our Alamo, Mrs. Rand?"

"I hope not, sir," she said. She screwed up her courage. "In fact, quite the reverse; *I believe the Luftwaffe will lose.*"

Dowding opened his eyes wide. "How have you reached such an extraordinary conclusion, in light of the statistics you've presented?"

"I've used a branch of mathematics known as zero-sum game analysis or minimax theory, sir. It's been developed to analyze probabilities in games like chess. I've applied it to our battle, sir."

Dowding pondered. *Now,* she thought, *he'll cry "Rubbish!" and berate Park for exhibiting poor judgment and wasting his time. Now I'll be sent to the Outer Hebrides to supervise an RAF laundry. Now I have disgraced the community of mathematicians and let down Keith Park and Harry Pound.*

"Tell me more, Mrs. Rand," Dowding said, after a long moment.

She almost sobbed in relief, although she realized she really shouldn't be surprised by his interest. After all, Dowding had ordered three hundred Spitfires before the prototype had concluded its trials; he'd built twenty or more RDF stations before they could be proven to be worth the investment; he'd asked for VHF radios before the technology even existed. He believed in scientific innovation—apparently he'd even give minimax a fair hearing.

"Minimax theory demonstrates that the key to winning is not to lose," she began, the words tumbling out of her mouth. "Each move should be designed to give the opponent the least favorable outcome, to deny the enemy the opportunity to win, and therefore to win oneself."

She grabbed a breath and rushed on. "We're doing—you're doing—everything right. The key to the battle is preventing the bombers from bombing effectively, and therefore the key engagement is Hurricane against bomber. We're winning that fight by wide margins, in large part because the Spitfires are keeping the 109s away. Unfortunately, there are simply too many 109s and not enough Spitfires, but the strategy remains correct, as our favorable victory margins prove."

Dowding held up his hand. "It's all right, Mrs. Rand; take your time—I'm listening."

"Yes, sir, thank you. The Luftwaffe also appears to be doing everything right. They're pounding the airfields. At some point enough fields may be out of operation for gaps to appear in our defenses. That will decrease our interception rates and increase their penetration rates, because we won't be able to get our fighters where they're needed quickly enough."

Dowding nodded, and Eleanor went on, like a locomotive with a full head of steam.

"11 Group has seventeen operational airfields, sir; eighteen if you count Oldchurch. That means we have eighteen locations from which to intercept the enemy, and the probability of interception can be translated into time calculations—how long it takes the Luftwaffe to reach their targets versus how long it takes our fighters to reach the Luftwaffe. Using these calculations, we can predict interception rates versus airfield availability. We can be confident of those predictions because we can apply the model to past history, to factual interception rates, and measure how accurate the model is."

"What's your conclusion in that regard, Eleanor?" Park asked.

"The model is accurate within five percentage points, sir. If we lose more than two fields at any one time, I calculate our interception rate will decline by ten percent per airfield, because you simply won't be able to reach the raiders in time. So, if five airfields are out of operation simultaneously, our interception rate will decline to fifty percent. From there on it's a vicious cycle: more unopposed raids, therefore more airfields lost. Under those circumstances the battle would be over in three days."

"In three days?" Dowding asked. "If we lose five airfields, we'll lose in three days?"

"You'd have lost your ability to thwart Kesselring, sir. You'd have lost critical mass."

"Er, 'critical mass,' did you say?" Dowding interrupted. "I'm not familiar with that term."

"It's a term used by a scientist named Leo Szilard in atomic physics, to describe chain reactions of particles, sir. In our case it means that each airfield you lose prevents you from defending others and so on, like a self-fulfilling prophecy or a chain reaction, and if you lost five at once, you'd lose your ability to defend any."

"And therefore Kesselring would have won," Park said.

"True, sir, he would, but not yet," she said. "In fact, Kesselring knows he's not winning; he's losing forty aircraft a day. He's lost almost nine hundred aircraft in twenty-three days. Admittedly he has vast numbers of aircraft—far more than we have—but he can't continue to sustain those losses indefinitely."

"Then he's in the same boat that we are, except he's got a bigger boat," Dowding said.

"With respect, sir, he's not in the same boat at all," Eleanor said. "Since August 18 your loss rates have been constant, at a little less than twenty aircraft per day on average. However, look at Kesselring's position. In the first eleven days of all-out effort, he lost four hundred aircraft; in the last eleven days, he's lost five hundred. He lost thirty-five yesterday, thirty-one the day before, forty-eight the day before that."

Dowding and Park remained silent.

"Let me make my points, gentlemen, if I may. First, this is asymmetric warfare. We don't have to win; all we have to do is not lose. Mathematically we have to be able to maintain the current level of interception rates, and we are succeeding in doing that. Kesselring, on the other hand, has to win; he *has* to knock us out of the southern skies. Each day he sends over hundreds of aircraft; each day we intercept them."

She took a deep breath. "Therefore, I believe Kesselring thinks he's *losing!*"

"Good Lord," Dowding murmured. "I've often tried to put myself in their position, but I've never reached that conclusion. It is, however, a perfectly logical analysis."

"Yes, sir, I believe it is. I must admit I've been fixated on attrition rates and aircraft availability rates—I report them to you every day. Now I realize that interception rates are much more important, and, in that respect, we're getting better, not worse, as the battle continues. An enemy bomber intercepted and turned back, even if unscathed, is just as great a victory as an enemy bomber shot down."

Park and Dowding looked at each other. Eleanor, in a moment of elation, saw that they were in silent agreement with her assessment.

"If he thinks he's losing, what do you think Kesselring will do?" Dowding asked finally.

"To answer that, sir, I have to step outside the realm of mathematics into areas I'm not qualified to judge. So I have to proceed on unverified assumptions."

"That's all right; go ahead, Mrs. Rand. Your guess is probably as good as mine."

"I very much doubt that, sir," she said, meaning it completely. Dowding had been in uniform for almost thirty years. His anticipation of what it would take to defend England against air attack had been nothing short of brilliant. She hadn't even been born when Dowding received his pilot's wings, yet here she was, analyzing the enemy's intentions.

She plunged on. "Obviously I don't know anything about the German leadership, other than what I read in the newspapers, and I'm sure that's almost entirely propaganda and claptrap. However, I assume that Hitler is not a patient man. He's used to exerting extreme force and getting quick results. It worked in Poland, Norway, the Low Countries, and France. I further assume that Göring loves flair and drama—although I admit that's a completely unfounded assumption, based solely on the ridiculously operatic uniforms he wears."

Dowding chuckled. "Not far from the truth, even so."

"Kesselring commanded the First Air Fleet in Germany's invasion of Poland, and the Second Fleet in the defeat of Belgium, Holland, and France. He's used to winning. In both cases he was up against brave but completely outnumbered opponents, and he used strategic bombing with brilliant success. I assume he's a very able man. However, on this occasion he's been unable to dislodge Fighter Command, even though we're heavily outnumbered and even though he's been at it for weeks on end, and he's taking very heavy casualties."

"Interesting," Dowding murmured. "Pray continue."

"If I take the combination of Hitler's impatience, Göring's taste for the dramatic, and Kesselring's frustration at his apparent lack of success over England—all suppositions, of course—and combine it with the statistic results we've obtained from minimax calculations, which are not suppositions, I am drawn to a strong conclusion: the Germans will change their strategy in the next two or three days."

"What will they do?"

"Well, sir, from a minimax perspective they've already made at least two major errors. The first was reducing their attacks on the RDF stations. By doing so they ceded us ten minutes of intersection time. That's sixty miles in level flight or twenty-five thousand feet in height. Those are huge numbers in the context of the battle. If they'd have continued to pound Chain Home and ignored every other target, even the airfields, we'd have been blinded, and we would have lost already. Perhaps they don't realize what the stations do; in any case, I think they found it was hard to knock down the towers with high explosives and lost interest. It wasn't working, so they moved on."

"Thank God they did," Park murmured.

"They seem to have made their second major mistake ten days ago. All the squadrons are reporting that the 109s are now flying with the bombers as close escorts. That's robbed the 109s of their independence, their speed, their maneuvering options, their superiority above twenty thousand feet, and our need to split our Spitfires and Hurricanes. They've chained their racehorses to their cart horses, as it were."

She warned herself not to get carried away by the excitement of the occasion. Dowding and Park did not need unnecessary analogies.

"I think they did that because they thought their original tactics, with their 109s up above and the bombers beneath, were resulting in too many casualties, particularly on August 18, when they lost a hundred aircraft in a single day. But, in fact, their casualty rates have since gone up, not down."

She felt a compelling need to smoke but dared not do so without Park's invitation.

"They've been pounding our airfields for the past ten days, since the twenty-fourth. But we're still intercepting over eighty percent of their raids because they have been unable to knock out enough airfields for long enough to keep us away from the bombers. Even that eighty percent belies our effectiveness, because eighty percent includes the nuisance raids by 110s that Air Vice-Marshal Park ignores. If we exclude the raids we ignore, our interception rate is over ninety percent. Therefore I believe that Kesselring and Göring will lose confidence and try a different approach."

"What will they do?" Dowding asked again, with a hint of impatience.

Eleanor realized he'd asked her that question five minutes ago and she still hadn't answered it. She took a final deep breath.

"I believe they'll go back to what they think works—from their perspective, what they *know* works. They'll go back to blitzkrieg. They'll give up attacking the airfields and bomb London."

"Good Lord!"

"By doing so they'll abandon the correct strategy for an incorrect strategy. They will make it more likely that we won't lose, in zero-sum terms, because bombing London weakens them significantly but doesn't weaken us. It is irrelevant to control of the English Channel. And not only will they leave 11 Group undefeated, they'll also bring 12 Group and its Big Wings into the battle. London will be a predictable target, allowing 12 Group time to organize. London is also at the extreme range of the 109s, and they won't be able to protect the bombers."

She allowed herself a dramatic pause.

"Therefore, gentlemen, I believe they'll lose."

"Good Lord!"

1100 hours, Saturday, September 7, 1940
RAF Oldchurch, Kent, England

Shaux set down Eleanor's paper slowly, as if laying down a sacred manuscript. He pushed his rickety chair back from his tiny desk, which he had improvised from an abandoned steamer trunk, stood, stretched, and stared vaguely through the window.

It was another beautiful day, and sector still hadn't called on them, even though it had to be 1100 by now. Perhaps it was raining in France.

Potter had devised a game called mini-cricket, using a bat with a cut-down blade and a moth-eaten tennis ball, in which the players were obliged to kneel at all times, and 339 was crawling about on the grass field, hooting with laughter. Digby was the umpire, seated in a deck chair reading a manual on Scottish birds of prey. He claimed his phenomenal eyesight was such that he didn't have to look up to observe the action.

"You're out by a mile," he roared at the batsman, without lifting his eyes from the text.

Shaux smiled and sat down again, tilted his chair back, and stared up at the roughly painted roof above his head.

Last night he had likened Eleanor's work to discovering wild strawberries found in a hedgerow, recalling the most vivid, beautiful memory of his childhood. Pound had called it seminal—energetic and exciting. Now he had had the chance read her paper—once to get the general drift and then a second time to study each line—he realized that both definitions were wrong.

It was like a mighty river. It had a sense of inevitability, of unstoppable force. He tried to recall what Churchill had said in one of his speeches about a process that couldn't be changed. "Like the Mississippi, it just keeps rolling along," he'd said. "Let it roll. Let it roll on in full flood, inexorable, irresistible …"

Eleanor's paper was like that. Each formula followed inescapably from the one before. The formulas marched down the pages in perfect logical progression. She had not faltered or commented, however remarkable the conclusions were. When the reader reached the end, he had been battered into submission by her intellect.

Each step was modest and irrefutable, forming a link in an unbreakable chain. The links flowed, one to the next, and the chain lengthened. Each "it therefore follows that" could not be contested. The whole thesis rolled on inexorably.

He recognized the boldness of her conception as a quality he had seen at Oxford, but there was also a sort of economy to the logic, as if everything that was extraneous had been stripped away, leaving only the bare bones of the underlying truth. It was ... puritanical in its stark simplicity.

This was not like the intellectually adventurous Eleanor, who liked to entice the reader with hints of as yet unproven and unexplored side paths. This sparseness must be the impact of Kristoffer W. Olsen, the Norwegian American mathematician with whom she laughed all the time and for whom Shaux had developed an immediate and overpowering jealousy. They had shared the intimacy of their thoughts. He had imposed his will over her exuberance, while she must have egged him on to explore his imagination. Neither could have dominated the other; each had turned the other's strength to their mutual advantage.

Shaux willed himself to stop. He had no right, none, to question her choice of collaborators. Jealousy was simply another whip with which to scourge himself. The only thing he had a right to judge was the fruit of their cooperation.

Last night she'd kept asking him about his past. In her own case she had now put down a sign, a monument, that in all probability other mathematicians would admire and build on for decades, so that no future textbook on applied mathematics would be complete without some reference to her work or some inference drawn from it, just as no such book would be complete without an explanation of Poundian harmonics. While she had thus added to the store of human understanding, he, Johnnie Shaux, would be no more remembered than a snowflake—a transitory thing, created and extinguished in the blinking of an eye and leaving no trace of its existence.

A snowflake consisted of random molecules of water that crystallized into a unique pattern in the sky; the flake fell and soon melted, and the molecules again became indistinguishable from any other water molecules. In the same way, he was born, grew up, flew a Spit, and would soon die, and there would be nothing to mark his passing.

There was no more to his life than that of the snowflake. One did not ask a snowflake about its childhood or whether it had anyone to love it when it was a baby. Snowflakes came and went without trace, and, in similar fashion, there was nothing to say about his own life.

JOHN RHODES

He was destined to die, perhaps today. It was his job, his duty—his obligation to society, as Mrs. McKinley would say—to fly into conditions in which death was all but inevitable and continue to do so until the inevitable occurred. He could only do so with equanimity if he had nothing to lose, nothing to look forward to. He had not asked Pound about his father, because he didn't *want* a father, particularly a father who had been a fighter pilot.

He did not want the burden of having to live up to a father's imagined expectations or standards. He didn't want Pound to say, "Your father would have understood" or "Your father would have been proud of you" or anything in that vein. He did not want a past.

He had not responded to Eleanor's questions, because if he had, he would have started to hope she was interested in him, and hope, however far-fetched, would be a load too heavy to bear.

The logic of his existence must be as spare and ruthless as Kristoffer W. Olsen's mathematical logic, with no what-ifs to trouble him in his last moments, such as, *What if she might come to love me?* or *What if I could be happy?* If he entertained these notions, the years to come might not seem a waste of breath, and when death came, he might meet it in despair rather than with indifference.

He shook his head to clear his thoughts and looked down at the paper. He particularly liked the way she'd ended it, almost abruptly, in a final intellectual coup de grâce: "But, as has been shown, theta is *not* the inverse of epsilon."

Bang! The knockout blow! Asymmetric zero sums QED!

She must have loved writing that, knowing that her logic was impeccable, knowing she hadn't refuted von Neumann's insight but enhanced and enriched it. Perhaps she'd written it with Kristoffer W. Olsen in a moment of shared intellectual triumph, a moment of intimacy in which their minds had been fused into one.

Perhaps … Again he tried to shy away from that thought, but Yeats—or John Donne, perhaps—drove him on.

She had shown very clearly there was no future for "Eleanor and Johnnie." She had postulated it by choosing Rawley and then proven it by marrying George. There was no role for Johnnie in her life beyond that of occasional old friend, on those rare occasions when such a friend was needed temporarily; indeed, by her actions she had proven she would take as a lover anyone but him. And therefore he had nothing to hope for and could climb into his Spitfire with indifference. QED! He flew, that's all, because he had nothing better to do and no other future.

But alas, just as Eleanor had robbed him of hope, Hitler had robbed him of his only other love, the pure, unalloyed joy of flying. No more could he "mount up with wings as eagles," as the Bible put it, no more delight in his "chariot of fire": Hitler had beaten 109s out of plowshares and condemned him to death.

She had conquered minimax and opened a unique portal into the nature of the battle raging in the skies. He, on the other hand, was making good progress in modeling the rate at which rainwater filled teacups. Such a life was truly a waste of breath.

"When I say 'seminal,' do I mean seminal?" Pound's voice roared from his doorway.

Shaux jumped and, for a perilous moment, almost fell over backward before recovering. Pound, in his excitement, failed to notice.

"Keith Park just telephoned. She knocked his socks off! What's more, she knocked Stuffy Dowding's socks off as well! Stuffy wants me to go up to London tomorrow, to add gravitas and gray hair to her algorithms—they're going to parade her round Whitehall."

He was bouncing on the balls of his feet, his cane forgotten.

"God, if I was half my age and wasn't married, I think I'd fall in love! Unfortunately, one condition is unchangeable, and the other I do not wish to change."

He sobered. "How was dinner last night, by the way?"

"Dinner? Oh, fine, sir, very good, thank you," Shaux said. Dinner brought up unhelpful memories, like "I suppose I've always taken you for granted, but I've realized you are the only real friend I have. Can't I be interested in my friend?"

Pound was too wise to press him—youth, as they said, was wasted on the young.

"It's very quiet today, sir," Shaux said, steering the conversation into neutral territory.

"True; I hope they're not building up for a big one ..." Pound said, automatically looking out the window to check the sky. "You know, I sometimes think that Digby really can see out of the back of his head."

1600 hours, Saturday, September 7, 1940
11 Group Headquarters, Uxbridge, Middlesex, England

Eleanor was still recovering from her meeting with Park and Dowding—she'd hoped for encouraging interest at the most but had received overwhelming agreement and support.

"That's really remarkable, Mrs. Rand, most instructive, thank you!" Dowding had said at the end of the meeting, and his lips had carefully formed themselves into a little-practiced but unquestionable smile.

Yesterday Pound had described her work as seminal, and he was coming up to London tomorrow at Park's request. Perhaps he really might leave his job at Oldchurch and move up here to work with her ... Perhaps her work really was good ... She had floated through the rest of the morning as if she had had too much to drink.

She gave Kristoffer and Millie the day off, and she saw in their expressions how they'd probably use it. She walked over to the library to borrow a book, just to unwind a little. Then she returned to her desk, closed her eyes, and luxuriated in a moment of complete idleness. Her paper was finished, meaning minimax would not nag her for a while, and Millie had so charmed the 11 Group sectors that their reports came in automatically. At least for an hour or two she could luxuriate in sloth.

All was not right, however. Her evening with Johnnie had been a disaster. He had been genuinely sincere in his praise for her work and delighted by her accomplishment, but he had also been distant and obtuse, unwilling to talk about anything other than mathematics unless she dragged it out of him. Something had changed since Oxford; something had made him defensive.

Perhaps he'd fallen for Dottie, that proprietary WVS lady. Perhaps Dottie eased the tension of battle in the most traditional of all ways. Johnnie was so placid and unassuming—she'd be able to twist him round her little finger.

But Johnnie was not a pushover. He was a rising star in 11 Group, in a profession that required an iron will. He was also highly intelligent, at least as intelligent as herself—no, he was better. Surely he wouldn't have ... Besides, he was completely self-contained; he didn't seem to need anything or anybody. He'd brushed aside her tentative gestures of friendship at dinner as if he were shooing away flies.

"Me? Oh, nothing new—I just fly, that's all."

He'd walked out to his Spitfire yesterday afternoon with such assurance ... He'd led his squadron into the air and turned toward the enemy, and his men had followed in perfect formation. Such a man did not dally with WVS ladies, surely?

How sad he must have been in the orphanage! How alone and unloved! She imagined him as a little boy, walking by himself in the rain in Wellington boots and a big, floppy rain hat, plodding through mud patches, splashing through puddles, walking, walking until he was too tired to care whether he was lonely or not.

"How awful!" she'd said, when she'd discovered he was an orphan.

"Not really," he'd said with a shrug.

The little boy had grown a suit of armor to protect himself from the world. Hopefully it was proof against WVS ladies. It had certainly been proof against her own questions!

"Who is your favorite mathematician, besides von Neumann?" he'd asked her at one point, toward the end of the evening, when they'd migrated to the bar for a nightcap.

"Me!" she'd laughed. "Who's your favorite artist?"

"R. J. Mitchell."

"Mitchell? I don't think I've seen any of his work."

"Oh, yes you have, Eleanor. You saw it today. He's the chap that designed the Spitfire."

"Oh, that's cheating, although I see what you mean!" she'd laughed. "Who's your favorite poet?"

"William Butler Yeats," he'd answered with surprising finality. She wouldn't have guessed that clams read poetry.

The book she'd taken out of the library this morning was a volume of Yeats's works. It lay on her desk, and now she opened it idly and riffled casually through the pages.

And then, very suddenly, there it was, like the Rosetta stone, the key to unlock Johnnie Shaux: a poem about a fighter pilot expecting to die—no, waiting patiently to die.

> I know that I shall meet my fate
> Somewhere among the clouds above...

"Oh, God!" she gasped, scarcely daring to continue, squinting sideways at the lines at random in order to evade the full impact of what she was reading. When she'd been a little girl, she'd read report cards and examination results the same way, fearful in case the news was bad.

> Those that I fight I do not hate
> Those that I guard I do not love
> No likely end could bring them loss
> Or leave them happier than before

"Oh, Johnnie," she whispered, and the words on the page seemed to drift in and out of focus.

> Nor law, nor duty bade me fight
> Nor public man, nor cheering crowds,
> A lonely impulse of delight
> Led to this tumult in the clouds

"Oh, Johnnie," she whispered again, and summoned the courage to face the final lines of the verse.

> The years to come seemed waste of breath
> A waste of breath the years behind
> In balance with this life, this death.

"It literally is a waste of breath" he'd said of his life, and he had indeed meant it literally. She reread the poem slowly, line by line, and each line was more difficult to read than the last.

"Me? Oh, nothing new—I just fly, that's all." *That's all,* she thought. He fought without hatred for his enemies or any particular love for his countrymen, to whom his death would mean nothing, or with a strong sense of duty. He was a pilot, and so he flew—that's all. He had no past to cherish and no expectations for the future either, for he had no one to love him and never had. He would fly until he met his fate, all alone, just as the little boy in her imagination would walk until he could walk no more.

Even the title was wrenching: "An Irish Airman Foresees His Death." A big, fat tear fell splat in the middle of the page, landing on the word "lonely." This morning she had been on top of the world. Now she was staring at despair. He'd said ...

A clerk appeared beyond the tearstained verse, and Eleanor jerked upright.

"Excuse me, ma'am, the AOC would like to see you in the operations room."

"What? God, I almost dozed off," she said, aping a yawn to justify her tears. "Right, I'll go immediately, thank you."

She cleared her throat and blew her nose several times. Hurrying across the worn grass to the bunker steps, she blotched her nose with seldom-used powder, for fear that Park might see her with a red nose and wonder why.

"I thought you might be interested, Eleanor," he greeted her, not taking his eyes from the map. "Something big is brewing above the enemy coast."

She looked at the outline of the coast of France, Belgium, and Holland. The WAAFs were pushing a horde of enemy markers into position.

Park picked up the telephone to Fighter Command at Bentley Priory, which had the responsibility for assembling accurate assessments and eliminating redundant reports.

"My map is getting covered in markers," he said. "Are you sure of your information? You're estimating several hundred aircraft."

He listened grimly.

"Very well," he said, and replaced the receiver as if it were a hot potato. He lifted another telephone and ordered six squadrons into the air. Eleanor's eyes went to the squadron ladders on the far wall; 339 was not among them.

"This is going to be a big one," he told her. "You predicted a change of strategy; maybe Kesselring's going to try to swamp us with overwhelming numbers. Today's been very quiet so far, although the weather's been fine. Perhaps he's been getting his chaps organized."

Another telephone interrupted him. Eleanor kicked herself. The model had not predicted mass raids. How could she have missed it? It was so obvious. If Kesselring sent two hundred aircraft against each of five southern airfields simultaneously, a thousand bombers in all, 11 Group might be overwhelmed even if Park put fifteen squadrons in the air. If Kesselring knocked out five airfields, even for one day, Park would lose critical mass, and then Kesselring would grind 11 Group into chopped meat by Tuesday.

Perhaps, as sometimes happened, the RDF filtering process was off-key, and there weren't really hundreds of aircraft stacked up over Calais. Sometimes RDF mistook clouds for Luftwaffe formations. In that case the six squadrons Park had scrambled, almost eighty aircraft, should be enough.

Park was staring at the map—the six RAF markers fanning out to cover the south and east coasts of Kent, and the gaggle of Luftwaffe markers across the Channel, now lined up like a picket fence.

He reached a decision and picked up a telephone again. This time she saw 339's status lights change from "Available" to "Ordered to readiness." Park was not taking any chances, and Johnnie would be pulling on his flying gear and walking out to his Spitfire. Pound would be calling "Good hunting!" after him.

"Good luck, Johnnie," she murmured under her breath. "Please, please, be careful!"

1615 hours, Saturday, September 7, 1940
RAF Oldchurch, Kent, England

339 solemnly lined up behind the huts and urinated downwind. Pound had told them that an exceptionally heavy raid was brewing across the Channel. Several squadrons were already forming a reception committee over the coast, and 339 would be part of a second line waiting inland for the raiders who got through.

Shaux led his pilots out to their Spitfires and strapped in. He was scarcely conscious of going through his preflight checks, firing up the Merlin, and taxiing into takeoff position at the eastern end of the field near one of Pound's improvised defensive gun turrets. He'd done this so often it had become second nature, like cleaning his teeth or brushing his hair.

He sat impassively behind his rumbling Merlin waiting for the Very pistol to signal them into the sky.

He'd spent the early afternoon attempting to reconstruct his operational flight log—the original had been destroyed when Christhampton was bombed. It was a tedious and painful task, but it had served to keep his thoughts away from Eleanor. The Defiant ground crew sergeant had been with Shaux all the way in Holland and France, and the 339 IO had somehow managed to get hold of copies of the operational reports of his old squadron.

In all, he calculated, he'd flown eighty operational sorties over France, Holland, and Belgium. His memories of these sorties had merged into a kaleidoscope of disjointed fragments, but some incidents were etched sharply into his memory.

He'd been posted to France on May 10, the day the Germans attacked westward toward Holland and Belgium. He'd left a month later on June 14, the day Paris fell. During the intervening thirty-six days he had witnessed at first hand unmitigated catastrophe on the ground and in the air.

From his very first encounters with the enemy, it had been overwhelmingly apparent that the Luftwaffe Messerschmitt 109s were the dominant aircraft in the skies, the top predators, overpowering even the Hurricanes and making mincemeat of Defiants. RAF strategy had quickly reduced itself to skulking around trying to avoid 109s. Fighter Command had sent no Spitfires.

Although it was all a bit of a blur, a "cataract of disaster," as Churchill had said on the radio, some incidents were burned into Shaux's memory indelibly.

Four days after he arrived, the Luftwaffe had attacked Rotterdam, the great Dutch port on the North Sea, with Stuka dive-bombers. Although terrifying from the ground, like giant flying pterodactyls summoned from the past, the Stukas were ungainly aircraft in normal flight, and even Defiants could defeat them. Over Rotterdam he'd learned to hunt them down, following them when they pulled out after their steep diving attacks and zigzagged away across the burning city at low altitude. He'd learned to pull into close formation beside them so that his gunner could pour machine-gun fire into their exposed flanks and cockpit.

Those had been his first "victories." He'd felt no sense of exultation or even satisfaction. He had been flying above an ugly foreign city of which he knew nothing, attacking aircraft manned by men about whom he knew even less. The brutality of the situation had been matched by its futility; he'd felt he was trapped in some macabre medieval vision of hell, some hideous modern version of Dante's *Inferno*. Everything—the grimy city stretched beneath him, the sea beyond, the oily smoke billowing up from bombed-out buildings, the Stukas twitching this way and that and skittering away, the sky above them—had been painted in shades of gray.

"Here, sir, have a smoke." The ground crew sergeant had clambered onto his wing and interrupted his reverie. He handed him a lit cigarette, and Shaux fumbled it a little in his thick flying gloves. "Mr. Pound said to tell you sector says ten more minutes. Otherwise they'll have to stand you down again before the Merlins overheat." He leaned in though the open canopy and checked the engine gauges.

"Good luck, Mr. Shaux," he said and touched Shaux briefly on the shoulder before jumping down. Shaux returned to later days of May.

Days after the fall of Holland, the British army had been trapped with its back to the sea at Dunkirk, ringed by panzers and strafed mercilessly by the Luftwaffe. An impenetrable haze of smoke hung over the beaches, so that it was impossible to see the coastline from the air. Hurricanes and Defiants had fought vicious battles above the pall, but the swarming 109s had overwhelmed them. Shaux's Defiant had been trapped by three 109s. His gunner had been killed and his engine set on fire. He'd jumped, floating down on his parachute through the haze. He saw the defeated British army he'd been fighting to defend for the first time as he struggled with his parachute lines and searched for a safe place to land.

He stood in an endless line of British and Allied soldiers on the long breakwaters—"moles," they called them—waiting patiently for a ship to rescue them. At some point, after he'd been queuing for many hours and inching toward the sea, a group of staff officers pushed their way to the front. One of them glanced back as he shouldered his way onto the next ship: it was Rawley Fletcher. Their eyes met, but Rawley's eyes moved on quickly; he was too busy yelling at the waiting soldiers to get out of his way to acknowledge Shaux's presence.

Finally, finally, finally, it had been Shaux's turn to clamber aboard an elderly tugboat and receive a mug of hot, sweet tea. The old tug had trundled out into the black waters of the Channel, and in due course the cliffs of Dover had appeared on the horizon as a gray smear, the most beautiful sight Shaux thought he had ever seen. But moments later a Stuka had also appeared, bent upon vengeance, and had blown the tugboat into three separate pieces.

He wasn't really certain what had happened next, although it had taken several hours and involved a lot of very cold seawater. Besides, it didn't really fit in an operational log book.

Three days later he'd been back in France with a new Defiant squadron cobbled together from a ragamuffin group of survivors and had thereby been given a ringside seat to witness the final collapse—not only of the French army, but of French will to fight.

After France, Shaux had been sent north to Lincolnshire for Spitfire conversion training at RAF Kirton in Lindsey. It had been a period of tranquility, almost like a summer vacation, during which he had met and fallen in love with the Spitfire. It was as if he'd had a holiday courtship with a beautiful woman, a woman who was strong and willful and daring and yet utterly submissive to his demands. But, Shaux thought, how could he possibly suppose such an analogy, since he had never had a summer romance, or any romance at all for that matter, far less a submissive woman in his arms?

Then he'd been posted to 339 at Christhampton, and on August 14 hell had broken loose for a second time. Since then he calculated he'd flown—

A flare rose from the control tower to interrupt his thoughts, and Shaux pushed the throttle open. His Merlin roared, and the aircraft accelerated rapidly as it bumped over the uneven turf; the tail came up, and he could see where he was going for the first time. There were tiny figures on the control tower balcony; he thought he recognized Pound and Dottie Brown.

Then came the moment of exhilarating expectation, when the stick was light in his fingers and the Spitfire was ready to fly, like a galloping horse gathering itself to jump. He waited one long second and then let the aircraft leap into the air, as if it, too, was exulting in the moment. He sat back and let the Merlin pull him up effortlessly as the altimeter wound itself up and 339 arranged itself behind his wingtips.

Behind and a little to his right was Digby, with A Flight behind him. Digby liked to fly a little higher than the rest of the squadron, so that he had a better field for his phenomenal eyesight. He was like having an airborne RDF station. Shaux wondered idly whether they'd ever invent an RDF system small enough to fit in an aircraft.

Behind and a little to his left was Potter, with B Flight behind him. Potter liked to fly a little lower than the rest of the squadron; contrary to conventional wisdom, he believed attacking in a climbing attitude led to greater success. As his record of victories grew, fewer people argued with him. This morning Shaux had recommended both Digby and Potter for the DFC, even though he had been awarded his own only yesterday; Pound had endorsed both recommendations emphatically.

Shaux knew he was automatically searching the skies, even though his concentration was wandering. Perhaps, when death came, he just didn't want to realize it was coming ...

Where had he been? Ah yes, in France he'd flown eighty sorties, and in the last three weeks he must have flown, at a rate of, say, three per day on average, another sixty. That gave him a total of 140 sorties, and he'd heard the average life expectancy of a fighter pilot was less than ten. So the odds against him surviving any given flight were down to about 14 percent ... That was why he had wanted to make sure that Digby and Froggie Potter got the recognition they deserved, because he wouldn't be around to do it if he waited any longer.

At least Eleanor would get the recognition she deserved; unlike a Spitfire, a mathematical theory was indestructible.

1630 hours, Saturday, September 7, 1940
11 Group Headquarters, Uxbridge, Middlesex, England

Eleanor stared down at the map. The thicket of markers along the coast of Europe had now sprouted tentacles that were inching their way across the Channel and the North Sea toward southern England.

A thin line of six 11 Group squadrons awaited them above the coast of Kent while six more—339 among them—were climbing in reserve. The board reported "Left ground" as 339's status. Eleanor was reminded of the opening moves of a chess game, in which a few pieces pushed boldly forward from the serried ranks before each player, except in this case one side had far more pieces than the other.

Park hung up the direct telephone line to Fighter Command.

"Jesus wept," he said, his soft voice belying his uncharacteristic verbal violence. "They're estimating upwards of eight hundred enemy aircraft—perhaps as many as a thousand."

Kesselring had sent swarms of aircraft across the Channel before; the most Eleanor could recall was on August 18, when he had sent up to six hundred. But those aircraft had come in waves, with intervals between them, giving 11 Group brief opportunities to refuel and rearm. He'd almost always sent independent groups of fighters, 109s and 110s, in *freie Jagd*, or "free hunts," to act as decoys. He'd always tried to keep Park off balance by splitting his forces, trying to make Park commit to defending particular airspaces so that other formations could slip through the holes to reach their targets.

The battlefield had thus been full of open spaces. Park had used his squadrons as marauders, chasing back and forth to cover as much territory as possible and employing hit-and-run tactics, employing just enough force to keep the bombers from their targets, but keeping enough in reserve so that he was ready for the next raid.

Kesselring had never sent so many aircraft all at once. Luftflotte 2 would outnumber 11 Group by seven or eight to one. The air lanes leading to each target would be dense with aircraft. Hundreds of enemy aircraft would get through to their targets. Dozens and dozens of bombers would attack each airfield. High explosives would rain down for minutes on end.

Eleanor thought of the gun turrets Pound had taken out of his Defiants and scattered round the perimeter of Oldchurch in a gesture of defense and shook her head. She thought of explosions bursting among the buildings he had so ingeniously purloined, eruption upon eruption upon eruption. Within an hour Kesselring might have returned Oldchurch to its former condition as a sheep meadow, and all Pound's efforts would be revealed as gestures of futility.

The tentacles advanced, a hydra-headed monster. Park picked up the seldom-used telephone that connected him to Leigh-Mallory at 12 Group headquarters in Watnall in Nottinghamshire.

"I need your help," she heard him say. "The day of the Big Wing may finally have dawned."

History was filled with accounts of small forces overcoming much-larger armies, Eleanor thought—Horatius at the bridge, David and Goliath, three thousand English archers defeating thirty thousand French knights at Agincourt, Drake's little ships against the mighty Spanish armada—but unfortunately the record of larger forces crushing smaller ones was much, much longer, as Voltaire had said.

Park had fought a brilliant fight, harrying Kesselring's formations with lightning encounters, parrying each thrust, deflecting each blow, with just enough aircraft to disrupt the enemy and thwart their attacks, living to fight another day, eking out survival. But now he faced a juggernaut. The 11 Group markers would soon be engulfed among the enemy markers crowding in toward the skies of Kent and Sussex. She looked at the enemy markers and thought of the minimax calculations of which she was so proud, and it seemed as if the markers—representing real aircraft, real bombs, real cannons—were sneering in derision at her vaporous formulas that represented no more than ethereal thought.

Churchill had said, "The whole fury and might of the enemy must very soon be turned on us. Hitler knows that he will have to break us in this Island or lose the war." She saw the fury and might bearing down on 11 Group and wondered whether the breaking point had come.

She glanced round the room. Normally she saw it as the nerve center, the cerebral cortex, of the fight against the Luftwaffe. She often found herself marveling at the concentration of modern electrical and communications technology this room represented and the abundant signs of inspired ingenuity.

Now she saw it in a different light. The wooden stairs up to the balcony level were cheaply built and absurdly steep, so that people frequently fell down them. The WAAF who updated the lighted status boards was jammed into a tiny space behind the stairs and could not see the big boards directly. The control rooms were so cramped one had to duck in and out of them, and the desks were a ramshackle collection of discarded office furniture.

The design of the status boards was illogical and counterintuitive. Why were the highest levels of action halfway up the list, instead of at the top? Why did the lights progress downward as readiness increased? The room was too dark. The WAAFs updating the markers on the table continually obstructed Park's view. The elaborately curved balcony windows—curved to prevent reflections—were ridiculous; why did Park need to be separated from his staff by glass?

Was this jerry-rigged contraption of a control room the best they could do against the whole fury and might of the enemy?

A WAAF leaned across the board and moved the 339 marker to Dover. The 339 status ladder moved to "In position." The nearest enemy markers to 339 were only two inches away. What was he thinking, the little boy who had walked through the puddles in the rain, who had grown into a solitary man and finally had disappeared into a verse by Yeats and been subsumed? What was he thinking as he waited among the clouds above? "Me? Oh, nothing new—I'm just flying, that's all."

1645 hours, Saturday, September 7, 1940
RAF Oldchurch, Kent, England

The southeastern sky was *thick* with aircraft; there was no other way to describe it. Shaux could see long smudges of enemy formations above the coast like a bank of clouds, like a rain squall bearing down on England. He could see two 11 Group Hurricane squadrons rising to his right and left. It was very unusual for 11 Group to have three squadrons in such close proximity on the same bearing; it reminded him of a 12 Group Big Wing. Eleanor's boss Park must be *really* concerned by the scale of the Luftwaffe assault.

Still, it didn't really matter how many aircraft there were altogether; in the end combat very quickly came down to a small volume of immediate airspace. You could be alone against ten 109s, and a mile away there could be ten Spitfires chasing one lonely Dornier; it all depended on the luck of the draw, and you played the hand you were dealt.

There were contrails all around them; there must have been numerous engagements in the last half hour—long, ragged skirmishes tracking northwest in the general direction of London. Shaux guessed those earlier raids had been directed toward 11 Group's inner ring of airfields—Biggin Hill, Kenley, Croydon, and Gravesend … Shaux wondered whether the incoming storm cloud would attack the same airfields for a second time or swing toward the southern airfields like Manston, Hawkinge, and Oldchurch.

At 11 Group HQ Eleanor would be able to see it all laid out on the map; it was ironic that people on the ground always knew far more about an air battle than the people actually fighting it.

The controller's voice vectored them toward the center of the oncoming squall, but with so many enemy aircraft it was going to be a question of choosing a formation at random and then pointing and shooting. Shaux kept 339 climbing as hard as they could. The enemy seemed to be stacked in layers between twelve thousand feet and seventeen thousand. With so many aircraft in the air, the Luftwaffe must be worried about traffic jams.

The 109s and 110s would be in the upper levels, with the bombers below them. If he had time to get above the upper levels, 339 could keep the 109s occupied while the Hurricanes attacked the bombers.

The two Hurricane squadrons were diverging and maneuvering to attack the enemy from its flanks. Shaux kept 339 spiraling upward. It was essential that the upper level of 109s were not left free to pounce on the Hurricanes below them.

However, as 339 climbed higher, Digby's telescopic eyes allowed him to see the structure of the enemy formations. This was not a standard formation with 109s and 110s above the bombers; Digby reported there were 110s and 109s mixed in with the bomber formations at every height.

Shaux wondered, as he had wondered before, why the Luftwaffe would be so foolish as to rob their fighters of so much tactical advantage. The 110s, in particular, would be vulnerable; they were defenseless against attacks from above, and their only evasive option would be to dive. Therefore, if 339 attacked a formation of 110s from above, they'd be forced downward, and the nearest 109s would have to follow them to protect them, leaving the bombers vulnerable to the Hurricanes. So be it.

Shaux knew from long experience that the first attack was always the most decisive, because both sides were in formation—the attackers had their maximum concerted firepower and could deliver a powerful blow, and the defenders were bunched together, offering the most targets. As soon as an attack started, the formation under attack would begin to disintegrate, as if the attack were sending a shock wave rippling through it. If the attackers could restrain the temptation to scatter in pursuit of the enemy and stay in formation, they would retain a huge tactical advantage.

"Follow me," he said. He knew that Potter and Digby would follow him come what may and keep their flights together until he ordered independent action. He felt a moment of exhilaration; 339 would stick together, twelve Spitfires moving as one, ninety-six machine guns bearing as one. All the training, all the discipline, had produced a single team, and all he had to say was "Follow me" to know they'd follow.

There was a passage in the Bible about a Roman centurion that Shaux vaguely remembered. "For I am a man under authority, having soldiers under me: and I say to this man, Go, and he goeth; and to another, Come, and he cometh; and to my servant, Do this, and he doeth it."

I say to 339, he thought giddily, *follow me, and they followeth.*

He climbed until the first enemy wave passed beneath 339. At its center was a bomber formation of thirty Dornier 17s, supported by 110s to its right and 109s to its left. The 109 leader must have spotted 339, for the 109s started climbing steeply. However, if Shaux had planned his attack correctly, they were simply taking themselves out of the battle, because every second they climbed toward 339, they'd fall farther and farther behind the bombers and the 110s.

Shaux waited for a minute, until the 109s had lost a mile in their futile attempt to reach 339, and then led 339 into a steep, banking turn down onto the 110s. Tracer began to sparkle around the 110s as 339 came howling down on them—339 had a closing speed advantage of over a hundred miles per hour—and the 110s dived in self-preservation.

"Follow me," Shaux said again as 339 flashed down through the altitude of the bombers. He pulled up sharply, letting the 110s escape, and circled back upward. None of the 110s had been damaged, as far as he'd seen, but they were now several thousand feet below the bomber stream and would take several minutes to regain altitude. They were out of the battle.

That left the 109s and the bombers. There were thirty Dornier 17s in the nearest formation. The 109s that had started climbing to intercept 339 had lost a minute—perhaps two miles—and were now diving to try to catch up.

The Dorniers were therefore unprotected. The Spitfires of 339 were still together, as if they were putting on a close-formation flying display. Shaux led them into a long, climbing flank attack. He opened fire at three hundred yards, calculating he had ten seconds to engage before 339 had to pull up to avoid ramming the 17s. One of the nearest 17s staggered and began to lose height. Smoke erupted from a second. Shaux led 339 above them, climbing steeply to gain height over the 109s for a second time.

The leader of the 109s must be an idiot, Shaux thought. He'd missed the initial attack on the 110s by trying to climb, he'd missed the attack on the 17s by being left behind, and now he had opened himself up to an attack by 339.

Jump on the 109s or go back for another go at the 17s? Where were the 17s going? Glancing down, Shaux saw they were over Maidstone; the 17s were plodding northwest on a track that would lead them to Dartmouth and the 11 Group airfield at Gravesend. He looked southeast and saw the dark line of more and more enemy formations following in their wake.

Shaux made up his mind. He'd take a quick squirt at the 109s. If he could break them up, the 17s would be defenseless against any Hurricanes that found them.

"Follow me," he said yet again and turned toward the hapless 109s. It was an almost frontal attack, with 339 descending on the 109's right quarter and the 109s trying to turn up toward 339 to return fire. Of all the maneuvers the 109 leader could have selected, this was the most inept. The 109s were presenting themselves as the largest, slowest targets possible in the circumstances. 339 swept down on them without a single answering shot.

Shaux saw his tracer rounds peppering the leader's engine cowling and cockpit canopy. Fire burst from the 109's Daimler-Benz engine as one of Shaux's rounds severed a fuel line and high-octane fuel sprayed the white-hot surfaces of the 109's exhaust manifolds. The pilot was probably never aware of this, for the cockpit canopy disintegrated immediately afterward.

"Follow me," Shaux said for the fourth or fifth time—he'd lost count—and pulled his aircraft into yet another climb. Glancing back, he saw that the 109 formation had been shattered into individual aircraft flying in all directions and that three of them, including their leader, were spiraling down out of control.

If he could keep this up—weaving in and out of the bomber stream, climbing and swooping—and if 339 stayed together, they could rake formation after formation. As long as the 109s and 110s stayed down with the bombers, and the enemy marched forward in a column less than ten miles wide—only a minute to a Spitfire—339 could attack at will and escape upward.

He started to look for the next group of 109s or 110s.

1700 hours, Saturday, September 7, 1940
11 Group Headquarters, Uxbridge, Middlesex, England

The control room map was a jumble of markers strewn across Kent. There were so many enemy formations and so many sightings being reported that the information-screening process had been overloaded. All that could be said for certain was that hundreds and hundreds of Luftwaffe aircraft, in dozens and dozens of subgroups, were streaming northwest across England.

Park's Spitfires and Hurricanes were darting among them, throwing themselves into the bomber streams like barracudas ripping into schools of fish. Reliable observers were reporting *hundreds* of contrails scrabbled like chalk across the sky, and *clouds* of bombers above them.

Very little damage had been reported on the ground. The southern airfields had been bypassed. The obvious targets were being ignored. Even Eastchurch, which had been pounded seven times in previous days, had been given a reprieve.

Eleanor counted the number of markers and extrapolated from the known sizes of a few of the formations. She'd started some statistics attempting to provide an accurate discount for double counting by observers—20 percent was a rough working number. That meant …

"How many?" Park asked when she opened her eyes, clearly having guessed what she was doing.

"It's just a guess, but I'd say approximately four hundred bombers and six hundred fighters, sir—over a thousand aircraft in all, discounting for a factor of double counting in the observer reports."

"All of them holding their fire and headed for London, so it would seem."

"So it would seem."

Park frowned. "This is what you predicted, Eleanor; Kesselring and Göring have changed their tune, it seems. If—"

Park's attention was diverted by his telephones, and Eleanor watched the markers advancing toward London, a city with a population exceeding eight million, the greatest single concentration of humanity on earth.

Attacks on London had long been anticipated, and there had been efforts to evacuate the young and vulnerable—"Operation Pied Piper," Eleanor thought it was called. Apparently the whole thing had been a bureaucratic fiasco. The only smooth part of the operation was the move of senior civil servants—and their extensive government files—to pleasant hotels in England's finest seaside resorts.

Park looked grimmer than she had ever seen him.

"Leigh-Mallory doesn't have his Big Wings formed up yet. Our chaps will start coming down soon to rearm and refuel. There's so much trade up there they're finding targets everywhere they turn. It's like the traffic in Piccadilly Circus on a Saturday night."

He gestured at the board. "London will be underdefended—almost undefended. Leigh-Mallory's Big Wings won't be waiting to meet them. As you pointed out, that's not entirely his fault, since he can't see what we're seeing. The only good thing is that the 109s will be at the limit of their range and will have to turn back soon. Our chaps will get back up with full tanks and full magazines. The enemy will be very vulnerable."

"That's cold comfort for London, Keith," said Dowding from the doorway. Eleanor knew he preferred to leave Park alone in the heat of battle, but the monstrous tidal wave sweeping across southern England must have compelled him to come back to Uxbridge.

"Yes, it is," Park agreed somberly. "If I were a civilian, I'd hope the RAF would shoot the enemy down *before* they bombed me, rather than afterward."

"Well, young lady, you predicted this," Dowding said. "What are your thoughts?"

"They're doing what they think will work," Eleanor said. "They've failed to clear the skies for an invasion, so now they're going to try to bomb Churchill into a surrender. They're trying to prove they've beaten us because we can't stop them bombing London."

Dowding and Park looked doubtful.

"But that's a delusion," she pressed on. "A thousand bombers over London don't put a single pair of German boots on the ground of England. And every bomber we shoot down is one less bomber to attack an RDF station or an RAF airfield and thus makes their victory even more difficult to accomplish."

"That's still cold comfort for London," Dowding said again.

Where was the boundary between objectivity and callousness, Eleanor wondered. At what point would she be *glad* that London was going to be bombed and that hundreds of Londoners would die horrible, undeserved deaths to prove her right or to prove that Kesselring had made a serious mistake?

Well, Park hadn't hired her to be a Pollyanna; he'd hired her to make arithmetically accurate measurements of just how bad "bad" really was, even if that meant she had to be a callous bitch.

"The first bombs are falling in East London, in the docks," Park said quietly, looking up from the telephone. "A mixture of incendiaries and high explosives. We're getting casualty reports."

"And may God have mercy on their souls," Dowding murmured.

She looked down at the map and saw the WAAFs moving enemy markers over London. She saw Park cringe as they did so. Another WAAF rearranged a cluster of markers around Maidstone, and the 339 marker was moved a little south, toward Ashford, into another thicket of enemy markers. She looked for another 11 Group marker in the thicket but could find none. 339 was alone.

"Amen," she whispered.

1730 hours, Saturday, September 7, 1940
RAF Oldchurch, Kent, England

In the end there were simply too many 109s. In the end 339 encountered a 109 *Schwarm* smart enough or lucky enough to catch 339 as it wove its way through the enemy formations.

Shaux had decided they had fuel and ammunition for one more attack before heading for Oldchurch—if Oldchurch was still in operation. He was checking the sky above them for 109s one more time when Digby gave a brief warning yell. Shaux looked to his right and saw 109s coming straight at him, *huge* in the sky.

He yanked back on the stick in his emergency escape maneuver, but the 109s were far too close to miss him. *Whack-whack-whack.* Pieces of his right wing were ripped off by cannon shells. *Whack-whack-whack.* The Spitfire shuddered as cannon shells tore through the fuselage behind him. The radio went silent. The Spitfire's right wing dipped as it stalled out.

The 109s flashed past. Shaux tried to correct for his right wing, but it was immediately obvious that the aircraft could not fly. The rudder bar offered no resistance to his feet; the control lines to the tail had been severed. He had ten seconds—fifteen at the most—before the Spitfire began to spin and centripetal forces pinned him in his seat.

Thank God the hatch locks opened. Thank God the canopy slid back. Thank God the Merlin—still roaring, although now useless dead weight—had not been hit and he was not engulfed in fire.

Get the seat straps off. Take one precious second to check the parachute harness. Struggle up into the howling gale as the Spitfire cants over like a drunkard. Hope nothing gets caught and entangled. Hope the tail misses. Let go the seat back and get sucked out into the maelstrom. Fall headfirst in the frigid air. See an onrushing 109. See cannon fire erupt from its wings. Fall below its field of fire. Think, That's not the act of a gentleman! *Giggle. Reach for the parachute rip cord. Look at the clouds—these clouds are finally, finally the actual "clouds above," Yeats's own clouds above. Shout into the uncaring wind, "Goodbye, Eleanor!" Hope Kristoffer W. Olsen will make her happy. Pull the rip cord. Perhaps it will work, perhaps not. Feel the massive, bone-shaking jolt as the canopy opens. Reach up and grab the canopy control lines. Look up to see if the lines are tangled. Feel cold in the crotch and realize what has happened. Think,* That's not the act of a gentleman either! *and giggle again. See the 109 coming round for a second shot. Look down to estimate the distance to the ground. Calculate the time the drop will last, using a formula for free-fall acceleration of 9.8 meters per second squared, offset by the drag of the chute, in order not to think about the 109. See the 109 lining up. Feel relief—a kind of calm in the maelstrom—that the days and weeks of waiting for the inevitable are finally over. Swallow deeply and watch the 109 silhouetted against the clouds. This is how it ends. Death will be a chance to relax and worry about nothing, in calm of mind, all passion spent. Forever, that's all.*

See the 109 open fire again, but away to the right. He's already missed once; perhaps he isn't a very good shot. See two Spitfires behind the 109. See the 109 burst into flame. See the letter codes on the Spitfires as they howl by. Recognize them as Digby and Potter. Think, Well, I told them to follow me! and giggle again. Say sternly, "Get a grip, Shaux." Start looking for a landing site without trees.

Shaux landed in a freshly harvested wheat field. He lay for a long moment without moving and then stretched his limbs one by one, just as he did every morning as he drank his tea. Nothing seemed to be broken, and, by some miracle, he hadn't twisted his ankles or dislocated his knees. He released his harness and stood up, but his knees felt weak, and he sat down again heavily. The stubble of wheat stalks scratched and poked at him.

This was the second time he had been shot down and had escaped unhurt—as far as he could tell. The odds against that were so long that they approached infinity … It was also remarkable that he'd felt no fear, not even when the 109 was shooting at him. He hadn't really thought or felt much at all; perhaps his fatalism really had insulated him from fear of the inevitable. Or perhaps, he realized with a jolt, he'd believed he'd live and therefore had no need to fear. Perhaps his longevity as a fighter pilot was a proof of immortality, rather than a proof that imminent death was inevitable. Perhaps he was Fighter Command's Methuselah. If that was the case, then …

"Are you all right, sir?"

A small boy was crouching before him, breathing heavily, staring at him with huge eyes. The sun turned his hair to gold.

"I saw you coming down, and I ran all the way."

"I'm fine, thank you," Shaux said. His voice sounded harsh in his ears, and he swallowed and cleared his throat.

A look of concern clouded the boy's face. "You're crying, sir. Where does it hurt?"

"Sorry, I didn't know I was." He brushed his tears away. "I'm fine, really."

A fresh worry struck the boy. "Excuse me for asking, but you're not a German, are you?"

"No," Shaux chuckled. "I promise I'm as English as you are."

The boy's face cleared. "We live just over there in that cottage," the boy said, pointing. "Would you like a cup of tea?"

"I'd love one," Shaux said. "Thank you for inviting me."

"Can you stand up, sir?"

"I think so."

Shaux stood; his knees had almost regained their strength. He gathered up his parachute and clumsily wrapped the lines around it. The boy took him by the hand and led him across the wheat field, as if he felt that Shaux needed support and reassurance.

A woman appeared in the cottage doorway as they approached, and the boy ran ahead, shouting to his mother to boil some water for tea.

"Whatever do you think you're doing, Bobby, running off like that? How many times do I have to tell you not to leave the—"

"I went to help this pilot," the boy explained as Shaux appeared. "I saw him come down on his umbrella."

"Your son was very kind and very brave," Shaux told her.

Shaux was immediately immersed in hospitality. Bobby had a tendency to wander off, he learned as tea was poured, and was altogether far too independent for a six-year-old, in his mother's opinion. Bobby's father, it seemed, was also something of a wanderer, for far more reprehensible reasons.

Bobby was, however, trusted sufficiently to be told to run to Wilson's farm up the lane to fetch Mr. Wilson, who duly arrived with a horse and cart and who would be glad—honored, in fact, it was the least he could do—to give Shaux a ride down to the village.

Bobby's primary concern, it transpired amid all this running, was that his friends at the village school would never believe the story.

Shaux asked Bobby's mother for a pair of scissors, snipped off the thread attaching his pilot's wings to his uniform, and presented the badge to Bobby.

"You've been a great help, Bobby," he told the boy. "I'd like you to have this as a keepsake. Now your friends will believe you."

Shaux shook the boy's hand solemnly and thanked his mother. On an impulse he shoved the untidy ball that had been his parachute into her hands.

"I'm sure you can find a use for the silk," he said. "Thank you again for the tea."

As he rode down to the village on Mr. Wilson's cart, listening to Mr. Wilson's weather forecast—never wrong, if he made so bold as to say so himself—Shaux stared into the sky, still crisscrossed with vapor trails. How strange it must be, he thought, to be down here looking up at the battle, helpless to affect the outcome as two air forces grappled for control of the sky above your head. Occasionally a plane or a bomb or a pilot might fall out of the sky, but beyond that the only evidence of the battle was those fleeting white trails …

Down in the village Shaux persuaded the local postmaster to telephone to Oldchurch, even though it was a trunk call, even though it was a weekend, and even though Shaux had no money with him and could only promise future payment. It transpired that the only vehicle available to transport him back to Oldchurch was an elderly Humber hearse, which set off at funereal speed. Shaux arrived in Oldchurch village at eight o'clock, as night was falling, and walked into the inn.

"It's the skipper," Potter yelled, and Shaux was engulfed.

It was clear that 339 was far from sober. Shaux eventually escaped and joined Pound and Dottie at a table near the fire.

"We're celebrating your survival and young Potter's eighteenth birthday," Pound told him. "It seems he lied about his age when he volunteered."

"I'm glad he did," Digby said, joining them.

"Is it true?" Dottie broke in. "Is it true the bastards tried to shoot you as you came down on your parachute?"

"Well, they missed, Dottie, so there's no harm done. Froggie and Diggers chased them away."

"I *hate* them," she snarled. "Trying to kill you and bombing London and all!"

"What?" Shaux asked. "London?"

"I'm afraid so," Pound said. "They ignored the airfields and attacked the East End en masse. The BBC is reporting heavy damage, but it's too early to get a clear picture."

"What does 11 Group say, sir?"

"They're estimating that three hundred bombers got through. Keith Park is taking it very personally, I'm afraid. Eleanor Rand telephoned. Her minimax model had predicted it, of course, and now she feels it's all her fault."

"I'm sorry, sir, I'm not following you."

"No, I'm sorry, Shaux, I'm not being clear," Pound said. "Eleanor used her model to predict a shift in Luftwaffe tactics. She reported that to Dowding and Park, and now it's turned out to be true. It's caused a great fuss, apparently. We have to go and see Churchill tomorrow afternoon. She's coming down tomorrow morning to prepare. She—"

He was interrupted as several struggling pilots crashed into the table and sent it flying. Potter, it seemed, was resisting the 339 tradition that pilots should remove their trousers on their birthdays and then be dumped half-naked into the village horse trough. Shaux assumed that Digby had invented the time-honored tradition five minutes before.

Peace was restored when the melee burst through the front door and continued on the village green outside, with most of the crowd following to observe.

Shaux righted the table and bought himself another drink. Dottie sat down beside him.

"They could have killed you," she said in a low voice. "It made me feel awful!"

"Now, Dottie," Shaux said in a voice he hoped was reassuring, "it wasn't that bad; nothing a good hot bath won't cure."

"Then come home with me," she said urgently. "There's plenty of hot water."

"That's very kind of you, Dottie, but I couldn't possibly impose myself on—"

"I want you to, don't you see?"

Shaux gaped at her. Surely she was not suggesting …

"What's the point of life if you don't live it?" she demanded.

Shaux could not think of a single thing to say.

"I'll go first, and you follow. That way nobody's any the wiser. You'll be back up at the airfield first thing."

"Dottie, I'm very grateful, but I couldn't," he heard himself say.

"Why ever not?"

Why ever not, indeed? Why not celebrate his survival in a naked woman's arms? Why not find out, finally, what it was like? Why not? Why not? Because he'd feel he was betraying Eleanor, he told himself, even though she'd shown no interest in him, at least in that way. He'd be betraying the *idea* of Eleanor.

"I'm sorry, Dottie, I'm spoken for …" he told her. "I've got an understanding with someone …"

She sat back, crestfallen, and he feared he had insulted her.

"It's the nicest thing that I can think of, but …" he began, trying to think of some polite way of escaping without embroiling himself more deeply in lies or giving himself an excuse to change his mind.

He was rescued by Potter, who burst through the door with his trousers around his ankles, only to be grabbed from behind and pulled out again. Shaux jumped up and followed, giving Dottie what he hoped was an infectious grin.

"Let's see what's going on!" he said hastily and bolted through the door.

Most of 339 was scuffling round the water trough, surrounded by a ring of bemused villagers. A loud splash marked Potter's defeat.

"Dammit!" Potter spluttered. "The water's freezing!"

"Here, Froggie, have a pints, bitter, to warm you up," Digby said solicitously.

"It's the least you could do," Potter said and drank deeply.

"What's all this commotion?" a loud voice demanded, and the village constable pushed his way through the crowd.

"Now, then, what's going on?" he asked. "What is that officer doing?"

"He seems to be sitting in the horse trough without his trousers, Constable," Digby replied.

"How did he get in there?"

"Here, let me show you exactly what happened," Digby said, and 339 descended on the policeman.

2230 hours, Saturday, September 7, 1940
11 Group Headquarters, Uxbridge, Middlesex, England

Eleanor sat beside Park in his staff car as it threaded its way through the darkened streets of London toward the docks, which stretched eastward for miles along the Thames beyond the Tower of London.

Park, it seemed, simply could not get over an overwhelming sense of personal failure. It was his job to defend London, and, regardless of the circumstances, he had failed to do so. 11 Group had definitely shot down over sixty German aircraft, and probably damaged another forty, while losing forty-four of their own.

That should have been a highly significant victory, but none of that mattered to Park. The East End of London was in flames, and therefore he had failed in his most important duty. He had to go to see it for himself and had asked Eleanor to go with him.

The night sky was clear, Eleanor saw. Not content with the afternoon's assault, Kesselring had dispatched more bombers—RDF estimates put their numbers at two hundred—to fly under cover of darkness to bomb the fires that still raged from the afternoon's carnage.

They passed through the crooked streets and tall buildings of the city of London, the home of England's banks, stock brokerages, and exchanges, and drove past the massive stone walls of the Tower of London.

Eleanor began to smell the bitter odors of burning buildings as they approached the docks. An ambulance clanged past them ringing its emergency bell. There were more and more Londoners in the streets hurrying toward the fires to offer help.

The streets were crowded with rescue workers and emergency vehicles. They came to a wrecked, smoldering building that was too badly damaged to be salvaged. Eleanor saw that the whole front wall was sagging outward over the street at an improbable angle; soon the entire edifice would collapse.

The police had cordoned off the street. They abandoned the car and continued on foot, coming across more and more destruction, more and more fires. The whole East End was burning, or so it seemed to Eleanor, and picking their way through the fires were armies of scurrying volunteers—policemen, firemen, soldiers, sailors, air-raid wardens, ambulance workers, nurses, Boy Scouts, even nuns—and dazed dockworkers wandering amid the destruction of their livelihoods and homes.

In some places the gas mains had been ruptured, setting off uncontrolled fountains of fire. In other places it was the water mains, so that the frustrated firemen had no pressure for their hoses and volunteers had to form long lines passing buckets. In yet other places the stench told of broken sewer lines, so that whatever water was available would not be fit to drink. Many of the streets were in darkness, festooned with broken power and telephone lines. Dense smoke shrouded every scene. Everyone was ashen-faced and coughing.

Park groaned at each fresh sight of the destruction he had failed to prevent.

All the pubs—and it seemed there was at least one on every corner—were open. The police were apparently ignoring the technicalities of licensing hours, and Eleanor heard that the publicans were offering free beer and cigarettes to the rescue workers.

They came to a row of narrow houses set directly on the street. Somehow a bomb blast had stripped off the front walls while leaving the rest of the dwellings intact and unscathed, so that she and Park walked, feeling like intruders, past neat front parlors and glimpsed cluttered kitchens beyond. The bedrooms on the upper floors were open to the night. Three small children in pajamas stared down at them from one such upper room. The wallpaper was bright with a nursery pattern of cats and dogs.

Eleanor smiled up at the children as she and Park walked by.

"Do you know where Mummy and Daddy are?" the oldest called down.

Eleanor stopped. "No, but I'll try to find them. What are their names?"

"Mummy and Daddy, of course!"

Eleanor smiled again. "Yes, of course, but do they have other names as well, like Joe or Jim or Mary? What do they call each other?"

"They're called Dear and Darling!" the smallest child piped in triumph, the first to solve the riddle.

Park groaned beside her.

"You stay there where it's safe," Eleanor called up, hearing a crack in her voice. "Keep away from the edge, and we'll find someone to look after you until your parents come home."

Perhaps she should ask Park to go on alone while she stayed with the children. But Park was obviously emotionally distraught, and her first duty was to him.

"Someone will be here soon," she called up. "Don't worry! Just stay back from the edge so you'll be safe."

At the far end of the street they found an exhausted policeman, who frowned in frustration.

"There's a lot of corpses as were carried out of that street," he said, his voice thick with fatigue and strained from smoke inhalation. "I'll report it, but until this muddle clears … and even then … Meanwhile, I'll ask the wife to look in on the kids."

They reached a building that had been reduced to a smoking pile of broken bricks and blackened beams. Rescuers were digging frantically in the rubble for survivors.

Next to it a church served as a makeshift hospital. Through the doors Eleanor saw a surgeon at work, bending over a torso while two volunteers held flickering flashlights so that he could see his scalpel.

A line of coffins stood beside a curb. A dog sat patiently beside one of them, whining softly and scratching gently at the woodwork with a tentative paw, waiting for its master to wake up.

A burly policeman stood in an intersection and organized a party of volunteers to search a damaged building down an alley. Eleanor watched him lead his party into the shadows. There was a strange, loud, whistling noise from the sky. Park yelled something that she didn't understand. He reached over and roughly dragged her to the ground.

As he did so, there was a brilliant flash that illuminated the dark alley, and then the loudest noise that Eleanor had ever heard. A geyser of dust and rubble exploded from the alley, and in the midst of the flying debris she saw the limbless trunk of the policeman. The buildings on each side of the alley shook and trembled. Sharp shards of shattered glass erupted from their windows and rained down on them like arrows; slates burst from their roofs and exploded around them like grenades.

Then came a moment of complete silence, and Eleanor wondered whether she had been deafened; but immediately the silence was broken by a thunderous *whoosh*, and a tall column of fire erupted from the wreckage. Park dragged her to her feet, and she stumbled after him to safety.

They found an open tea shop and stopped to catch their breath. There were more explosions, but these were muffled by distance and too far away to hear that terrifying whistling sound. Park's face was covered in soot; he had lost his uniform cap, and his tunic was coated in thick gray grime. It was impossible to recognize that he was in uniform. One of his hands was bleeding from flying glass. She wondered what Smiling Albert Kesselring would say if he knew he'd almost killed his nemesis. Would he curse his luck at missing or be glad that Park had escaped, out of professional courtesy?

She saw her fingers were leaving black marks on the tea mug; she must look just as bad as Park—and only a few hours before she'd been worried about a red nose! She glanced round the crowded room, which was lit by guttering lanterns, and saw that everyone was in the same condition.

"Where's the bloody RAF?" a large man at another table asked the room at large. "Where were the bleedin' Spitfires when we needed them?"

"Sat on their bloody asses doin' sweet Fanny Adams!" another man said.

Eleanor reddened with embarrassment beneath the grime—not because of the crude cockney slang, but because 11 Group, her group, had failed to stop the attacks. She dared not look at Park.

"How'm I goin' to earn a living if my job's gone up in bleedin' smoke?" the first man demanded.

"What about my house with no bleedin' roof?" the second responded. "Bloody RAF! What a load of old rubbish they turned out to be!"

"It's not their fault," a small woman objected. "They're doin' their best, you mark my words!"

"Well, then, their bloody best ain't bloody well good enough!" the first man roared back. "They're a bunch of bleedin' wankers, if you ask me! Whoever's in charge ought to be taken out and shot." He pushed back his chair and shouldered his way through the door.

Park leaned across the table and spoke so quietly she could scarcely heard him. "Tell me again why all this represents a terrible mistake by Kesselring and a glorious victory for us?" he asked her grimly.

More bombs exploded in the distance, and an ambulance clanked past.

"Kesselring could have destroyed 11 Group as a fighting force today, sir," she replied in the same undertone, trying to convince herself as much as him. "Biggin Hill, West Malling, and Christhampton are already out of operation; he only needed to knock out two more airfields to gain air superiority south of the Thames. With a thousand aircraft he couldn't have missed, even if we'd shot down twice as many of his aircraft as we did. You'd have been forced north, and Leigh-Mallory is too far away to defend our southern airfields. We would have lost."

Park nodded wearily, not persuaded. She continued as urgently as she could.

"Instead, sir, tomorrow morning you'll still have critical mass, and he'll have sixty less aircraft than today and two hundred less aircrew. With due respect to that large man, let's hope that something—rage, stupidity, arrogance, who knows—keeps sending the Luftwaffe back to London."

She heard the enormity of her whispered words, watching the faces of the Londoners around her, but pressed on.

"Judging by Mr. Churchill's speeches, attacking London will stiffen his resolve, not weaken it; he'll never surrender. In the meantime, if Kesselring keeps this up, you'll grow stronger, and Kesselring will grow weaker. In a week or ten days, no more, you'll be victorious."

Park said nothing.

"I may sound like a callous bitch, sir, spouting highfalutin theory in the middle of a disaster, but it's still true."

She lit a cigarette and sucked on it greedily, emotionally and physically exhausted. Park's thoughts seemed to have turned inward, while hers careened from one calamity to the next. She should have wished Johnnie good luck yesterday afternoon. At dinner she should have told him how proud of him she was, how much she admired his stoic bravery, instead of asking stupid prying questions. She should have stayed with those children this evening until help came. What kind of woman walked away from three frightened little kids in the wreckage of their home? And now she was pleased that helpless civilians were being slaughtered by the dozen! Was she completely incapable of a single decent human emotion?

Johnnie was all alone, her thoughts lurched on. He'd been alone all his life. When he climbed into his Spitfire, he was all alone in the dangerous skies. He asked for nothing, expected nothing. What kind of woman walked away from a man with nothing, not even hope? Surely she should …

More customers entered the tea shop, and she and Park left to make room for them. Park stopped in the street and looked at the wreckage that surrounded them.

"If this is what victory looks like, I'm not sure I can bear it," he said.

SEPTEMBER 8, 1940

0430 hours, Sunday, September 8, 1940
RAF Oldchurch, Kent, England

Johnnie Shaux awoke an hour before dawn. He dressed, got his tea, and sat down outside the A Flight dispersal hut to drink it in the enveloping darkness.

The tea scalded his tongue. He lit a cigarette, and the smoke tasted harsh and acrid in his mouth. *Plus ça change, plus c'est la même chose.* The more things change, the more they stay the same.

Yesterday had certainly been very strange. The central fact of being shot down and surviving unscathed was not in itself remarkable—that was simply a random event, like the unpredictable movement of an electron in the new science of quantum mechanics.

Far more significant was his reaction. He'd swung from fatalism, in which he looked at imminent death with indifference, to convincing himself he was an Olympian immortal and would live as long as Methuselah! Who was the cartoon chap in the new American comic books who was invincible? "Superman," was he called?

Shaux had long since decided he'd die a bachelor. Eleanor had never given him the slightest clue she might be interested in him, and no other woman could possibly compete with her—or his myth of her, to be more exact—and it wouldn't be fair to marry someone he thought of as second best.

However, dying a bachelor in his old age was a far more dreary and forbidding prospect than dying a bachelor in the next few days. Longevity had its drawbacks. If he lived until he was seventy-five and thought of her, say, five times a day on average, he'd think of her … more than ninety-eight thousand times, without considering leap years.

If he confessed his feelings and she rejected him, as he expected, then their friendship would be shattered, and he'd be miserable for the rest of his life. If he remained silent and their intermittent friendship continued, he'd also be miserable for the rest of his life. Worse, as her friend, he'd have a front-row seat to witness her next love, her happiness in someone else's arms, and the brood of someone else's children she'd bear.

He thought of an American expression he'd heard from an exchange student at Oxford: "Life sucks, and then you die." His fate would be worse: "Life sucks, and then you don't die."

He had been *stupid* to reject Dottie Brown's overture. He should have gone back with her. He could have been sitting here replaying the scene in his mind's eye and planning their next encounter. He could have filled his waking thoughts with happy realities rather than ephemeral fantasies. In time, the practical immediacy of Dottie's reality could have crowded out the theoretical possibility of Eleanor.

Yet, when Dottie had made her offer, not only had he rejected it like a scalded cat, he'd rejected it on the absurd basis that he had an understanding with Eleanor! How delusional could he be?

He'd been shot down over Dunkirk. He'd been bombed in the English Channel. Now he'd been shot down again. He'd survived all three encounters and numerous other near misses—so many near misses he couldn't begin to come up with a realistic estimate. It seemed he was fated to live, but to what purpose, to what end?

339 must have attacked well over a hundred aircraft yesterday, weaving its way through the clouds of enemies, showing outstanding discipline and resolve, leaving disruption in its wake. It had been exhilarating to know that the squadron was behind him, sticking together, playing follow-my-leader regardless of the odds and the tracer flashing all around them. Digby was so calm and professional, exuding confidence … Potter was a natural, a great leader … 339 had been a broken squadron when it arrived at Oldchurch, decimated by losses, led by a man who needed the assistance of a whiskey flask to climb into his cockpit … A ramshackle squadron on a ramshackle airfield …

Now 339 was a team—not that Shaux could take the credit, of course. He thought of Potter and Digby jumping on the 109 that tried to shoot him in his parachute—and then de-trousering that unfortunate copper and dumping him into the horse trough. It would take all of Pound's diplomatic skills to smooth that incident over … What would the charge be? Assaulting a police officer with intent to cause a public act of indecent exposure? Misappropriation of government property? After all, presumably the poor man's uniform trousers had been issued to him.

339 had knit itself into a team, and teams had a much-greater chance of survival than individuals. But losses were inevitable. They'd been incredibly lucky yesterday—he'd been the only pilot shot down. Thank God for that—not because he'd survived, but because he wouldn't have to suffer the anguish of writing to bereaved parents and wives. He thought of the pathetically inadequate letter he'd written to Protherow's parents the day before.

"Dear Mr. and Mrs. Protherow," he'd written. "Please accept my deepest condolences on the death of your son." He'd stopped. Protherow had been in the squadron less than twenty-four hours. He'd scarcely spoken to him. He'd had to check to find out his first name. What could he possibly say? "Even though Percival was with us for only a short time, he impressed all of us in 339 with his courage and determination."

The vision of Protherow's face leaped into his mind, the terrified eyes ringed with fire, the open mouth screaming in silent agony, dying far too slowly. He'd never even seen the 109s that got him. "It may be of some comfort to know that he died instantly and felt no pain, bravely defending his fellow pilots and his country." Today someone else was scheduled to replace Protherow, and he would be reduced to a forgotten statistic.

Shaux had hardened his heart and rushed to get the letter finished. "We will remember him with honor. Yours sincerely, John Shaux, Commanding Officer, 339 Squadron, RAF."

He remembered a verse by Ovid, or Horace, or some Roman poet or other—"*Dulce et decorum est / Pro patria mori.*" "It is sweet and honorable to die for one's country." He doubted Protherow would agree.

Shaux had no next of kin to receive a similarly deceitful letter written by someone who scarcely knew him. He'd left that box blank on his RAF personnel form. Occasionally he'd thought of putting in Eleanor's name—after all, it would make no difference after he was dead, but she'd be embarrassed and annoyed by his presumption.

Why didn't he just tell Eleanor he loved her and take his chances? How could he lead 339 through enemy formations without a qualm but be unable to summon up the courage to confess his adoration? His father must have done so, and his two grandfathers, and his four great-grandfathers, and his eight great-great-grandfathers, and so on, back through time. Why did he, Shaux, lack the moral fiber to do the same?

At Oxford George Rand, Eleanor's husband, had once called him a "stolid stoic" with "celebrated sangfroid." In truth he was less a stoic and more a coward, it seemed.

She was coming down today, according to Pound, so that they could prepare to meet Churchill. Churchill, no less! Her work, her insight, her creativity, were becoming part of national strategy at the highest levels, it seemed, and deservedly so, because the notion of applying game theory to human conflict was an obvious step—obvious now that Eleanor had taken it.

Her eyes had a tendency to become unfocused when she concentrated, and she'd nibble her bottom lip, but only on the right side ... When she took her glasses off, it seemed like an act of intimacy, as if she were baring her mind ... What would it be like to wake and find her sleeping beside him? Did she sleep curled up in a ball or spread-eagled? What—

"Sector's been on the phone," Pound's voice said, and Shaux almost leaped out of his chair. The cold remnants of his tea went flying.

"Sorry to startle you, old chap," Pound chuckled. "Anyway, group is gambling that the Luftwaffe will take the day off to lick their wounds; they've lost over a hundred aircraft in two days. 339's being stood down for twenty-four hours. The squadron will fly over to Boscombe Down and take the day off."

"The chaps could certainly use a break, sir," Shaux said.

"You should stay here, if you would. I'd like you to join me with Eleanor Rand in the minimax discussion and then stay on to cover for me while I'm up in London visiting the high and mighty."

"Should I go and see that policeman, sir, and apologize on behalf of 339?"

"It wouldn't hurt," Pound said. "I'll do the same, the first moment I have. He's a decent enough bloke; I doubt he'll bear a grudge."

"Very well, sir."

"By the way, Eleanor's bringing the American chap, Kristoffer someone, with her. It should be interesting."

0630 hours, Sunday, September 8, 1940
11 Group Headquarters, Uxbridge, Middlesex, England

Eleanor stared at the group adjutant as if he were an alien from another planet attempting to communicate an indecipherable message. He repeated the words, but they simply would not register.

"What do you mean, sir? They're dead?"

"I'm sorry, Mrs. Rand—I know it's a great shock. Millie's aunt telephoned to say that Millie and Corporal Olsen were at her parents' home in the East End when it was bombed last night."

Effervescent Millie, conqueror of men's hearts with a mere glance, conqueror of synthetic division of polynomials by dint of sheer determination … Kristoffer, with his elegant mind and wry wit … How could they be dead? How could some mindless bomb, mindlessly dropped, have pulverized their lives, their love, and their future?

It was only two days ago that she'd asked Millie what she did to her uniforms to make them less like bales of cotton.

"Nothing, ma'am," she'd replied. "I just wear them."

"But they look so much better than mine."

"It's not the uniform, if I can say so without offense."

"What then, Millie?"

"My advice is to accept what you've got, ma'am, and enjoy it. There's girls aplenty who'd be envious."

She remembered the time Kristoffer had edited one of her minimax papers, his honeyed voice at once lazy and yet energetic.

"Lookee here, ma'am, at these sad lines of hog manure," he said, jabbing at the rows of formulas. "Up here you created an elegant formulation that stands on its own. Then you seem to doubt your work, even though it's obviously correct, because you proceed to pour all kinds of doo-doo on it until it dies of asphyxia at the bottom of the page."

"But it's not hog manure …"

"Ma'am, I grew up on a hog farm. Never, ever doubt a North Carolina hog farmer's ability to recognize and categorize excrement."

What a life Millie and Kristoffer would have lived together …

Eleanor walked blindly toward the operations room. The endless flights of concrete stairs led downward. Kristoffer had always made a point of climbing these stairs behind Millie, creating gales of sotto voce giggles. The long, grim tunnel at the bottom was festooned with wires and conduits. She entered the operations room, already a hive of purposeful activity.

She took an automatic glance at the squadron ladder boards; 339's status was "Released." Park must have given them the day off; Johnnie would be safe.

On the wall beside the door was the wooden holder for Park's reports, so that he could look through them as soon as he entered. She pulled out this morning's minimax report and glanced through the summary data, missing Millie with every line. Would the sectors fall over backward to call the data in, now that Millie's eyes flashed no more? How would this data get into the model, now that Kristoffer was gone? He had so refined the model that it would take her days to puzzle it out. She'd have to find a replacement for him—no, nobody could replace him; a substitute. As for Millie, someone else would do her job, but that would simply emphasize her absence.

Eleanor flipped through the pages to the squadron details, sector by sector, and came to 339. Sorties flown, current availability, victories claimed, operational incidents reported, pilots and aircraft lost ...

1700 hrs.   Shot down by enemy fire   Acting S/L Shaux, J.

If she'd been up on the balcony, she'd have toppled over. As it was, she grabbed at the map table to steady herself. The ladies' lavatory was down the corridor; she'd never make it. She wondered whether she'd vomit on the map of 10 Group's area of responsibility in the West Country.

Stand up straight, Eleanor. Say "Good morning" to the senior WAAF on duty. Answer "Yes, please" to the offer of a cup of tea. Take a deep breath. Test walking by taking one step while holding on to the table. Remove hand to check whether it's trembling noticeably. Pick up the sheaf of reports before anyone notices—placing anything on the map table surface is strictly forbidden. Do not look at the sheet that says, "1700 hrs.   Shot down by enemy fire   Acting S/L Shaux, J."

Hear a flurry of greetings of "Good morning, sir." Realize Park has entered. Turn, touching table with back of waist in case support is needed. Smile.

"Good morning, sir."

"Good morning, Eleanor," Park said. "Where do we stand this morning?"

He took the sheaf of reports from her hands and glanced down at them.

"That chap Shaux's got more lives than a cat," he chuckled. "Shot down, bailed out, and got home in time to participate in a minor imbroglio with the local coppers, so I understand."

"He's all right?" she managed to ask.

"He's as right as rain; I just got off the telephone with Harry Pound—speaking of whom, you'd best get going down to Oldchurch."

He looked at her face, reached out, and squeezed her shoulder gently.

"Look, Eleanor, I heard about your team; I'm very sorry. I'd like to write to both sets of next of kin, if I may?"

"I'm sure they'd be very grateful, sir." It was typical of Park to take such trouble, even in the heat of battle.

"Well, it's the least I can do. Now, I'll see you and Pound at 10 Downing Street—don't be late, for God's sake!"

Say "Goodbye." Walk to the ladies' lavatory. Lock the door. Kneel in front of the toilet and vomit. Decide that crying is a self-indulgence to be indulged later. Get up. Look closely in the mirror. Decide to accept what you've got, ma'am, and enjoy it, in memory of Millie.

1030 hours, Saturday, September 8, 1940
RAF Oldchurch, Kent, England

Oldchurch looked deserted. The Spitfires were absent, and the only operational aircraft in sight was one forlorn Defiant at the northern end of the field. At least it still had its gun turret to give it a modicum of self-respect.

No Spitfires meant no Johnnie, she thought.

In the car on the journey down to Oldchurch, she'd decided to confront him, to offer herself as an alternative to his hopelessness. He'd never shown any interest in her except for that one time in the punt on the river in Oxford, when she'd thought she'd seen something in his eyes. But the more she thought about it, the more she became convinced.

Besides, if she'd yielded to Rawley and George, why not to him, a better man than either of them? Johnnie was not the pushing type; he'd never made a move to which she could react. She'd have to break through his clamshell armor and make him react to her initiative. *Exactly so*, she'd thought grimly, *just like he didn't react when we had dinner!*

She'd twisted uncomfortably in her seat. She was about to meet with Pound, England's most eminent mathematician, in preparation for meeting with the prime minister—and yet her mind was as preoccupied as an adolescent's. Feeling like an idiot, she pulled out a paper and pencil.

"Let's settle this once and for all," she muttered to herself.

"Is he a decent man?" she wrote. "Do I find his company pleasant? Can I imagine him as a constant companion? Do I find him attractive?"

The first three questions were easy to answer, but she paused on the last. It all depended on defining attraction. Since she'd never felt it consciously enough to recognize it, how could she answer the question?

Well, she thought a little wildly, *if I can't observe it directly, can I infer it?* Both Newton and Einstein had demonstrated the existence and properties of gravity without being able to observe it, by analyzing its attractive effects on other things that they *could* observe. She chuckled; she must be the only girl in England trying to decide whether she loved a man by applying the general theory of relativity, and probably the only girl in Europe.

Still … she certainly thought about him with increasing frequency; when he hadn't returned with the other Spitfires, she'd felt sick to her stomach; this morning she'd felt she would faint. These were not signs of indifference. If the earth attracted the moon by the laws of gravity, then surely Johnnie must attract her by the fundamentals of biology?

Rawley's absence pleased her. George's unfortunate death saddened her, but she felt no sense of irreplaceable loss. How would she feel if Johnnie died? Not well, judging by this morning.

As for that elusive passion, that chaotic racing of the blood she had sought without discovery in Rawley's and George's arms, how was she to know without the obvious practical experiment? *If I knew he was coming to my bed tonight, would I be pleased, indifferent, or horrified?*

Rawley had presumed her love, and George had asked for it, and she had been unable to summon it for either of them. If, on the other hand, it was she who did the asking, perhaps she'd find it. Pound had said his harmonic equations had been there all along, waiting to be discovered; perhaps her love for Johnnie had also been buried treasure, and she'd been too blind to see it.

Very well; so be it.

Her mind made up, she'd slumped back on the cushions and let her mind drift. In some bizarre fashion she knew Millie would be pleased … Rawley would be furious, as would her mother: "You threw over a viscount to marry an orphaned nobody? How *could* you, after all I've done for you?"

An image of a young boy had leaped into her mind, her future son, with Johnnie's eyes and Johnnie's solemnity, splashing through the puddles. Her heart had ached with an unexpected surge of emotion so fierce it hurt. That little boy would never be alone, she'd sworn to herself, never abandoned, never unloved.

Now she was here in Oldchurch, and Johnnie apparently was not. There was an overwhelming irony that, upon her having decided to make an indecent proposal, its recipient was not here to receive it. She'd have to settle for Pound and minimax.

But when she entered Pound's office, Johnnie was also there, leafing through the notebook containing her work.

"I'm sorry about your team, Eleanor," Shaux said immediately. "It must be an awful shock."

"Are you all right?" she demanded, as if he hadn't spoken.

"Of course," he said. "Why ever not?"

"You were shot down."

"Oh, I'm fine, not even a scratch," he said, as if he had simply stumbled on a stair. "More to the point, I've had the chance to go over your thesis several times. It's fantastic, Eleanor! I also think I can see traces of your colleague's work. He must have had great clarity, great simplicity; I'd have liked to have met him."

Johnnie, as usual, was diverting attention away from himself, as if his brush with death was not worth talking about. With Pound in the room, she couldn't push him for details, far less make her proposal.

Pound pressed tea and cigarettes upon her and then began to expound on the direction he thought her research should take.

"You know, it's almost Darwinian—the survival of the fittest," he said, stoking up his tobacco pipe. "Or perhaps the carnivorous food chain would be more apt. The bombers get attacked by Hurricanes, the Hurries get attacked by 109s, and the Spits attack them! What's that old verse? 'Big fleas have little fleas upon their backs to bite 'em, and little fleas have lesser fleas, and so ad infinitum.' If Kesselring had sent his thousand aircraft against us, instead of London, we might have lost our remaining Spitfires. In those circumstances, minimax theory suggests—"

He was interrupted by the station warrant officer, who flung open the door. "Sector says there's 110s headed our way, sir. Sneak attack. Only minutes away!"

"Follow me," Pound ordered.

The four of them piled into his elderly car and set off, with remarkable speed, for the western end of the field, where a Defiant turret stood on a platform surrounded by tall walls of sandbags.

Pound manned the turret with practiced ease, swinging up one leg and swiveling on his cane. The warrant officer seized a thick electrical wire and connected the Cowley's engine to the base of the turret.

"We're too old to fly, but at least we can still shoot." Pound grinned. "Makes us feel we're making a contribution. The Cowley's electrical system powers the turret, thus making it a supplementary military vehicle, therefore enabling it to make a contribution also. I put it in the station inventory as a 'MAG', an abbreviated version of 'mobile auxiliary generator, dismounted Defiant turrets, for the use of.' It may look like an elderly Bullnose Morris to a casual observer, but it's a MAG nonetheless. Now, keep your heads down."

He clamped his pipe between his teeth and searched the heavens. Within seconds Eleanor heard the deep rumble of approaching air engines. Shapes appeared in the southern sky.

Shaux reached out and gently pushed Eleanor's head below the top of the sandbags. He crouched beside her.

"I can't see what's going on," she protested.

"You won't be able to see at all if your head gets blown off," Shaux said.

"I have to talk to you," she said as the approaching aircraft grew louder. "Now?"

"It won't wait, Johnnie. I want to get it off my chest. I've been doing a lot of thinking, and I—"

Pound opened fire in the Defiant turret, drowning out her voice. The ground shook as explosions sounded from the station buildings, and the dark silhouette of a 110 thundered overhead. Pound swung the turret around as the 110 flew over them, and his four machine guns barked up at its retreating tail.

There were strange thudding noises in the sandbags around her, dull but loud at the same time, and Eleanor realized another 110 was firing at them. Shaux pulled her into his arms and pressed her down against the ground. Her ears were filled with a cacophony of noises—the roaring 110 engines, the stammering of enemy fire, the thudding of cannon shells, the whining of the turret hydraulics, the barking of Pound's machine guns.

Pound ceased firing. The last 110 roared overhead. Eleanor raised her head in the sudden silence. She noticed Johnnie was holding her hand. She looked up toward Pound, who was staring into the sky.

"Dear God, he's hit!" Johnnie shouted and leaped up.

Pound was lying back in his seat as if he were stargazing; his pipe was still clamped between his teeth, but a dribble of blood ran down his jowl beside it. Shaux reached into the turret and lifted him out as if his portly frame weighed nothing and laid him gently down so that Pound's head was pillowed by the sandbags. The chest of his uniform was saturated with blood.

Eleanor knelt down beside him and gently removed his pipe.

"Thank you, my dear," he whispered. His eyes were wide open, as if he was seeing more than just her face.

She looked around for Shaux. He was bending over the warrant officer, who was slumped against another wall of sandbags, clutching his arm.

"I'm all right," the warrant officer said through gritted teeth. "It's just a flesh wound. How's the wing commander?"

Shaux looked across at Pound and shook his head slowly.

He can't possibly be right, Eleanor thought. It was inconceivable that

Pound could die; he was far too full of life. He was an improviser of successful RAF stations and of improbably fast cars. He was the discoverer of Poundian harmonics and a man whose advice Albert Einstein had sought. He was a man who could see into men's souls, who—

"Please tell my dear wife I love her," he whispered.

"I will," Eleanor said. She reached out and cradled Pound's head in her arms. She bent down to his face to catch his words.

"Look at a map of Europe, my dear," Pound said, his voice even lower than before.

"A map of Europe? What do you mean?"

"Put yourself in Hitler's position. Consider his assets and particularly his shortages and liabilities. Build a new model based on that premise. It's what I was going to suggest to Churchill."

"A strategic model?"

He closed his eyes, and for a second she thought he'd gone. Her eyes filled with tears.

"He needs raw materials to feed his war machine," Pound whispered. "He's short of oil, for example. Use the economic asymmetries to conclude what he'll do and what we have to do to stop him."

She had a thousand questions but said nothing.

"Look after Johnnie Shaux, for me, will you?" he breathed.

"I will."

"I worry about him. It occurred to me that he's never had anyone to love him …"

"I'll try, I promise."

"Tell him his father would have been proud of him."

"I will," she murmured.

"Please tell my dear wife I …"

He sighed, and Eleanor knew he had slipped away.

She laid him down as gently as she could. Shaux knelt beside her.

"How can he be dead?" she asked him, feeling tears coursing unchecked down her cheeks. George, Millie, Kristoffer, and now Pound; it was as if the Luftwaffe was deliberately killing everyone she knew as a punishment for developing her model, leaving her isolated in an uncaring world. Moreover, they'd almost killed Johnnie yesterday, and last night they could have easily killed Park when that bomb exploded in the alleyway. She'd have been like a lost child in a world of strangers.

Johnnie was staring down at Pound. He'd taken Pound's plump hand in his, as if to shake goodbye. He was just as alone as she was.

"Don't leave me too, Johnnie," she said. "I need you. We'll stay together and make the best of it."

He looked at her, and she knew he'd say something self-obliterating.

"Pound asked me to look after you, and I promised I would, and so you have no choice."

Johnnie opened his mouth to reply, but the warrant officer interrupted him. He'd struggled to his feet and was looking upward, his head cocked to one side.

"I hear the bastards coming back," he shouted.

Shaux jumped up. He took one look at the turret and a second at Pound's car.

"This turret's useless. They got the Cowley."

Eleanor scrambled up also. She could hear the threatening hum of approaching engines. Poor Pound's beloved motorcar was riddled with bullet holes—it had died with its master. Looking across the field, she saw that half the station buildings were on fire.

"What shall we do?" she asked Shaux.

Without replying, Shaux ran to the lone Defiant left with a turret and scrambled up on the wing. Eleanor ran after him.

"What are you doing?" he yelled back at her.

"I'm coming with you," she said, following him up onto the wing.

"It's much too dangerous, Eleanor!"

"If you're going, I'm going. Besides, how are you going to fire without a gunner?"

He groaned in frustration. "Well, that's true, dammit, but you might get killed."

"So might you."

"That's different!"

"No it's not. Stop arguing. Either I come, or you don't go. You can't fire the guns without me, and the warrant officer's wounded. Come on, we're wasting precious time."

He made a gesture of helplessness, and she pushed past him. The turret was turned sideways, and the only way in and out was through its rear opening. She clambered into the turret, hitching up her skirt to her thighs. The interior was incredibly cramped and stank of oil and other odors she didn't recognize. Shaux looked after her, clearly trying to think of a way to stop her.

"If you keep staring at my bottom, you won't be able to concentrate," she called back, giddy with fear and excitement, still trying to grasp that Pound was dead. "Now, fly!"

Shaux shook he head in frustrated defeat and climbed into the pilot's seat. Eleanor inspected the turret. She could scarcely fit in. The four machine guns were placed very widely, at the extreme side edges of the turret, so that they could fire forward along the sides of the cockpit or backward past the tail. Most of the available space was taken up with incomprehensible machinery for the hydraulic systems. There was only just enough space to sit down in the uncomfortable canvas seat.

"Strap in!" Shaux yelled.

The engine started with a deafening roar, and the airframe shook. She tried the hydraulic pedals tentatively, and the turret swung wildly. A leather flying helmet, hanging from one of the gunstocks, slapped her in the face. She felt a bolt of terror that she might be thrown out of the turret through the gaping opening behind her.

The aircraft lurched forward. She struggled to center herself in her seat and pull on her harness, but the angle of the bouncing fuselage tilted her sideways and made it much harder. The pitch of the engine rose, and the aircraft bumped harder and harder across the turf. Every time it bumped, her feet moved the pedals, and the turret abruptly swung this way and that. Every bump made the gun mounting bounce, and protruding controls threatened to knock her out. She grabbed at them to steady herself, and the guns pivoted upward, dumping her down on her knees.

Without a shred of dignity left, she lifted her rump over the edge of the seat and pushed backward until she righted herself. The canvas webbing safety harness seemed to have too many straps, and the big brass buckle made no sense. This was absurd. Far from helping Johnnie, she couldn't even sit in her seat and strap herself in.

"Calm down," she said to herself aloud. "This is a simple exercise in topology. There are five straps and therefore a total of ten surfaces. The apparatus must be symmetrical with the buckle at the intersection of the *x* and *y* axes. It is, in effect, a simple two-dimensional object arranged about the point of origin." The straps finally revealed their secrets, and she tugged them tight. Her hands were shaking, and she gripped her knees to steady herself.

The aircraft slewed round as Shaux reached the airfield perimeter, and the sound of the Merlin, already deafeningly loud, rose to a high-pitched scream. The bumping grew harsher, and even over the engine roar she could hear the undercarriage creaking in protest. Within seconds she felt the tail of the aircraft rise beneath her feet. She looked out of the turret for the first time. She was astonished to find she was facing backward toward the tail, unable to see where they were going, unable to see Johnnie, alone in a tiny, noisy, vibrating cylinder with the chill wind howling through slits in the turret. The trees that lined the field were already rushing by. Two more harsh bumps and the aircraft rose into the air.

The bumping ceased instantly, replaced by a deep vibration, as if the aircraft was shaking itself apart. They rose astonishingly quickly; by the time they reached the far end of the field, they were already several hundred feet in the air. The aircraft banked onto its right wing, and Eleanor almost shrieked as her stomach performed a cartwheel. The airfield was a perfect miniature of itself, complete with burning buildings and aircraft.

She heard a tinny voice yelling at her, and she realized it was Johnnie's voice coming from the leather helmet. She crammed the gunner's helmet onto her head. The aircraft righted itself abruptly.

"Put on the helmet," his voice sounded in her ears. "Can you hear me? Eleanor, put on the helmet. Eleanor? Can—"

"Yes, I'm here."

"Are you all right?"

"Yes, I'm fine," she lied.

"Okay, there's no need to shout, Eleanor. Just speak normally. Strap in securely and then try to get a feel for the turret controls. You don't need to use much force."

His voice was completely calm, as if he had said, "Try the buttered scones." She tried using different levels of pressure on the pedals and found that a gentle dab was all that was needed to move the turret. Suddenly the aircraft banked again. She stamped down against the angle automatically, and the turret rotated wildly.

"*Shit!*" she yelled in fear and exasperation.

"Don't fight the aircraft," Shaux said without condescension. "You're part of it; go with it. Let it carry you."

"I'll try," she said doubtfully.

"You're feeling centripetal force, accelerating the aircraft relative to the center of our turning circle. Acceleration equals velocity squared over radius—remember?"

How could he be quoting Newtonian laws of motion while they were flying on one wing? The aircraft righted itself, and the turret stopped spinning.

"I'm going to fly round the airfield at two thousand feet," Shaux said. "Imagine we are at the center of a clock face. The nose of the aircraft is at twelve o'clock; the tail is at six. Your job is to search the sky behind us from three o'clock to nine o'clock; I'll search the forward semicircle. Do you understand?"

"Yes, I understand," she said.

"Search slowly and methodically. Start at the horizon and work upward."

"Yes."

"If you see anything, say the bearing and the height. Say, for example, 'Aircraft at five o'clock high.' Got it?"

"Got it."

"Can you point the guns out to one side and aim upward?"

"Wait a second ... yes, okay."

"Release the safety catches—they're on the stocks above the trigger guards. They're labeled 'safe' and 'fire.' See them?"

"Yes, I've done it."

"Fire a short burst to get the feel of it."

She squeezed the trigger, and the guns barked, *whack-whack-whack*, jumping in her hands. The cockpit filled with the bitter smell of cordite, and her ears were ringing.

"Yes, all right," she said.

"Don't shout."

"Sorry."

"Now, return the turret amidships facing backward and search the skies."

They circled the airfield. Eleanor realized she was panting. Her heart was racing, and her hands were sweaty. She took a deep breath and tried to relax, leaning back into her seat as Shaux banked the Defiant once more.

"This is crazy, Eleanor," Shaux said. "You shouldn't be here."

"I want to be with you."

There was a long moment of silence.

"Why?" he asked.

"Because … because it seems right."

He made no reply. She took a deep breath and plunged on.

"I read the poem by Yeats about the airman, Johnnie. I think you decided you'll die, and you shut down all your emotions, all hope for the future, so you could accept it."

He was still silent. She was having the most important conversation of her life strapped into a shaking, freezing metal canister talking to a man she couldn't see through a smelly intercom.

"Say something, Johnnie."

"I … I can't talk about it."

"Yes you can. I'll go first. I've made some huge mistakes, especially over Rawley. But I'm not like you; I can't pretend I'm not human. You're all I've got. I realize I …"

"What?"

A second ago it hadn't been there, and now it was pointing straight at them, with the sun glinting off its cockpit.

"There's an aircraft on my right at seven o'clock, er, medium high."

The menacing silhouette changed, as if it was beginning to dive.

The Defiant stood on its wing as Shaux dragged it into a sharp turn. Her stomach protested, but she tried not to fight the turn.

"Describe the aircraft. One engine or two?"

Suddenly there were more shapes behind the plane above them.

"Two engines, and there are two aircraft, no, three of them. Now they're at three o'clock."

"Now I see them; they're 110s," Shaux said. "We're going to fly under them. Aim your guns forward above the cockpit canopy and wait. They'll have to point upward at fifteen or twenty degrees."

She told herself to be calm and aimed the guns as he had told her.

"Keep the guns steady, and I'll do the aiming. You can't shoot straight forward, only at an angle above the prop. When the time comes, we'll shoot upward into their bellies. Don't try to aim too, or we'll confuse each other. Wait until I tell you to fire."

"Will we be all right?" she whispered, realizing that the war had suddenly ceased to be something that happened to other people; now it was happening to her.

"Of course," he said. "Piece of cake."

She realized he was probably lying. She didn't know the odds for one Defiant against three 110s—probably not good.

The Defiant straightened out, and now it was headed toward the approaching enemy. Something bright was flashing on the nose of the leading aircraft. A line of light approached her and flashed by, followed by another and another, like shooting stars. But these were not natural phenomena, bits of meteors falling through the upper atmosphere; these were white-hot cannon shells attempting to kill her and Johnnie too.

"Shall I fire?" she asked, fighting panic.

"No, wait, please," he said evenly. It was as if he'd said, "Please pass the sugar."

The Defiant was climbing. The enemy was rushing down on them. How could he be calm?

"Fire now," Johnnie said quietly but distinctly, and she pressed the trigger. Her guns barked and shuddered, and now lines of light—parabolic curves—stretched upward to the enemy. Johnnie lifted the nose of the Defiant a fraction, and she saw sparkles playing on the enemy's nose.

"We're hitting him!" she shouted, feeling a fierce exultation. Johnnie lifted the nose as the distance closed, and the sparkles played along the enemy's underbelly. *This is for Pound*, she thought, *and for Millie and Kristoffer.*

"Stop firing."

"But ..."

"Stop firing. Wait for the next one."

The first enemy flashed overhead, huge and malevolent, and the next 110s were already firing. Shaux adjusted their direction a fraction, so that they were aiming at the one on the right.

"Open fire," he said.

Again the lines of incandescence flashed between them, cutting transitory geometric patterns in the sky. There was a wonderful elegance to the display ... She recalled the basic physics of parabolic trajectories ... *Bang-bang-bang!* She jumped in horror as the Defiant rocked. The elegant lines were tearing through their left wing.

"God help us!" she cried.

"Stay on target, please, Eleanor; that's just superficial."

The 110 on the right seemed to be changing course, almost as if the pilot intended to ram them. *Bang-bang-bang-bang-bang.* The Defiant rocked again. There was something black coming out of the 110's left engine as it careened down upon them spitting death. The Defiant was tiny in comparison to the 110, and she was trapped in the steel prison of the Defiant's diminutive turret. Her palms were slippery with sweat, her stomach was in knots, her whole body was shaking violently, and she gagged as she recognized the stench of terror. Collision was inevitable, violent death a certainty. She was firing with her eyes shut tightly, waiting for the moment of impact.

"God help us!" she cried again.

Suddenly the Defiant was standing on its tail as Shaux wrenched the nose upward. She watched the huge 110 flash beneath them, trailing smoke. The Defiant staggered and plunged earthward like a stone. She was hanging from her straps. She screamed.

"It's all right, Eleanor," Johnnie said. "Just a controlled stall."

As if on cue, the Defiant's free fall became a controlled dive, and then the dive became level flight.

"Sorry about that," Shaux said calmly. "I needed to take evasive action. Can you see them?"

She stared about wildly, but the sky seemed empty.

"Search slowly and methodically."

She was weeping, she realized, and she was fairly certain she'd wet her underwear.

"I … I can't see anything."

They were approaching the airfield. Now she saw the wounded 110 far below them, trailing a long plume of oily smoke. It hit the ground as she watched, bounced, and bounced again, as if a giant had flipped it onto the airfield and sent it skipping like a flat stone across still water. Each time it bounced, a puff of flame burst from the fuselage, so that it was progressively transformed from a bouncing aircraft into a bouncing ball of fire.

They swept over the wreckage, which had come to rest against the western gun emplacement. Pound's body was being cremated. There would be nothing physical for his widow to grieve over, nothing but her memories of him and echoes of his features in her children's faces. Had she stayed, Eleanor would have been down there too … The wounded warrant officer …

She shuddered. Her hands were gripping the gun controls like white talons. She felt acid bile rising in her throat.

"It's over, Eleanor," Shaux said quietly. "It's all over. You're safe. Just keep checking the sky for more aircraft."

Even in this moment of crisis he was still flying, still searching the skies, still looking for the enemy, seemingly oblivious to their encounter with death.

"Stretch your arms and legs out one by one to release the tension," he said. "It helps."

His voice was a lifeline amid the chaos.

"Promise me you'll never leave me," she demanded to the gun controls. She realized that she was sobbing uncontrollably.

"Look, Eleanor, you can do a lot better than me …"

"No, I can't. I need you. Promise me."

"Search for the other 110s. They may come round again."

"I will, but you have to promise me—that's more important."

His voice was silent.

"Promise me," she demanded.

Still silence. He was only a foot away, but it might as well have been a mile.

"Forget Yeats! Promise me you'll live and be happy. Say it—say the words!"

"Look, Eleanor, you're in shock …"

"Don't evade the issue! Don't pretend you don't want me! Say the words."

She heard him groan.

"Say it!"

"I promise I'll live and be happy," he sighed.

"And you'll never leave me."

"And I'll never leave you," he whispered.

"And I will never leave you."

They flew in silence for another ten minutes, absorbing their commitment. Everything had changed.

There were no more 110s.

Eventually they landed and taxied, bumping and bouncing, to the line of blazing huts. Pound's handiwork had burned with him. Shaux shut off the engine, and the silence was as deafening as its roar. He opened the canopy, and they were surrounded by ground crew.

"You got the bastard, sir!" the senior warrant officer crowed. Eleanor stared at him as if he were a ghost. He had survived; his face was white from loss of blood and his arm was in a crude sling, yet nevertheless he insisted on helping Shaux down from the wing. Shaux was encircled by airmen clapping him on the back. The dramatic end to the 110 had obviously given them a strong taste of sweet revenge.

"Well, thanks, chaps," Shaux told them, "but the credit goes to my air gunner."

Eleanor emerged from the turret, acutely aware of her state of dishevelment, hurriedly pushing her skirt below her knees.

"Well, my sainted aunt!" said the warrant officer, slack-jawed with astonishment. "Is that really you, Mrs. Rand?"

"Well, I'll be a monkey's uncle," said the IO.

"Stone the bleedin' crows!" said Sergeant Jackson.

They rushed forward to help her down.

"Three cheers, lads," yelled the warrant officer, and the assembled ground crews roared out their approval.

"Drinks all round tonight, Mrs. Rand!"

"Thanks, thank you all," Eleanor said unsteadily. She felt the ground was moving under her feet, and she wondered afresh whether she was going to vomit. No, she mustn't—she had to see Churchill in a clean uniform.

"I'd love to join you," she managed to continue, "but I must get back to London immediately."

They all but carried her to her car. She climbed in, and Shaux began to close her door. She stopped him and said quietly, "Come up to London tonight. Come to ... come to the Charing Cross Hotel." She had passed it last night on the way to the East End, and it was the first thing she could think of. "Ring me up on the house telephone. Come at nine o'clock. Promise?"

"Look, in moments of great tension people say things they don't—"

"I mean every word, dammit! Do as I say! Now promise."

"I promise," he said.

1530 hours, Sunday, September 8, 1940
10 Downing Street, Westminster, London, England

Churchill's office on the second floor of 10 Downing Street reeked of cigar smoke, and the air was so thick that the prime minister seemed to generate his own private fog, or perhaps, Eleanor thought wildly, his magnetic force of personality cast everything around him into shadows.

He sat behind his desk, wearing a scowl above his old-fashioned bow tie. He seemed older than his photographs, and his massive shoulders were more rounded, as if they bore an almost unbearable weight. When he stood to greet her, he was shorter and far stouter than she would have imagined. The cartoon artists often depicted him as a bulldog, but Eleanor thought a bullfrog would be more accurate.

When he spoke, it was as if a skilled actor were giving an impersonation of his unmistakable voice. "Mrs. Rand, I presume?" he inquired gravely.

"Yes, sir."

He turned to Park. Eleanor thought she saw a flicker of amusement cross Churchill's face.

"I am advised that there has been a gross breach of military discipline this day, Air Vice-Marshal," he said to Park with ponderous formality. "To wit, I am advised that unauthorized personnel have been flying in Royal Air Force fighter aircraft. Are these reports accurate, pray tell me?"

"I fear they are, sir," Park replied, equally as gravely.

Eleanor was almost certain that Churchill was jesting, but not quite. His massive head assumed a look of belligerence.

"If young women form the general impression that they can shoot automatic machine guns with impunity, then the balance of the sexes may be unhinged, and every Englishman will henceforth enter his home in trepidation, for fear of encountering a Browning .303 in the hands of his beloved spouse." He shuddered theatrically. "I would certainly approach my own abode with a sense of grievous apprehension, for I fear I have done much to warrant such a confrontation. What is to be done, Air Vice-Marshal, I pray you?"

"I leave it in your hands, sir."

Churchill smiled, and his scowl was transformed into an impish grin, as if the burdens of office in the midst of a desperate national crisis had been overcome by the sheer joy of being alive.

"In that case, I think the immediate award of a Military Medal appears the best solution. I congratulate you, Mrs. Rand."

He wears his emotions on his sleeve, she thought as his eyes twinkled at her. *He's like a little boy playing games.* For a moment she really had thought she was in trouble!

"I shall see to it at once, Prime Minister," Park said, grinning at her.

"Pray sit down, Mrs. Rand."

She sat down. Churchill returned to his desk and retrieved his massive, smoldering cigar.

"I am not a mathematician, Mrs. Rand, nor yet a scientist. I must therefore rely on the judgment of others, who advise me that you have devised a remarkable analytic tool; a tool, indeed, that predicted these dreadful air raids?"

"I can't predict the future, sir, of course," she said, trying to pull herself together and answer him coherently. "All I can do is project future actions based on past performance, and the projections may well be inaccurate. These raids on London were a mathematically probable event. All we can do is measure probabilities."

"I understand your caution, Mrs. Rand, but what is your prediction for the course of the present battle?"

It might be best to equivocate, but Churchill did not seem like a man who welcomed wishy-washy thinking. She took the plunge.

"These daylight attacks on London will continue until Luftwaffe losses become too high for them to continue. At present attrition rates, that will probably take ten days. Perversely, the harder they try, the quicker they'll fail. Then they'll give up intensive daylight bombing and revert to nuisance bombing at night. The current raids have no strategic value, other than trying to rattle your resolve, sir. Hitler is trying to break the Londoners' will, in order to break yours."

He frowned, and his bullfrog's chin lifted pugnaciously. She hurried on.

"If they can't defeat Fighter Command, sir, and they can't defeat you, then they'll have to abandon their plans for an invasion, at least for the foreseeable future."

"What will they do instead?"

"I have no idea, sir. I haven't considered it. I've simply attempted to model the current battle in isolation."

"The fate of this island is teetering is the balance, Mrs. Rand."

"I know, sir." There wasn't anything else to say.

He pondered for a moment.

"I know you're not a gypsy fortune-teller with a crystal ball, Mrs. Rand, nor yet a savant with a pack of tarot cards. Nevertheless, I want you to paint with a broader brush, to look beyond the immediate. I shall give you whatever resources you may require, and you will extend your analysis as widely as you can."

What did he mean? He might just as well have told her to design a rocket ship to the moon—but this was not a moment for equivocation.

"I ... I'll do my best, sir."

"As shall we all, Mrs. Rand, as shall we all, with gathering skill and might, until, in the fullness of time, Herr Hitler and his monstrous ménage lie choking in their own vile excrement."

He really does talk that way, she thought as Churchill stood to wish her goodbye. She'd heard he tried out various phrases in normal conversation and then used the ones he liked in speeches to the House of Commons.

She wanted to ask him what he meant—a broad brush, but a painting of what? She'd been lucky with minimax on a small scale, with a finite number of variables, but if she tried to extend it, would the logic hold together? Pound had told her to start with a map of Europe ...

Outside, in Downing Street, she turned to Park.

"What should I do, sir?"

"You should think, Eleanor—you're very good at it."

She left Park and walked up Whitehall toward Trafalgar Square, turning the prime minister's words over and over in her head. She had wanted to hand minimax over to Pound and Kristoffer and anyone else who wanted to pursue it. She wanted to devote her attention to Johnnie; this morning she had given him her commitment, and tonight she intended to consummate it. She did not want to leave Park while the battle teetered in the balance. She did not want to be sequestered in some gloomy, drafty old country house trying to second-guess the deranged stratagems of Adolf Hitler, surrounded by quirky, self-absorbed mathematicians with bad teeth and pimples. But if that was Churchill's command ...

She glanced up before crossing Whitehall and saw Rawley was coming in the opposite direction. There was a brief moment to observe him before he saw her. His hurried gait seemed to lack its old self-assurance, and his face no longer radiated its unique brand of complacency. He seemed diminished, preoccupied.

She turned away, hoping he wouldn't notice her, but he called her name. She turned back reluctantly, and he bore down on her and grabbed her arm.

"Good God, Eleanor, where the hell have you been?" he demanded. "I've been trying to find you for days. I have to talk to you. Let's find somewhere to have some tea."

She had just left the prime minister, and now Rawley was demanding her attention. *From the sublime to the ridiculous in five minutes,* she thought. If she refused, he might make a public spectacle. *But I am not concerned,* she thought. *This time I have Johnnie Shaux on my side, and I am therefore immune.*

"Very well," she said, and her curtness surprised them both.

They went to a Lyons tea shop on the corner of Trafalgar Square and found a place to sit on the lower level.

"Look, old girl, I'm off to Canada," he said as soon as they sat down. "Organizing support, waving the flag, and so forth. I've been trying to see you before I leave."

She lit a cigarette while he complained to a waitress that the cutlery was dirty. The waitress shrugged and walked away, and the cutlery remained in place.

"*Canada,* Eleanor; did you hear me? I needed to talk to you before I leave."

"Yes, I see," she said. "Tell me, Rawley, do you still think the RAF will be defeated and the army will have to fight?"

"There's no question of it," he replied, brushing the question aside as if it were unimportant. "These raids on London prove the Luftwaffe can't be stopped. There'll be an invasion, for sure."

A pretty girl at a nearby table overheard him and looked at Rawley with apprehension. If a staff officer was forecasting doom …

"I don't agree," Eleanor said with emphasis, to counter the girl's concern.

"Everyone says so." Rawley shrugged. "Churchill's just whistling into the wind."

"And, while we fight, you'll be safe in Canada?" she asked him.

"That's unkind! Someone has to go …"

"And you volunteered?"

"That's not fair. They needed someone with a bit of dash to impress the factory girls and so forth, and a medal for bravery, and …" He stopped abruptly and almost managed to look ashamed. "But that's not what I wanted to talk to you about," he hurried on. "Look, old girl, I know you said no when I offered to marry you, but I hope you've reconsidered my offer. Someone needs to keep an eye on the old man if I'm away. If there's an invasion, someone needs to look after the estate."

Now the pretty girl's interest was riveted.

"I said no because I meant no," Eleanor said coldly.

He must be desperate to raise the issue again in so public a place.

"Look, the Germans respect the aristocracy," he said. "Half their government ministers are Prussian nobles. With a title you'll be a lot better off, just in case the worst comes to the worst."

"I'll take that chance."

"Don't be so hasty. As George's widow … Well, to be frank, George was of Russian blood and might even have had a bit of the Israelite mixed in, if you see what I mean. He was certainly rich enough to be. The Germans don't like that at all. They might confiscate his money. If it's mine, it'll be safe in Anglo-Saxon hands. Pure Aryan blood and all that, and I must admit the Germans have got a good point in that regard. That's why I wanted to see you—I'm offering you protection by marrying you."

He leaned across the table and attempted to grasp her hand but succeeded only in knocking his cup and saucer to the floor. The pretty girl giggled.

"*Goddammit!*" he snarled.

"Look," he said, leaving the mess where it lay and oblivious of the girl's attention. "I admit I may have taken you for granted. I admit I was wrong. I admit I need someone I can trust with Dad and the estate and all that. I even admit I need George's money. I need you as my wife. There! I've said it all! I hope you're satisfied."

She stared at him without speaking.

"Besides, I must admit I've missed you, old girl," he said, as if confessing a shameful secret, and Eleanor knew his final confession was his first lie.

His eyes slid away from her gaze. In other circumstances she might have been sorry for him, but her heart had turned to stone. *In a moment he'll tell me he misses humping me,* she thought.

Last night Millie and Kristoffer had been killed. This morning Pound had died in her arms. She'd been certain she'd be killed in that Defiant turret. She'd committed herself to Johnnie. She'd just spoken to the prime minister.

She ground out her cigarette and spoke clearly, not caring whether she was overheard or not.

"You need a wife because you're too lazy, or too incompetent, or both, to manage your own affairs."

The girl giggled in delight.

"And what do you need?" he shot back, stung into a semblance of his old arrogance.

The girl awaited her answer with interest.

"I need a man I can admire, a man I can trust, a man I want to go to bed with. You fail on all three counts, Rawley."

The girl all but applauded, and the waitress loomed over Rawley's shoulder.

"What's all this mess?" the waitress demanded, overriding whatever Rawley might have been replying. "Who do you think you are, Captain Dirty Cutlery?"

"It's Maj—" Rawley began but stopped.

"Oh, excuse me, *Major* Dirty Cutlery!"

Rawley cringed under her onslaught.

"Goodbye, Rawley," Eleanor said.

"Now then, Major High and Mighty," the waitress continued loudly, "you're going to bloody well clean up your own mess."

Eleanor strode away from the public spectacle Rawley had created without looking back and walked the short distance to Charing Cross railway station. She entered the hotel that stood above the station and booked a room for the night. When the unpleasant receptionist began to create complications, she drew a pound note from her pocketbook and silenced him. Then she walked down Villiers Street and caught a London Underground tube train as far east as bomb damage permitted.

She emerged into a pall of acrid smoke. In some places fires were still burning from the night before; in others unchecked rivers ran from broken water mains. The side streets were littered with debris. Rows of houses and shops were rudely interrupted by gaping, smoking holes. Emergency workers were still everywhere, but they looked exhausted and overwhelmed by the scale of the damage. She had expected everything to look better by daylight, but it did not, and the haphazard nature of the destruction made it all the more appalling.

Worst of all, she knew this was only the beginning; this would go on and on and on, and if—when, she corrected herself—11 Group made daylight bombing too expensive for Kesselring to afford, he would continue by night, when 11 Group could not stop him. Darkness would protect his bombers but would also reduce their accuracy, so that Londoners would be subjected to random acts of violence without a purpose beyond gratifying Hitler's spiteful proclivity for inflicting pain.

After stopping to ask three times, she found Mons Terrace, and halfway along it she found a large crater where Millie's family's house had once stood. She stared at the heap of debris that still hid Millie's and Kristoffer's remains. They had been robbed of fifty years together. Millie would have gone off to America with him after the war. She'd have lived in a big white American house with a pillared front porch and driven a big American car shiny with chrome. She'd have had American children and grandchildren. She'd have …

At least she'd died in his arms. At least she'd found love. Millie would have wanted Eleanor to have the same thing … Her memorial to Millie would be to live her life as Millie would have wanted.

She turned away and began a second search. At last she found the row of houses without front walls, and from there she found the local police station. The exhausted policeman she had seen last night directed her to the home of the three small children's grandfather.

She knocked on the door, not certain what to say, and the youngest of the three answered.

"I came to see if you were all right," Eleanor said. "Do you remember me?"

"Mummy and Daddy went to heaven," the child explained calmly, as if her parents had gone out to the cinema. "So now we're staying with Grandpa."

An elderly man appeared, and Eleanor explained herself. He invited her in with elaborate courtesy, and they sat awkwardly in his tiny front parlor amid lace and chintz.

"The children haven't really grasped it …" he said slowly. "I haven't grasped it … It's as if they're going to walk in at any moment."

Eleanor remained silent, not knowing what to say.

"How'm I going to manage them? The wife passed on three years ago … How's my pension going to stretch?"

Eleanor pulled out her purse and took out the pound notes she had.

"Look, sir, buy whatever you need. If that's not enough, I'll send more."

"Goodness, madam, I can't take this! It's very kind of you, but …"

"Please take it, sir. I don't need it, and the children do; it's that simple."

"But …"

She put the money on the table and fled before he could object. He called after her from his doorstep, but she waved and continued walking. The money would never compensate for the loss of their parents, but it might make the children's life a little easier. She would arrange with the bank to send money to the old man on a regular basis.

She found herself passing the tea shop where she and Park had stopped the night before, and entered. The same large man occupied the same chair and was addressing the other customers just as he had the previous night. She bought her tea and sat down, conscious of the fact that on this occasion her uniform was not disguised by soot and grime.

The man eyed her. "Where was your lot when we needed them?" he demanded belligerently.

"Leave her alone, you daft ninny," a woman replied for her. Eleanor recognized her also. "It ain't her fault, for God's sake!"

"Well, it's someone's fault," he growled. "Where was the Spitfires?"

"There were eighty Spitfires available yesterday," she heard herself telling him, and the tea shop went silent as she spoke. "Every single one flew."

"How the hell do you know that?"

"Shut up, you big ape," the woman said, coming to Eleanor's support. "We want to hear. She obviously knows what she's talking about."

A murmur of approval from the rest of the customers supported her.

"There were eighty Spitfires but over six hundred Messerschmitt 109 and 110 fighters," Eleanor continued. "The odds were seven to one against. That wasn't the pilots' fault, but—unlike you—they didn't complain and blame other people. They just got on with it."

"Don't you use that tone of voice with—" he started, but Eleanor cut him off, and he gaped at her speechlessly.

"Many of the pilots died trying to stop the bombers reaching London, trying to protect you, and the rest fought until it was too dark to see. Almost one in four of our pilots died. The rest fought until their guns were empty, landed and rearmed, and went back up again."

"Well—"

She overrode him again. "I have a friend who's a pilot. He ran into a squadron of enemy fighters. He shot down two of theirs before he was shot down himself. He was up there again today and shot down another one. Just because you can't see them doesn't mean they're not fighting."

"I told you so," the woman said.

"You shut your cakehole," he snapped at her over his shoulder, before turning back to Eleanor. "What am I going to do for a job, now the bleeding dock's up in smoke?"

"Volunteer!" she snapped back, saying the first thing that popped into her head. "Join the RAF and do something for your country."

"Volunteer? Are you half-crazy or completely stupid? I'm in an essential trade, I'll have you know. I'm in a reserved occupation."

"How can you ..." Eleanor started and then gave up. *He has a lot in common with Rawley,* she thought and smiled inwardly at how much the comparison would infuriate both of them.

"Ignore him, Miss! What do you think's going to happen?" the woman broke in, and Eleanor saw the other customers lean forward to hear her answer.

"It will go on. Hitler's failed to beat the RAF, so he's turned on London. He's trying to break our will to fight. He thinks he'll win if he bombs enough of us out of our homes and kills enough of us."

"Screw him!" the woman spat.

"So he'll keep bombing," Eleanor continued. "It will take a week or two, but his losses will get higher and higher as the RAF shoots down more and more of his aircraft. Then he'll have to bomb at night, under cover of darkness. When he stops bombing by day and bombs only by night, you'll know he's lost the war."

"How will we know that?" the woman asked.

"Because it will mean he can't stand up against the RAF by day, which will mean he can't bomb the Royal Navy out of the Channel, which will mean he can't invade, which will mean we'll have a chance to rebuild the army; and one day, in a year or two or three, we'll regain our strength and invade Germany and defeat him."

"So, if we put up with this, we'll win?"

Strictly speaking, Eleanor thought, *according to minimax theory, if we put up with this, we won't lose, but still ...*

"Yes, we'll win."

The woman paused to check Eleanor's logic, just as Pound might have done.

"Well, then, let him do his worst," she said. "In fact, if you'll excuse my French, fuck Adolf Hitler, and fuck the Luftwaffe for good measure."

2100 hours, Sunday, September 8, 1940
Charing Cross Hotel, London, SW1, England

Eleanor waited for Shaux in her hotel room. She'd rushed back to her palatial old apartment for fresh clothes and then had arrived at the hotel in time to take a bath. She'd put on silk pajamas, changed her mind, and dressed again in her dowdy uniform. She'd put on makeup and removed it. She'd settled for a little French perfume she'd bought in Paris last year. She'd turned down the bed, dithered in indecision, and remade it. Her glasses, she'd finally decided, would remain off.

She seldom drank, but now she longed for a strong glass of whiskey to settle her nerves. She wanted to smoke, but then she'd have to clean her teeth again.

He was due in two minutes. He wouldn't come—he'd had a tug-of-war with Yeats and lost. He'd wanted to come, but the train had been canceled because of the air raids. He'd come all the way to the hotel, walked into the lobby, and then lost his nerve at the last moment; now he was downstairs in the bar drowning his sorrows.

The telephone rang.

"Eleanor?" his voice asked uncertainly.

"Room 302—come up."

"Look, you were under enormous stress. If you want to change your—"

"Come up now."

She searched her face in the mirror. Her children would have Johnnie's eyes; which of her own features would she see reflected in their faces?

He knocked on the door.

Hours later, she awoke to the distant but unmistakable sound of Big Ben tolling the hour of three in the morning. She supposed they had slipped into a satiated sleep, still entangled. She fumbled in the darkness to light the candle that stood on the nightstand, moving cautiously for fear of disturbing him.

In the candle's guttering light she saw that his face had been wiped clean of all anxiety, all fear. Released—at least for this moment—from his daily encounters with imminent death, he wore the face of a man at peace with himself, without the need to demand attention, without the need to dissemble, without greed or envy; a man sufficient unto himself, needing no explanation; a man committed to giving; a man who would never ask what she would not gladly give. She knew he was not dreaming.

He slept like a child, his chest gently heaving. He had remarkably long eyelashes. There were tiny lines etched around his eyes by endless hours of staring into brilliant skies. She examined him at her leisure, as if seeing him for the first time. This morning she had thought him dead; now she put her ear to his heart and heard its steady beating.

She was bone weary and yet brilliantly awake. She had made a long and circuitous journey to his arms, lost and befuddled on fruitless sidetracks to Rawley and George, but now, at long last, she knew she had reached her destination. She had sought mathematical asymmetries; now she had found human symmetry. She had been trapped in the reeking, claustrophobic Defiant; now she was free. She had walked the shattered streets of the East End; now she was at peace. She had struggled for purpose; now she was staring at it. She had made a promise to Pound; now she had fulfilled it.

She exulted in her newly discovered love, now triumphantly consummated; she dreaded his return to 339.

"You will not die," she whispered fiercely. "You will not die somewhere up there, alone."

He would survive; he would endure. Their lives would be fused into one, forged in the crucible of passion but tempered and strengthened by long companionship and shared experiences, merged and indissoluble. Yeats would have no further dominion over him, and when death finally came, they would die after lives in which not a single breath had been wasted.

EPILOGUE

1030 hours, Wednesday, September 18, 1940
Australian High Commission, Aldwych, London,
SW1, England

The Australian prime minister's representative greeted Eleanor politely. She was a lot better looking than he remembered. The first time he'd seen her, he'd guessed there was fire beneath the surface, and this time he was convinced of it.

"It's nice to see you, Mrs. Rand," he said. "Thank you for coming to see me."

"It's nice to see you too, sir," she replied, in that prim and proper voice of hers.

He offered her a cigarette and made a fuss of lighting it.

"Now, Mrs. Rand, how goes the battle? These air raids on London are terrible … terrible."

"Yes, they are, sir, and the fact that they're completely pointless just makes the pain and suffering worse."

"Pointless, Mrs. Rand? Don't they demonstrate the Luftwaffe's superiority?"

"On the contrary, sir. Mr. Churchill has made it very clear that he won't be cowed into submission. Ordinary Londoners are frightened, naturally, but they're not giving up. Since nineteen bombs out of twenty are falling on wasteland or in areas of no military or economic significance, the raids have virtually no strategic value at all."

"But—"

She overrode him.

"It therefore follows that the Luftwaffe must send twenty bombers to deliver one useful payload. We are shooting down two out of every twenty bombers. Therefore, it costs the Luftwaffe two lost aircraft for every one even vaguely useful bombload."

"But—"

"Every time you hear a bomb drop, you are hearing a step toward Hitler's defeat."

"But—"

"There are approximately ten thousand significant sites within London. It would cost the Luftwaffe twenty thousand bombers to destroy these targets. The Luftwaffe doesn't have twenty thousand bombers, sir; it now has less than five hundred."

He paused to absorb the numbers, not doubting her accuracy. Granted, the Pommies had put up a surprisingly good fight, fair dinkum, and granted, the Germans had lost a lot of airplanes, but surely …

"Look, Mrs. Rand, let me be frank," he said. "I think you're trying to talk a defeat into a victory, just as you British did with Dunkirk. You're all caught up in Churchill's rhetoric. This is not your 'finest hour,' I'm afraid— more like your last hour."

She stubbed out her cigarette.

"I don't know whether it's our finest hour or not, sir. All I know is that it is mathematically impossible for the Germans, who have lost over a thousand aircraft since we met a month ago, to gain air superiority over southern England. Therefore there will be no invasion, and therefore we have won the air battle."

He tried to think of a counterargument but could not. He'd heard it said she had correctly predicted the course of the battle … Perhaps she was right. Joe Kennedy, the American ambassador, had predicted Churchill wouldn't last three months; in fact the prime minister was wildly popular and seemed to reflect the mood of the nation perfectly. Maybe Joe Kennedy was wrong about an inevitable English defeat …

"Sir, we met exactly a month ago, on the eighteenth of August," Eleanor said.

"I remember."

"Do you remember the old fairy tale I told you, sir—about the condemned man and the king's horse and the one month?"

"I remember it well, Mrs. Rand."

"Do you know what's happened, sir?" she asked, and a grin dispelled her prim and proper mask, as if she were showing him her true self for the first time.

He grinned back—he simply couldn't help it.

"The horse talked?"

"Exactly so!"

AUTHORS NOTES

The Battle of Britain took place in 1940. In the company of a handful of other great World War II battles—such as the D-day landings in Normandy, the Battle of the Bulge, the Battle of Iwo Jima—it has captured the popular imagination ever since.

This popular image arises in part, I believe, from a desire for moral clarity in war. Unlike more recent conflicts, World War II was unequivocally fought against very bad people for very good reasons, and even if the good side committed an atrocity or two, the bad side's actions were demonstrably worse, and the bad side's ultimate defeat was absolute and their surrender unconditional.

The Battle of Britain was the first and perhaps the most decisive of all aerial campaigns in history. It pitted the David of Dowding's RAF Fighter Command against the Goliath of Hermann Göring's Luftwaffe. It was, quite literally, the battle that determined the course of World War II. Britain survived and fought on for another fifteen months until the United States entered the war following Pearl Harbor.

And, of course, the Battle of Britain was immortalized by the unparalleled rhetoric of Winston Churchill.

The battle produced many exceptional pilots on both sides—Douglas Bader, Adolf Galland, Sailor Malan, Werner Mölders, Stanford Tuck, and Helmut Wick, to name but a few. The vast majority of pilots, however, were not flying aces but simply very ordinary young men placed in very extraordinary circumstances. My fictional protagonist, Johnnie Shaux, is an example of one such man.

The primary characters in this book are fictitious. When I have placed real historical figures in imaginary circumstances and given them imagined dialogue, I hope I have done so respectfully. There was no 339 Squadron, and there was no RAF Oldchurch. The events of the two three-day periods covered in this novel are also fictitious; however, the general scope of the fighting on those days—the numbers and types of aircraft involved and shot down, the targets attacked, the timing and elevation of the bomber raids during the day, the weather conditions, and so on—reflects historical records.

The Battle of Britain

By June 1940 Hitler had been successful in gaining control of almost all of western and central Europe. The one remaining part of the jigsaw puzzle, at least as the jigsaw puzzle was then defined, was Britain, which he intended to invade as soon as the Luftwaffe gained air superiority over the English Channel and southern England.

The Battle of Britain was the Luftwaffe's attempt to defeat the RAF and took place from July to September 1940.

The climactic battle occurred on September 15, which is now celebrated in Britain as Battle of Britain Day. Massive Luftwaffe daylight attacks on London were met by intense resistance. 11 Group harried the attackers in its customary manner, and 12 Group, with adequate time to prepare, was able to put its Big Wings into action with devastating effect. The Luftwaffe lost eighty aircraft on September 15, a blow so severe that even the Luftwaffe's numerical superiority could not absorb the damage. Thereafter, daylight raids decreased sharply, and in October Hitler abandoned the attempt to invade Britain.

The story of Johnnie Shaux and Eleanor Rand begins on August 18, known to the Luftwaffe as Adlertag (Eagle Day), and ends on September 8, the day after the first major attack on London. During that period, the Luftwaffe lost an estimated eight hundred aircraft, and the RAF almost five hundred; the combined losses of the two sides averaged sixty aircraft per day.

The history of the RAF during the first year of World War II is summarized below.

The "Phony War" and the Battle of France

Hitler invaded Poland on September 1, 1939. Poland quickly succumbed to Hitler's invasion from the west and Stalin's attacks from the east—Germany and Russia were allies in the early stages of the war.

Britain and France declared war on September 3. France mobilized its army, which was then the largest in the world, and the British sent the British Expeditionary Force of approximately 250,000 men to reinforce it. While the two sides faced each other on the French-German border without engaging, Hitler focused to the north. The Soviet Union occupied Finland, and Germany occupied Norway and Denmark. Finland, Denmark, and Norway were all neutral, but Stalin and Hitler were not bothered by such technicalities.

On May 10, 1940, the German army abruptly attacked westward with crushing effect. Luxemburg collapsed immediately, the Dutch surrendered on May 14, and by May 24 Belgium had also surrendered and the BEF had been forced back on the port city of Dunkirk, from which it was evacuated. The scale and rapidity of the collapse of the Western Allies was so great that the Royal Navy could not possibly evacuate the stranded British army, but a fleet of private civilian vessels manned by volunteers—tramp steamers, tugs, fishing boats, ferries, pleasure yachts—crossed the North Sea and rescued them.

The German army now launched a frontal attack on France, savaging the French army. On June 14 Paris fell, and the last French resistance collapsed on June 22.

The RAF deployed approximately 250 aircraft in France during the Phony War and the Battle of France, primarily Hurricanes, Defiants, and Battles.

My fictional hero, Shaux, flew his Defiant during the futile attempt to defend the Low Countries between May 10 and May 25, when he was shot down over Dunkirk. He was evacuated with the BEF, survived when his rescue vessel was sunk, and returned to France to participate in the second ineffectual attempt to stop the Germans. He escaped in his Defiant on June 15 as the French army collapsed before the German advance.

The Battle of Britain, Phase 1, Kanalkampf, (Channel Battle) July 10 to August 11

With continental Europe defeated, Hitler prepared to launch Unternehmen Seelöwe (Operation Sea Lion), the invasion of England across the English Channel. A key part of the plan involved destroying the RAF. Hitler wrote that the RAF must be "beaten down in its morale and in fact, so that it can no longer display any appreciable aggressive force in opposition to the German crossing."

The first phase was to gain air superiority over the English Channel and drive British shipping out of it. The Luftwaffe succeeded, using an effective combination of dive-bombing and 109 fighter cover.

My fictional Shaux took no part in this campaign. He was in the north of England being trained on Spitfires.

The Battle of Britain, Phase 2, Adlerangriff, (Operation Eagle) August 12 to August 23

It should be noted that at this stage of the conflict the Luftwaffe had won every campaign it had waged since the beginning of the war, and the RAF had lost every campaign. Thus German confidence was running high as the Luftwaffe prepared to "beat down the RAF" as Hitler had ordered.

The Luftwaffe assault on mainland England began on Adlertag ("Eagle Day") with a series of punishing attacks against the Chain Home RDF stations and 11 Group airfields. These attacks continued with great intensity until August 19, when bad weather caused a break in the conflict.

The Luftwaffe was in shock. They lost over 350 aircraft in six days, including 96 on the eighteenth alone, a day they dubbed "the Hardest Day." In spite of Luftflotte 2's great numerical superiority, 11 Group had been able to counter almost every raid. Spitfires, in battle for the first time, had proved to be superior to 109s. Every other German aircraft type was also vulnerable to Hurricanes.

As we now know, the Luftwaffe failed to grasp the significance of the RDF stations and the Fighter Command control system. The Luftwaffe had destroyed over 50 percent of 11 Group's strength, and yet, as if by magic, 11 Group seemed as strong as ever.

In this novel, my fictional Shaux is heavily engaged in this battle; my story begins on August 18, when the fictional 339 Squadron is bombed out of Christhampton and transferred to Oldchurch and when Eleanor meets Park for the first time.

The Battle of Britain, Phase 3, August 24 to September 6

During the week of bad weather that followed August 18, Göring and Kesselring reorganized the attack. The fearsome Stuka dive-bombers were withdrawn—they'd proved to be as inadequate against the RAF as the RAF's Defiants and Battles had been against the Luftwaffe. The 110 heavy fighters had also proved vulnerable—from now on they'd only fly with 109 protection. The 110s and 109s were to be used primarily as close escorts for the bombers.

Finally, Göring, who (as noted) did not understand the significance of RDF, ordered raids on Chain Home to be discontinued.

On August 24 the weather cleared, and the assault on 11 Group airfields recommenced. The results of Göring's and Kesselring's reorganization were as catastrophic as before; the Luftwaffe continued to lose over forty aircraft per day, and, in spite of repeated attacks on 11 Group airfields, 11 Group continued to send up surprisingly large numbers of fighters.

My fictional Shaux fights throughout this phase of the battle while my fictional Eleanor pores over the results and develops her minimax theory.

The Battle of Britain, Phase 4, September 7 to September 15

By September 4 the German high command was losing patience. Hitler and Göring ordered attacks on London, apparently for two reasons. First, Hitler hoped that a series of devastating attacks would break British morale and force Churchill to the bargaining table. Second, Göring and Kesselring, who kept expecting Park to run out of fighters, hoped that 11 Group's remaining forces would be drawn into a decisive battle against overwhelming odds and decimated.

It was a critical mistake. Luftwaffe forces had put 11 Group under severe pressure, and Churchill wrote later that "the scales had tilted against Fighter Command."

Intense attacks on London began on September 7 and continued until September 15. Although the Luftwaffe inflicted widespread damage, there was no evidence of civilian panic or that 11 Group was weakening. Worse yet, from a German perspective, London was in range of Leigh-Mallory's Big Wings, and it was at the range limit of the 109s. Thus the bombers faced increased opposition and sharply decreased defenses.

On September 15 the Luftwaffe launched one more all-out effort, only to lose eighty aircraft.

The Luftwaffe had now lost over a thousand aircraft over England since August 12 without visible evidence of progress. Two days later Hitler postponed Operation Sea Lion. Although German raids continued for months, it was clear to both sides that the Luftwaffe could not gain air superiority over southern England and that an invasion was impractical.

My fictional Shaux fights in this phase of the battle; he is shot down on September 7. My fictional Eleanor uses her minimax model to predict the attacks on London.

Thwarted by 11 Group, Hitler turned his eyes eastward. On June 22, 1941, less than a year later, he launched his vast and infinitely brutal Operation Barbarossa against his former ally Russia.

The Commanders

Winston Churchill

So much has been written about Churchill that it seems foolish to attempt to summarize his tremendous and tempestuous career.

Suffice it to say that he was summoned to power in May 1940 (at the age of sixty-six) when defeat or surrender seemed imminent and inevitable, and he left power five years later when victory had been won. The election of July 1945, two months after VE Day, was a bitter blow to Churchill; despite his inspiring leadership during the war, he was routed in the polls.

The series of speeches he gave during his first few months in office are, arguably, the most powerful examples of oratory ever delivered, by any leader in any language on any occasion. It was Churchill who coined the term "Battle of Britain," which encapsulated the existential nature of the struggle. Years later, on his eightieth birthday in 1954, he said, "I have never accepted what many people have kindly said—namely, that I inspired the nation. Their will was resolute and remorseless, and as it proved unconquerable. It was the nation and the race dwelling all round the globe that had the lion's heart. I had the luck to be called upon to give the roar."

Air Chief Marshal Sir Hugh Dowding

"Stuffy" Dowding was a successful fighter pilot and squadron leader in World War I. He assumed command of Fighter Command in 1936. A visionary thinker, he devised the command and control system that enabled the RAF to deny the Luftwaffe victory in 1940. He championed the early development of radar, IFF (identification, friend or foe), VHF radio, and many other technologies still basic to aerial combat; he also pushed a reluctant government to invest in modern fighter aircraft, the Hurricane and Spitfire in particular.

In the early stages of the war he resisted immense pressure to squander RAF reserves in a futile attempt to defend France, thus preserving Fighter Command as a fighting force. He made sure Park was left alone to fight the Battle of Britain without political interference, but he did nothing to heal or resolve the deep rift between his two key lieutenants, Park and Leigh-Mallory, thus weakening Fighter Command's effectiveness.

He was by all accounts a remote and intolerant man; he seems to have been respected but not liked, for evidently he was not very likable.

Ironically, as soon as the Battle of Britain had been won, both he and Keith Park lost their positions in the political infighting that ensued.

He retired in 1942 and was raised to the peerage as Baron Dowding of Bentley Priory. In his later years he became deeply interested in spiritualism and believed in reincarnation. He died in 1970.

A bronze statue of Dowding stands beside St. Clement Danes church in the Strand in London. The inscription reads, in part, "His wise and prudent judgement and leadership helped to ensure victory against overwhelming odds and thus prevented the loss of the Battle of Britain and probably the whole war. To him, the people of Britain and of the Free World owe largely the way of life and the liberties they enjoy today."

Reichsmarschall Hermann Göring

Hermann Göring (also spelled Goering) commanded the Luftwaffe throughout World War II. Although he is often depicted as an outlandish figure, rather like Shakespeare's Falstaff, he was a genuine war hero and a shrewd and successful politician.

Göring was a fighter pilot of great distinction in World War I, rising to command Jagdgeschwader 1 after the death of Manfred von Richthofen, "the Red Baron," and receiving Germany's highest award, the Pour le Mérite. He was enraged by Germany's defeat and the humiliating terms of the Treaty of Versailles and became one of the first members of the Nazi Party.

He was central to the rise of the Nazis. He became a member of the Reichstag (Parliament) in 1928 and was its president in the crucial years of 1932 and 1933 when Hitler was consolidating his political power. He may have been responsible for arranging the Reichstag fire, the critical event that established Nazi political supremacy. Thereafter he held many military and civilian positions of power and remained in Hitler's innermost circles until almost the very end.

Returning to the catalog of the bizarre: he may or may not have been the illegitimate son of a Prussian nobleman; he was addicted to morphine, which impaired his judgment as a wartime commander; he was given to extravagant costumes and uniforms; he collected titles and honors; he had a long affair with a married Swedish noblewoman named Carin, Countess von Fock, and built a vast estate named Carinhall, named in her honor, which he decorated with plundered artworks and surrounded by an extensive hunting reserve stocked with bison and elk; at the very end of the war he attempted to oust Hitler, only to be sentenced to death, a fate he evaded by surrendering to the Allies; he committed suicide in 1946 by taking cyanide rather than face the humiliation of hanging as a common criminal.

For the purposes of this book, he personally made two errors as head of the Luftwaffe during the Battle of Britain: he directly ordered the end to attacks on Chain Home, failing to understand their significance, and he ordered the 109s to fly in close support of the bombers, thus robbing them of their strategic advantages and raising their casualty rates. The decision to bomb London was Hitler's.

Generalfeldmarschall Albert von Kesselring

Albert von Kesselring—"Smiling Albert," as he was known—commanded Luftflotte 2 in the Battle of Britain.

He spent the first thirty years of his career in army staff positions, eventually rising to become administrative head of the newly formed Luftwaffe in 1936. Thus, unlike Park, Dowding, or Göring, he had no experience of aerial combat and therefore no sense of what actually happened when the two sides met.

He commanded Luftflotte 1 in the Polish campaign, where his forces overwhelmed the Polish air force—and no wonder, for not only did Kesselring have fourteen hundred aircraft facing four hundred Polish aircraft, but in addition the best Polish fighter, the PZL P.11, was not only far slower than Kesselring's 109s but slower than the German bombers as well!

He must have been supremely confident at the beginning of the Battle of Britain. Once again he had enormous numerical superiority. He began with approximately sixteen hundred bombers and eleven hundred fighters, spread across airfields in northern France, Belgium, and Holland. Park had only three hundred fighters to oppose him, and even though most of these were modern Hurricanes and Spitfires, they had not been able to prevent the Luftwaffe from seizing control of the skies of Western Europe during the Battle of France.

Unfortunately for him, Kesselring was facing Dowding's organizational genius and Park's tactical brilliance. He was also saddled with Göring's poor judgment and Hitler's catastrophic decision to bomb London. And no one in the Luftwaffe seems to have made note of the fact that, even though the Polish PZL P.11 fighter had been hopelessly inferior, it had still managed to shoot down as many German aircraft as the Luftwaffe had shot down Polish aircraft.

As this book suggests, the Battle of Britain was not so much won by the RAF as lost by the Luftwaffe.

Kesselring's career did not suffer as a result of his defeat in the Battle of Britain. He became C in C of all German air forces in the Mediterranean theater (where, in the Battle of Malta, Park defeated him in the air for a second time) and subsequently of all German forces in Italy, where he is said to have conducted a brilliant defensive campaign as the Allies fought their way northward. He also declared several Italian cities "open," thus preserving the antiquities of Rome and Florence.

In March 1945 he was placed in command of all German forces fighting the Allies in Western Europe, but by then defeat was inevitable. He was sentenced to death for atrocities committed by German troops under his command in Italy but was subsequently reprieved and released. He died in 1960.

Air Vice-Marshal Sir Trafford Leigh-Mallory

eigh-Mallory's reputation has suffered in comparison to Park's and Dowding's, perhaps in part because he was killed during the war and wrote no memoirs. He has champions, such as Sir Douglas Bader, and detractors, such as Field Marshal Lord Montgomery, who is reputed to have described him as a "gutless bugger." For the purposes of this book I limited my characterization to his unquestioned quarrels with Park over fighter strategies and the Big Wing controversy.

During the Battle of Britain he commanded 12 Group, which was based in the Midlands to the north of London. It was not until the late stages of the battle, when the Luftwaffe were sending large formations with predictable flight paths against London, that 12 Group and its Big Wings made any notable contribution.

Following the battle, Park (although victorious) was stripped of his command, and Leigh-Mallory replaced him at 11 Group. Leigh-Mallory subsequently became AOC in C of Fighter Command (Dowding's old position) and C in C of the Allied air forces—including the US Army Air Force—for the D-day invasion. Each of these appointments was surrounded by controversy, adding to his reputation as an ambitious schemer.

He was killed in a flying accident in 1944 while on his way to take up a new command. Ironically, this new position was filled by Keith Park.

Air Vice-Marshal Sir Keith Park

have given Park a significant role in this book, including extensive imaginary dialogue and emotional reactions. I hope that I have not caused offense by so doing. My first objective was to bring to the fore his unquestionable brilliance as a tactical commander, which he displayed in an unprecedented situation—there had never been an air battle remotely like this one, in which Park was "writing the script" as he went along and facing overwhelming numerical odds against him. My second objective was to provide a strategic overview (through the eyes of my Eleanor) to balance the close-up view of the battle experienced by the pilots (such as my Shaux).

Keith Park was a New Zealander who fought with distinction in World War I, serving in Gallipoli and on the western front. He was so seriously wounded in 1918 that he was invalided out of the infantry, but he immediately volunteered to become a fighter pilot. He received four awards for bravery, the citation for one of which reads, "For conspicuous gallantry and devotion to duty in accounting for nine enemy aircraft, three of which were completely destroyed and six driven down out of control."

He took command of 11 Group on April 20, 1940, and within a month had to deal with the explosion of German forces into Western Europe, when Hitler launched his blitzkrieg against the Low Countries and France. It is often written that he and Dowding abandoned the British and French armies to their fate, particularly by failing to commit Spitfires. In fact, the RAF had stripped half its forces to defend Europe and lost almost two hundred aircraft defending Dunkirk alone.

Then, of course, the Battle of Britain commenced in August. By the end of September it was clear to both sides that, despite all odds, the Luftwaffe had been defeated—and Park was immediately relieved of his command in favor of his nemesis Leigh-Mallory!

Park was out of favor for almost two years. Then, in July 1942, he assumed responsibility for the air defenses of the island of Malta in the Mediterranean. Although less well known, the Battle of Malta was as strategically significant as the Battle of Britain, because Malta was the key to controlling Mediterranean airspace, at exactly the time that Rommel, the "Desert Fox," was locked in his epic battle for North Africa against Montgomery, Bradley, and Patton. Just as he had in 1940, Park organized a brilliant defense against overwhelming odds in the German air assault code-named Operation Herkules and then went on the offensive, providing air support for the Allied invasions of Sicily and Italy.

As noted before, he ended the war in the position for which Leigh-Mallory had been intended, as the commander of all Allied air forces in Southeast Asia. He retired to New Zealand and died in 1975.

Park is often described as "prickly," and he may well have been so. On the other hand, he had a strong relationship with Dowding and was enormously popular with his pilots (unlike Leigh-Mallory). He kept a Hurricane for his personal use and often flew to meet his pilots.

As for his dispute with Leigh-Mallory, suffice it to say that Park's strategy of sending small, nimble forces to disrupt the bombers before they reached their targets was designed to minimize bomb damage, while Leigh-Mallory's Big Wings, which took time to assemble, certainly brought much more firepower to bear but often only after the bombers had reached their targets and were returning home.

And as for an epitaph, Lord Tedder, the chief of the RAF, wrote of Park, "If any one man won the Battle of Britain, he did. I do not believe it is realised how much that one man, with his leadership, his calm judgement and his skill, did to save, not only this country, but the world."

The Aircraft

Boulton Paul Defiant Mark I

The Defiant was a single-engine fighter with a rotating gun turret. It could therefore attack aircraft to each side or above it but not directly ahead, behind, or below. In effect, to bear on a target, it was necessary for the pilot to position the aircraft in the right attitude and for the gunner to aim the turret, which proved very difficult to coordinate.

In general terms, the Defiant was comparable to a Hurricane, with the same engine, but it was almost 1,600 pounds heavier and therefore much slower and far less maneuverable. It was disastrously ineffective against 109s and 110s. Its vulnerability was revealed in the Battle of France and over Dunkirk, and it was subsequently flown only in emergences.

It is curious to note that an early prototype did not have a turret; instead it had twelve guns in the wings firing forward, like the 109, Hurricane, and Spitfire. In this configuration it was almost as fast as a Spitfire and might have been a valuable asset, instead of a death trap for its crew.

This is the aircraft my fictional Shaux flew in the Battle of France and in which Shaux and Eleanor make their desperate defense of Oldchurch.

Dornier 17 Z-2, Heinkel He 111 H-1, Junkers Ju 88 A-1

These three *Schnellbombers* (fast bombers) were the primary offensive weapons used by the Luftwaffe in the Battle of Britain. All had certain characteristics in common: they had crews of four (occasionally five); they had two engines; they carried between one and two tons of bombs, depending on their configuration; they flew at laden speeds a little above 250 miles per hour; and, although they sprouted several guns, they had poor defenses against fighters.

They had all been designed in the mid-1930s to be fast enough to outrun fighters, and as empty prototypes they were; but at operational weights they were slow and cumbersome. The slower they flew, the more armament they needed to defend themselves and therefore the more weight they had to carry and therefore the slower they flew … The speed of the Ju 88, for example, declined from 360 miles per hour (faster than a Spitfire) as a prototype in 1936 to 260 miles per hour in the production model used in the Battle of Britain.

In spite of numerous attempts and promising starts, the Germans never produced a great fast bomber. Ironically it was the British firm De Havilland, without being requested to do so, that produced a bomber for the RAF that could truly outrun fighters—the extraordinary Merlin-powered Mosquito, which was constructed from plywood, built in part by piano makers, and which could exceed 400 miles per hour. So fast was the bomber that it was converted to a single-seat fighter, the Hornet, capable of flying at almost 500 miles per hour. Göring, the champion of the fast bomber, was beside himself. "It makes me furious when I see the Mosquito. I turn green and yellow with envy."

This history is significant because it dictated the architecture of the battle. The slow speed of the bombers gave 11 Group Hurricanes time to scramble, climb, chase the bombers down, and intercept them. This forced the 109s into close-escort duties down at the same speeds, making them accessible to 11 Group Spitfires, which in turn forced the Luftwaffe to send two fighters to defend each bomber.

The Dornier 17 started life as the fast and elegant "flying pencil," with a sleek, pointed nose, and ended life with a bulbous nose stuffed with ineffectual machine guns. Approximately six hundred were built before the type was phased out in favor of the Ju 88.

The He 111 was the primary bomber used by the Luftwaffe in the Battle of Britain. It proved to be rugged and flexible, and a total of seven thousand were built before it was phased out in 1944.

The Ju 88 A-1 was supposed to replace the slower Dornier 17 and He 111, but it was not fast enough to make a dramatic difference. It proved to be a versatile aircraft in other roles, and a total of fifteen thousand were built.

Hawker Hurricane

The Hurricane's reputation suffers from its lack of glamour in comparison to the Spitfire. It fact, it was the workhorse of 11 Group, accounting for 70 percent of RAF victories in the Battle of Britain.

The Hurricane was strong and stable, with the best gun arrangement. It was easier to manufacture than the Spitfire, which accounts for its greater numbers. It was superior to all Luftwaffe aircraft except the 109. As a consequence, Park used the Hurricane to attack bombers whenever possible, relying on Spitfires to keep the 109s away.

Rolls-Royce Merlin Mark II and Mark XII

The Merlin engine was so important that it deserves a place in its own right. It was a 60-degree V-12, with a cubic displacement of twenty-seven liters, developed by Rolls-Royce in the mid-1930s. The Merlin Mark II, the most widely used variant during the Battle of Britain, developed 1030 horsepower.

The engine was superbly reliable. Rolls-Royce literally ran Merlins until they broke and then strengthened whichever part broke and ran them until another part broke. The Merlin powered the Hurricane and Spitfire. The engine also proved to be extremely flexible; by the time Merlins were finally phased out of production, they were developing 1500 horsepower. The Merlin's m7ajor weakness, its tendency to stall in a dive attitude, was eventually solved by replacing the carburetors with fuel injection.

More than 150,000 Merlins were built, and they powered not only the Hurricane and Spitfires but also such legendary aircraft as the Mosquito fighter-bomber, the Lancaster heavy bomber, and the mighty American P-51 Mustang fighter. The Merlin-powered P-51 was very fast and later in the war would fly all the way to Germany escorting US Army Air Force B-17 bombers to their targets—exactly what the 109s could *not* do over London in the Battle of Britain.

The Luftwaffe equivalent of the Merlin was the monumental thirty-four-liter, 1100-horsepower, fuel-injected Daimler-Benz 601, which was used in the Messerschmitt 109s and 110s.

Most of the additional power of later versions of the Merlin came from using higher and higher octane fuel, which the British imported from the United States. The Germans had no equivalent source of supply and could only get more power by increasing engine size and weight—obviously a self-defeating tactic. Instead they turned to alternative fuels and, by the time the war ended, were far ahead of the Allies in rocket power and jet engines, producing the V-1, the first successful cruise missile; the V-2, the first successful ballistic missile; and the Messerschmitt 262, the first operational jet fighter. One wonders what my fictional Eleanor might have made of this asymmetry in fuel supplies and how it shaped the war in Europe.

The demand for Merlins far outstripped Rolls-Royce's production capacity. They reluctantly outsourced some manufacturing to the Packard motor company in Detroit—reluctantly because Rolls-Royce craftsmen hand-built every engine and hand-polished every working surface, whereas Packard used production line techniques and employed a largely unskilled female workforce (shades of Rosie the Riveter). The Rolls-Royce engineers were therefore amazed (and doubtless chagrined) to discover that the quality and reliability of Rosie's Packard-built Merlins was even higher than their own.

Messerschmitt Bf 109 E-4

The Messerschmitt Bf 109 E-4 was the primary fighter used by the Luftwaffe in the Battle of Britain. Known to its pilots as the "Emil," it was only marginally inferior to the Spitfire and was superior in some situations, particularly in diving.

In the early stages of the battle, the 109s were allowed to roam free, flying high above the bomber streams and diving down when 11 Group Hurricanes arrived to attack the bombers. This proved highly effective.

When Göring changed this strategy in late August and required the 109s to fly close escort, he reversed the situation; now the 109s became prey for Spitfires diving down on them. It was one of Göring's greatest mistakes, made over the objections of his 109 pilots.

The 109 had a severely restricted range and could stay over London for merely ten minutes or less before abandoning the bombers. This meant that Hitler's decision to bomb London exposed the Luftwaffe's bombers to the RAF without defending fighter cover.

While it may have lacked the Spitfire's beauty, the 109 was a spectacularly successful aircraft. More than thirty thousand 109s were built in all, and the 109 shot down more aircraft than any other type on either side—including one 109 that shot down seventeen aircraft in a single day. So great were the aircraft's strengths that it continued to be produced even after the appearance of its replacement, the Focke-Wulf Fw 190, the aptly named "Butcher Bird."

Messerschmitt Bf 110 C-1

The 110 was a twin-engine heavy fighter, known as a Zerstorer (Destroyer). It had six guns mounted in the nose and had a top speed of more than 240 miles per hour—faster than a Hurricane and almost as fast as a Spitfire. However, it was not a very maneuverable aircraft and could not survive encounters with 11 Group.

Kesselring initially used the 110 for *freie Jagd* (free hunts), sending formations of 110s to look for targets of opportunity or to act as decoys, as well as bomber-escort duties.

In the end, the 110's vulnerabilities compelled Kesselring to use 109s to defend 110s—a grossly inefficient use of resources.

Although the 110 was outmatched against single-engine fighters, it did survive in production for other purposes and had successes, particularly as a night fighter.

Supermarine Spitfire Mark I and II

The Spitfire was developed from a line of racing seaplanes in the mid-1930s. It married an exceptional airframe design by R. J. Mitchell with a superb engine, the Rolls-Royce Merlin; the union of the two created the iconic Spitfire.

Although the Spitfire's performance was occasionally matched by other aircraft, the basic designs of both airframe and engine were so strong that it was continually upgraded through World War II. The final combat versions were almost one hundred miles per hour faster than the Mark Is and IIs used in the Battle of Britain. Specialized versions reached speeds of over six hundred miles per hour and heights of over fifty thousand feet. Over twenty thousand Spitfires were built, and the aircraft remained in service until 1955, ten years after jet fighters were introduced.

Part of the Spitfire's mystique is its graceful and distinctive design and the fact that it was exceptionally easy to fly—both are in sharp contrast to the 109.

It is generally supposed that the Spitfire won the Battle of Britain, but it was hard to manufacture and never made up more than a third of 11 Group's strength. The less glamorous Hurricanes flew more missions and shot down far more aircraft. However, the Spitfire was the only aircraft that could outperform the 109 in terms of speed and maneuverability, and in that regard it was indeed the king of the skies.

In his memoir *The First and the Last*, the great Luftwaffe ace Adolf Galland wrote of a meeting with Göring at the height of the battle:

> The theme of fighter protection was chewed over again and again. Goering clearly represented the point of view of the bombers and demanded close and rigid protection … We received many more harsh words … Finally, as his time ran short, he grew more amiable and asked what were the requirements for our squadrons. Moelders asked for a series of Me109's with more powerful engines. The request was granted. "And you?" Goering turned to me. I did not hesitate long. "I should like an outfit of Spitfires for my group." Such brazen-faced impudence made even Goering speechless. He stamped off, growling as he went.

The Influences

Given the influential roles of Yeats, von Neumann, and others in this novel, and the liberties I have taken, it seems only fair to include them in my notes.

John von Neumann

To the best of my knowledge, John von Neumann played no part in the Battle of Britain, nor did anyone attempt to apply his mathematics to the battle. Mea culpa if I am wrong.

Neumann János Lajos (1903–1957), known as Jancsi (meaning Johnnie), was born in Budapest in Hungary and immigrated to the United States in 1930. He settled at Princeton and was a colleague of Albert Einstein. He made numerous extraordinary contributions in many scientific and mathematical fields, including quantum mechanics, computer science, and economics. He published his theory of minimax in 1928, but his classic work on game theory did not appear until 1944. Therefore my fictional Eleanor would have been building on an incomplete early version of his theory, guessing at where von Neumann might be headed.

I have found no reference to a theory of asymmetric zero sums—nor, indeed, to Poundian harmonics, whatever they might have been!

William Butler Yeats

William Butler Yeats (1865–1939) was an Irish poet and dramatist who won the Nobel Prize in Literature in 1923. He wrote the poem that dominated my Shaux's thoughts following the death of Major Robert Gregory, the son of one of Yeats's closest friends and supporters, Lady Augusta Gregory. Gregory was shot down and killed by friendly fire in Italy in 1918 during World War I.

Yeats wrote his own gaunt epitaph, and it is inscribed on his headstone in Drumcliffe, County Sligo, Ireland:

> Cast a cold eye
> On life, on death.

Horseman, pass by!

One cannot but imagine that Shaux would have approved—until Eleanor came to his rescue.

Other Quotations and Allusions

Thomas Hardy

Thomas Hardy wrote *Jude the Obscure* in 1895, a novel studying the disappointments and frustrations of its unfortunate protagonist, doomed to a life of mediocrity and obscurity by his own weaknesses. Shaux would have read the book at Oxford, in which it is set, and stolen the allusion to describe his own circumstances.

Saint Jude was one of the apostles; Saint Jude the Obscure was a lesser saint now lost in the haze of medieval hagiography.

Publius Ovidius Naso

Ovid, as he is known in English, was a Roman poet who lived from 43 BC to approximately AD 16. He wrote, *"Dulce et decorum est / Pro patria mori."* ("It is sweet and honorable to die for one's country.") The quotation is inscribed—apparently without irony—on the wall of the chapel of the Royal Military Academy at Sandhurst, the British equivalent of West Point.

The British poet Wilfred Owen quoted Ovid bitterly shortly before he was killed in World War I. His graphic poem describes a soldier dying hideously from a poison gas attack and ends:

> My friend, you would not tell with such high zest
> To children ardent for some desperate glory,
> The old lie: *Dulce et decorum est*
> *Pro patria mori.*

Perhaps Shaux was thinking of Owen's verse as he wrote to Protherow's parents.

Isaiah 2:4

And he shall judge among the nations, and shall rebuke many people: and they shall *beat their swords into plowshares,* and their spears into pruninghooks: nation shall not lift up sword against nation, neither shall they learn war any more" (KJV, emphasis added.)

This verse is inscribed on the wall across from the United Nations Plaza in New York City. In my story, Shaux reverses the meaning in the Bible: Hitler had created instruments of war out of instruments of peace.

Jargon and Slang

AOC: Air officer commanding (senior officer, such as Park).

AOC in C: Air officer commander in chief (such as Dowding).

Buckley's chance: (*Australian*) No chance at all.

Cock-up: (*British*) A serious mistake.

DFC: Distinguished Flying Cross. Awarded to pilots for distinguished service. Although it was awarded for single feats of bravery, it was often given in recognition of cumulative success (as in Shaux's case). Higher awards for gallantry included the Distinguished Service Order (DSO) and the Victoria Cross (VC). Only one VC was awarded in the Battle of Britain.

Fanny Adams: (*Cockney rhyming slang*) Fuck all.

Fair dinkum: (*Australian*) Fair, honest.

MM: Military Medal. This medal was normally awarded to noncommissioned officers and privates in the army. However, occasionally it was also used to recognize the services of women, because all other awards for service in action against the enemy were explicitly reserved exclusively for men! For example, two WAAFs were award the MM for their courage during an attack on the RAF station at Detling on August

13, 1940. Therefore, when my imaginary Churchill wishes to recognize Eleanor's bravery, he uses the only medal available to him.

Pommie: (*Australian*) An Englishman, derived from the letters POHM (Prisoner of Her Majesty) that were sewn on the clothes of convicts sent to the Australian penal colonies.

RNoAF: Royal Norwegian Air Force.

WAAF: Women's Auxiliary Air Force. The RAF did not accept women into its ranks until 1949, but "Stuffy" Dowding, in another of his prescient insights, insisted that women be judged on their talents and promoted accordingly. There were 4,500 WAAFs in Fighter Command during the battle. Eleanor's rise in the administrative ranks would not have been exceptional.

Excerpts from Hitler's Führer Directives

Führer Directive 16, July 16, 1940

Since England, in spite of her apparently hopeless military situation, shows no sign of coming to terms, I have decided to prepare a landing operations against England, and, if necessary, to carry it out. The aim of this operation is to eliminate the British homeland as a base for the further prosecution of the war against Germany, and, if necessary, to occupy it completely … The British Air Force is to be so beaten down in its morale and in fact, that it can no longer display any appreciable aggressive force in opposition to the German crossing.

Führer Directive 17, August 1, 1940

The Luftwaffe is to overcome the British Air Force with all means at its disposal and in the shortest possible time. The attacks are to be directed primarily against the planes themselves, their ground installations, and their supply organizations, also against the aircraft industry.

Excerpts from Churchill's Speeches

Churchill gave his speeches to the House of Commons, and so they were heard only by a small audience of politicians and were not recorded or broadcast on the radio. Given their dramatic role in the history of the war, this might seem like a colossal waste.

However, it should be remembered that Churchill was chosen as a compromise prime minister, and at the time of the Battle of Britain he was new, unproven, and highly controversial. He was heading an uncertain and fractious coalition government, and the vast majority of the political and intellectual establishment did not agree with his policy of fighting on against overwhelming odds. Almost everyone of influence advocated negotiating with Hitler.

Therefore his rhetorical firepower was aimed primarily at stiffening the limp resolve of his fellow politicians, rather than the resolve of the British population.

Churchill did not mince his words. He told the cabinet at the beginning of his ministry, "If the long history of our island is to come to an end, then it shall only end when every last one of us is beaten to the ground and lies choking in his blood."

It should also be remembered that Churchill's speeches were given at a time of unparalleled military disaster, a "cataract of disaster" as he described it, when defeat seemed inevitable—to everyone but him.

Churchill subsequently repeated his speeches on the radio as addresses to the nation, almost as an afterthought, and it is these repetitions that were recorded and history remembers.

American readers will also note his references to the United States as the ultimate savior of Europe. This was a year and a half before Pearl Harbor and four years before D-day, and Joseph Kennedy (the father of the future president) typified American determination to stay out of the war. (I should note that seven US pilots fought in the battle as volunteers. The Australians never wavered in their support of Britain, and thirty-two Australian pilots participated in the battle. Two Norwegian squadrons were formed in 1941 and served with distinction.)

In the following excerpts I have emphasized the portions of Churchill's speeches I used in the book.

May 13, 1940, inaugural speech as prime minister to the House of Commons

I have nothing to offer but blood, toil, tears and sweat. We have before us an ordeal of the most grievous kind. We have before us many, many long months of struggle and of suffering.

You ask, "What is our policy?" I will say; "It is to wage war, by sea, land and air, with all our might and with all the strength that God can give us: to wage war against a monstrous tyranny, never surpassed in the dark lamentable catalogue of human crime. That is our policy."

You ask, "What is our aim?" I can answer with one word: "Victory— victory at all costs, victory in spite of all terror, victory however long and hard the road may be; for without victory there is no survival."

June 4, 1940, speech to the House of Commons

I have, myself, full confidence that if all do their duty, if nothing is neglected, and if the best arrangements are made, as they are being made, we shall prove ourselves once again able to defend our Island home, to ride out the storm of war, and to outlive the menace of tyranny, if necessary for years, if necessary alone.

Even though large tracts of Europe and many old and famous States have fallen or may fall into the grip of the Gestapo and all the odious apparatus of Nazi rule, we shall not flag or fail.

We shall go on to the end, we shall fight in France, we shall fight on the seas and oceans, we shall fight with growing confidence and growing strength in the air, *we shall defend our Island, whatever the cost may be, we shall fight on the beaches, we shall fight on the landing grounds, we shall fight in the fields and in the streets, we shall fight in the hills; we shall never surrender,* and even if, which I do not for a moment believe, this Island or a large part of it were subjugated and starving, then our Empire beyond the seas, armed and guarded by the British Fleet, would carry on the struggle, *until, in God's good time, the New World, with all its power and might, steps forth to the rescue and the liberation of the Old.*

June 22, 1940, speech to the House of Commons

What General Weygand called the Battle of France is over. *I expect that the Battle of Britain is about to begin.* Upon this battle depends the survival of Christian civilization. Upon it depends our own British life, and the long continuity of our institutions and our Empire. The whole fury and might of the enemy must very soon be turned on us. Hitler knows that he will have to break us in this Island or lose the war. If we can stand up to him, all Europe may be free and the life of the world may move forward into broad, sunlit uplands. But if we fail, then the whole world, including the United States, including all that we have known and cared for, will sink into the abyss of a new Dark Age made more sinister, and perhaps more protracted, by the lights of perverted science. *Let us therefore brace ourselves to our duties, and so bear ourselves that, if the British Empire and its Commonwealth last for a thousand years, men will still say, "This was their finest hour."*

August 20, 1940, speech to the House of Commons
(This is the speech that my fictional Shaux and Eleanor listen to on the radio.)

Rather more than a quarter of a year has passed since the new Government came into power in this country. What a cataract of disaster has poured out upon us since then! ... Meanwhile, we have not only fortified our hearts but our Island. We have rearmed and rebuilt our armies in a degree which would have been deemed impossible a few months ago ... The whole Island bristles against invaders, from the sea or from the air ... The stronger our Army at home, the larger must the invading expedition be, and the larger the invading expedition, the less difficult will be the task of the Navy in detecting its assembly and in intercepting and destroying it in passage; and the greater also would be the difficulty of feeding and supplying the invaders if ever they landed ... Our Navy is far stronger than it was at the beginning of the war. The great flow of new construction set on foot at the outbreak is now beginning to come in.

Why do I say all this? Not, assuredly, to boast; not, assuredly, to give the slightest countenance to complacency. The dangers we face are still enormous, but so are our advantages and resources. I recount them because the people have a right to know that there are solid grounds for the confidence which we feel, and that we have good reason to believe ourselves capable, as I said in a very dark hour two months ago, of continuing the war "if necessary alone, if necessary for years." ...

The great air battle which has been in progress over this Island for the last few weeks has recently attained a high intensity. It is too soon to attempt to assign limits either to its scale or to its duration. We must certainly expect that greater efforts will be made by the enemy than any he has so far put forth ... It is quite plain that Herr Hitler could not admit defeat in his air attack on Great Britain without sustaining most serious injury. If after all his boastings and bloodcurdling threats and lurid accounts trumpeted round the world of the damage he has inflicted, of the vast numbers of our Air Force he has shot down, so he says, with so little loss to himself ... if after all this his whole air onslaught were forced after a while tamely to peter out, the Fuhrer's reputation for veracity of statement might be seriously impugned. We may be sure, therefore, that he will continue as long as he has the strength to do so ...

... It must also be remembered that all the enemy machines and pilots which are shot down over our Island, or over the seas which surround it, are either destroyed or captured; whereas a considerable proportion of our machines, and also of our pilots, are saved, and soon again in many cases come into action ... We believe that we shall be able to continue the air struggle indefinitely and as long as the enemy pleases, and the longer it continues the more rapid will be our approach, first towards that parity, and then into that superiority, in the air upon which in a large measure the decision of the war depends.

The gratitude of every home in our Island, in our Empire, and indeed throughout the world, except in the abodes of the guilty, goes out to the British airmen who, undaunted by odds, unwearied in their constant challenge and mortal danger, are turning the tide of the World War by their prowess and by their devotion. *Never in the field of human conflict was so much owed by so many to so few.* All hearts go out to the fighter pilots, whose brilliant actions we see with our own eyes day after day ...